MW01241740

The Torenium Chronicles

Book 3

Man Eater Wars

By

T. David Sergent

TABLE OF CONTENTS

PROLOGUE
Many Years Ago

"WHERE THE PUCKERING HELL IS PRINCE, CARRUM?!" Bastion yelled at the soldier in his grip. There was a thud and the soldier jerked forward. Bastion let go, the soldier fell, and Bastion saw the crossbow bolt piercing the soldier's back armour. He looked over and saw the big easterner barbarian loading another, presumably for him. He charged, but a knight on a horse trampled the barbarian and Bastion jumped back out of the way.

"You need to come with us, Commander!" The knight shouted over the sound of the battle around them.

"The Prince, where is he?" Bastion commanded.

"Sir, we haven't much time!" The knight pleaded.

"THE PRINCE!" Bastion growled.

The knight signalled to another knight behind him and he jumped off his horse and handed Bastion the reins.

"I will take you to him but we must hurry."

"Do it." Bastion said, jumping into the saddle. "GO!"

Bastion was led to a tent just outside the battlement. Soldiers lay around it either bandaged or dead.

"He's hurt?" Bastion asked of the knight as he jumped off the horse. The knight just pointed to the tent.

"Stupid impulsive puckering dark pig headed-" Bastion paused as he swung open the flap of the tent. Prince Carrum was on a cot with a doctor shaking his head and another in a black cloak leaning over The

1

Prince and moving his hands over him as he spoke soft words deep in his hood.

"What is this?" Bastion demanded, pulling his sword. "Get the dark hell away from him!"

"He is dying." The doctor said, lifting his hands as if to say he did not know what was happening.

"You, Mr Mumbles, back away or lose your head!" As the words left his mouth, two more cloaked figures seemed to materialize out of the shadows. They wore red cloaks and eyes glowing red in their hoods. They raised their hands and Bastion felt an invisible force pushing him back.

"Oh, no you don't." Bastion said and tried to push back on whatever was driving him back. He started to gain momentum and the red figures exchanged a surprised glance.

"Bastion-" Prince Carrum moaned. Bastion looked up to his friend, met his eyes, and he pushed forward.

"I am here, Carrum!" Bastion said and growled as he pushed forward, getting closer to the prince and the chanting man in black.

"If it is not me that..." The Prince coughed blood and vomit to the side of his cot. "-you send it back. Promise me-" The Prince managed a breath. "-you must promise me!"

"I promise you - and that these puckering asses will follow!" Then there was a flash and Bastion felt himself propelled backwards through the tent flap and onto the hard ground beyond. Then only darkness.

Bastion woke to find the doctor looking down at him. "What-" He managed to say but the words felt like salt on a wound in his throat.

2

"Drink some water, Sir Bastion. All is well. The day is won!" The doctor said soothingly.

"No-" Bastion tried again and sat up, taking the water and drinking. "-where is he?"

"The Prince?" The doctor asked, smiling. Bastion just looked at him and the doctor cleared his throat and stepped back.

"No need to worry, there." The doctor explained, forcing a smile on his lips. "It seems the wounds were much less severe than thought. He is on his way back to the Great City and expected to make a full recovery!"

Bastion took another drink while maintaining his stare with the doctor watching every reaction.

"Is that so?" Bastion finally said.

"Oh yes, Sir Bastion. He was most fortunate that we ... that is I, was able to get to him so quickly." The doctor smiled cheerfully. Bastion could see that smile did not continue to his eyes.

"And your friends?" Bastion asked.

"Friends?" The doctor asked back, trying to look confused.

"HORSE!" Bastion yelled out. "WHERE IS MY HORSE!"

CHAPTER 1

Miska leaned against her small room wall, fighting off the image of the piercing grey eyes in her head. Guilt and longing washed over her. She breathed, trying to clear her mind the way the Head Mother had taught her. The thought of Sebastion faded, but the feelings remained. She walked to her small window, opened the wooden shutters, and the sunlight slammed into her like a hammer, but at the same time it was soothing, and she stood a moment to enjoy it.

She ran her fingers down her now long hair as it was now tied tight behind her as was the way of the Lady of Light's novice-priestess. A gentle breeze blew in, and she closed her eyes letting it wash over her as her simple brown dress flapped. She was just a novice now and could not not yet wear the white gown of a priestess. As she felt the sun's warmth comfort her, she let the memories of when she first came here take her.

Nundra, the kind older woman who found her on the docks of Endrea, brought her to see the High Mother as soon as their ship had made port. Miska remembered sitting in the receiving room of the biggest building she had ever seen. The enormous red chairs faced long embroideries of The Lady of Light and her priestesses. The images were overwhelming, and some were even scary. One, in particular, had stuck out to her from the rest. It was a priestess holding back a bear-like beast with one hand and holding a large curved knife in the other. Children were on the other side of the image, cringing and screaming as they

4

looked on. Miska could not tell if the priestess held the bear at bay with a knife to save the children, or had brought the monster to them.

She remembered that the room was silent, and when the door began to creak open, the noise filled the big room, echoing off the walls.

"Do not be afraid, child." Nundra had said then in that gentle way she had about her. "She will see you now, my dear. Be respectful but do not be afraid." Miska remembered how she had put her hands on her shoulders. "You have nothing to hide here. She will surely see how special you are, as I do."

Well, The Head Mother must have seen whatever Nundra had because not long after their meeting, Miska found herself the youngest priestess in training. Although most saw it as a significant honour, others were jealous and gave her angry looks when she was brought to the novices' corridors and assigned a room with a window. Miska, however, noticed little of it. She had felt as if she was in some dream she had no control over. The trip from Endrea to the Lady of Light's church had been the longest in her life. The days of solitude had given her time to think about all she had lost and left behind. As soon as she stepped onto the deck of that ship, she felt she was making a mistake. She even turned to walk back down the plank to the dock, but Nundra was there. She had grabbed her arm like a python and held her. It was nothing like the gentle hands the older woman had here. Miska remembered it was as if the priestess had sucked the strength from her body. Miska had fallen to her knees and wept as the other women filed onto the ship, stepping around her, some of them crying openly. Nundra had lifted her to her feet that day and hugged her like a mother. Miska remembered crying so hard that she soaked the kind woman's high collared gown. Nundra did not seem to mind but had rocked her back and forth, soothingly. Miska thought it felt so good that she won the urge to turn and jump into the water and swim back to the docks as the plank was pulled away.

She remembered whimpering Sebastion's name into Nundra's white gown. She did feel as if she was betraying him by leaving. He had said he would stay with her forever, but now it was she leaving him. But the strangest thing is she didn't know why. It was as if something was pulling her towards that ship that morning—something she could not resist.

That first night under the sails, watching the water rush by, she had decided that as soon as the ship made land she would start her journey back to him and Morakye. Whatever had driven her to the vessel, The Lady of Light disappeared as that plank was pulled away. The lulling ship and the women getting sick over the side were no comfort. She slept with the others in the bottom of the ship. The priestesses would lock the door behind them, "So the men about the ship are not tempted by sin." But Miska suspected it was just as much to make sure none of the women stole one of the small boats and tried to make it back. She even suspected some would throw themselves over the railings in despair.

It was not a good voyage to the house of the Lady of Light. It was long, lonely, and full of regret. All she could do was plan her trip back to Sebastion. She knew he was going off to find this Bashor, and she thought she could find some information on him and start there. The man-eaters would probably overrun Endrea by then. She had no doubt those awful barbarian man-eaters would leave little to nothing left in that city. No, she would have to find Bashor.

That had been before she met the High Mother. Much had changed when Miska met the leader of the Church of the Lady of Light. That feeling of being drawn to something had returned along with a hunger to learn and become a priestess. The small amount of reading Sebastion had taught her had given her the foundation that she quickly built on. She was always busy now with reading, writing and, of course, praying.

She was taught skills now, and some she could not understand why they were a part of her studies. There was some amount of fighting and self-defence skills but what was strangest were the ways of war. Some classes dealt with specific battles and the techniques to win. She was taught the history of significant conflicts and then tested and what had won the day. There were battalion positioning and the art of supplies and the moral in armies and why it was necessary. She couldn't help but have little interest in these classes and would have instead been reading something more interesting and even praying than breaking apart the pieces of skirmishes that happened long ago. But as much as she disliked it, the priestesses drilled it into her head. She had no idea why a priestess would need to know the Gworkin Battle Manoeuvres or the Shashwin Hidden Spear Assault. At times, her head would float back to the Dempsies and their freedom, but most of the time they went to the time she had spent with Sebastion. There were times when she thought of running away but others when she felt she was finally where she was supposed to be. Slowly she made friends, and even the older girls started to accept her. She never forgot Sebastion, but as the weeks slipped by, her heart felt less broken. However, she knew there would always be a hole there that only he could fill.

It was morning, and the bells rang that it was time to wake. Miska stretched and heard strange voices in the courtyard. She tried looking out the window, but it was at the wrong angle. The voices sounded like they were getting anxious, so she threw a blanket around herself and stepped into the hallway. She saw a group of other girls standing around a large window in the hall peering out excitedly, so she moved in closer and tried to see. She saw a wagon being unloaded with injured people and what looked to be many dead bodies. The Head Mother stood a distance off and Miska thought she looked glum and sorrowful as if every one of those people was a direct relative. The Mother suddenly looked up and the girls squealed and ran off, leaving only Miska standing there, returning the sad stare. Miska finally looked away, seeing an injured child lifted off the cart. It was a little girl wrapped in linen-stained red from either her blood or that of someone she had ridden with. Miska moved closer to the window, trying to see more of the poor child.

As she stared, the little girl's head moved to reveal her face. Miska's breath caught in her throat, and she put her hands over her heart. It was the same perfect, beautiful, dark-haired girl she had seen with the Dempsies long ago. Miska ran from the window to the door leading to the courtyard outside. She sprinted with her blanket billowing behind her. When she got to the cart, she had to look around for the child. She saw a man who worked at the compound holding the child with one hand and pulling bodies out of the cart with the other.

Miska ran over to the man and ripped the child from his arms. The child that looked up at her was not the little girl she had seen, but somehow she knew it would not be. From her time spent with the priestesses, she knew about signs. Somehow this girl she held in her arms was meant to be in her embrace.

Miska lifted her blanket and stripped the child of the dirty linen. She wrapped the blanket around her and held her close. The girl started to whimper, and Miska soothed her by brushing back her dirty hair from her face.

"Shh," Miska cooed. "It's all right now. You will be safe here, little one. It's okay. Don't cry." She spoke softly, bouncing her gently on her hip. The child looked up, and Miska used a corner of the blanket to wipe blood and grime from her face.

No, this was not the child she saw from the window; this one was thin and malnourished and looked close to death. The blank look of hopelessness in her eyes burned a spot in Miska's heart as if tattooed there forever.

She stared down at the girl and tried to smile encouragingly as a cold feeling penetrated her body. A hand touched her shoulder, and instead of jumping, she felt warmth returning. "What do you see, my child." The Head Mother asked her.

Miska looked up, feeling the tears in her eyes. "I see misery. I see the loss of hope, and it breaks my heart." The Head-Mother put an arm around her and also looked into the blanket.

"What did you see that made you run out here?"

Miska looked down at the little girl that had blank eyes, stroking her cheek." I saw a child I have seen before. A dark-haired child. The most beautiful little girl I have ever seen. She looked at me from the eyes of this child. I am certain of it." she said, thinking she sounded a little silly and thought that the Head Mother might think she was lying.

"You have a gift."

"It is no gift to see these poor people broken and battered, Mother." Miska said, tears running down her cheeks but smiling bravely for the little girl. "I know what you're thinking. You are thinking that I am seeing some image of The Lady. I don't know if that is true, but I would give that up if I could make all this killing stop."

The Head Mother nodded knowingly. "And that is why she has chosen you, my dear."

"Chosen for what?" Miska asked.

The Head Mother leaned in and kissed Miska's forehead gently. She smiled down at her with her kind, wrinkled eyes. "That is between you and The Lady of Light. I believe you are destined for something important. Do not try to swallow down the world's pain. Not even I can stomach that. There are times when you will be pushed, and that is when it is best to move out of the way." The Head Mother reached with her wrinkled hand holding Miska's chin, so she was facing her. Miska watched the older woman's eyes go from kind and motherly to very hard. "Then, there are times you push back."

"I do not understand, Mother." The woman let go of Miska's chin and became the kind old woman again. "But you must, my dear. I fear there is precious little time. The barbarians are coming, and there is no doubt you will see quite a bit more of what you have there." She touched the child's cheek. Miska looked into The Mother's face.

"Are you saying I should fight?"

10

"The answers are within you, child. I can only lead you to the well; it is you who must drink the water." The Mother smiled.

Miska nodded, not fully understanding. The Head Mother took the little girl from her and held her close. "I believe you have a class now." The Head Mother gave her a nod, smiling. "On your way, then."

"But-" Miska started, but that same stern look came to the old woman's face, and Miska saw no room for argument. She turned and headed back, turning once at the door to see the Head Mother watching her closely.

CHAPTER 2

The Man-Eater Barbarians were moving across the Empire like a creeping disease, Torenium Empire. They were systematically burning and destroying everything they came across on their way west. All the Empire's major cities were now full of hungry and battered refugees from the Kingdom's outskirts. Food and clean water were in short supply, and the people waited for the Great City army to come and save them, but the opposite was happening. The Advisors were pulling all the armies from the other cities to come and strengthen their defences. Only once had an army of Torenium come out and faced the Barbarians. And it was the small army of Endrea, and their defeat rang across the Empire like the bells of death. The empire desperately looked for help from the Great City, but all that could fight had left under the King's Advisors' command to strengthen the Great City's army. Hope was gone, and so was any will to fight. Everyone but the Advisors thought it was just a matter of time before even the Great City would fall, but they in their ignorance thought building their armies meant they could be safe indefinitely. They were sure they could hide behind their soldiers for as long as it took for the Man-Eaters to have their fill of the outskirts to realize their folly of attacking the Great City and go back to the east from where they had come.

The problem, of course, was that the Advisors were not military men and not wise men, either. They were simple men spending almost all of their time squabbling and fighting for land and gold. They held all power and left everything to a vote among them, which they rarely did, and they never got much of anything done. None were very interested in ultimate power; they wanted gold and made sure one did not get more power than the next. It had been like this for years as Torenium crumbled around them. The Great City was the last city to hold any image of the once-great Empire, and even that was now a façade. Only the houses surrounding the King's castle were still big and majestic as if they were in another time. Almost all the windows faced each other as if to not see the depredation beyond their view. In their degradation and ignorance, they did not know or care about how to manage an army. Now that they had sent for the other armies and the city was flush with the military, there was less rule now, and the little that once went to the poor went to the armies that protected the wealthy. The Advisors gave very little to care for them, but the poor gave all.

Desperation fostered mistrust, then anger, and finally, violence. The men in the armies were growing very pensive about being brought here and not being able to defend their own homes. Most thought they were putting together a great defense to run the Man-Eaters out of Torenium for good. Still, the truth became more evident as news circulated more and more of their hometowns and cities going up in flames. The Advisors had to make examples of soldiers to keep them from running back to their families. Cages hung above the wall with dead men being picked apart by the fat blackbirds that were circling the city of late.

The powerless leaders of the armies watched the birds, knowing what that could only mean—the Barbarians were getting closer. The birds followed death, and now it was coming to their city. Doom hung over them like a thick blanket. Each day the sun rose; the people of the

Great City counted as just another drop of sand in the hourglass to their end. No longer did children play in the streets, or was there music in the local taverns. The Great City was holding its breath, waiting for the inevitable. Only the fat Advisors thought they could keep their good thing going.

The main streets were almost always silent, but many could hear from the distance laughing and music deeper in the city. It was faint, and the people would at times stop and the smell of meat roasting would wash over them, sending their mouths watering and their stomachs growling. Anger would have overtaken them all if they hadn't already felt so hopeless.

The King sat in his chair by the window, as he always did at this time with a fine animal skin blanket covering his lap. He stared out the window at the party going on below. The image of it was making him feel sick, but he didn't know why. His thoughts were always just beyond his grasp, and he now felt more than ever. He watched one of the fat Advisors walk beneath his window; the man stopped and looked up, saluted him, and then fell over, spilling his wine on his white tunic. The young woman with him giggled in delight and helped him up. They laughed as they walked on without looking up at him again. Anger shot through the King, but the reason why he did not know. He brought his old hands to his face and felt his cold cheeks. He pulled his hands away and looked at them. The skin was yellow, wrinkled, and full of brown spots. It was so thin he could not believe it still held his blood underneath. A sudden urge of desperation shot through him, and he put his hands on the arms of the chair, pushed, and his body began to rise, and excitement filled him.

"Hold on there, old man!" A voice came from behind him. He was sure he had heard it before but had no idea from where. "No reason to get excited." The voice said, sounding closer to him now. He felt a hand on his shoulder, pushing him down and back into the chair. He tried to resist, and the hand pushed down hard, making the King fall back down heavily into his chair.

"If you fight me, my liege,I will be forced to tie you down again…" Red-hot anger flowed through him, and he felt his old hand twitching at his side where he was sure he had once worn his sword.

"I think its medicine time," the voice said. He tried to make a sound and could even feel his numb lips move, but no sound came out. He tried again, but a wooden spoon was forced into his mouth with a familiar foul-tasting liquid. He pulled away and coughed.

"-no." He was finally able to whisper. There was a sharp intake of breath from the voice in the room. "-no … more." He could only whisper, his throat burning. He then felt the room temperature change suddenly, and then there was a banging followed by someone running down the hall. He somehow knew he was now alone. A face came to his mind, surprised by the feelings the face brought up. He felt the wall of numbness coming, so he gripped his chair and concentrated on that face. He knew it. He was sure of it. The name of the man who had that face floated around his mind playing some relentless game of tag with him … thick brown hair and grey eyes. The old King concentrated on those light eyes and thought he had it. That's when he saw another

15

vision floating behind the face. It was a shield, and it was an emblem he recognized. It was two gauntlet fists. It was the crest of...

"-Bastion ... help me! Come to me, my loyal knight. I ... need ... y-" Then a wall of darkness washed over him like a crashing wave, and all thoughts were gone.

The royal physicians slammed open the door, leading a short man with a pointy nose over to the old King who was sitting in the chair slumped over.

"He looks out of it. Are you sure he spoke?"

"Yes, yes! I heard him clear as day." The pointy-nose man gave the physician a sideways doubtful glance, angry to be dragged away from the party. His wife had gone home early with a headache, and there were at least two young serving girls he wanted to introduce himself to.

"What did he say?" The Advisor asked.

"He said 'no' and then 'no more.'"

"Are you sure it was not just him making some noise that sounded like that?" The man brushed crumbs from his stained white robe.

"It was clear." The doctor insisted.

"Fine-fine, then. Up the dosage and watch him. If he does anything unusual, tie him to the chair."

The doctor frowned and nodded in agreement.

"What's wrong?" The man frowned, looking longingly at the window where the party continued.

"You expect me to sit here all night watching a decrepit old man when everyone else plays?" The doctor asked, following the Advisor's gaze. The pointed-nose man sighed and waved the comment off. He whirled his stained white robe dramatically as he turned and left. The door slammed shut, echoing along the walls of the small room.

"I think we would all be much better off if you would just die already, old man." The doctor muttered bitterly, coming next to the King to stare out the window at the party below. "Though none of those bastards want the responsibility, your empire has gone to shit."

CHAPTER 3

Even the air felt different on this side of the black mountain and Lara couldn't help feeling that she should not be here. They had found an old trail and they followed it through a pass through rocky terrain. The way was painfully slow, and she was not sure the boy would make it. His skin was ashen now, and his eyes were twitching like he was having some kind of fit. She thought it would have been unfortunate for him to have survived The Dark Lord, dragons, and evil mages just to die here on this bleak, rocky path. It would have almost been better if he died before they had to drag him up and down that stupid mountain. The man-child weighed as much as an ox!

I will be happy never to set eyes on another mountain in my life!

She reached up and wiped away the sweat that threatened to drip into her eyes and sting them. She looked around and thought these woods seemed older than any she had ever seen. The trees were more prominent, and the plants that grew there looked stronger and somehow … intimidating. She had seen some small strange creatures crossing their path, and she could not help but worry how the bigger ones might look.

Baran was taking his turn and suddenly stopped looking behind at the litter that held Killian's Nephew. Sebastion was having another convulsion, and his body twitched violently, his eyes frantically moving under his lids as if he was having a nightmare.

"Best you run ahead and get da' boy's uncle," Baran said, looking down sympathetically.

"Right," Lara answered, jogging ahead to find Killian. Killian had been moving further forward, looking for anything that may have slowed them down. This was a chore for him as he had to come back often to hold Sebastion's head and soothe him. It was only Killian that was able to do this. He would rest his hand on the boy's cold chest and sing some song. At times, Lara would listen as he sang about some silly man and a hog.

Strangeness does seem to run in the family.

She did not have to run ahead far to catch up with Killian as he was heading back in their direction. She couldn't help but notice that some of the wrinkles were returning after his miraculous change to youth. What she saw in his eyes was unstoppable determination and what might be a hint of guilt. He was no longer wearing the leather armour he once had but now preferred the simple green shirt and cloak tied behind him. He still wore the leather gauntlets with throwing knives tied on each hand. And with two big swords sticking up over his head and on his back, she thought he did look very much like the dangerous man he was. As he got closer, she noticed he had a more worried look on his face than usual.

"Is something wrong with the trail?" She asked, catching her breath.

"Found some marks on the trail, but they're probably nothing."

Lara shook her head, unconvinced from his tone.

"Your Nephew is at it again. I think we need to hurry and get to that witch of yours."

"Yes, it's not much further from here." He said, breaking into a jog to get to Sebastion's side. "Don't go too far ahead alone," Killian yelled over his shoulder at her.

Yeah, sure. Probably nothing, she thought, frowning and watching him go.

"And watch for that damn cat!" He yelled before disappearing down the trail. Lara couldn't help coughing out a laugh at that. Killian had been calling Morakye 'that damn cat' since they first crossed the mountain. It seems this area reminded Morakye of his home, and he had been jumping through the trees and disappearing and reappearing like a ghost which was scaring the puckering shit out of all of them. To Lara's surprise, she decided she liked the little Fangor. He was always upbeat and never seemed to think that the boy would not get better. He kept calling him his brother and 'the one.' Morakye would get anxious when Sebastion had his fits, but she was sure Morakye did not think Sebastion would die.

There was a rustle of leaves, and Morakye was there like he had known she was thinking of him. She knew the rustling of the leaves was a courtesy not to scare her. Lara put her hands on her hips and shook her head at him as if scolding a child.

"You're past your curfew, you bad little cat."

Morakye smiled at her, but Lara didn't see the smile follow into his yellow eyes as it always had. "What's wrong?"

"Rifkins," Morakye said as if Lara should understand. Lara shook her head, having no idea what he was talking about. Morakye pointed to a mark on the ground and repeated. "Rifkins." This time he said it as if even the sound of the word left a bad taste in his mouth. Lara looked at the ground and saw an indent in the thick green grass but could understand none of it.

"What in the puckering hell is a Rifkin, Morakye?"

"Rifkins be bad," Morakye said, shaking his head. Lara nodded and made a motion with her hands in front of her for him to continue.

"Me thinks they look be like children of your kind but darker-skinned and very … eh, more mean."

"They're mean?" Lara asked, raising a brow.

"Me do not know another word in your language to … describe them." Morakye looked at the ground, trying to think. "In Morakye's tribe, when someone did something bad to another, they call it a Rifka. Do you know?"

"I think I get it," Lara said, starting her walk back to the others. Morakye grabbed her wrist and held her.

"Me's not done yet … sorry," he said, his pointed ears twitching and looking around nervously. Lara smiled and stroked his soft cheek. They had been together for only a few days, and she was surprised how comfortable she was with him, despite his strange looks.

"Sorry, Morakye. What else is there?" She asked, smiling.

Morakye frowned up at her. "They's are following us. They's should catch us by tomorrow morning."

Laras did not like the serious look in his eyes. "You're sure?"

"Morakye is sure," he answered, putting a clawed hand up to shade his eyes so he could remain looking up at her.

"They are bad?" She asked.

"Bad." Morakye nodded slowly.

"Great." Lara sighed.

Killian sat next to the litter grasping Sebastion's hand. He soothingly told him that they did not have much longer to go and that they would get help. Truth be told though, Killian had not been to see the witch in a long time, and there was even a chance she was no longer there or even alive. But he could think of no other that could help and he was sure they had no other choice.

Lara and Baran had no ideas on how to help a boy that had been spat upon with dragon's blood. In fact, they were still processing the whole thing in their way. Killian was sure Lara never believed in the gods, but then she had had one standing in front of her. It happened to be the bad one, but a god nonetheless. He knew when she saw him, there was no question as to who he was. Killian could only imagine what she was thinking.

"I need to talk to you," Lara announced, breaking his thoughts and walking over quickly.

"What is it?" He asked without looking up.

"Perhaps in private." She said, not making it a question. Sebastion was more restful now, so Killian stood up and walked a few paces away. Lara waved to Baran, and he came over to them too, rubbing his shoulder that had not long ago had a Barbarian arrow through it.

"Morakye says we're being followed by something called Rifkin's, or Ripkins, or something like that." Killian frowned and looked over at Morakye, who had taken his place beside Sebastion. He angrily moved his fingers in the silent language.

'You are just spooking them.' Killian signed.

22

'They have a right to know.' Morakye signed back, not looking at him.

"STOP DOING THAT!" Lara whispered harshly through her teeth. "That is rude, and we're all in this *together*."

Killian smiled at her sympathetically. "Sorry, I just didn't want you to get worked up if you didn't have to about our coming guests. That's all." He scratched at his dark beard thinking. "It's been some time, but if I remember, the witch's hut should only be a day and a half from here."

Lara looked over at Morakye and he caught her eye. "Morakye said that they would catch up with us by morning."

Killian crossed his arms and scowled at the ground. "You sure?" He asked, without looking over at the Fangor.

"Morakye is *very* sure, though he wishes he wasn't. Morakye does not like Rifkins."

"And what by da' dark hell is a *Rifkin*, may I ask?" Baran looked around, confused.

"-little pain in the asses that have been known to work with the Barbarians," Killian answered, scowling.

"Dat's great," Baran nervously looked around at the trees.

"Let's keep moving until we come up with something, shall we," Killian said, walking off down the trail. Baran quickly picked up the litter and moved with him, and Lara ran forward to catch up with Killian.

"Don't worry about me, I got it," Baran called after them sarcastically. He looked over at Morakye, who was walking beside the litter to be near Sebastion. "I don't suppose you wanna take a turn, eh?" He asked.

23

"Morakye is so small, and you are so large..." Morakye said, smiling and showing off his pointy fangs. Baran shook his head, grumbling, and marched on.

"So we haven't spoken of what happened back at that castle," Lara said, walking side by side with Killian now.

"You sure you want to get further involved?" Killian asked seriously. Lara thought a moment before answering. A few days back, she would have told him he was too worried about her and Baran ... but now.

"Yes, I'm in. I can't speak for Baran."

"The dark you can't!" Killian laughed.

"Alright, maybe I can." She laughed too. "We're in."

Killian stopped and looked deep into her eyes. They were far enough ahead that it didn't disrupt Baran and the litter. He liked her dark eyes and how the corners lifted slightly like a cat. He smiled, taking her in. Her long dark hair was tied tightly behind her, hanging down to the middle of her back. She wore her black leather trousers and sleeveless shirt. Killian started losing track when he realized what he was doing and looked up again to meet her eyes. She opened her eyes wider as if to say, 'get to it, already!'

"I can only tell you what I know, which isn't much, and most of it is only what I suspect." Killian started walking again. "My old ... boss, Bashor, wanted this." He reached up and pulled The Eye of The Gods crystal from beneath his shirt. "He knew my father had it, but he didn't know where. So he needed someone who would find it for him. He knew none of us would ever deal with him, so he..." Killian was trying to find the right words. "-created, one of us that would. He and his evil

24

under-wraith pets convinced me that I had killed my brother. Not knowing where to turn with the weight of it on my shoulders, Bashor came to me. He told me there was a place for me and that I could work for him. Understand, all I really wanted to do was die. The guilt was crushing. I was lost and confused. All he asked in return was my allegiance, oh, and if I *happen* to come across the Eye ... that would be nice, too."

Lara laughed at his sarcasm. "So, he changed your memories?" She asked, confused. "Where does the boy come in?"

"I'm getting to that," Killian said, waving at her impatiently.

"Oh, and who was-eh, Mel-"

"Melodia," Killian finished for her, scowling into the trees around him.

Lara looked over and saw a sadness wash over him that made her remember him as the old man who first came to her home.

"You loved her?" Lara realized the truth of it seeing the pain in his face.

"Yes." He answered simply and taking a moment before continuing. "When we were young." Killian took a deep breath. "I had already joined up with Bashor. I had so much pain in my heart that I went to the Great City and prayed to The Lady of Light for help. I remember kneeling in that damn temple, weeping, and asking for guidance. My mind was being tortured by the memory of killing my brother. It consumed me. Day and night, it played again and again in front of me." Killian reached up and ran his hand through his now long, thick hair as he walked. "I was lost and prayed for death. And then she was there. I had not even seen her enter the temple where I prayed. I remember it like it was yesterday. She was wearing the white gown of a priestess. Her hair was so red it looked like it was made of fire. But it was her eyes that trapped my heart that day. They were the purest blue I had ever seen. There was extreme kindness there mixed with an inner strength that I envied ... even today. We talked for days, though I never revealed my secret. In time, we realized that we were in love, and we became inseparable." Killian stopped and walked in silence a time before going on.

"Well, to make a long story short, I finally told her what I thought I had done, and she could not accept it. Not that I blame her. I left, and we did not speak again for many, *many* years. She walked in the Light of the Lady and I under the shadow of Bashor, who was in the service of the Dark Lord."

"But she was there-at Bashor's castle?" Lara asked, confused. She saw Killian swallow hard before answering.

"Bashor said she came to free me from his service. I do not know the truth. I think she might have come to me in my dreams ... but that could have been more of Bashor's tricks, I don't know. What I do know is she is dead, and that Bashor is responsible for it ... not to mention my brother and very nearly my Nephew."

"And all for that fancy crystal?" Lara asked.

"Not all of it," Killian said, turning to her. "Bashor and the Dark Lord had their plans for Sebastion. Though I think they were separate ones. Somehow, he is the center of all this." He glanced at her, seeing the confused look in her dark eyes. "I think that is enough for now. It comes down to this. First, we help Sebastion; then I hunt down Bashor and separate that puckering dark bastard's head from his shoulders."

"Sounds like a good plan." Lara nodded, frowning. "Solid."

"Why do you want to come?" Killian asked her, serious now. "What is there to gain from following me into this darkness and death?"

Lara frowned, thinking a moment. "Because right now I choose too," she answered defiantly. "My destiny is my own, and right now I choose to go with you." She turned to him, returning the stern gaze, and making it evident there was no room for argument.

"Very well, then." Killian shrugged. "It would be a very long road without you and your mule." He nodded at Baron, who was struggling with the litter. Lara snickered and kept walking. She used the silence to think about the things Killian had told her.

The sun was starting to set, but they knew better than to stop. Killian had taken his turn pulling the litter to give Baran a break. The truth was that he did not know how far the witch was from here. It was a long time ago, and much of the landscape had changed. Morakye had disappeared into the woods, returning with some strange-looking fruit that they ate as they continued. As the darkness approached, Baran started nervously looking behind. Killian could also feel the approaching danger. Every time the wind blew, they jumped and put a hand to their weapons. Their nerves were on edge waiting for the Rifkins, who could come at any time. A strong breeze blew through the trees, and Baran turned and pulled his sword from his hip.

"Dat's it!" He exclaimed. "I cannot just wait for 'dose bastards ta' put an arrow in my damn back!"

"Calm down, Baran," Killian said, putting the litter down. "According to Morakye, we still have time."

Baran looked over to where Morakye had been walking, but he was gone. "Oh 'dats just great," he said, throwing his hands in the air with his sword. "Dat's just perfect."

Lara did not miss the worried look on Killian's face as he looked around at the trees.

"He'll be back." She said, trying to sound confident. She was sure the little Fangor did not come all this way to run off now. "He always comes back."

"Yeah, but he ain't always possessed little children thingy's after 'em." Baran countered.

"Rifkins," Killian said, picking up the litter again.

"I'll take 'dat," Baran said, walking towards him. "Better that I'm using some of 'dis nervous energy."

Killian had to admit he was thankful as his arms felt like they were on fire from pulling. His Nephew had gained a lot of weight since he had first seen him and pulling was strenuous ... at least for him. Baran lifted the two handles and quickly walked down the trail.

They had not gone far when Morakye appeared ahead of them like a ghost in the coming darkness.

"AHH!" Baran yelled, startled, dropping the litter and struggling for his sword. Killian had been trailing behind to watch for Rifkins when he heard Baran's response. He ran up the trail, jumping over Sebastion, who had rolled off. Killian landed on the ground near Baran, his sword ready, looking for danger. He saw Morakye ahead, standing still in the fading light and holding a bow with a quiver of arrows and three spears on his back. He had what looked to be a hard leather vest with strange designs that seemed to be burned symbols across his chest.

28

"Where'd ya get 'dat?" Baran called out, angrily.

"Is there anything else around us?" Killian asked, searching the treeline with his eyes.

"Just me's … for now," Morakye said, smiling.

"For now? What does that mean?" Lara asked, moving closer to the Fangor to admire his new weapons. Morakye turned his back so she could see. "I take it you borrowed these from a Rifkin, then?" She asked him, raising an eyebrow but letting a half-smile touch her lips.

"He no longer needed it," Morakye said, his yellow eyes catching the moonlight and turning to Killian. "Will's you be picking my brother off the ground now?" He asked, looking up at Killian.

"We need to talk, Fangor," Killian said, turning to help Baran lift Sebastion back onto the litter.

"Me think's the rest is still several hours away," Morakye said, crossing Sebastion's arms across his chest. "These things-" Morakye indicated his new weapons, "-belonged to what I think you people call a … scout."

"Do we need to worry about this scout?" Killian asked.

Morakye gave him a confused look before answering. "He be very dead."

"You're sure?" Killian asked again, seriously.

"Morakye is not proud of what he did, but what was done is done completely." Morakye made a sucking noise through his teeth waving a hand as if saying 'that is enough of that.' Lara covered the smile on her face with her hand.

"Alright, then," Killian said, a little taken aback. "I don't suppose you've seen the witch's cottage in your disappearance?"

"Yes," Morakye answered.

"Next time you plan to take a- "Killian stopped. "What did you say?"

"Morakye said *yes* to you." Morakye shrugged. Lara laughed out loud this time, and Killian gave her a look that made her clear her throat and cover her smirk.

"Where is the witch's cottage?"

Morakye pointed up the trail in the moonlight. "Just over that hill." They all looked up the path, but it was too dark to see the hill.

"Why didn't you just say so?" Killian asked, stomping off.

Morakye shook his head, turning to Lara. "Me think's these two humans are most definitely related." Lara laughed and, saying nothing more, followed after Killian.

With their goal in sight, the group moved quickly down the hill. Morakye ran next to Sebastion, making sure he did not fall out again. As they got closer, they could see there was light coming from a window in the cottage. Sebastion suddenly sat up slightly and looked around before laying back, twitching again. They stopped and watched him, surprised by his sudden animation. Killian came over and touched his temples for a short time, and Sebastion seemed to become more restful, as he always did.

"I think we should hurry," Killian said worriedly. "His skin is so cool I don't know what-" He ran his hand through his Nephew's hair. "I just don't know." He looked over at Morakye, who was looking up the trail. Killian followed his gaze and saw a figure leaning against a stick and watching them in the darkness. "Nobody move." He whispered.

"wha-" Baran started, but followed Killian's gaze and also froze.

30

"My name is K-"

"I have *no* care what your name is." The figure in the dark cut him off in a deep husky woman's voice. "Leave now or die. Those are your choices."

"My Nephew is sick. I can pay you..." Killian pleaded.

"You have nothing I want." She said back. Then Killian saw Morakye's fur rise upon his neck in the little light.

"A Fangor!" The woman exclaimed, seeing Morakye for what he was for the first time and stepping slightly forward. "Can it be that one survived?"

"One does," Morakye answered cautiously.

"Step towards me, little one," the woman said.

"Will you help my brother?"

"Brother?" The witch asked excitedly.

"Yes, brother but not of my blood," Morakye said, striding towards what he presumed was the witch.

"Hold there," Killian said, pulling his sword and walking confidently towards the figure in the darkness. He stepped around Morakye to stand in front of her. Now that he could see her better, she was not what he expected her to look like now. She was tall and not as old as he had thought she would be. She had hard but intelligent eyes with long grey and black hair that fell across her cloak.

"How is it you do not feel?" She asked him.

"What?" He looked at her, not knowing what she meant.

She looked at him in fascination. Killian looked behind him to see if he was missing something but just saw terrified looks on Morakye, Lara, and Baran's faces.

31

"What is it?" He asked, but was sure now what or who it was coming from. "I will make this simple for you," Killian said, looking at the shocked witch. "Release them from your spell, or *I will*. Do you get my meaning?" He positioned his sword, ready to strike.

"If you kill me, who will help your boy there." The witch answered, smiling.

Killian smiled back. "Who said anything about killing you? I was thinking of lopping off your ears ... then perhaps your feet." Killian let the smile leave his face and he became all serious. "Look into my eyes, witch. Do you see any hesitation?" The witch did look into his eyes and must have seen enough because she waved a hand and Killian heard someone fall to the ground. "Thank you. I would like you to take a look at my nephew."

"Curious bunch, you are." The witch said, leaning on her stick and shaking her head. "Bring the boy and the rest." She added, heading back to her cottage. "Oh, make sure not to step on the rocks," she said over her shoulder.

Baran gently lifted Sebastion off the litter and carried him around the rocks scattered on the ground in front of the cottage. Lara walked behind him to make sure he didn't make a mistake. They entered the cabin and stood in a semi-circle around Sebastion in the little room.

"What's wrong with him?" The witch asked, looking down to where Sebastion lay on the floor.

"We were hoping you could tell us," Killian said, scratching nervously at his now-thick beard. The witch knelt and looked at him more closely. "He looks like he's been poisoned." She reached out and touched his head. A light sparked and she flew backward. Everyone backed up to the wall, searching the room. The light faded, and Sebastion was back to twisting and turning as if in a bad dream.

"WHAT BY THE DARK HAVE YOU BROUGHT TO MY HOME?" The witch cursed, staring wide-eyed at Sebastion.

"What was that?" Killian asked her, his back still against the wall.

"He surely is poisoned," she whispered, shaking her head.

"Make sense, woman!" Killian growled at her. The witch looked back and forth at Sebastion and Killian. "He has magic in him and..."

"And what else?" Killian demanded.

"I don't think it's a what, but more like a ... who, I think." The witch shook her head as if mystified. "Most with the magic die either in the womb or shortly after birth. How is it he is so old?" The witch demanded.

"He has had no magic that I know of," Killian said, stepping to Sebastion to calm his whimpering.

"If the magic is not reined in, it will consume him, and he will die. There is nothing someone like I can do." She said, getting up from the floor and brushing off her clothes.

"That's it?" Killian asked with anger building up inside of him. He grabbed Sebastion's hand in his own and tried to swallow the frustration. As he leaned forward, The Eye came out of his shirt and hung over Sebastion, glowing slightly.

"What is that?" The witch asked, coming to Killian slowly but cautiously, keeping him between herself and Sebastion.

"That, my lady, is not of your concern."

33

"I know that. I have seen that..." The witch pointed a long finger at it, stepping closer. She suddenly turned and went into a room and the four of them exchanged confused glances at her quick exit.

"What if 'dat old hag can't help?" Baran asked, sadly looking over at Sebastion.

Killian hung his head and sighed. "I don't know. I just don't know..."

"We may have to face the fact that she may not know how to help him, Killian," Lara said. "And let us not forget, our little friends are on the way."

"I have not forgotten anything. NOT ONE PUCKERING THING." Killian growled, rubbing a knuckle into his aching forehead. Just then, the witch came out of the room, excitedly carrying a book. "It's right here. If it is truly what I think it is, then-" She pointed in the book for them to see. "Could it truly exist!?"

Killian looked in the book and recognized the image. "Yeah, that's it." He shrugged. The witch only looked at him unblinking. "What?" He asked. The witch shook her head, amazed.

"That is the Eye of the Gods." She said, still staring at him.

"Yes, I know that" Killian said back, his eyes wide, sarcastically mimicking her look. "Now tell me something useful. Like how to help my Nephew from laying there like some damn vegetable!" The witch slammed her book shut and placed it on the railing above the fireplace as she took a deep breath.

"Perhaps the answer is already with you. But let me ask you something first." She stepped forward to face Killian squarely. "Why should I help you? What's in this for me?"

"I have coin," Killian said, red-faced.

"That's good for you. What else do you have?" She asked, crossing her arms. Killian looked to his companions, but they returned his blank look. He had not thought about payment up to this point. All his thoughts were on Sebastion and his condition. "What do you want, witch?" He asked, now feeling foolish.

"Firstly, that you call me Parla, which is my name, not 'witch.' Witches are presumed to have magic. I just use the powers around me. Not of my own. And secondly, that your traveling companions take a seat and not stand around as if they are going to attack me at any moment." Killian tried to relax some and nodded to Lara, who smiled at him, as surprised as he was by the woman's response.

"Is there a third?" Killian asked, trying to make his voice calm.

"Most assuredly, but for now-" Parla swept an arm dramatically around the cottage, meaning for them to sit. Lara and Baran found chairs, and Morakye sat on the floor near Sebastion's side. Killian remained standing, facing her.

"Time is something I do not have a lot of," Killian said, crossing his arms and frowning at her.

"Or patience, I see," Parla remarked. Lara laughed and Killian gave her a side-eye look.

"We are being pursued," Killian said, finding a chair and sitting near the table.

"Yes, yes-the Rifkins. I know about them."

Killian could almost feel Morakye's ear twitching at that. "Then you know time is of the essence. We can take you with us until we get to safety if you like. But first-"

35

"First, do not worry about the Rifkins," Parla said, cutting him off. "They are a superstitious bunch, as are most on this side of the mountain. The little folk think I can curse them and so keep their distance." She scratched at her underarm, eyeing Killian thoughtfully. "Why do they pursue you?"

"I don't know."

"Don't you?" She answered, obviously unconvinced. "What other secrets do you strange people have?"

Killian looked away, his face turning red, this time from anger. Lara recognized the look and shifted uneasily in her chair. *Here we go.*

"I will make this simple for you. I am guessing that you may have information that may lead to helping my Nephew. My bargain is this. Tell me what I need to know, and in return, I will not kill you. And 'firstly' before you respond to my deal, as we shall call it. Know this, my patience has run out, and I have faced bigger things than you, and I am not having a good TIME OF IT!" He slammed a fist onto the table, knocking some jars and small objects onto the floor.

Parla sat back as if profoundly considering Killian's offer. She tapped her chin and looked at the ceiling thoughtfully.

"Oh, for the love of light, woman!" Killian swore.

Parla put up her hands soothingly. "Alright, alright."

She smiled. "The answer is already with you."

"Yes, you said that."

Parla smiled wide, showing off her crooked yellow teeth. "What you have around your neck is one of maybe a handful of magical items that still exist in this world."

"I don't care," Killian answered between clenched teeth.

36

"But you will," Parla said confidently. "The Eye is a filter of sorts that absorbs magic. It acts differently according to any situation, like any other magical device, the laws of this world do not burden it. One of the obvious things I see by looking at your friend there and nearly being fried by the light, I might add, is that the man is consumed by magic. I find that rather peculiar as almost all that are with magic-die. There is talk of one girl surviving until nearly seven years old once, but I suspect that is only folklore. Since the cleansing, there has there been any as old as him with any significant power. So, I have to admit that it makes me very curious. Who is he?" She asked seriously.

Killian shook his head 'no.'

"Then, I ask for only one thing more for the knowledge I can give you."

"Speak it," Killian said, leaning in his chair, thinking he knew what it was going to be and not for a second going to let it happen.

"Tell me, what is going on here all of it. I ask that you give me your word to tell me everything you know and anything the others know. I want it all." Killian looked at her, surprised.

"That's it?" He asked, leaning forward.

"That's it. But all of it, though." She warned, wagging a finger at him. He looked back at the others and Baran shrugged his vast shoulders with a frown on his face. Lara prodded him on with her hands.

"Agreed."

"Take the Eye from your neck and put it on your nephew." She went on sitting forward in her chair now. "I believe that will at least help his condition. I believe it will be chicken soup to a cold, but it should at least help him. Do it now."

Killian looked at her, unsure. "No tricks" he said, reaching around his neck.

"I cannot promise the result as all this is new to me as it must be to you. But- " She raised her hands in the air, not finishing. Killian frowned and stepped to Sebastion. Morakye's eyes narrowed and twinkled from the light of the candles that lit the room. Killian looked into those eyes and saw the desperation and frustration that must be mirrored in his own. He exchanged nods with the Fangor before reaching out and placing the crystal around Sebastion's neck. He held the small, pointed crystal in his hand before letting it rest gently on the skin of Sebastion's chest. The crystal immediately began to glow red from the inside. Sebastion's eyes opened wide, and he stared at the ceiling from his back. He reached up and placed his hand over the crystal. His body shook gently. His head turned slowly, and his eyes came to rest on the witch. Then there was another flash of light that blinded everyone and knocked them from their seats. When their vision returned, they could see Sebastion moving slowly on the floor. Morakye was there at his side.

"Wa-" he tried to speak and painfully swallowed. "Wa-water" he croaked.

CHAPTER 4

The chilly night air was penetrating the witch's cottage. Baran fed a small fire and the others watched as Sebastion shovelled anything put in front of him into his mouth. The only words he had spoken thus far were 'water' and 'more.' They were down to stale bread and overripe fruit that the witch had tucked away. Morakye watched him like a mother hen, and Killian was beaming from ear to ear. Lara watched the two of them, fascinated by their similarities. She had noticed them before, but now that Sebastion was awake, the obvious traits were all the more evident. She stood over them, arms crossed, staring down with her dark eyes, amused by it all. She wondered how these two would now react to each other. Sebastion had so obviously changed since Killian had last seen him. Killian had described him as an emaciated small boy, but that was not who was now swallowing down food like a wolf. The man here was tall, muscular, and had a look in his eye that looked far older than his years. She couldn't put her finger on just what she saw there, but it was not the innocent look of a boy of his age. She sensed movement and looked over to see the woman, Parla, struggle with a door on the floor that led to the rest of the food stores. She had remained silent since Sebastion was brought back, and Lara watched her suspiciously.

Parla came up out of the door with a piece of salted meat. Sebastion eyed it hungrily.

"I will need a coin or two to replenish what he has swallowed?" Parla said to Killian as she placed the tray of meat in front of him.

"Yes, of course. We will give you that and more."

Parla nodded, rubbing a spot in the middle of her forehead painfully. "I think I will get comfortable before this headache takes over me. Any objections?" Killian shook his head without looking at her. She plopped into a chair and got comfortable. She reached up to a shelf that was nearby and pulled off a small pipe. She packed it with dried leaves and sparked it to life. She puffed silently before leaning back. The smell of the smoke was different than Killian had ever smelled, and he sniffed it curiously.

"A little something to get the tongue wagging." Parla chuckled, seeing his look and leaning back and crossing her legs. "Such an interesting day ... so very interesting."

"What was the 'cleansing' you were talking about?" Lara asked, taking a seat across from her.

"Ah, yes. Thank you." Parla nodded to her. "The cleansing, as it is written, was a time when the wizards walked this world. The story goes that they found the secret to immortality and a way to preserve it. To ensure their absolute power, a group of wizards destroyed all other magic users, all things magical, and the ability of a person with the gift to survive childbirth. Thus 'cleansing' the world of magic ... other than their own, that is. This ensured their total rule. But as time went by-," She took a big puff off her pipe before going on, "-they became bored with themselves and explored ways to expand their powers, and inevitably there became contention among the wizards. Two fought, and their destruction of the world from their fighting led to the others having to choose. To save this world, they had to combine their strength to destroy both fighting wizards. From that time on, they swore to never fight amongst themselves again. However, their ambitions once again overcame them, but this time they found a new way to fight each other without breaking their oath … or the world. They used the people to fight their battles for them. The world became their great chess game, and they moved people as their game pieces at their whim. They became gods to the people, and they were more than happy to be worshipped. There were wars, then alliances, then more significant wars, which continued for a long time before the world inadvertently became chaos. Too many of their pawns were dying, and they found that it was no fun without them. A balance had to be made to keep things from spinning out of control, again. They brought their powers together and, in their arrogance, allowed two to be born of powerful magic. Two equal twins. Separate in everything, including their sex.

These two were going to be the class of gods beneath them to fix their mistakes. These two would be the ones to interact with the people of the world. They would keep the living from becoming too destroyed so that the wizards, now gods, could still play their games." Parla stopped a moment and rubbed her head, looking confused. "I swear I hadn't known that before. How strange…"

Killian looked over at her curiously as Parla rubbed her head silently.

"Perhaps if you go on, Parla," Lara suggested. She had been listening, very interested in what she was saying.

"Yes … sure. Uh-the twins." Parla took another suck from her pipe. "They grew, and not just in body but in power. They were supposed to be the watchers of the people but became more interested in the ones

41

who created them. They were jealous of the thirteen powers, although minus the two, and found that soon their magic was as powerful as theirs. It did not take long from there for the twins to find out they were even more powerful. As time went on, the wizards became lesser gods, and the twins ruled. Still, like the ones before them, they looked to the people of the world as nothing but entertainment. The twins' power over the lesser gods comes from each other. Only together do they have the power to control the lesser gods. If one is destroyed, then they both are destroyed." Parla leaned forward and looked surprised. "I do not know how I know this, but something else is happening in the world. "She paused, looking up at the ceiling, thinking. "Something bigger than the twins. Something that has them scared ... change." Parla looked at Sebastion and he stopped chewing to return her gaze.

"You are the catalyst to that change. Somehow ... I ... feel it."

"I ... have to go," Sebastion mumbled through the food in his mouth, still staring at the witch.

"It is night, and we don't know what's out there." Killian answered patiently, "I think we should wait until morning."

"No, I have to go now," Sebastion said, getting up from the table. Killian got up as well and gently put a hand on Sebastion's shoulder. "What is it, Nephew. Why do you need to leave now?" Sebastion nervously looked around the room. For the first time, Lara saw the innocence in him now that she was unsure he had left.

"Rayor ... eh, Killian, I need-" he leaned forward and whispered into Killian's ear. A smile spread across Killian's face and he laughed, waving Sebastion to the door.

"Out back, just beyond the trees," Parla called after him as he opened the door and flew out. Realization of the situation ascended onto everyone, and they laughed. Morakye, too nervous to lose his brother again, followed Sebastion outside.

CHAPTER 5
The March

There was no need for cages and the people marched behind the huge temperamental war horses. If someone fell, they were dragged until they got up again. If someone did not get up, the Barbarians would cut the binds, and they would have wished that they had gotten up. Their meals were small and considering what they suspected was in the lumpy stew, disheartening at the least. They had no idea where they were going, but most no longer cared. They had all given up and were now only walking husks of their former selves.

The groups had watched their cities burn before their eyes. Fighting the man-eater horde was impossible. The Barbarians were too strong and vicious for the Torenium people to stand up against. Besides, most men able to fight were ordered away to the Great City in its defence. The wall of Endrea was breached just a few short hours after the battle began. The Endrean army, which was just a small number of older or injured men left behind by the Great City, was easily and quickly crushed by the Barbarians.

Towards the end, the small number of soldiers who were still alive turned and ran back to the wall in desperation. The Barbarian's rode them down to the last man. Not one soldier made it back to the fleeting safety of the walls of Endrea.

With no one to fight them, the man-eaters pounded the gate until it too could no longer take their beatings and collapsed. Some hid, others jumped into the ocean and preferred a cold death to what waited for them. Some foolishly begged for mercy, and they were the first to find the fires and spits. The Barbarians would viciously laugh when the Endorians grovelled and begged for their lives. The ones they thought were strong enough to walk were roped and taken away. The others prayed for a quick death as the Man-Eaters prepared a great feast after which no living soul remained in Endrea.

As the Barbarians left the dead city, the flocks of blackbirds descended and ate any dead flesh that was left behind. In a short time, all that was left of the once lively city was bones and empty streets. A bell on a float near the dock would echo through the open city as the wind blew waves onto the white sandy shore. Seagulls looked sadly onto the once busy beach, and hungry rats ran freely, looking for the last bits of food they could find. Endrea was dead. The last of the people unable to buy passage out of the now silent city marched north with ropes around their hands and necks.

One rather small man marched with the others but hid the fire that burned in his eyes. He kept his gaze low and unseen, but his rage grew with every awkward step. Every time the dry and frayed rope around his neck stretched and split his skin, vengeful determination pushed him on. Every rock he tripped over brought focus to his raging brain.

Ishma knew the man-eaters well. He had once been a slave of them until winning his freedom. He had to fight for his release, and now he was in the same damn puckering situation. Long ago, he had saved his master's life by killing a big bear with only his knife. They had been hunting, and the bear surprised his Barbarian master, jumping out from the close by brush. It knocked him to the ground and bent its maul to finish the job when Ishma jumped on the back of the bear and stabbed it in the neck and head so many times that eventually it fell to the ground, twitching and breathing out its last breath. The next day his master freed him, having Ishma's teeth ceremoniously sharpened in the way of the man-eaters. The tattoos came later on the docks of Ruthar. He was never accepted among the Barbarians and left to find his fortune in the West. There he picked a trade he knew something about, the slave trade. The work was easy, and the money was good. Everything was going well until a damned skinny boy appeared out of the woods. It seemed as soon as *he* came into his life, everything went to puckering hell.

When Ishma had arrived in Endrea, he could not sell his slaves and so he couldn't raise the money to board a ship. He had to free the slaves into the city because he ran out of money to feed them and pay the guards that watched them. Ishma quickly found himself in a doomed city about to be invaded by man-eaters with no way out. The last of the money he received from the big knight he spent in a dark, depressing bar. The owner eventually hopped a ship and left his wares to anyone dumb or poor enough to still be there. The last few days in the city he spent so drunk he couldn't remember much of it. There was only one thing that stood out in his mind. It was on the same day of the man-eaters' attack but earlier in the morning. He had heard a commotion outside in the streets and went out to see which was uncharacteristic of him. What he saw was a crowd of people by the docks. He then saw a man flung into the air above the people's heads, screaming. Ishma had climbed onto a barrel and then the small overhanging roof to get a better view. What he saw was the creature he had caught and caged. It was clothed and flinging around sailors like rag dolls. Finally, a sailor had gotten a lucky strike, and the creature yowled like the beast it was. That was when *he* appeared again. As if haunting him, the boy, now a tall and well-built man, because of *him*, ran into the circle of men and cut them down as if he was butchering pigs for a Sunday feast.

Ishma remembered watching as *his* slave became covered in blood as he killed like a beast. He could not get the crowd's gasping out of his head as to how they started mumbling some nonsense about demons. Although even he had to admit the boy did look like some monster from the Dark Lord's hell as he stood there blood-soaked and wild. From that roof, he could see his eyes gleaming as if from ethereal light through his bloody face. He felt the power of that moment, and it made him hate the boy all the more. He wanted to forget this Sebastion, that dark, damned furry creature, and even the puckering pretty girl with the big brown eyes that had caused him so much trouble. He had enough of them for a lifetime, but there he was again. Feeling disgusted, he had jumped off the roof and found himself an abandoned bottle to keep him company. He had tried to take his thoughts away from the rotten son of a whore, but they would come back as if he was haunted. He remembered throwing the bottle against a wall and then hearing the battle horns of the man-eaters. He had closed his eyes and let the alcohol take him. When he had awoken, he was lying among a line of dead bodies. He remembered his mistake, jumping up startled, looking around and catching the eye of a Barbarian nearby who had gotten off his horse and roped him into a line of slaves.

Now he was in this mess trying to keep his gaze low and, with his small legs aching, trying to keep up with the others. Ishma refused to be a slave again, and he needed a plan to escape but, every time, his mind kept going back to *him*. To a disgusting, puckering bastard slave that had ruined his life! Part of him knew he would have gone to Endrea whether or not Sebastion crossed his path, but he was sure that the boy had cursed him in some way. The hate for him filled him with rage and that gave him the strength to put one step in front of the other.

If I ever see that puckering bastard again, I'll cut him to pieces ... PIECES!

The big Barbarian rode past them and the bound man in front of Ishma started pissing himself. Roped as he was, Ishma had to step in the river of urine as he walked.

"Keep your cowardly fluid to yourself, you worthless waste of flesh!" Ishma whispered sharply at him. The man's only reaction was to stiffen slightly and cast a nervous glance behind him, as much as the rope would allow.

Someday our paths will cross again, cursed boy. One day...

Chapter 6 – Thieves of Magic

The marble floors echoed with their voices. They sat facing each other. The chairs were on a slight stage with the black marble flooring separating them. Their bodies still the age they had been when they had found their immortality. Some looked young and others older with grey and some with no hair, but all now wore worried looks on their faces and a few even seemed frightened.

"We should listen to what he has to say." A woman said, straightening her green robe and trying to look confident. She looked of middle age, with short greying black hair. Her most noticeable feature was her huge nose that seemed almost to take over her entire face. The people that worshipped her found the nose to be the most beautiful feature of the body. People with enormous noses were regarded as the most beautiful of their land.

"And risk the Twins' wrath?" Another asked in a more timid voice.

"What are we supposed to do? Are we all to live in fear of The Twins forever?!" A dark-skinned man asked, rising from his chair.

"You are brave here hidden beneath the world, Taglien. But what song will you sing when we are at the surface again?" Another asked. "Will you be the one to lead us against the twins?" Taglien humphed and took a seat, crossing his arms defensively.

"I agree with that; we should at least hear what the mage has to say" Said a short, bald, and ugly man, his face littered with acne scars. His beard grew in patches around the battered flesh.

"I have heard the twins have separated paths," another spoke up. "Now could be our only chance to take back what is rightfully ours."

"These two were our mistake, and we should now make things right again" a fair-haired woman said, putting her pretty chin in the air.

"Things have come a long way since then." The short ugly one said disdainfully. "How are we to challenge them? Even apart, they are stronger than we. What do you propose we do?"

"I don't know … but the mage may."

"If the twins find out," one cautioned.

"Oh, spare me the warnings! We know what the twins would do." Taglien said, rising again. "Let's take this to a vote already and see?"

The room of lesser gods, as the twins had named them, looked around, agreeing.

49

"All those in favour of speaking with the dark mage raise a hand," Taglien said, sitting again. He looked around the room before raising his arm above his head.

"The decision has been made." The woman with the big nose said. "Taglien, you have taken an active role in the outcome here. Will you contact the Mage and inform him of our decision?" She asked. Taglien looked at her, wide-eyed.

"You want me to contact him?"

"It seems appropriate," the woman said, and the others around the room nodded in agreement.

"Okay, fine then. I will be the one to find the Mage." Taglien wiped a bead of sweat from his dark brow with a cloth that he pulled from a pocket in his long robe.

Taglien sat by the waterfall that fell from the sky and disappeared just beyond the rocks in his courtyard. The lesser gods found a way to live in the world but on another plane of existence and this allowed them their privacy and security. They manipulated the physical world enough to give themselves every comfort. Taglien's castle was large and glowed a pleasant pale white. The landscapes around it were constantly changing as it floated through many separate planes. For one moment, it would be mountains, and then another surrounded by calm seas. Taglien sat in a cushioned chair, staring into a crystal suspended above his lap. It showed him a time long ago with him looking the same, dancing and playing with children that looked almost identical to him. He stared at them and leaned back into the thick cushions. The crystal floated around with him, keeping the same distance from his eye. The image changed, and a woman was there with similarly dark skin but with delicate feminine features. Her face filled the ball, and she smiled. Taglien stared back at her longingly, and he reached a hand up and caressed the cold, smooth surface of the crystal. "I miss you..." He whispered to the image. The image of the woman smiled wider and nodded to him.

"If I knew you felt that way, I would have come sooner," Bashor said, coming into the room and bowing.

"WHAT!" Taglien yelled, standing up quickly. The ball was knocked aside and fell to the ground with a thump. "How dare you invade my privacy?!" He yelled to the tall, emaciated man in black before him.

"Now, Tag, don't get all worked up. You have decided to meet with me ... and here I am."

"How do you know what we have decided?" Taglien asked, composing himself.

"That is not important. What is, is that I am now here. I will meet with the others. How's tomorrow?"

"Such *arrogance* for a mage with limited power," Taglien said, crossing his arms and smiling wryly.

Bashor crossed his arms as well, mimicking him. "Limits? Yes, I have limits. But don't we all?" He asked, smiling back and winking. "My powers will grow ... but you must know that or you wouldn't have decided to summon me." Bashor walked over to the wall made of stone and looked out the window. "Neat trick with the waterfall."

"How did you know that we decided to speak with you, Mage?" Taglien asked, sitting back down in his cushioned chair.

"Come now, my dear deity; I am not dumb. Even a mere mortal like myself could tell that the twins are splitting and will undoubtedly turn their wrath on you now that they are fracturing. They cannot have you plotting against them in your dark corners, can they?"

Taglien was not so easily provoked this time by Bashor's demeanour. He sat back and took in what the dark Mage had said. Could it be true that the twins have finally split? Up to this point, the lesser gods had only speculated. Was the Mage making all this up to fulfil some plan of his own? Most assuredly, he has something planned in all this.

"How can you be sure the twins have split?" Taglien asked, rubbing his chin and thinking.

"Do you not think that question should be answered with the rest of ... your kind," Bashor said with such disdain that Taglien looked up, raising an eyebrow.

"Why do you have such hate for us? We have done nothing to you. The dark twin is the one who stripped you of your magic; why hate us?"

Bashor stared down at the dark-skinned lesser god as if looking into a barrel of cow droppings. "It is your *nothing* that disgusts me. The two that now threaten you are the same you and your lot of nothing-ers created by your complacency and ignorance. Power was stripped from you easier than lifting a Langorian female's skirt." Bashor finished the last swallowing as if he suddenly had a terrible taste in his mouth.

"We will see you tomorrow afternoon," Taglien said coldly. "Leave now, Mage."

Bashor bowed low and dramatically disappeared.

The Mage was going to be more trouble than help. Taglien knew at some point the annoying Mage will need to be eliminated; indeed, before he grows in power. He thought it best to see what he has to offer and then contemplate his demise.

"That mortal is truly un-likable!" Taglien said out loud, lifting a hand in the air. His crystal ball shot into his palm and the wizard, now a god, leaned back and once again brought back images of his time as a mortal himself.

CHAPTER 7
The Mage

I t was winter and the cold wind was blowing hard into the cave with snow drifting in and leaving a pile just inside the hole leading in. The wind whistled and made groaning noises that bounced off the rock fissures and peaks. It was mid-day but the sun barely peeked through the clouds.

A man squeezed into the cave. Covered in fur, he pulled many bags in with him. He was bent from the cold and held his arms as close to his body as the bags would allow. He walked purposefully to the back, stopping and looking behind him before touching the wall in a pattern and mumbling under his breath. A piece of the rock wall slid open, and Bashor quickly stepped in, letting the rock close behind him.

Bashor had moved enough of the black rock here from the black mountains to keep him safe. He had done it a very long time ago before the Dark Lord had stripped him of his powers. This provided the perfect cover for his hiding; however, there was nothing left of use inside. Even the small amount of ancient furniture was either crumbled or too fragile to touch. He had made a pile of blankets in a corner for his bed, and there were two protruding rocks from the ground on his desk. With his servant, Grothar, now dead, he had to go out and find provisions himself. That, of course, meant casting temporary spells to keep him hidden from the twins. He was nowhere close to being as powerful as he once was, but now with the magic in the boy's blood extracted into his own, he could feel the power returning ... or at least he convinced himself that it was. It felt so good that he could almost forget his decrepit home in the cave, almost.

He pulled out what fruit he could find in the town and some dried meat. He needed his strength to enter the other planes again and he unenthusiastically stuffed what he had into his mouth. Many of the books had disappeared with him when he left his castle. He had long ago made sure that if he were displaced, the books would go with him. He now stared into one of them, practicing the words and the inflection that brought the magic to life. He disliked using spells like this, but now he had no choice with his power so limited. In time, he would no longer need spells and tools to help his dealings with magic. In time, he would be powerful enough to bend the world as he saw fit. The thought comforted him as he practiced the words. He thought about how his life would have been different if he hadn't slipped into this plane of existence where magic was restricted and stolen by a group of fools. He had no desire to go back from the dreary place he had come. The powerful magic users from his home would have made short work of these idiots playing gods. Though he did have to admit the twins they created were quite powerful, and very much in the way of his total control of the magic here. He needed the eleven remaining gods and their powers to finish the twins, and then he would destroy the others … and then it will all be his. All the magic this world had would be his; the things he could do and places he could see outside this miserable world.

It was slightly past mid-afternoon, and Bashor decided he had made the lesser gods wait long enough. He did not want to provoke their anger to action but only to keep them off balance. He placed the candles around the circle he had already drawn and stood in the middle. He crossed his palms together and chanted the words he had been practicing. The candles around the circle flared up and began to pulsate to his heartbeat. Bashor blew all the air out of his lungs and jumped into the air. When he landed, he was standing on the marble floor between the waiting lesser gods. He sucked in his breath and looked around. They all looked irritated, and some looked full-out angry. Perfect, he thought as he put on his best arrogant smile and swept into a dramatic bow. He noticed Taglien and saw he looked haggard and nervous.

The idiots were probably ready to turn on him, thinking I was not coming. Good. Their inability to be cohesive will make them easier to control.

"Good afternoon," Bashor said, smiling.

"Afternoon! You were to be here in the morning, Mage!" The short god cursed.

"He is nothing but a cheap magician looking to up his reputation by meeting the gods," Chelcor said in his high-pitched voice, brushing his robe and looking at the jewellery that adorned his fingers.

"You agreed to see him, same as us. Maybe you can shut your big mouth and let us get this over with." Larko shouted out to him. He crossed his big arms and looked down his nose and across the room at the feminine little god.

"You do not scare me, Lark. We all know your people are animals, and my people know what to do with animals. That I can assure you."

"You flaky little piece of dung!" Larko spat. "Let's see what you do to an animal then, heh? Why don't we settle this now? No more rules to bind us. Just you and me." Larko got off his chair, being held back by two others.

"You all know the rules!" Grastor yelled out and stood. He was the oldest and, at times like this, assumed the peace-making role. His head was bald, and he wore his beard long and down to his chest as white as snow. "Let us hear what the Mage has to say." He said in an almost pleading tone. Larko gave the little Chelcor one last look before sitting down and composing himself. Chelcor rolled his eyes and concentrated on the Mage standing patiently between them, watching like a hawk ready to plunge onto its victim.

"What can you tell us, Mage?" Grastor said, still standing and running a hand through his long beard. Bashor smiled again at them and took his time. When he did start talking, he walked along the marble floor as if he had been there his whole life. He told them about the Dark Lord's plan to use him and about how both twins had planned to use a certain boy for some purpose but, luckily, he had intervened and rid the world of the horrific creature. He explained carefully that the twins are splitting and that they would soon turn their attention on them as their feuds raged on. He explained that it was inevitable that they would sooner or later rid themselves of the lesser gods. He was empathetic about the need to create them once to handle the details of being gods and he even feigned remorse when he spoke of when the twins took power over them. His delivery was flawless, and the lesser gods soaked it up. He enticed them with the thoughts of bringing down the twins, and the lesser gods exchanged excited glances.

"We did have need for them once," Silsen said through her big nose. "What if we do take back the power? Then we are back where we started." She said, shrugging her shoulders.

"Not necessarily," Bashor said, stepping closer to where she sat. "I know the work it takes to keep the world in balance. It's an annoying game of power and finesse. I know just the man for that job." The others nodded knowingly and exchanged worried glances.

Bashor smiled at them. He knew he had them right where he wanted them. He could feel a piece of the puzzle falling into place. He was one step closer to having it all.

CHAPTER 8
Rifkins

Parla, the woods witch, invited them to stay the night. However, Killian knew he would be up most of it, telling her all he knew, as was the agreement. Sebastion was quickly becoming his old self again and sulking and staring into the fire. As best as Killian could understand from him and his furry little adopted brother, the young man was heartsick. Some girl or other had left him at Endrea. Killian knew well that the young could do stupid things in the name of love and watched him closely. He had many questions around why Sebastion was with Bashor, why the Dark Lord wanted him and for god's sake The Dragon! But there were more pressing things right now like getting out of these woods and away from the Rifkins and witch.

Sebastion and Morakye spoke quietly together, and Lara and Baran paced the floor. It was a small hut, and their constant pacing was making Killian anxious. Every time one of them passed a window, they would look out as if expecting to see the Rifkins running over towards them at any second. The witch said the Rifkins were superstitious, and they hoped she was right and stayed away. Killian had no idea how many or even what they wanted from them. Even if they did not come to the hut, they could very well surround it and wait for them to leave. They could not stay here forever. He sighed and brushed his hands through his hair. When he looked up, he found Parla's watery brown eyes looking back at him.

"What?" He asked.

"I'd hear more about the Great City and the king specifically," Parla said, crossing her arms.

Killian felt a pang in the pit in his stomach. He looked over and saw Morakye curiously looking back at him. He whispered something into Sebastion's ear and he turned to look at Killian as well.

"Go ahead," Sebastion said, shrugging at his uncle. "Your master told me who I am. I know about the king being my grandfather and how my brother had been killed as an infant by his hands." Killian sat back in his chair, frowning deep and putting his feet in front of him. He bobbed his head up and down, trying to think of what to say next.

Lara felt tired and had to admit it felt good to have a roof overhead again, especially with what looked to be a storm coming. She heard the distant thunder and the lightning flashed nearby. Her legs would not let her rest, however. She rubbed her sweaty hands together and looked out the window. She had looked out the window so many times that she was sure her eyes were now playing tricks on her. Now the distant branches seemed out of place, and rocks near the cottage seemed to have multiplied. Thunder cracked loudly overhead, and everyone instinctively ducked. The lightning flashed outside the window, and Lara was looking into the eyes of what seemed to be an angry child. She yelped and moved backward. The window went dark again, and she put a hand to her mouth as she pressed her back against the wall. Killian ran to the window and looked out. The lightning came again, but he saw nothing.

"What was it?" He concentrated, searching the darkness.

"I'm not sure," Lara answered, pulling her short sword from her side. "It could have been some lost child or something."

"Child?" Morakye asked, his ears rising to the top of his head.

Baran leaned forward, also now staring into the darkness outside. "Yeah, didn't we say these 'lil toadies look like children?" he asked, pulling his sword free.

"How many did you see and-" Killian stopped and started counting. "Parla, how many large size rocks do you have outside your door?"

"This is ridiculous." She snorted. "Rifkins do not come this close to my home. Never in my-" Killian asked the same question again, interrupting her.

"There are ten stones in my yard." She huffed.

"There are now fourteen," Killian said, his eyes narrowing as he concentrated out the window.

Parla got off her chair, looked out the window, and saw the four rocks that should not be there. One of them got up and ran off into the woods.

"I think the Rifkins may have overcome their fears," Killian said, watching the other three for movement. The others in the room were coming to the window, but Killian angrily waved them off.

DAMN IDIOTS!

"Get away from the window!" Killian growled at them. "Grab all the blankets you can find and give them to me … NOW!" He pulled his blanket from his pack. There was already a ragged cloth hanging from nails over the window, so he threw his blanket over that. The others figured out what he was doing and did the same to the other windows.

"We're like sit'n ducks," Baran complained, his colossal head moving from side to side, waiting for an attack.

"This is my house!" Parla said, stomping towards the door.

61

"WAIT!" Killian yelled. Lara, who was closest to her, tried to grab the witch, but Parla was too fast. She swung the door open and put her hands on her hips.

"HOW DARE-" A small spear thudded into her chest and she took two steps back into the hut, still angrily staring out the door. All was silent when two more flew into her. Parla looked down and then up and out the door before falling back onto the floor, dead. Lara, who was behind the door, kicked it closed as another hit it with the blade slightly protruding through. She quickly put the beam across it and stepped away.

"What now?" She asked Killian.

Killian looked down at the witch. Lara looked around the group, but everyone else was as confused as she was. She started to ask again, but Killian held up a hand for her to stop. He rubbed his chin, thinking. They heard a scratching noise on the rear wall.

"They be on the roof," Morakye said, his ears twitching.

"The witch said the Rifkins are superstitious," Killian said, going to Parla's body. He put a foot on her stomach, grabbing the spears one by one and jerking them out of her body. The spears were in far and Parla's body lifted, and he had to use his foot on her chest. As the last one pulled free, he looked up to the others who were staring at him, wide-eyed.

"Lara, you're not going to like it ... but you're going to have to put on that dress..."

"The puckering hell I am!" She said, shaking her head. "That is covered in blood, and I ain't ever wearing a dress ... there ain't no way, sweetness. Ain't happening ... no way."

"Can I at least tell you the plan?" Killian asked, spreading his arms disarmingly.

"Go right ahead." She said, crossing her arms defiantly. Killian could see her blushing to her exposed arms.

"Look, this is what I am thinking." He made sure everyone was listening. Morakye squeezed in with the rest of them to hear. "These Rifkin things have been scared of the witch in the past, right?" Everyone nodded, agreeing. "Alright, then we give them something to be scared of. We bring the witch back to life." They exchanged a confused look. "I also have some fire powder in my pack to make a show. We do some acting in here, and then we throw open that door, and we give those little bastards something to run from."

"What 'den?" Baran asked in almost a whisper.

"Then—" Killian whispered back. "Sebastion and I slip out first during the flashes from the powder. And *then* we kill everything that's from here to the trees on the other side." Killian suddenly got a dark look in his eyes. "You three follow close behind with Morakye at the back with his bow."

"I'm not wearing a dress," Lara said again.

"You're wearing it," Killian said back at her.

"Nope, need a new plan." She said, shaking her head, her dark eyes narrowing.

They all screamed in the house and banged on the walls. They gurgled and choked and then went deadly silent. Sebastion flung open the door, and Killian threw out the two flaming bags of powder. They flashed one right after another. Morakye came out in the witch's bloody dress, screaming almost perfectly like a crazed woman.

The three Rifkins curled up and, pretending to be rocks, stood and screamed back at him, eyes wide. Baran had suggested Morakye put an old sack on his head for effect. It seemed to work because the Rifkins dropped their weapons and ran as if they were the small children they resembled. Killian and Sebastion whirled past Morakye with identical swords in their hands, Morakye directly behind them, and then Baran, then Lara in the back with Morakye's bow in hand. They ran for the trees as fast as they could. Lara was slower as she would run backward from time to time to see if there were any on their heels. They made it without incident. When they were in the trees, Baran, carrying all the packs, handed them out, and everyone put them on. They ducked down and Killian leaned forward to speak when an arrow hit the tree where his head had just been.

"RUN!" He yelled, jumping up.

CHAPTER 9
Revelation

The Lady of Light sighed deeply as she sat in her favourite chair, staring ahead but not seeing anything. Even with all her powers, she couldn't help feeling that things were spinning out of her control. Her dark-hearted twin had said the boy was dead; that could only mean that chaos was returning to the world. She feared whatever power working through the boy would now find another way, and it would be entirely out of her control. At least with the prophecy, she could be somewhat aware of what could happen ... even though it was just a guess at times. But her pig-headed brother believed he could change the way of things. In her time of existence, she has always known there was another ruling force on top of the other. She was not sure it ever ended or even if it genuinely existed for that matter. She could only surmise that those powers were there, but what she was sure of was if those powers did exist then the prophecy engraved in those rocks were somehow connected. But the boy was dead now, so perhaps all her theories were wrong.

She leaned forward and put her head in her delicate pale hands. How could it just be over? How could her brother have so easily thwarted such a, presumably, powerful prophecy? She spun her hand in the air in a half-circle, and she was suddenly in a thick green forest.

Insects buzzed loudly, and a gentle stream ran busily from nearby. She stepped lightly from her chair and through the underbrush towards the water. She rubbed her temples, trying to ease the worry there. Her forehead wrinkled and looked foreign on her perfect face. A gentle breeze blew her long black silky hair behind her, and she breathed it in. A large tree had fallen and blocked the path she was following. Instead of stepping around it, she walked through it, making it shimmer back in place behind her. The fact was that it might not have been there any longer. She was traveling in a time that was already lived. She looked up and spotted the thing she had come here to see—a small boy sitting on a rock looking into the water and smoking from a small pipe. The Lady moved closer and sat next to him, looking into his blue-grey eyes.

"Where have you gone to, little Sebastion?" She sighed sadly. Sebastion suddenly looked up as if seeing her, but the Lady realized he was looking through her at a family of squirrels hopping around the ground. The large one barked at him almost playfully and went back to her little family. The Lady looked back at the boy and saw a smile on his face as he watched the tiny creatures go about their business. The Lady waved her fingers in the air again, and she was beside the same boy, slightly older, in a room lying bruised and bleeding on a bed.

She watched and recognized what must have been the boy's ancient uncle carefully tending to the boy's wounds and feeding him a milky liquid that made the boy's speech slur. She loomed over the two of them, watching. The uncle had a dangerous look in his eye that even gave her a chill. She closed her eyes and went back for a moment to see what happened. She was back instantly and understood the uncle's deep anger.

Such cruelty in this world. Instead of following Sebastion's life trail this time, she tried to attach herself to Killian, and she found herself in darkness. Confused, she pushed herself harder with her magic, but as hard as she pushed, the darkness pushed back. Confused and now very curious, she came back to her chair and thought about this. Never before had she been magically beaten by anything other than her brother, and she was sure this was not him. She would have recognized the feel of her brother. She stood up and paced her room, which was made up of simple, comfortable chairs and a big fireplace. Even the walls were bare. She stopped walking suddenly, having a thought.

Perhaps if I didn't push but rather … gently brushed? She closed her eyes and opened her mind gently and let her mind wander off. She then steered it softly and calmly to the image of Killian. Nothing but darkness appeared before her eyes, and she was about to give up when she thought she could see the light far off in the dark. Like a stalking cat, she ever so gently glided herself towards it, careful not to scare it off. Soon she was able to make out images in the light. A woman was sitting on a table in black leather. She was sitting uncomfortably as if her backside hurt her. She was talking to someone else in the room. The Lady tried to get closer and she could make out a man in the room with her. He had long brown hair and broad, muscular shoulders. There was something familiar about him, but she could not make out his face as he was turned away from her. The woman facing him seemed to be hiding anger in her eyes, and the Lady observed her over the man's shoulder. Suddenly, the man turned and the Lady caught her breath.

It cannot be! It was the boys' uncle Killian … only much younger. There was no mistaking the eyes. Suddenly the image flashed, and she was in a courtyard filled with smoke and Barbarians. She watched as a colossal Barbarian stood looking into the smoke. Suddenly, the uncle jumped out of the darkness, cutting a line in the big man's face, and was gone. The image of Killian jumping into the air was frozen into the Lady's mind. Not because of the man but because of what slipped from between the man's shirt as he jumped. There was no mistaking it. She suddenly knew there was more going on than she had thought. She opened her eyes and found herself sitting on the cold floor, staring up at the ceiling, smiling.

A sudden feeling came over her, and she closed her eyes and reached out once again with her mind. Ever so slightly, a familiar presence came to her. It was weak, but it was there. The Lady of Light stood and laughed. A smile started to spread across her face, erasing the lines as if they had never been.

Oh, my dear little friend. What are you up to?

CHAPTER 10
Church Life

Miska lay in her tiny room, listening to the wind play its sad song through the wooden shutters of her window. She thought it such a miserable sound that it made her cry. She held the blanket to her nose, but she could not get warm. It was as if the wind somehow found a way under her blankets and right into her skin. She could hear the tree branches brush against the stone walls outside. Tears ran down her face, and her fingers felt cold against her cheeks when she brushed them away. When she used to feel this way, her father would wrap her in his big arms and tell her stories until she forgot about the sadness. But he was dead now. The only other one that loved her she had betrayed and left in a doomed city and is probably also dead. Barbarian man-eaters were not far off, killing and eating people, and she was here in her small cold room, feeling her hot breath on her hands under the covers. She wept, burying her face so that no one would hear. She prayed to the Lady, convinced that she should have died with her father. This way, she would not feel the loneliness and heartache crushing her like it was right now. As if by answer, the calm grey eyes filled her mind, and with the guilt, she lost herself in her misery. Hours passed, and there were times that she thought there might have been knocks on her door. There were no locks and anyone could enter a door in the church of the Lady, so everyone was respectful, and no one would enter without being invited. She may have yelled something out but could remember none of it. She undoubtedly had been missed in classes, and final blessings were about to begin. She was sure to get interrupted from her escape into self-pity at prayer time. There was a timid knock on the door.

"GO AWAY!" She yelled from under her blankets. There was no answer, so she thought whoever it was had gone, but another more timid knock came. "By the light, find some other to harass!" She cursed a few more words she had learned from her father under her breath. The door opened slightly, and Lithra poked her head in the door.

"Uh … eh … sorry, Miska. I don't mean to-you know-" The girl sounded about to cry and guilt crashed into Miska again, but this time for a different reason.

"No, no. I am sorry." Miska said, smiling slightly from her blankets.

"Are you ill?" Lithra asked, concerned.

Miska shook her head miserably. "I don't think so. I just want to be alone." Miska started to weep again.

"I-eh-have orders to bring you to the Head Mother, Miska. I am sorry, but the priestess who sent me made it seem important."

Miska could not help but roll her eyes at the mention of the priestess who probably sent Lithra to her. The woman was a cruel and soured old crow that was not shy with the contempt she had for Miska, jealous of the attention she was getting from the Head Mother. The looks that came from her and some of the other priestesses were sometimes pure hatred. Most were good and kind here, but not all.

"If the Mother has sent for me, then I will come." She sighed, rubbing her arm across her eyes. "Come in, Lithra," Miska said, pulling the blankets off and sitting up. Lithra looked around nervously and Miska looked at her, confused, then realized what the problem was.

The shirt she was sleeping in was open and she was bare-chested. Lithra was too shy to have said it. Since she had met Lithra, the shy girl had never wanted to be noticed nor make anyone uncomfortable around her. Lithra, at times, had a talent for disappearing altogether. Not in a magical sense, but in a way that people would just forget she was even there. The girl was not ugly but plain and featureless so that she could blend into any environment.

"Is it time for blessings?" Miska asked her. Lithra nodded nervously. "Then go and say a prayer for me, won't you, my friend?" Miska asked, smiling at her. Lithra smiled back widely. "Of course, I always pray for you." She said and disappeared out the door. Miska was surprised by her response. 'I always pray for you,' she had said.

How could the other girls here be so mean to Lithra when she was such a kind soul? She shook her head, trying to clear the thought away. She had not bothered to change into the cream-colored dress of the novice priestess. She was no longer just a novice but now a novice priestess. She was the youngest by many years, another reason for some of the church's women to dislike her. The Head Mother had insisted she be put through the ranks even if it caused a significant disruption with the others.

Miska put on her thick blue cloak and pulled the hood tight. She did not have to go outside to get to the Head Mother's apartments, but the corridors were cold, and she already could not chase the chill away. She kept her gaze on the ground both to hide her swollen eyes and so she wouldn't have to speak to anyone. She was thinking of how her life had changed in such a short amount of time. Not that long ago, she was a Dempsy that lived day to day in freedom and play. The Dempsies did not give much thought to personal possessions and shared everything, making them feel like part of a big family. Then things changed, and she was forced to be a slave, then happily a lover, and now a novice priestess in the Church of the Lady of Light. Her head spun from it, and she did not realize how quickly the big red double doors leading to the Head Mother's chambers appeared in front of her. There were two giant white statues of the Lady on either side, and she bowed to both as was customary. When she was leaning up from her second bow, the door opened slightly, and she caught the eye of the Head Mother's chief handler, Priestess Blith. She was a tall woman with light blond hair tied behind, as was customary for a priestess. Her skin was tight over her bony, darkly tanned face that Miska thought looked like stretched leather. She faced Miska with her arms crossed over her white dress and her typical scowl of disapproval. She stared down at Miska as if she were a kitchen mouse.

"The Mother does not like to wait ... *especially* for a novice," she said with her tight lips hardly moving. Miska looked back to the ground. Priestess Blith took this as a submissive move and snorted out a short laugh.

What was happening was Miska was trying with all her power to swallow her anger. It was not the day for Blith's berating. "I am sorry, Governess," Miska said in the manner that was expected of her.

"That's right, little novice. I *am* the governess. It will do you well to remember that." Miska knew that she was more than a novice now. She was a novice priestess who was just one level below a full priestess, but she did not want to push things with Blith.

72

"Let's see your eyes, novice," Blith said, reaching out to pull Miska's hood from her head. Miska stepped back too fast, and Blith took in a sharp breath. "How dare y-" Blith said. But Miska moved like a cat around the big woman into the inner chambers. She looked up and saw two other priestesses standing, watching them curiously. She moved quickly towards the door where she knew Mother would be. The one nearest to the door saw what she was trying to do and grabbed at her. Miska was small and fast and got to the door. She opened it quickly, and the others froze.

"AH! There you are, my dear!" The Head Mother's voice said from within. Miska looked back quickly to see the priestess' evil stares that could have been daggers buried into her back.

"Good day and the light of the blessing, Mother," Miska said, shutting the door behind her and pulling back her hood to reveal her face.

CHAPTER 11

"Come sit." The Head Mother said, indicating an identical chair across from her by the fire. The room was big, the walls lined with books. Above the fireplace was a painting of a man and woman holding each other close in the woods, nude, lost in each other's eyes. The image was so large it dominated the room, and Miska had trouble keeping her eyes from it. She looked up at it quickly and down again only to see the motherly woman looking at her curiously over her reading glasses. Miska felt her face go red and looked to the ground.

"Does that painting make you uncomfortable, dear?" She asked curiously, raising a brow.

"Uh, no ... mother." Miska suddenly wished she was back in her room.

"Well good, then." The older woman pulled her glasses from her face and rested them on a table. She leaned back and crossed her arms in front of her. A small smile spread across her wrinkled face. "That picture, you see, is a representation of something we here in the Church of the Lady stand for." The Head Mother looked up at the painting and stared. Miska looked at it and, for the first time, let her eyes not only go to the prominent parts of the image but to the eyes. The couple was staring passionately at one another. Miska thought there somehow seemed to be a range of different emotions in the eyes and faces. She recognized need, want, anger, desperation and, of course lust, all at once. She felt the artist must be very talented at conveying all those emotions in one look and one painting. Her eyes followed the woman's naked arms to her hands that were clutching the man's forearms. The man's hand was on the woman's breast but seemed to not only be there for pleasure but to push her away at the same time. Miska suddenly realized what she was staring at and looked over to the Mother and found she was staring at her just as curiously. Miska felt the blood return to her face.

"What do you see there, child?"

Miska swallowed hard, wishing they could talk of something else. "I see many feelings being … uh, felt through that painting."

"Tell me more. What do you think the artist is trying to express." The Mother smiled wider as if thoroughly enjoying Miska's unease.

Miska looked into her face and had no choice but to feel the woman's smile pass through her too. "I don't know," Miska answered, shrugging.

"That is not an answer." The Head Mother said, mimicking Miska's adolescent response. Miska laughed and sighed as if clearing her mind, stood up, and stepped closer to the painting. There was landscape behind the couple embracing, but she concentrated on the line of the bodies. After some time, she looked back to the Mother, who watched with a raised brow, looking for a response.

"I see…" Miska began. "I think-" She stuttered, but the Head Mother shook her head.

"Don't overthink it, my dear. What do you see?"

"I see … life."

"HA!" The Head Mother clapped her hands in front of her, excited. "Very good!" The old woman said happily. Miska jumped from the noise of the clap. "I have asked many others about what they saw there, and you could guess the things I have heard. Love, lust, the power of the light. Sins of the flesh … blah blah blah."

Miska laughed at that and took the seat across from the leader of the church. "You have seen what I have seen and all those things the others have and so much more … life. Life is lust, pain, love, and many more things. This little exercise just confirms what I believe."

"What's that, Mother?" Miska asked, confused. The Head Mother smiled wide again, and Miska watched as it led up to her eyes. She was unsure if she was projecting her thoughts from the painting but thought she saw sadness in the woman's eyes along with joy. "That you are different … special, my child. That is why we have progressed your status here. We could fill your head with a great many things within these walls, but-" The old woman winked knowingly. "The spark can only be fostered by us. We cannot create it. I believe that very spark exists in you." The woman leaned forward, looking deep into Miska's eyes. "And I plan to fan that spark into a *roaring* fire." Her warm smile changed to a look of complete commitment and determination.

"I am … honoured-"

"Oh, I'm sure you are." The Head Mother said, leaning back and chuckling to herself. "For now, go and get yourself cleaned up. We're going to see the Advisors."

"We?" Miska repeated, her big brown eyes wide.

"You have fifteen minutes."

"But-" Miska stared, wide-eyed.

"And this time, try not to look so weepy and sad, child. We are going representing the church and the Lady of Light." She winked again.

"Okay, off you go then." The Head Mother said, dismissively waving her hand and putting her reading glasses back on. Miska saw no room for argument and quickly went to the door, still numb with the Mother's words, in shock.

The Advisors. Why would the Head Mother take a novice priestess like herself to see them? And what was that about fanning the flames? She knew nothing about such flames. Her head spun. It was apparent that the woman liked her, and Miska had to admit it felt good. She, at times, felt lost in the big compound. She shook her head, trying to lodge some sense out of what had happened, and opened the door. Blith was there, staring at her in disbelief. It was suddenly apparent to Miska that she had been standing there listening to their conversation the whole time. Miska stepped through, and then Blith closed the door behind her.

"You little rat!" The tall, blond-haired woman said, scowling. She swore under her breath so her voice would not go past the door, grabbing Miska's arm. "I have dedicated my life to that old woman, and never have I asked for a thing." She tightened her grip and pulled Miska closer to her. "And you go with her to the Advisors? What spell have you cast over the old crow?" Blith hissed in a whisper. Miska tried to pull free, but the woman's grip was firm. "Why, you?" Blith asked, bringing her face close to Miska's.

Too late to hold back, don't... Miska felt the familiar heat of anger. She knew it was no use pushing the feeling down. She knew she shouldn't show her anger to a priestess. Especially Blith, who she knew very well would hold it against her forever.

Miska's eyes narrowed, and she reached over and grabbed the woman's hand that was squeezing her.

"I do not know why the holy mother has asked me to accompany her." The sound of her anger only gave her more momentum. "But what I do know is that *she* believes in me, and I also believe she favours me in some way." Miska let her nails push into the woman's leathery skin. "She is old, as you say; where do you think that will leave me?" Miska stared back at the woman into her cold blue eyes. Miska smiled coldly up at her, and Blith loosened her grip. Miska took advantage of the opportunity and turned on her heel, letting her hood fly close to the woman's face. All Blith could do was watch as Miska quickly and confidently walked out the door without turning back.

CHAPTER 12

She was still smoothing her long hair when she came to the Head Mother's rooms again. The big double doors were left slightly open, and Miska tied her hair behind before opening them further. She had put on her thick white shawl that hung around her dull-white dress.

She gingerly poked her head in but saw nobody in the rooms, so she waited patiently. In a few minutes, the Head Mother, with her handlers, came into the room from a side door. Lithra was with them, but she would not catch Miska's eye.

"Are you ready, my dear?" She asked Miska, smiling. Miska noticed an intense, confident look in the Head Mother's eye. She imagined it was the same look a great general might have while riding into battle.

"Yes, Mother," Miska said, bowing. The Head Mother smiled and came to her, taking her hand. Blith made a barely audible sound of disgust in the back of her throat at the open sign of affection.

"It is not far, but it is cold, so we will take a cart to the castle." The old woman said, leading her down the corridors of the church. "When we meet the Advisors-" The Mother saying *Advisors* like it was a dirty word. "-just stay behind me, not saying a word. However, do try to take in everything you see and hear. Be attentive to every detail of this meeting. Do you understand?"

Miska looked up into the old wise woman's eyes and nodded. "Good. I do not savour these moments consorting with these lost souls. But there are many things someone in my position must do for the good of the light." The Mother seemed to reflect for only a second before squaring her shoulders and quickening her step. Miska could not help feeling proud of the Head Mother. She thought to herself that she would like to embody this image of confidence and grace like the Head Mother. She did her best to copy the woman's walk, still holding the older woman's hand tightly in her own.

It was a short carriage ride, but the wind was cold and pulled at their wraps as they entered and exited. They were greeted at the castle's door by a bald and bent old man that looked even older than The Head Mother in blue velvet formal wear. He smiled a wide toothless grin when seeing her, and she touched his shoulder gently, smiling back.

"Can you tell *them* we are here?"

"Certainly, My Lady. And may I say you look as beautiful today-"

"Oh, yes, I'm sure." The Head Mother cut him off. "Just a picture of beauty I am." She said, laughing lightly. The old man smiled back. Miska thought she saw a twinkle in his eye. He walked off and Miska watched him curiously. She looked back at the Mother and saw she was also watching him go with a strange look in her eyes.

"Who is he, Mother?" Miska asked quietly. The Head Mother did not answer right away with a faraway look on her face. "I was not always Head Mother of the Church of the Lady of Light, my dear." She looked back into Miska's eyes. "Sacrifice is part of our blessed life, I'm afraid." She sighed. "But you already know that." She turned to Miska and smiled knowingly but kindly.

"Yes, Mother," Miska answered, looking down and not sure what emotion she felt when her face turned red.

The old man came back and took them to another large room with many chairs and statues. The man seemed angry now and left again, whispering something into the Head Mother's ear. The old woman's face became pale and angry. "Oh, So they want us to return to the church." She put her hands on her hips. Miska started to turn to leave.

"Hold it." The old woman commanded. "You stay with me, my dear. We will face these idiots together, whether they want to see us or not," She said, crossing her arms and frowning. The older man looked around quickly to make sure no one heard her.

"We will be waiting here for as long as it takes for them to see us. Tell them that, my sweet. Tell them we will wait for the king. Tell them the church will pray for our king right here and, if need be, bring all the members of the church and the faithful here to the castle to pray for the king's quick return to health." She faced the older man squarely. "See if that puts a cramp in their fat bellies." She finished, winking at him. The older man smiled hesitantly, shaking his head.

"They will see you soon would be my guess, My Lady."

"They had better." The Head Mother said in a way that sent a chill up Miska's back. The older man in the ancient suit left quickly. He came back in just minutes, ushering Miska and The Head Mother politely into another room.

Miska and the Head Mother entered the room behind the man as he dramatically opened the doors for them. Miska was taken aback by the room as it was nothing she had expected. A large table in the centre overflowed with exotic foods, most she had never seen before. Much of it lay on the floor, discarded. Several people walked around the table, ignoring them. One rather fat man in a stained white robe sat behind a

81

full roasted pig with a large thigh of meat in his hand. He absently stared at them as he ate. Miska took it all in. There were many extravagant paintings and tapestries on the walls. Her eyes caught one tapestry in particular, and she concentrated on it. It was an image of what must have been the king, swinging a great sword and keeping some vicious-looking beasts at bay. It immediately reminded her of the tapestry in the church's waiting room when she was unsure whether the priestesses of light kept the creatures away or brought them towards the people. Here it was apparent that the king was fighting them off. The beasts were like some kind of possessed bears, snarling and frothing at the mouth. There was a knight there pulling one of the creatures away from the king. The animal almost had the king in its fearsome maul, but the big knight had the beast's face in his hand and was forcing it to the ground with a sword plunging down on it. She looked at the visible eyes between the slits of the helmet and felt her heart skip a beat. It was like the blue-grey eyes of Sebastion were there in the canvas. She stepped forward, but the Head Mother grabbed her shoulder, making her jump.

"What is it, dear?" The Head Mother asked in a whisper. Miska looked at the older woman for a brief second, then back to the familiar eyes.

"I know that man in the painting ... in the armour."

"That's ridiculous. That man lived a long time ago."

Miska looked at the Head Mother again and looked into her eyes. "I know that man."

"It is a resemblance. That is all. Will you be alright?" The old woman asked her, concerned.

"I am fine, but somehow ... that is him."

"Alright, dear. We'll talk of this when we get back." The woman looked up, studying the image herself for a brief second before turning back. "For now, follow my lead and don't say a word ... even if spoken to." With that said, the Head Mother walked confidently up to the table's edge and loudly cleared her throat. Everyone in the room turned to look at her.

"I am here to speak to the king." She said confidently and loud enough to fill the room and echo off the walls. The fat man stopped chewing and looked at her sternly before rolling his eyes. Instead of swallowing what was in his mouth, he turned his head and spat on the ground.

"The king is busy with other important matters. If you have anything to say, Doria ... say it to me. And I will *advise* him." He said, smiling a greasy smile folded many times with the fat that sat heavily on his face.

"I would prefer to speak to the king directly, and I have not used that name in many years, Tith of Hogs Town." She said the last putting her nose into the air. Miska saw redness run up the fat man's neck as the smile left his face.

"What do you want?" He ,asked simply, getting up and whispering something to a young man. The man disappeared behind one of the tapestries that Miska surmised must be a hidden door.

"I want you to open the doors to the refugees outside. They do not stand a chance out there alone and you know it."

"Why should we care about those cowards that ran from their homes to our walls for protection? They left their towns and cities to

83

hide like mice here. And like mice, they came to eat all the food we have spent months storing."

"I am no fool, Tith. I know that all the armies of Torenium are here to protect you." She said, pointing an accusing finger.

"Not just me, My Lady of light's blessings, but all of the great city … including the Church of the Lady of Light. Do not forget-"

"I forget nothing." The Head Mother interrupted angrily. "I have not forgotten that it was the same people that beat the doors of the great city for entrance, with babies clutched in their arms, that built this city and the empire. It was their families that made up the army that is here to protect them. You had taken away any hope in beating back the man-eaters when you took their army. How can you just let them stay out there and die? By the light, these are *your* people!"

"*Our* people." Another man corrected, pushing open the tapestry and stepping in. Miska thought she heard a woman's laughter behind the tapestry when he stepped through the doorway. The man smiled, straightening his robe. It was much cleaner than the others yet still too tight around the middle. He brushed his thick greasy black hair from his face as if waking from a nap. He walked over to a doorway close by and lifted his robe. He looked over at Miska and winked as he started urinating on the wall. Miska looked away, blushing and disgusted. "*Our* people are inside these walls too, Mother." The man said, rolling back and sighing. The Head Mother turned away from him and waited for him to finish. When he finished, he dropped his robe and walked to them. He walked past the Head Mother and came to Miska, who was still looking at the ground. When he stepped in front of her, she noticed his new-looking sandals withlong yellowed toenails protruding. He cleared his throat for her to look up. She did and noticed he was taller than she had thought. His eyes were narrow and cruel. She recognized the look in his eye.

"Leave her, Flaz." The Head Mother said, low and full of menace. The man reached up with a thick-fingered hand and touched Miska's face. His hand was wet and smelled of urine. Miska pulled away, stepping back. Flaz laughed and looked back at the other Advisor who was now eating again. He also laughed and urged him on, grunting. The tall man reached out again.

"Do not touch me," Miska said, staring back into his eyes.

"Touch you?" The big man asked sarcastically. "Yes, little one, I will touch you." He reached his hand forward but was stopped by a massive hand on his shoulder. Miska saw the black and gold armour on the arm and followed it up to the familiar face.

"You?" She asked, stepping back from him, surprised.

"You have been getting around, milady," Lehgone said, bowing slightly but not letting his eyes leave hers.

"This has gone far enough!" The Head Mother said, taking Miska by the arm and pulling her away from the two men staring at her. The Advisor got his senses back and reached for Lehgone's hand.

"How dare you touch me!" He yelled, trying to pull away, but Lehgone held on easily, still looking at Miska. Finally, he turned and looked down at the smaller man standing next to him, trying to get free.

"If you ever touch me again-" The man started, but Lehgone ignored him and crossed his arms, frowning down at Miska.

"So tell me. What brings you here to our fine city? You do know the scenery has been less than-pleasant of late?" He asked, raising a brow. "I find it … peculiar that we meet again, especially with the company *you* keep." He looked her up and down, letting his eyes rest on her dress. "You are now of the poised and virtuous, then?"

"She is one of the light and one of *mine. And* we are leaving." The Head Mother said, reaching a hand out for Miska to take.

"I will walk you out, ladies," Lehgone said, leaving no room for argument and putting a hand on his big sword and walking to the door.

"You had better watch yourself, knight," Flaz yelled threateningly after him. Lehgone ignored him again, holding the door open for Miska and the Head Mother to exit. He smiled courteously into his long moustache, but it did not continue up into his dark eyes. He closed the door heavily behind them and Miska jumped. They turned to face him, and Lehgone crossed his arms again, suspiciously looking down his long nose.

"Who are you?" The Mother asked him, crossing her arms.

"I am the most powerful man in this city." He said, slowly looking away from Miska and meeting the Mother's eyes.

"More powerful than the king?" She asked, raising a brow. Lehgone laughed bitterly at that. "Yes, more powerful than the royal invalid who does not have enough sense to die."

"Those are brave words." The Mother said, returning his look.

"I control the armies now. The Advisors could not do it. So I do. Without me, this city … and the empire, I would wager would not have a chance in the darkest hell of survival. I am the last and only hope for those fat wastes of flesh behind this door … and they know it."

"Then it is you who I should be talking to." The Mother put in cautiously now. Lehgone turned to Miska. "Have you heard from your friends?" He asked.

"Not since I left. Do you know if they are alive?" Lehgone saw the desperation in her face. "I have no idea. The boy and the monster seemed capable enough, so I suppose they could be alive." Lehgone knew it was a lie as soon as the words passed his lips.

"Monster?" The older woman asked curiously.

Lehgone laughed. "So much for confessing to the light, eh little one?" He smiled.

A dark look came over the older woman. "Can we meet away from the smell of the-" She didn't finish the words but jammed a thumb in the direction of the door they had just come through.

"I will come to you later in the evening," Lehgone said simply and put his hand on the door to open it but turned back. "Make sure she's there." He said, looking at Miska. "I do not believe in coincidences." With that, he turned back to the door and stepped through, closing it hard behind him with a bang.

"He could very well be one of the darkest people I have ever met." The old woman said, looking at the door. "There is a certain aura a soldier gets when he's been through a battle. Then there is quite another one someone gets from cold-blooded murder." The Mother's eyes narrowed and turned to Miska. "You two seem to be friends, though." She said accusingly. Looking down at Miska, she thought she looked more like a bird of prey now than the head of a church of light. "I would like to hear how that came to pass, my novice priestess. I would be very interested to hear more of that."

"I have not lied to you, I saw-"

"Not here!" The Mother interrupted her angrily, "Save it for when we get back to the walls of the light." She took Miska by the arm and walked off. Miska couldn't help thinking how different this was from how they had stepped in.

CHAPTER 13

Baran could feel the trail tipping down in the darkness as he ran fullout ahead of the others. He would put his foot down, hoping to find ground each time, until he didn't. He flipped forward and landed on his pack and started rolling. In his tumbling, he heard someone falling behind him.

Killian saw the dark image of the big knight go down and he tried to throw out his feet in a desperate attempt to control his fall but it was too late. Baran could feel himself getting nauseous from the rolling; then there was a crack that echoed through his skull. Killian was grabbing for anything to stop his rolling and then his foot snagged a root, and he heard a crunch that sent a chill through him. And then the pain shot up his leg and exploded into his brain. It was all he could do not to scream. He rolled on the ground, holding his leg and trying to be silent; Rifkins and all else forgotten. Lara slid down the hill with Sebastion at her side. She had to jump to stop hitting Killian and landed in some brush before rolling to a stop. She felt a sting on her bare arm and, when she stopped falling, put a hand to the spot and felt the dampness there.

DAMN!

Morakye came last, jumping into the air and sliding down the hill with his claws deep in the ground, slowing him. He immediately ran to Lara, took his Rifkin bow and the remaining arrows and, in a single fluid motion, he turned and let an arrow fly. A cry and a lifeless Rifkin came skidding down the hill with an arrow deep in his eye.

89

"I think we've got a problem, boys," Lara said, looking at the dark-skinned, dead Rifkin that stopped rolling at her feet. Killian stopped moving and stared up at the sky, trying to get the pain under control.

"Me thinks there are more on the way," Morakye said, his yellow eyes unblinking and glowing in the moonlight as they stared up the crest of the hill.

"That puckering hurt," Killian said between clenched teeth from the ground, taking deep breaths.

"No time for reflecting, handsome. I think we better be moving on." Lara looked around nervously. "Where's that lazy hunk of flesh?" She asked. Baran raised a hand, sitting up against a tree. "You resting again, bull?" Lara asked, getting to her feet, but Morakye pushed her back down.

"Why make's it easier for them?" Morakye said without looking at her.

"Damn cat," Lara said, imitating Killian's deep voice. Killian chuckled despite the pain, still holding his leg up. "How many, Morakye?"

"It matter any?" Morakye answered, obviously not wanting to answer. They all picked up on it and fell silent for a moment.

"They's are at the ledge now, and Morakye has only three arrows left."

"D'ats great," Baran sighed. He rubbed his head gingerly and looked up to see Sebastion staring off into the darkness, his eyes almost as bright as Morakye's.

"Uh ... Killian. I think da' boy's doing something."

"I am not a boy," Sebastion answered in reflex, not looking over.

90

"Are you, alright?" Killian asked, rolling onto his side. Lara had crawled to him and tried to see the ankle in the darkness.

"Can anyone else see it?" Sebastion asked.

"See what?" Killian asked, trying to look in the direction where Sebastion was staring, but he would have had to roll over and Lara was still feeling his ankle for breaks. Suddenly a shooting pain ran through him, and he sucked in the air. "For the light's sake, woman!"

"Is it tender there then?" She smiled at him. He looked back at her, eyes wide.

"Oh, I think I'd rather take one of d'ose arrows then keep listening to you two," Baran said, leaning back and shutting his eyes.

"We're heading for the cave." Sebastion suddenly said.

"What?" Baran asked, opening his eyes.

"The cave. On top of that hill. That's where we're going ... there." Sebastion kneeled, pointing like a hunting dog.

"I don't see nothing 'er, Sebastion," Baran replied, squinting in the direction.

"Okay, everyone up," Sebastion commanded. "We don't have much time. They are getting ready to rush us. Let's go!". Lara exchanged a glance with Killian. "I don't see a cave." She said, frustration in her voice.

"Do you doubt the Rifkins are getting ready to charge us?" Sebastion asked, looking at her. She thought his eyes too bright for being in darkness. Lightning flashed and Lara jumped back as the look on Sebastion's face was heightened in the light. "Alright. I get it."

"Can you move?" She asked Killian.

"I have no choice, so let's go." He answered, leaning on a nearby tree for support.

"No time," Sebastion said and picked Killian up like a child in his arms. "We have to make it to that cave or be killed." He said, already running as he said it.

"PUT ME DOWN!" Killian yelled, his face red with embarrassment. But Sebastion did not and kept running. The others followed behind.

"They be coming," Morakye said quietly, following after them.

They moved slowly up an incline that was riddled with broken tree branches and holes, but the urgency of their situation spurred them on. Twice they heard the thud of what must have been arrows hitting the trees around them. Finally, Sebastion stopped in front of a large rock.

"There!" he said, pointing to a hole in the ground just under it."

"D'at's your cave!" Baran said, falling on his knees. "A dark blasted hole in the ground for rats!"

Sebastion went to his knees without saying a word and disappeared into the hole like a rabbit. Killian followed pulling and groaning, then Lara right after him. Then Baran, grumbling loudly, and finally Morakye. Inside, it opened up slightly for them to move more freely, but not much. It was dark, damp, and the rocks on the bottom were jagged and sharp on their hands and knees.

"Sebastion, wait up!" Killian called after his nephew, hearing his progress far ahead in the darkness. The cave opened a bit wider and Morakye slipped by them all to catch up with Sebastion. Killian, Lara, and Baran swore at him as he pressed by them. Morakye had the most challenging time getting by Baran with his big belly.

"Stupid damn furry beast!" Baran swore at him as he struggled to get by him. "W'at by the damn puckering dark hell are ya doing!" Baran's head was thrust back by Morakye's rump as he slipped by. The others swore just as vehemently. Morakye made no apologies as he clawed his way forward, pushing and shoving.

"Could you please control your cat," Killian angrily called ahead into the darkness. His ankle ached with every move he made.

"Someone's up here," Sebastion answered back, his voice echoing in the darkness.

"Yes, I know," Killian answered back, annoyed. "It's Morakye. He's charging forward like some-"

"No- "Sebastion cut him off. "There's someone else here with us."

"WHAT! Who?"

"A man," Sebastion answered, invisible to them all in the dark cave. "I think he's dying."

"Alright, hold on. You two get that?" Killian asked behind him.

"Someone up ahead dying. Got it." Lara said, miserably.

Killian felt the air was cooler and the air moving more freely and knew it was open just in front of him. "Sebastion?"

"Yes, we're here." He answered, so close Killian jerked back, sending pain up his leg.

"Alright. How big is the opening?"

"Morakye's height and maybe three Barans across," Sebastion answered.

Killian slipped into the opening, reaching around. The man is in front of you, just beyond your reach."

"You can see him?" Killian asked, surprised.

"Um, yes. I can see pretty well here."

"Like how you saw the cave?" Killian asked carefully.

"Yes," Sebastion answered awkwardly.

"When you girls are done catching up and all d'at," Baran said, falling into the opening. "Maybe we can figure out what ta do now, heh?"

"Can you describe the man in here with us, Sebastion," Killian asked.

"Yes, I will try. He is wearing what looks like rags." Sebastion paused. "His knees and hands are covered in blood as if he has been crawling for a long time. He is probably dying of thirst as he drank both mine and Morakye's water to the last drop."

"You gave a dying man the last of your water?" Killian asked, angrily.

"I did not know for certain he was dying," Sebastion said defensively. "He was pleading for water."

Killian could see nothing in the cave but somehow knew Sebastion was shrugging his shoulders.

After everything, he's still just a boy.

"He can talk?" He asked.

"Yes, and he is listening to you right now."

"Who are you?" Killian asked into the darkness.

"Go on. It's alright." Sebastion said to him gently.

"I am ... Kirslem." The man said in a hoarse and pained voice.

"Why are you here?" Killian was trying to pick up on the accent.

94

They all heard the man swallow, trying to wet his throat. Then they heard him take another swallow of water. "I thought you said he drank all your water?" Killian asked Sebastion.

"He did," Sebastion answered back coldly. "That was yours." Lara laughed softly, echoing off the walls.

"The women ... do not last long here." The man croaked painfully.

"What do you mean?" Killian asked.

"They cannot work as hard ... digging, and *they* prefer them to the men." Kirslem went into a coughing fit.

"Who are *they*?"

"*They* eat the women and ... the young ones first. They only keep us alive for digging. They feed us..." The man began to gasp and whimper.

"Who are *they, damn it*?" Killian asked again in a warning voice.

"*They* feed us our own." The man began to sob. "The man-eaters. The Barbarians. The darkest, cruelest beasts ... from the deepest dark lord's hell!" The man coughed again, choked violently, and fell silent. They heard Sebastion shaking him but knew then that the man was dead.

"What now?" Lara asked. Then there was the strange noise of something banging off the walls behind them. "They have found us now," Morakye said.

"This way!" Sebastion said.

"WAIT!" Killian cried out. "Not all of us can see in this blasted dark cave!" Sebastion reached through an opening in a wall and grabbed Killian's hand. Killian jumped at his touch but grabbed it and took Lara's hand behind him then she reached back and grabbed Baran. They quickly crawled away from the dead man. Then they felt the cave getting smaller and the air getting thinner.

"You sure 'bout this?" Baran called ahead nervously. "I can't see noth'n. There could be those little bastards right behind me." His voice was cracking as he said it.

"You know, I just had a thought," Lara said back to him quietly over her shoulder. Baran didn't answer, but she could hear his irregular breathing. "Do you remember the festival week?" Still he didn't answer. A particularly sharp stone stabbed her hand, and she swore under her breath in the darkness. "Maddy was her name. She lived in town and she would bring sweet meat pies." She took a moment, bringing herself back to that time that seemed so long ago to her. "The flaky crust and the oh, so sweet warm meaty grease that would burst into your mouth when you bit down. Ooh, those were some of the best meat pies I had ever had ... the best anything I've eaten, I think. Do you remember what was in those, Bull?" She asked but still no response. "I think it was the pie crust or the combination of spiced red meat and pheasant together, I think?" She suddenly heard Baran's stomach growl, and she knew she was getting to at least part of him.

"Corn." He said finally.

"What was that?" Lara asked back.

"You forgot the corn." He mumbled. "That was what gave d'at sweet taste ... was the corn."

"Yes ... you are right, I think. I remember that now." Her stomach growled now and they both chuckled. "If I remember correctly," She went on. "You passed out in the courtyard that night." Baran cleared his throat.

"And If I remember correctly, maim, you made me walk the wall for twelve hours the very next day because of it."

"Yes, I did." She laughed. "And I would again, Bull."

"Yes, I believe 'dat you would." They suddenly heard Sebastion's voice echo back to them, but they couldn't make out what he said.

"Killian? Did you get that?" She asked.

"He said that the cave gets bigger further up and … well … I'll tell you the rest when you catch up." He called to her.

Lara was surprised by how far Killian had moved ahead of them when she and Baran were talking. "Alright, be right there," she called back. She hoped the cave didn't veer off anywhere because she and Baran were just traveling by feel. It was total darkness.

The cave did indeed felt more significant when Baran and Lara caught up with the others. And the air was cooler and more comfortable to breathe. Sebastion told them they were at the mouth of an even bigger opening, but the others had to take his word for it in the darkness.

"What's the rest?" Lara asked. Her question was met with silence. "Hello?" Lara asked sarcastically into the darkness.

"I'll let Sebastion tell you … Sebastion?" Killian asked.

"There is something ahead of us. Something big, I think."

"What d'a dark blazes does that mean?" Baran asked.

"If you are quiet, I think you should be able to hear it." They fell silent and held very still, and a slight clicking noise bounced off the walls.

"I thought 'dat was da Rifkins."

"No, they *are* coming but making much less noise,"

97

"So what is dat d'en?" Baran asked, not even trying to keep the annoyance out of his voice.

"Morakye knows what *d'at thing* is?" Morakye said, trying to imitate Baran's speech.

"What is it?" Killian demanded.

"It's a Murgan Tex." Morakye said emotionlessly.

"A Morga what?" Killian asked.

"Murgan Tex," Sebastion spoke up. "In our language, it would be Cave Killer or maybe Cave Death."

"I like d'a cat's name better," Baran said, sighing.

"So those are our choices then?" Lara asked, reaching to the hilt of her sword for reassurance that it was still there. "Either we turn back and face the Rifkins in the dark, or we take our chances with the Cave Killer thing?"

"Yup. That's about it." He could see her, but none of them could see him. He saw that she still had blood running down her arm, and he knew she had to get it bandaged quickly.

"How close is the Cave Killer now?" She asked.

"Alright. Hold on now, will ya." Baran interjected. "Maybe someone should tell us what a Cave thing-y is, heh?" He spread his hands wide, but Sebastion was the only one to appreciate the gesture.

"It's-" But Sebastion paused.

"It's what? What is it?" Lara asked.

Morakye let out a low growl.

"Tell me he's doing that 'cause he's hungry," Baran said.

"There must have been a shortcut through another passage," Sebastion said.

"Shortcut?" Killian asked, reaching for his sword.

"It's almost here," Sebastion answered, pulling his sword free.

"Okay, now I vote for 'em, Lil Folk," Baran said.

"Too late, me thinks," Morakye answered in a hiss-like whisper.

"Great idea to go into the caves. Just great." Baran muttered, adjusting his helmet on his big head, getting ready for whatever was coming next as he turned his head, looking blindly in every direction.

"Take me to the opening," Killian commanded, reaching out his hand. Sebastian took it quickly and pulled him to the opening that was just beyond them. He went to one knee and pulled a piece of cloth from his pack. He pulled his tinderbox free and sparked the fabric to fire. Everyone shielded their eyes until they got used to the light. He then twisted the burning cloth around his sword and held it up. He leaned on his good ankle and looked around. "Start ripping and lighting people. Make piles along the edges and BE QUICK ABOUT IT!" Everyone started making piles of anything they thought would burn and lighting them. Soon the opening was bright with flames.

"What now?" Lara asked.

"Now we make our stand." He looked at her in the light of the flame and saw the deep cut on her arm. "Use some to bandage that wound," he said,

"It's here." Sebastion said.

They saw him looking into a dark hole to his left. Morakye growled deeply again as two long appendages slowly reached out of the hole. Two large eyes followed them, moving independently of each other, and taking them all in. They didn't say a word, watching to see what it would do and how much more there was of it. There was a clacking sound as it moved into the opening. It was like a boulder with six long spiky legs and protruding red eyes that looked at each of them as if sizing them up. It stepped too close to one of the piles of flames and angrily hissed at it.

"D'at thing is really big," Baran whispered, looking up at it. The crab-like creature whirled at the sound of his voice, dancing side to side as if excited about a potential meal. Killian picked up another burning piece of cloth with his sword and thrust it between Baran and the Cave killer. "Get back, monster!" He swore at it.

"What do we do now?" Lara asked, her sword in one hand and her wounded arm close to her body. Morakye suddenly sprang into the air and onto the Cave Killer's back. He drove his claws down, trying to pierce the shell, but the shell was too hard. The Cave Killer screeched loudly in anger and shook Morakye off. He landed hard on his back and a shelled leg followed his descent, just missing crushing his skull as he rolled over and scrambled to a wall.

"I'm open to ideas here?" Killian asked Sebastion.

"I don't think it can see very well in the light." He said, scooping up another piece of burning cloth.

Killian ripped off what was left of his shirt beneath his leather vest. "This light won't last long. Anything else?"

"Baran, wait!" Sebastion yelled out, but it was too late. The big man started circling the giant crab and stepped away from a pile of burning cloth. The Cave Killer swung one of its legs widely and hit Baran in the chest. He was flung against the wall and fell to the ground with a loud huff of air. Lara ran to him, pushing her sword out in front of her, but the burning cloth fell, fizzling as it went out. Killian flung the burning

100

pile to the side of him into the air. The Cave Killer looked up, saw the flames coming down, and backed away.

"We've got a problem here!" Killian said, standing with Lara in front of Baran's unconscious body. Sebastion stood on the other side of the Cave Killer; his sword stretched out as the flames beside him began to fade. Killian frantically looked around. "Where's that damn cat now?!"

"I saw him jump in the hole we came out of," Lara said with her back to him.

"He left us?" Killian asked, looking at Sebastion. Sebastion shook his head, knowing that would not have happened. If anything, Morakye was more wounded and dying or even already dead in the darkness of the hole. Just then, his friend dived out of a hole in the wall, rolling with something tucked close to his body. When he stood, he had what looked to be a dead Rifkin with him. The little body hung limply in his claws. Morakye drove one of his clawed hands into the Rifkins' chest and flung it at the Cave Killer. The giant crab grabbed it out of the air with a pincher-like claw near its mouth. Another followed it, and the claws ripped the Rifkin in half. They all winced together at the noise it made as it was torn apart, including Baran who was now on his knees watching.

"Me's thinks we should be leaving now!" Morakye yelled, waving them into the opening through which the Cave Killer had come.

"Oh, I think I love 'dat cat!" Baran yelled, holding his chest and running for the hole.

"Won't it follow us?" Lara asked.

"The other Rifkins are coming, and me thinks they may be mad at me," Morakye answered.

"Let's hope the Cave Killer gets a taste for them," Killian said, climbing into the hole.

"Thank you, brother," Sebastion said, smiling and getting into the cave next. Morakye jumped into the hole last, hearing an arrow bounce off the walls of the opening.

"Too early for that, methinks," Morakye said, hurrying into the hole.

Soon, in the darkness, they were hearing the screaming of Rifkins behind them. The screams only helped them move along faster. The ground was less littered with sharp rocks here and they were all thankful for that. It also helped them move as fast as they could on their hands and knees.

"Keep up." Sebastion called to them.

"You are moving too quickly. We can't keep up." Killian called ahead, annoyed. "He moves like a puckering mole!" He swore into the darkness.

"Apparently sees like one too," Lara answered back low.

"There is light," Sebastion called to them, now far off.

"Oh, thank 'da gods for that," Baran said, huffing breath and trying to keep up.

"I'll be happy never to see a hole again," Lara said back to him.

"Let's not get carried away," Baran said jokingly.

"BARAN!" Lara yelled back, surprised by his remark. "Are you two trying to call the Cave Killer back for dessert?" Killian whispered harshly at them.

After a few bends, they did notice light. For the first time since battling the Cave Killer, they could see what was in front of them. "Is it a way out?" Killian cautiously called up. There was no answer from Sebastion or Morakye, so they waited. After a short time, they heard someone coming back towards them. As they got close, they recognized Sebastion's hunched-over frame.

"Well?" Killian asked him. "Are we out of here or what?"

"Sort of," Sebastion answered, sitting and leaning against the wall.

"You know some'n kid. You got's a terrible way of spitting things out." Baran grumbled.

Sebastion smiled at him apologetically in the faint light.

"The cave ends a short way ahead. Beyond that is a drop and..."

"For d'a light's sake, spit it out," Baran swore as he took off his helmut and rubbed his aching head. "What can be worse than those crab t'ings back there?"

"Man-eaters," Sebastion said seriously.

"Ah, hell." Baran said. "You win. You found d'a one thing."

"Are you sure?" Killian asked.

"Yes. They are just past this way. It's another large opening, and they have many people digging."

"Slaves?" Lara asked.

"Yeah, the man-eaters are working them hard."

Killian sighed and nervously pulled at his beard. He looked over and saw the large gash in Lara's arm that they hadn't had time to bandage. "You better get that covered now that we have a second." He said, looking at it.

"With what?" Lara asked, leaning her head back against the wall and trying to get her wind back. "We burned everything back there with the creepy-crawly, remember?"

"Oh, alright then. It seems we need to get out of here." He turned back to Sebastion. "How do we get out of here?"

"I don't know," Sebastion answered, putting his hands up.

"Can you try using d'at mysterious stuff you have again, then?" Baran asked.

"It doesn't work that way," Sebastion said, frowning at him.

"Let's see what's out there, shall we?" Killian said, finally breaking an uncomfortable silence.

They all silently crawled together to the edge of the cave. The light was flickering below. Morakye was on the edge of his stomach, watching. He lifted his head up and looked back, putting a claw to his black lips before they got there. They got the message and inched forward silently. Below was a fire in the centre of a big opening surrounded by rock walls. High above, there were several small caves like the one they were in. There were larger ones below them that had dirty men in rags coming and going out of them. The Barbarians lazily stood around, watching them and whipping the smaller frail-looking people from time to time to keep them moving. Off on one corner, there was a single line of men carrying baskets of rocks. Killian was thinking that could be an exit. A man fell, dropping his basket of stones and looking up at the Barbarians with a terrified look that pulled at Killian's heart. The man shifted and saw them looking down at him. They watched as his terror turned to confusion. The Barbarian jumped in front of him, raising the whip and then turning slowly. Following his gaze, they ducked back into the cave.

"Do you think he saw us?" Lara asked, whispering.

"I don't know," Killian said, looking over at Sebastion, who was staring deeper into the cave. "Don't even puckering say it," Killian said, leaning against the wall and rubbing his face with his sore and bleeding hands. "It's back, right?"

"Yes, and coming fast." He answered.

"What!? What is coming fast? What is d'at-" Baran stopped himself when he figured out it must be the Cave Killer coming. "This is not a good day," Lara moaned.

"Barbarians or Cave Killers?" Killian asked them, smiling sardonically, exasperated with their situation.

Morakye peeked over the edge again and quickly pulled his head back.

"Yeah, well?" Killian asked him.

"Eh, them are right there waiting," Morakye said, shrugging. "You mean they know we're here!" Lara asked.

"Morakye does not know why else they would be there with them arrows pointed here."

"Perfect," Killian said, laughing. "Just great. Anyone got any ideas?"

"Yeah, I do," Sebastion said.

"Not sure 'bout your ideas, kid," Baran said miserably. "That's how we all got here, remember?"

"We'd already be dead; if it wasn't for him," Killian reminded him, covering his face with his hands. "What's your idea?"

Sebastion explained and they listened carefully as the sound of the clacking got closer.

"Alright, let's do it," Killian said finally. Sebastion went to the edge and started yelling out in the language of the Barbarians. He told them that he had prisoners and wanted to come out without getting filled with arrows. The Barbarians asked his name and he didn't know what to say.

"I am ... uh..." He hadn't anticipated that question. How would he know what a Barbarian name would be? Unable to think of anything else, he yelled out. "CAVE KILLER!"

Morakye ran and jumped from the ledge into the air and over the heads of the Barbarians. The others slipped down the wall with Morakye's diversion and ran. Killian limped painfully moving as fast as he could. The barbarians detecting the movement, turned back and raised their huge bows. It was then that the Cave Killer jumped out and into the air over their heads. It smashed one of the man-eaters to the ground, landing hard on the rocky ground. The other Barbarians fell over each other, scrambling to get away from it. The slaves nearby screamed and ran as they scattered. Barbarians came to see what the commotion was shouting and knocking arrows.

Together they dropped their stuff next to a cave entrance and tried to blend in with the slaves. They had already ripped their clothes to shreds to set fires in the cave, so they did not have much trouble.

They ran with the group keeping their heads down, not knowing where they were going. Soon they realized they were inside another big cave. There were torches on the walls that lit their way, but the cave never seemed to end.

Killian's ankle was hurting so bad he was thinking that he was going blackout and most likely get trampled. Lara was picking up on it and as they passed a bend took Killian's arm, pulling him in the direction away from the crowd. Baran saw them and followed. They went further in before leaning tiredly against a dim-lit wall away from the scrambling slaves. Killian slid down, feeling that he might vomit.

"Okay, handsome," Lara said, soothingly rubbing his shoulder. "Take a breath … deep breath."

"I think we lost 'der others," Baran said, looking back the way they had come and trying desperately to catch his breath.

"Don't worry, Bull. I think that kid could find anyone or anything at this point." She said as she pushed Killian's hair from his face. Baran grunted his acknowledgment, leaning against the rocks and trying to slow his breathing.

Lara watched as Killian suddenly got a faraway look in his eyes. "Hey … hey stay with me now." Lara tried, but Killian rolled over sideways and passed out. She shook him frantically knowing they could be discovered at any moment.

Killian finally opened his eyes and winced from the pain. "I think it's only a bad sprain, but I need to get off of it. DAMN IT!" Killian sat up. "Not the best time to be puckering lame." He slammed a fist in the ground.

"I think we need to rest a bit anyway," Lara said, leaning against the wall. "This might get bad. I need my sword." As she finished, Killian started pushing himself to his feet.

"Whoa there, big guy!" Lara said, putting a hand on his shoulder to gently push him back down. "You're not going anywhere just yet." Killian groaned, reaching out and touching his leg.

"I'll get 'da stuff," Baran said, standing up straight.

"You're nuts! You can't go back there." Lara said, shaking her head. A piece of black hair that had escaped her long ponytail fell in her face, and she brushed it irritably. Baran started taking off what was left of his old mismatched armour and dropped it to the ground. Lara started again, but Baran held up a finger for her to stop. Lara knew this look, and she knew The Bull long enough to know when he was going to be as stubborn as his namesake. Without another word, he went around the bend and they heard a loud crack. Baran came back, dragging a big slave under the arms. He took the rags off the slave and put them over his clothes. He held his nose for a few minutes trying to control himself and then opened his arms dramatically for them to look him over.

"You would make a fine slave," Killian said, smiling.

"Thanks for d'at." Baran nodded.

Lara frowned at him. "I don't think this is a good idea." She said, shaking her head.

"Tell you what." Baran smiled at her. "If'n I get killed, you can make me walk the damn wall. How about d'atn then?" Baran winked at her and disappeared around the bend.

"I'm getting really sick and tired of being the only voice of reason in this group." She said, sitting.

"Don't flatter yourself," Killian said tiredly. "You're just as crazy and stubborn as the rest of us."

"Pucker off," Lara said, but gave him a quick smile.

"The big ones are gone," Morakye said, looking around. He had a rag over his head and another tied around his waist.

"What? Where?" Sebastion asked, stopping. Several of the running slaves slammed into him and he bounced off a wall.

"Back me thinks."

"This veers off just ahead. Let's get there and figure out what we're doing next." Sebastion pushed forward.

"Veers off?" Morakye asked, turning his head sideways, confused as to how he would know that. Sebastion gave him a look but said nothing else.

"Come on," Sebastion said, jumping back into the crowd of slaves. Not far off, Sebastion turned into what looked to be a little-used area. There was no light, and it smelled of human excrement.

"You be sure this is it?" Morakye asked, putting his face in the crook of his arm.

"Yeah, there's something here."

"Morakye thinks he knows what it is, brother." He said, coughing into his arm.

"No. Something else, something different. It's like- it's ... singing or something."

Morakye looked at him and Sebastion held the front of him; as he did this the eye of the gods glowed a dull red. He stepped forward to touch a rock on the wall and found his hands passed through it. He looked back and saw Morakye looking at the wall, wide-eyed. "I think we can pass through this," Sebastion said.

"We, brother?" Morakye asked worriedly.

Sebastion pulled a hand from the rock and grabbed the Fangor, stepping through the rock with Morakye in tow.

They found themselves in a dimly lit small room lined with shelves. On these shelves were various things ranging from books to small figurines of animals, people, and others that they could not recognize. The glow in the room did not seem to come from any one source. Each item on the shelf seemed to have a different song. Sebastion took in the room with his eyes and ears, trying to take it all in. As he did, he subconsciously put his hand around the crystal around his neck, and was surprised when the singing seemed to lessen to the point where he could think again. Then he saw a nude woman standing very still in a corner, watching them closely.

"Do you see her?" Sebastion asked Morakye, wide-eyed. Morakye's ears twitched and the hair on his back stood up.

"Morakye sees no one." He said, scanning the area back and forth with his yellow eyes. The woman moved from the shadows of a shelf, and Sebastion saw she glowed a pale green. Stranger yet, he could see through her.

"I see you." He awkwardly said to her.

"And I, you." She said back.

Morakye jumped several inches into the air. "I heard that, brother." He said, getting on his toes, ready for anything. The woman moved slowly and sensuously to stand in front of Sebastion. He tried with all his will to keep his eyes on her eyes.

"What are you?" He asked her.

"I am whatever you want me to be, sweetling." Her image faded slightly and then became focused again. This time Sebastion was sure her womanly curves were now more pronounced. Her lips seemed more full, and the rest of her wasaccentuated. "Do you like me?" She asked, licking her lips with a glowing, transparent tongue.

"Where is she?" Morakye asked, on the verge of jumping out of his fur skin. The woman turned to Morakye, smiling, and stepped in front of him. Sebastion watched as Morakye's narrow eyes suddenly focused on where she was standing.

"Torman tan luxer mor." He whispered, his eyes wide and full of wonder. Sebastion somehow knew what it meant. Morakye had said she was the most beautiful Fangor he'd ever seen. The woman thanked him in the same language, brushing what Sebastion saw as long human hair. He suspected Morakye was now seeing whatever the woman wanted him to see. She started to reach out a hand and an urgency ran through him so strong he stepped between them without thinking.

"No, brother," Sebastion said, pushing out an arm to hold the woman back. Morakye tried to push Sebastion out of the way, and the woman and Morakye touched him at the same time. There was a flash and he was somewhere else.

Sebastion found he was hiding in the woods, watching men on horseback ride by. On the horses' backs were dead Fangors bouncing up and down lifelessly to the horse's gait. He suddenly realized he was somehow watching what must be the past through Morakye's eyes. He watched the line of men ride by and suddenly recognized one of the Fangors as his uncle. Shock, terror, and grief gripped his heart so hard he wanted to fall to his knees. He knew his feelings were not his own, but it did not stop them from taking him over. He watched as the body with his beloved uncle's dead eyes seemed to look right at him as he bounced up and down. More bodies followed behind, but he was too afraid they would be his aunt or perhaps, worst of all, his sister. A sharp pain suddenly went through Sebastion, and he began to weep into his sharp-clawed hands. Through his tears, Sebastion heard the words of some ancient Fangorian wise woman in his head: *"You will meet a warrior that will carry the weight of prophecy with him. This man will be a dark slayer. He and you are connected in some way. You must seek him out."*

Sebastion could now see the old Fangor wrapped in furs. Her feline face was a mix of brown and white fur. Her eyes, as strange as they were, still looked to be full of sadness. "There is more." The older woman said in a whisper. Her sagging, pointed ears went lower on her head. She leaned in close for him so he would hear. "You will be the last of us. Sweet, boy ... you will not *join us on our journey. But like you, another one lost from his kind will you find. You will be the other half of one. You must leave tomorrow to the south."* Then, just as he was there, he was back in the room with Morakye.

"*My* memories," Morakye said, looking at him with an anger Sebastion had never seen there before.

"I was there," Sebastion said back, feeling the weight of it.

"No, Sebastion. You saw, but you did not live it. It was not yours to live." Morakye's eyes were narrow with anger.

Sebastion realized Morakye did not say brother and blinked, realizing his discomfort with what had just happened. "I felt..." He started but did not finish. "Where is she?" He asked, looking around. Sebastion looked over and his eyes met the eyes of the apparition, who was now squatting down in a corner holding her transparent legs close

112

to her bare chest. Her look was hate and terror in one. "Has she had any contact with you since I have been … eh, away?" Sebastion asked and immediately looked all over the room, his eyes bright and ears high above his head, twitching nervously. "You can't see her," Sebastion answered his question. "Tell me what you are?" He commanded the image of the woman, stepping towards her.

"You should not play games with me, dragon." She said venomously. "You know who I am just as I know who you are … regardless of your ridiculous appearance." She squeezed her legs tighter and looked away. "You and I would be the same if it were not for the mage and his magic that has bonded me to that horrible thing." She extended a long delicate finger towards a figurine on the bookshelf beside her. Sebastion walked towards it slowly to get a better look. It was just a simple stone carved into the torso of a woman. It was worn as if someone had spent a lifetime rubbing at it nervously.

"Bashor has bonded you to this, then?" He asked her, somehow knowing the answer before he asked it.

"I know of no one of that name, but if that is the name the dark Mage has taken now then yes. Are you patronizing me, lizard? You know as well as I of these things." Sebastion picked up the diminutive figurine in his hand and studied it. "You could free me…" The woman suddenly said in a desperate voice from the floor by his leg.

"You are Conslava," Sebastion said quietly and more to himself than to her, flipping the dark stone image of the woman's torso in his hand. He then suddenly stopped and sternly looked down at her. "You were a vile woman. You killed men for pleasure … and still will as what you are now." Sebastion squeezed the image in the palm of his hand. "You are nothing more than a weapon now."

"Help me, and I will be whatever you want me to be." Conslava smiled up at him, wetting her lips again. She then stood and Sebastion found himself looking into Miska's big brown eyes. She was wearing the man's clothing and the hat she wore in the city of Endrea. She looked up into Sebastion's face with her eyes batting, and Sebastion felt his heart skip a beat. Miska reached up to touch his cheek but stopped before touching him with a slight seductive smile on her lips. A smile that was not Miska's. Sebastion felt a rage come over him that he was not sure he could control ... or even wanted to.

"Brother?" Morakye asked, backing away from Sebastion slightly as the crystal around his neck flared up red. Miska's image disappeared and Conslava backed up to the rock wall, hissing like a cornered cat.

"Do that again, Nymph," Sebastion warned with fire in his eyes. "and I will make you wish you were one of those poor bastards you killed long ago."

"You are just as bad as that dark mage, dragon!" She said dragon as if it were poison on her tongue.

"My name is Sebastion. Do not call me dragon again." He watched as Conslava cringed in pain. Her image faded and then came back faintly. She looked at his hand, eyes wide and frightened. Sebastion looked down at his hand and saw the figurine was glowing white. He looked up at her and she caught his eye, lowering her head submissively. "I will do whatever you command ... master." She went to her knees before him, bowing her head low.

"I's can see her now," Morakye said, looking surprised and a little frightened. "What went on here, brother?" He asked, his ears points on his feline head. Sebastion looked into Morakye's yellow eyes and could almost read his thoughts.

"It is still me, my friend."

"Brother." Morakye corrected him. Sebastion smiled. "I am sorry I invaded your memories. Sometimes ... *it* ... takes me whether I want it to or not." He looked down at the woman at his feet. "I think this one is attached to me now somehow. Whether I want *this* or not." He looked at the figurine that was now just a dull piece of worn rock again. "I find myself having fewer choices of late."

"Morakye does not think that is wise, brother." Conslava looked up at the little Fangor and hissed again. Morakye took a step back. "Morakye thinks Sebastion should unattach himself," he said seriously, his yellow eyes large.

"She may be useful," Sebastion said and put his fists on his hips, looking down at the somewhat transparent, dangerous figure before him. "What can you do for me?" He asked her. She excitedly looked up at him from the ground. Sebastion looked down at her, suddenly feeling uncomfortable, and took a step back, taking his hands off his hips. He looked back at Morakye, and then he gave Sebastion a strange look. Sebastion cleared his throat and waved her up off the ground. "Alright, I need to find my friends. Can you help me?" Conslava looked around the walls and pointed at one of them with a long finger. "Two are there beyond these walls here. Can you not see them, d-" She stopped herself and looked back at Sebastion, who gave her a look that made her lower her head again. "And the other? The third?" Sebastion asked her. She quickly looked around again before resting her gaze on another wall.

"The fat one is running back to the others with three Barbarians close behind him." She stopped then, staring off in the same direction. "He is thinking of stopping before he gets to the others. He does not want to put the other two in danger." She stopped staring. "He has stopped. They will kill him."

"Take us to him NOW!" Sebastion commanded. "I cannot, master. That is beyond what I can do."

"Well, what by the puckering dark hell can you do?!" He yelled at her, taking a step towards her. Conslava breathed out a sharp breath, throwing up her arms and stepping back.

"If you command it, I could stall the Barbarians ... or worse." Sebastion noticed her face lighting up slightly.

"Then stop the barbarians from killing my friend by any means. DO IT NOW!" The image of Conslava flared and shrieked in delight before disappearing out of the room.

"Come, brother," Sebastion said, reaching out for Morakye. "Let us find the others." He took Morakye's hand, but Morakye pulled away. "What is it?" Sebastion asked, feeling a little hurt by the reaction.

"Does my brother Sebastion still exist?" He asked, cocking his head sideways. "Morakye will know if my human brother remains."

"Of course, I am right here," Sebastion said, touching his chest, not knowing what the Fangor meant. Morakye shook his head, not convinced.

"Too many changes. Morakye wonders what of the man I knew remains."

116

Sebastion sighed. "I'm not sure we have time for this, brother."

"The ... N-nymph," Morakye struggled for the word. "You called her? Morakye thinks she will be effective in slowing down any man. Even Barbarians-" He stepped close to Sebastion and looked up into his eyes. "These are not the same eyes as my brother. I see some of the same, but much of the difference is there as well." He looked and Sebastion returned his look. "Something there familiar ... something other than Sebastion."

"Yes, brother. I don't think I can fully explain it, but ... I think I am not alone here." Sebastion tapped his head slightly with a finger.

"Inside of you?"

"Yes. There is something else with me. Not something bad ... I think ... it's truly trying to help me ... us."

"The dragon?" Morakye asked as if he already knew the answer.

"Not exactly, brother. -More than that. I think Conslava has an idea of what. I think the other inside me was the one that bonded Conslava to me." Thinking of it caused a dull ache in his head, and Sebastion rubbed at it.

"The other plays a dangerous game with the evil ghost woman then," Morakye said in a harsh low voice. Sebastion shook his head in agreement.

"I think the other is desperate. I also think whatever it was is now changed inside me. We are becoming ... eh, um together ... I think ... you know?" Morakye looked at him, confused, so Sebastion tried again. "I do not feel like the other is changing me. I feel like we are ... becoming together. Becoming something different."

117

"Morakye likes you the way you were before." The Fangor's words were so sincere that Sebastion felt emotion run through him. "Morakye does not like or trust this ... different thing in you." Sebastion nodded his head, acknowledging his worry.

"I think we should go and make sure Baran is all right," Sebastion suggested, holding out his hand. Morakye looked apprehensive. "The other will not harm you ... I'm sure of it."

"Show me," Morakye said, still staring at Sebastion's outreached hand.

"What?" Sebastion asked, confused.

"Show me the other. Let Morakye decide if it is as good as you say."

"I'm not su-"

"Morakye has seen things Sebastion can do now." He said, cutting him off. "Try. Show me. Let your brother see the other. *Snoram cof tu oram*, brother."

Sebastion looked at the Fangor, surprised at what he had said in Fangorian and only slightly surprised now that he understood it. In the common language, it meant 'Share the load.' Sebastion smiled at that, and Morakye smiled back, showing his sharp teeth. Sebastion had to laugh, and Morakye took his hand. Sebastion shook his head, still smiling, and closed his eyes to try to do what Morakye asked. In his mind, he tried to pull forward the entity that shared his mind and body. It came quickly and willingly to the surface. Sebastion suddenly felt the Fangor's mind with him. The three were suddenly connected. The other with Sebastion seemed to recognize Morakye, and a feeling of warmth filled them both. It was a strange connection through raw emotion.

There were no words or pictures in their minds. It was all feeling and a contact neither Sebastion or Morakye had ever felt before. They felt sadness, regret, and a host of other emotions. But what neither Sebastion nor Morakye felt was maliciousness on either of their parts.

On the contrary, what they felt from their presence was like a family member watching over them. There were concerns and extreme worry. Sebastion had little to gauge this feeling, but as it was explained by Morakye's thoughts and memories, the meaning flowed to him. They both opened their eyes together as a single thought and stared a moment more.

"Me think's we have met him before," Morakye said.

"I know. But I cannot place it." Sebastion answered back. Morakye smiled. "We's can now find our friends."

Sebastion laughed and pulled the Fangor through the stone wall as if he had done it all his life.

CHAPTER 14

There was a light knock on the door, and Bashor looked up, surprised, and wished he hadn't as a feeling of wooziness passed through him. "Who is it?" He asked, angrily rubbing his head.

"Sir, I was told to bring you food," answered a timid male voice from behind the door. "I have bread, soup, and fruit … eh, sir."

Bashor threw open the door and the servant took two steps back. The man was wearing a simple brown monk's robe and a yellow rope with a talisman around his waist. Bashor couldn't make out which symbol of one of the lesser gods it was.

"To whom do you pray?" Bashor asked bitterly, reaching out and pulling the timid little monk into the room. The man nearly spilled the contents of the tray. When he was settled, he looked desperately for a place to put it down. He quickly lay it on the bed and stepped back away from Bashor, inching towards the door. He suddenly remembered the question and started stuttering.

"Forget it … it does not matter," Bashor said, catching the man's arm in his claw-like hands. The man tried to pull away, but Bashor held him tight. "HOLD STILL!" Bashor commanded, and the servant went still, his eyes darting around, terrified. Bashor pushed his thumbnail into the monk's flesh, drawing a bead of blood, and rubbed his thumb in it slowly, looking for any trace of magic. The man squealed, unmoving. Bashor pushed the arm away, disgusted. The man fell to the ground, finding he could now move again.

"There is nothing in you, maggot. Take your useless flesh from my sight." Bashor spat, pulling a cloth from his pocket to clean his hand, and again began feeling sick. "Wait," he said before the man could get through the door. The man froze like a rabbit that was stumbled upon by a hungry wolf. "Where would I find the closest church of either twin?" Bashor asked. The servant was silent and did not look back. "Answer now," Bashor warned.

"There,-there is a place not far from here, above us. Some say that there are sacrifices to the dark lord there. It is an evil place. Even the most wise and powerful god, Tigrien, would not go there." The man stepped the rest of the way out the door and closed it silently but quickly behind him.

Okay then, how do I get to the top? Pesky magical spells are protecting this place all over. The same spells that are keeping me safe from the twins are keeping me confined. He looked around the room and concentrated on his limited powers. He thought he saw a faint glow come off the mirror he waslooking into.

Of course! I am a fool. Those idiots are watching me through an enchanted mirror. Well, if they can use it, so can I!" He walked up to the mirror and casually stepped to the side so there was no reflection. He reached out a hand and gently pushed the mirror off the wall and it crashed loudly onto the floor.

Did they believe I would not know...? He pushed the shards of glass into a pile with his foot and took a deep breath. He put his hands together and closed his eyes. He concentrated on the broken, enchanted glass and pictured what he wanted them to do in his mind. The glass slowly began to melt together. Bashor unfolded his hands, pointing at the floor as the shards formed into a rectangular shape in front of him. He spread his hands and blew a breath at the glass and found himself looking at a pale sky.

"There I will find more of my magic nectar!" He said aloud as he dove into the image in front of him.

His momentum propelled him several feet above the ground and he landed hard. All the air left his lungs from the impact, and he slowly rolled, waiting to be able to breathe again. When he was able to sit up he looked around, sucking in the cool fresh air. A few deep breaths later, he stood and heard a woman screaming in the distance. He brushed at his trousers, scowling at the dirt and small pieces of grass stuck to him. The woman screamed again but was sharply cut off. Preceding the scream was a high-pitched laugh and then thick coughing. Bashor brushed his hair back from his face and went to investigate.

He seemed to be in a large field overlooking green meadows. If he hadn't been so hungry for the magic, he could even have thought it pleasant. The sun was high and birds chirped as they swooped around him as a pleasant gentle breeze blew around him. After spending so much time hiding in the cold, Bashor breathed in the air and let the sun warm his skin. He was not usually one to enjoy the sun, but today it felt good.

There was a large mound with grass growing up the side that seemed to be where the screaming came from. He walked cautiously around the side of it and saw large stones piled high and blocking the view of what was in the centre. He heard the rattle of chains and kept walking around until he found a crack to look through. What he saw was a large opening to the sky. There was a raised altar in the middle of the clearing. On it was a chained woman with a large, bleeding hole in her chest. On the ground next to her was a thin man wearing a bull's head or mask of some sort. He was sitting on the ground leaning against the altar, rubbing what looked to be the woman's heart all over his body, leaving streaks of blood on his pale skin. Bashor could hear him chuckling to himself and making sounds of ecstasy. His body under the Big Bull's head shook in the rapture of it. The man started rubbing his thighs and Bashor could see he was wearing only a black cloth tied around his waist. The dark mage saw where this was going and contemplated whether he even wanted to bother with this deranged man. There was a noise just on the other side of the crack in the rock he was looking through and something passed by his view. He stepped back, startled, but curiosity got the best of him, and he looked back through the hole again. He now heard the whimpering of at least two more women there, leaning against the same rock he peered through. He heard the rattle of more chains and knew the little bull-man had his victims waiting their turn. He saw the man get up and heard him say something in a high-pitched voice inside the hollowed-out bullhead. It echoed so much that he could not make out the words. Bashor watched the man walking towards the crack, and he heard the woman start crying and whimpering for help. He thought the man looked so frail that he wondered what prevented the women from just overpowering him. He deduced they must be drugged in some way.

The man came to the place where the woman were, and Bashor heard chains drop to the ground. Then he felt a familiar surge in the air. The man giggled beyond his view and then Bashor saw him. He was carrying the woman upside down with one hand around her ankle. He was holding her effortlessly off the ground as she fought to get free. The man had great strength in his scrawny body, and Bashor knew that could only be done with the help of magic. He smiled greedily and rubbed his hands together, excited as a smile spread across his lips.

Back inside his small room Bashor read from a favourite book of his that he often travelled with. It was the memoirs of a man that lived a long time ago. It described how the 'elite men' should strive for dominance over the sordid masses. He read, smiling and sipping from his wine glass that did not contain wine. He felt the expected return of energy going through his body. There was a sudden bang on the door as if someone had walked into it not expecting it to be locked and he heard a woman swearing on the other side. Then the door burst flying to the ground with a bang. Silsen walked in with her substantial bulbous nose pointed in the air. When she saw the little skinny man suspended in the air upside down and bleeding into a basin, she caught her breath in her hand. She saw the eyes of the little man look at her with fear and desperation. The man was obviously still alive but near bleeding to death. It was then that she realized what Bashor was sipping, as he contently sat reading on the small bed they had provided for him.

"What by the balance do you think you are doing?!" She exclaimed, looking at him as if he were a large rodent that had jumped out in front of her.

"Oh, *do* calm yourself, dear Silsen," Bashor said without looking up from his book. He held out a finger for her to wait and quietly finished the line he was reading before acknowledging her. He could feel the room get colder with his desired effect. "Ah, okay." He finally smiled up at her. "What is it I can do for you?"

"You can tell me why this man is hanging upside down, bleeding to death."

Bashor shrugged, closing the book and standing. "Simple." He said, taking another sip and rolling his eyes. "I do not have the luxury of naturally building magic. I need to extract it where I can find it."

Silsen looked at Bashor, raising her brow in confusion, and as the realization of what he was saying came to her, she focused on reading him with her abilities. Bashor returned her gaze, frowning.

"Your powers are limited still but..., somewhat more than when we first met." She said finally.

Bashor brought the glass to his lips and sipped, raising his eyebrows up and down. As if understanding for the first time, Silsen looked at him, horrified. Bashor smiled at her with blood-stained teeth.

"Who is he?" she asked, regaining her composure and indicating the man hanging upside down.

"I don't know exactly. I suspect he is a practitioner of the black magic and worshipper of the dark lord, or some sort of thing."

Bashor couldn't help but roll his eyes when Silsen's mouth fell open. He thought she looked like some type of fish-like creature.

A short time later, Bashor found himself once again in front of the lesser gods for an "emergency meeting." Bashor had drunk the last of the living blood from the man that contained a base amount of power. It was nothing compared to what he had gotten from the boy and the priestess some time back.

125

They had put a chair in the middle of the room as the lesser gods talked about him as if he wasn't there. It was fine with him, however. To him, the gods were acting like frightened sheep, with their ignorant hysteria. He knew they would eventually look to him for support. He had no doubt of it.

"The dark lord is looking for him right now!" One of the lesser gods yelled, and Bashor looked up to see who it was. It was little Chelco, the feminine man with the powdered face and short, tight robe.

"Perhaps we should give the mage to the dark lord and have done with it." Another said. Bashor did not even look to see who it was. He got up from his chair and dramatically yawned into his hand. The lesser gods exchanged angry looks, but none said a word. Finally, Bashor stretched and addressed them as if he had just walked into the room.

"Yes, the dark lord is looking for me." He said, flipping a hand at them as if to say the thought meant nothing. "He wants to kill me for the same reason he will be going after you ... in time." The lesser gods started talking among themselves again. Bashor let them talk for a few seconds to let it sink in.

"SO," he said loud enough for them all to hear over their worried banter. "That is why we are working together. Survival. Right?" He smiled disarmingly and opened his arms wide.

"Your survival, not ours, Mage." Larko, the short dwarf-like god, said bitterly.

"We've been through this, Larko, my friend," Bashor said, walking up to the dwarf's seat. "The dark lord will be coming for us all. That includes you." Bashor looked him squarely in the eye, but the little god did not give way. They stared at each other like this until someone cleared their throat uncomfortably. Bashor finally looked away, smiling innocently. "We're in this together. Like it or not."

"Let's say we are in this together." Silsen put in. "Will you be eating the dark lord's people only, or should we expect our decibels to be *drained* as well?" Bashor surprised them all by taking the question seriously and thinking about it. He stared at the floor, frowning deeply, contemplating. Finally, he raised his head, smiling tight-lipped. He crossed his arms behind him and winked before walking off and through the doors silently. The lesser gods exchanged furious looks at Bashor's apparent arrogance. "I will not have him draining *my* people," Silsen announced, trying to meet everyone's eye to make her point.

"Of course not, with *their* noses, they could *smell* him coming a mile away," Lutta said under her breath and brushing back her perfect golden locks from her face. Silsen, hearing her comment, stared daggers at the pretty little god. Brinka, Lutta's twin sister, chuckled into her small delicate hand.

CHAPTER 15

With the boy now dead, the time spent on his sister's prophecy seemed more wasted and foolish than ever. The Dark Lord paced a long corridor with walls lined with paintings of battles and vicious creatures of the past. He didn't even notice them as they blurred as he walked, using his magic to propel him faster than his typical long gait. His head was down, and his mind was full of storm clouds as he contemplated the many demises he had for the dark Mage.

The bastard had plunged a magical knife into my flesh. He had double-crossed me and made me look the fool!

The dark lord stopped and pulled a painting from the wall, slamming it to the ground where it exploded into pieces.

Where are you, Mage? What rabbit hole have you crawled into?

He ran his fingers through his hair, and it fell back into place instantly and perfectly. He stopped and turned, and a door materialized. He turned the handle and walked in as if he had always been there. The room was filled with windows on the walls. The images through them were all of cruel and dark things. The dark lord looked from window to window. He imagined all the things that were being done to the dark Mage and started to feel himself relax. He summoned a chair and it slid across the room and under him. He was saving his favourite window for last. This particular one never disappointed, and he had bestowed unique gifts onto this specific disciple of his. The man was a fierce and demented soul, and the Dark Lord had much respect for him. Some of the things the man came up with even he, the lord of darkness, would not have thought of. Smiling like a hungry child turning to his favourite part of a large meal, the dark lord spun the chair and looked at the place in the centre of the wall as he smiled with anticipation.

He watched there blankly as nothing happened. There was just a woman in what looked to be a white dress lying on an altar. The dress was nearly completely stained red except for the frayed end that hung over the stone. Her chest was carved open with her heart lying on the ground next to her, crumbled and as lifeless as the woman's body.

The dark lord felt the frustration coming back frominactivity. He knew the magic in the windows was powerful and should have taken him to his decibel no matter where he was. He concentrated on the power there, but the scene did not change. He suddenly knew something was wrong. The dark lord extended the window view with an outstretched finger and stepped through. As he arrived, he looked around for the man along the rocks. He saw two women chained to a wall. The women were alive and staring at him as if they were still in shock. They looked to have been that way for quite some time and, again, the dark lord suddenly felt something had gone wrong here. He stepped up to them and knew instantly that questioning them would be useless. They started whimpering loudly and pleading for his help. He couldn't concentrate with the noise and cut both their throats with a nail that grew instantly from his index finger. He walked past them, now appreciating the silence. He irritably gathered his power and pulled the past forward. He did not have to go far in time before he saw the familiar face of Bashor. His heart quickened, and he almost lost his hold on the magic but, with a grasp on his will, he kept hold and watched as Bashor froze the man in place and tasted the blood from his wrist with a long skinny pale finger. Bashor must have liked what was there because he tore off the bullhead and dragged the man by his long thinning hair out of the clearing. The dark lord followed behind the image of Bashor to a hole in the ground that glowed and buzzed with magic. Not just any magic, but the magic of the lesser gods.

So he is in league with them already, is he? The dark lord could feel his divine blood rush to his face.

Yes, it is time we dealt with these meddling wizards. Far too long have I let them exist in a world that has grown away from them. He knew he couldn't destroy them all without the support of his other half, his sister. But, he knew what he could do to manipulate them and have them destroy themselves as two of them had done long ago ... although their power of immortality was very strong, he did find a way to make them wish they were dead.

Okay, you puckering fools. Then Let it begin...

The Dark Lord watched the magical hole disappear as Bashor vanished with it. The image wasn't replaying what had already happened; he would have pulled the flesh from the Dark Mage's bones right there and then.

Did the idiot think I would not know if he killed one of my own? FOOLS, all of them!

Chelco sat slumped over with heavy eyelids in his red highback chair, letting his many worshippers admire him. He lazily looked them over in his big white castle and allowed his eyes to twinkle and his long black hair to shine with light. His skin was perfectly powdered. He sat disdainfully watching in his short robe. He had purposely shortened it

130

to show off his shapely calves. His worshippers of men and women looked on at him with full reverence and Chelco looked back in the quiet confidence of his full control over them. The highest-ranking of them would, at times, come to kneel at his feet and tell him how they have been blessed by having him in their lives.

Some he let think that they had touched him deeply with their words, and he would reach down and touch their heads ever so lightly. The truth was he found the act of physical contact with them disgusting, but he knew that sometimes one of his kind had to appease even the sheep. He had a basin of warm water near him, and he would wash his hands often, careful not to touch himself until he was well scrubbed.

This particular day of sitting and being revered was getting incredibly tiresome. His thoughts kept going back to the vile and arrogant dark Mage. Though in his dark reflections, he did have to admit that the Mage did have some excellent black riding boots. He smiled to himself at the thought. The group of people on their knees staring up cooed at him, thinking the smile was for them. His thoughts went to the days when he had many closets of clothing, shoes, and boots. He suddenly started feeling sad that his wardrobe now only consisted of short white robes, golden rope as ties, and sandals. He looked down sadly at his perfectly groomed toes in the sandals and sighed. The man near his feet looked up at him, horrified. Chelco reached down and touched the man's head to appease him, trying hard not to make a disgusted face. The man squealed with joy. Chelco forced a smile and reached into the warm water beside him.

Later that day, he retired to his private quarters away from the many groomers, servants, and worshippers and watched out his window as the scenery changed every few moments to some of the most beautiful places in this world. As much as he forced his thoughts to clothes and art, it always came back to the dark Mage.

Is it not bad enough that I am to see more of the scruffy Mage that I must now have his sickly image in my mind?

He looked up at the ceiling as a wave of frustration flowed through him and thought he saw a flash of light from the corner of his eye. He looked around but did not see nor sense anything. He returned his gaze to the window and now watched as thousands of blue and red flowers bent in a breeze as it swept across a vast natural field. He thought their dance in the wind was almost musical.

"Hello, Chelco, old friend." A deep voice said behind him.

Chelco cried out, covering his mouth and throwing out his other hand in front of him. When he turned, he was looking up into the cold and perfect eyes of the dark lord. Chelco couldn't help but take a moment to contemplate the perfection of his jawline and chin. Jealousy helped to feed the anger that was coming.

"It has been a long time since we last spoke, has it not?" The dark lord asked, smiling and showing off what Chelco thought were dazzling white, straight teeth. An uncontrollable wave of jealousy rushed through him. He turned away in an attempt to hide his face. The attempt had failed, however, and the dark lord smiled at the man's back, knowing he had found yet another weakness of this lesser god.

"My, my, you have startled me!" Chelco said, turning and smiling wide, letting his light eyes twinkle.

"Yes, it seems I have. But then how could I have not? You were not expecting company, were you?" The dark lord stared down accusingly at the smaller man. Chelco's face turned red as his thoughts went to the dark mage. He quickly turned away and made it as if he had planned to yell out for wine and cheese. When he turned back, he was composed. "I have not had guests for some time, my lord."

"Oh, I am not your lord, Chelco. Though I think perhaps some of your habits do fall into my colours, eh?" The dark lord said, smiling."

"Well!" Chelco said with a huff.

"Do not worry about these things. That is *not* why I am here."

"Why are you here?" Chelco asked, trying to smile, but he knew it came out weak.

"To see where you stand on the war, of course." The dark lord smiled back.

"The war in The Torenium Empire is beyond the lesser gods," Chelco said as if it pained him to able to do nothing. "As we agreed, we left that to you and your-"

The dark lord shook his head slowly, wagging a finger at him. "Must we play games? I would think we were beyond that." He took a glass offered to him by a female servant in a white robe like Chelco's. Her eyes never left her god's face until the dark lord casually reached out and squeezed one of her breasts. She jumped, dropping the tray, and gave him a shocked look. The dark lord then gave her a smack on the bottom that sent her several paces forward. "Why even have these around if you … eh, prefer the more equipped ones?" The dark lord asked, smiling.

133

"Games, my lord?" Chelco asked, trying to bring him back to their discussion. Chelco irritably waved the woman off with a hand. She looked back at him, sadly having heard the dark lord's words.

"The war is on, and everyone is picking sides. Do not make me sound a fool by telling you what you already know, Chelco." The dark lord put on his most sanctimonious scowl.

"I do not know about the sides." Chelco lied. He assumed the dark lord was speaking about their new alliance with Bashor and knew he had to be very careful.

"My dear little friend." The dark lord said, clasping his hands in front of himself and taking on the demeanour of a patient parent. "You know as well as I that Larko and his little gang of *much* lesser gods are plotting against you and whoever you are with." He said, shaking his head. Chelco smiled, but the dark lord knew his eyes were telling a different story. He had him.

"You are saying Larko is plotting against me?"

"You don't know?" The dark lord asked, an expression of disbelief on his face. "Surely your friends have warned you!" He said, turning up his hands in disbelief. Chelco said nothing but the dark lord saw the wheels turning.

"Who are the others Larko is plotting with?" Chelco asked, red-faced now. The dark lord became stiff as a board and stared down at the man as if he were a annoying gnat.

"It seems I have come calling to the wrong temple. I meant to speak of these things with someone..." The dark lord looked away, thinking before answering. "-Someone more knowledgeable of the recent situations."

Chelco's face went from red to now purple, his eyes flared and, for the first time, twinkled of their own accord. "I will not be ostracized." He said.

The dark lord laughed at him. "Do they still have you believing Bashor is there to help?"

Chelco could only stare, knowing he should say nothing more. "It seems they have big plans for you." The dark lord said finally, laughing and vanishing.

The dark lord arrived back in the room with the windows still smiling from his visit with the simple-minded lesser god. He could not see into any of the lesser gods' dwellings, but he, at times, did get an inkling of their goings-on from the happenings within their temples. He intently watched what looked to be a large house converted into a church as Chelco appeared, his face still red and angry. He looked around until he found an older man in a long green robe intensely reading a book on an altar.

"WHAT DO YOU KNOW ABOUT THESE IDIOTS' PLOTTINGS?" Chelco yelled in his high-pitched voice. The older man jumped, knocking the book off the altar and frantically looked around. When he saw Chelco, he fell to his knees with his hands palm up towards the angry god. "I have no time for your stupidity, old man. TELL ME WHAT YOU KNOW!"

"Oh, my Lord. I know little about the dealings of the gods." The man whined, not looking up.

"*Little?* Then you know some, eh?"

"My Lord … I know … I know something." The older man said hesitantly, as if the words gave him a great deal of pain.

The dark lord smiled and sat into his chair, looking up at the window where the scene unfolded. He wondered if the long, deep cuts on the older man's back were healing yet. He and the man in the green robe had already had a long discussion on how to handle the little god's questions. The seed of deception had been planted. Now, with the dandy little Chelco's lead worshipper in his pocket, all was working as planned. The dark lord put his hands behind his head and reveled in his genius.

I will have the slugs killing each other in days. Then the rodent mage will pop his little head up out of the hole and then... The dark lord excitedly smashed a fist into the palm of his other hand. I will have him ... and I will make it last. He unconsciously reached over and touched the place where Bashor had plunged the knife into him. Yes, I will make it last a very long and agonizing time. The pain I will inflict on him will be legendary. The idiot gods will destroy each other, and I will have the Mage. My sister can worry about words in stones, and I will expand my rule over the flocks the lesser gods leave behind. Everything is working out perfectly! The dark lord smiled to himself, now quite satisfied with himself.

CHAPTER 16

"Is that all of it?" The Head Mother asked, sitting back into her big chair by the fire.

"Yes, mother," Miska replied sheepishly, her throat burning from talking through her whole life in such a short period. The Head Mother of the Lady of Light put her hands together and touched the tips to her lips, thinking. Miska shifted in her seat nervously, letting her gaze rise to the painting on the wall, but that made her face grow as red as when she first saw it. She had told the Head Mother how she and Sebastion became lovers but seeing the two in the painting made her feel suddenly guilty, and then a wave of loneliness and regret overtook her. She felt the feeling wash through her like a cold breeze on naked skin.

"And you're sure the name was Bashor?"

"Yes," Miska answered a little more abruptly than she meant. The Head Mother seemed to have not noticed, and Miska breathed easier. The Head Mother finally looked up, smiling.

"I would very much like to meet this Morakye." She said, almost cheerfully. Miska looked at her, surprised. "I think he sounds simply irresistible."

"Um ... I guess he is," Miska answered, letting her mind fill up with the picture of the Fangor. She pictured when she had first seen him on the trail escaping the slavers and thought Morakye was far from 'irresistible' at that moment. She wondered where he was now ... if even alive. The Head Mother asked if he was still with Sebastion or if any of them were already dead in the currently empty city. She sighed and looked up, surprised to see the Head Mother's bright blue eyes on her. She then realized she had let her mind wander.

"Sorry," Miska said, lowering her head with embarrassment. Before her head dropped, she noticed the Head Mother was giving her a look she could not interpret.

"Your friend Sebastion sounds like someone I would also like to meet."

"I do not know if he is even alive any longer. After I..." Miska swallowed audibly in the big room before finishing. "-left." The Head Mother watched her for a moment before going on.

"I have always been fairly good at predicting things, and I predict we will see this Sebastion again ... and his friends." She added more lightly. "When I was a child, they told stories of Fangors." She smiled wide, and her eyes went far away. "Most of the time, the stories depicted them as savages or evil, but I always suspected that if they did exist, they would be much like the way you described Morakye." Miska thought it was strange having the Head Mother of the Church of the Lady of Light mentioning Morakye and Sebastion by name. "Is there anything else, child? Anything else I should know before we speak to this Lehgone character?" Miska shook her head, lifting a glass of water to her lips.

"What were your thoughts on the Advisors to the king?" The Head Mother asked Miska with an arched eyebrow and a frown.

"I do not think it is my place to say," Miska said, looking at the ground again.

"There is a great wheel turning in this world, my dear. And I believe you are more involved in that *turn* than you realize." The Head Mother said this in a severe, low tone that made Miska look up. "What did you think of the Advisors?" She asked again in a way that left no more room for hedging.

"I thought they were..." Miska paused, and the Head Mother cocked her head sideways, trying to elicit a response. "I thought they were horrible, Mother," Miska said, looking down again. "I'm sorry, Mother. But they were such a horrid bunch of men. They reminded me of the guards watching the slave caravan, mean ... disconnected men."

"Disconnected?" The older woman asked, sitting up on the edge of the chair now.

"Yes, disconnected from ... you know, people. They are living a life that is ... for themselves." The Head Mother nodded, pursing her lips. "I think that may have been the best description of them I have ever heard." She said, frowning, impressed. Miska shyly smiled at the praise. "Mother?" She asked in a small voice.

"Yes."

"Where is the king? And why does he not help his people?"

The Head Mother took a deep breath and let it out of her nose like a bull. She stood and went to a tall window that looked over the courtyard of the church. She held the curtain back with a wrinkled yet delicate hand that only just protruded from her white gown and looked out. A sad look came over the older woman's face, making Miska feel guilty for asking the question. "The king is nothing more than a shell now." She sighed. "The real king has not been around for a very long time. Our king would have been much better off if he was allowed to pass long ago."

"Why does he not?" Miska asked in such an innocent voice that the Head Mother looked up at her, smiling.

"That is a good question, dear." She let the smile fade from her face and stared at the ceiling before answering. "An evil has touched his soul, and I believe it has left him twisted and broken. I cannot know if the evil has left him or even if he is better because those fat selfish *disconnected* men you met keep him so looped up on drugs no one could know ... including himself"

"Why don't we find out?" Miska shrugged.

"Well, my dear. We can't just-" The Head Mother started but stopped. She looked at Miska, surprised. "Have you seen some sign or had some feeling that we should?" The older woman asked carefully. Miska looked back at her, confused. "Do you mean like if the Lady had asked or pushed me to do that?"

"Yes."

"No. I don't think so," Miska said, trying hard not to roll her eyes. "It just seems like if we need to see the king and the Advisors won't let us, then-" Miska shrugged again as if what she was saying was so obvious. "Then, we should just do it ... you know, anyway."

The Head Mother frowned, looking at her and nodding her head in agreement. "Sounds like a shrewd plan." She said, scratching her chin and sarcastically shaking her head. "But even with how ridiculous it sounds ... there is some logic to it, I have to admit." Miska couldn't help seeing a mischievous light come into the woman's eyes. "How do you feel about damp, dark places?" The Head Mother asked Miska.

"I ... uh ... like them?" Miska answered, starting to smile and feeling excited, seeing the look come over the older woman's face. The Head

140

Mother called out to have Nundra come to her chambers immediately. The priestesses nervously left the room to do her bidding. Moments later, Nundra went into the room with sleepy red eyes. Her white dress looked thrown on.

"Yes, Mother. You have summoned me?" She asked, bowing low and painfully.

"Could you please get my little friend and I here traveling clothes?" The Head Mother stopped then, thinking. "Um, make it men's traveling clothes and do not tell anyone what you are doing. Do you understand?" Nundra looked at them both, confused. "The *whys* do not concern you, old friend. Believe me when I say you will be better off not knowing." Nundra bowed again, smiling knowingly. "Yes, Mother." She said simply and left.

"I have a feeling this will only be the beginning of our adventures together, my dear Miska." The Head Mother said, smiling merrily and looking more excited than Miska had ever seen her. "We all have secrets, don't we dear?"

"I'm not sure what you mean, Mother," Miska asked, confused.

"Oh, sure you do. There are things we have that we do not share with others. That is fine, as long as they do not affect others negatively." The Head Mother explained. "For example, I do not enjoy singing."

"WHAT!" Miska loudly exclaimed.

"Do not get excited, child. I know that is a big part of what I have to do in each blessing, but..." The Head Mother shrugged, much like Miska had a few moments ago. "I don't like it. I think you may be the only one I told that to." The Head Mother laughed gently to herself at that. Finally, she looked back at her, the smile leaving her face. "There is a reason I am talking about secrets, little priestess." She said, walking up close and looking into Miska's big brown eyes. "I have another secret to share, but before I do, I must ask that you promise not to let anyone know of it." She looked hard at Miska and put her hands on her shoulders. "Now, you must promise."

"Y-yes, mother. I promise." Miska felt frozen in place, looking into the Head Mother's slightly cloudy and watery blue eyes. The older woman stepped closer, inches from Miska's face, so all she could see was the Head Mother's eyes looking intensely into hers. Miska studied the eyes as they seemed to get slowly brighter and less cloudy. Miska took in a sharp breath, watching and unable to move. She tried to step away, but the Head Mother tightened her grip on Miska's shoulders, holding her in place.

"There is no reason to be frightened, my dear." The Head Mother said in a voice that was hers but ... different at the same time. Then the older woman gently pushed Miska back into the chair, and her jaw dropped. The woman who stood in front of her now was nothing like the older woman there before. Except for the eyes that were still the blue, but now they were bright and clear and looking at Miska waiting for a response.

"I-just-I..."

"It is still me, child." The woman said, smiling. "I may have changed in the way you see me but, rest assured, it is still me." Miska could only nod her head as she stared. The woman before was now beautiful and strangely familiar though she could not place from where. The much younger Head Mother smiled, and Miska shook her head in amazement. The woman was now barely middle age, and her hair was long, deep brown with rich red highlights. Her skin was porcelain white and flawless. She was tall, and Miska strained her neck, looking up at her from her chair. She was still wearing the gown, but now the dress clung to her curvy but muscular frame.

"But how?" Miska asked, looking the woman over in amazement.

"It is one of the many gifts of the Lady of Light. And one that I take advantage of only on rare occasions."

"But … why, Mother?" Miska was finally able to get out. The Head Mother smiled wide, and Miska could hardly believe how beautiful the woman was now … and yet still familiar. The Head Mother was hardly ugly before, but now…

"My name is Doria when I am like this. And I will call you by your name, Miska. Okay?"

Miska nodded her agreement, still staring.

"As for why." Doria went on. "If you are asking why I do not look like this all the time, then I will give you the answer by asking you a question." Doria crossed her arms, looking down at Miska and seeming again very much the church leader of the Lady of ight … only younger. "How well does your youth and beauty serve you in life … or even today with the Advisors?" Miska looked down and thought about that. "I would wager-" Doria said, leaning closer to Miska. "-a gold piece that if you were plainer of face and-" Doria flicked a finger at Miska's taut firm body. "You would have had many different experiences to date."

"I may not have met Sebastion, mo-" Miska stopped herself before finishing, realizing what she had almost said to the Mother.

"So you think it was your looks that brought this man and you together?" Doria asked, raising an eyebrow. Miska's face turned red, and anger flared.

"My father has-" Miska looked to the floor for only a second, remembering. "...had a saying." She looked up to meet the Head Mother's now youthful bright eyes. "Take the blessings and forget the crass for those that hate can kiss my ... umm ... ass." Miska quickly looked at the floor, not believing she had just said that and wishing she had kept her big mouth shut.

You always lose your temper. You stupid, stupid girl!

She prepared herself for the Head Mother's wrath. However, what she heard from the Head Mother was not what she expected. First, it was a surprised, coughing type of laughter, but the laughter became deep and heartfelt as the shock turned to realization. Miska looked up to see Doria step back and lean on the chair as she laughed uncontrollably. Miska couldn't help but start laughing too as she watched the woman double over. Doria stopped a second after hearing Miska and tried to get sober but then started laughing again, even harder than before. Miska watched the Head Mother shaking her head, amazed by the now strange, youthful woman in front of her. Her laughter was so rich and pure; it made Miska feel better than she had in a long time. She suddenly felt some of the darkness leaving her heart.

CHAPTER 17

"So, you did it so everyone would take you more seriously?" Miska asked.

"Well, that is the biggest part of it. People respond to what they see." Doria gave a Miska a look as if to say 'as you know.' "Youthful looks do not as easily instill the confidence of wisdom and knowledge like the lines of age. And Ihave earned every line that you saw. It's just that the Lady has granted me the gift of youth. I am old enough to be the person you are used to seeing as the Head Mother, but I have also received a gift from the blessed Mother. One that I rarely take advantage of but a gift I enjoy just the same." Just then, the door opened, and Nundra came into the room with an armful of clothing. She looked at Doria and the Head Mother winked at her. Nundra smiled and placed the clothes on the chair before leaving the room as quickly as she had come

"She knows?" Miska asked.

"Nundra? Yes, she knows just about everything there is to know about me. She is a good friend and a faithful follower of the light ... *and* she can keep a secret." Doria said, raising her brow to make the point. Miska did not miss the gesture. "Shall we put these clothes on and go ask the king why he has been so absent of late?" There was such an overwhelming sound of excitement in the now younger woman's voice that Miska felt more eager than frightened. "Your father sounds to have been a special person."

"Y-yes, he was. He was my best friend." Miska said, looking through the pile of traveling clothes Nundra had brought. "What was your father like?" Miska asked, trying to get her thoughts off of her own before she started to cry again. She sensed Doria had stopped moving and curiously looked over. Doria was looking at her just as curiously. "What is it?" Miska asked.

Doria took a deep breath before answering. "I have not thought of my father, if you can call him that, in a long time. I never knew him."

"I'm sorry, Mother. I did not mean to pry."

"If you keep insisting on calling me *Mother*, people may think that I started far too early for a lady. If you know what I mean." Miska's face turned red. "And yes, I think you do." Doria smiled that broad, friendly smile again.

"Sorry ... uh, Doria."

When the two of them dressed, Doria pulled her soft boots onto her feet. "Feels good wearing pants and boots again. Sometimes I think my mother had it right."

"Your mother," Miska asked.

"I think you had enough of my going on's for one day, dear," Doria said, tossing a knife to her. Miska grabbed at it, fumbled, and it fell to the ground in front of her. "Okay then, it seems if we get in trouble, it will be up to me."

"You just surprised me, Mo- Doria," Miska said defensively with a hint of anger.

"Tuck that in your belt. Remember the things you were taught, including the knife, yes?"

"Yes, Doria," Miska said, tucking the small knife into her belt and heading for the door.

"This way," Doria called out behind her. Miska looked up to see a piece of the fireplace slide in where Doria pushed it. "You might as well get used to the dark inside," Doria said, brushing an arm in front of her for Miska to walk thru. "It's a way to the castle."

"Perhaps we can keep each other company," Lehgone said, stepping out of the darkness and into the room from the passage. Miska caught her breath, stepping back from him. "Have you forgotten me so quickly?" He asked, smiling into his long moustache, "Did we not say we would be meeting?" He put his hands on his hips and admiringly looked Doria up and down. "-there's something different about you, Mother." He said sarcastically.

CHAPTER 18

The slaves passed by them only a few feet away. They hid in a crevice, thankful for the dim light of a torch some distance off. Killian's ankle had swollen from being badly twisted in his escape from the Rifkins, but he hardly noticed it now. He and Lara had been anxiously waiting for Baran to come back with their packs and weapons. They sat in silence, listening to the slaves run by accident or not, their hands had found each other on the hard rocky ground. Their backs were against the cold stone wall as they sat there, waiting silently for the big man's return. The running people's sound was a background to their breathing as it bounced off the rocky walls. The warm touch of flesh was welcome from the hard times and even harder outlook that was likely awaiting them. They did not look over at each other at first as if savouring the moment without spoiling it with the logic and better sense their eyes would surely bring. Lara's long but delicate hand traced Killian's large and callused one in the dim light. First, it was she that brushed her fingers gently over his, and then it was his that just as delicately traced hers. Then, without warning, Lara threw a leg over Killian, and they were looking into each other's eyes. What they saw there was not logic but not just lust either.

Lara saw the vulnerability in him. She saw the long hard years that should have been on his flesh as well. She reached out a hand, touching his cheek that was thick with coarse hair. Killian reached his hands up and gently pulled her head to him and they kissed, their heads swimming. He let his hands brush down her bare muscular arms and felt her wince for just a second as he touched the place where the cloth covered her wound. She pulled away only slightly, and they looked at each other again to see if there was a reason to stop. Killian smiled an apology for hurting her, but Lara leaned in again before he could speak. Her hands went to his belt and unlatched it. She stood quickly and wiggled fast out of her soft leather pants. Watching her, he pulled his down and felt the cold, sharp rocks under him. Normally he would have flinched away but, instead, he hardly even noticed that they were there. He reached up and pulled Lara onto him. As she came down, she sighed a warm breath into his ear. He felt goosebumps run up his spine. He opened his eyes only slightly, and he thought he saw a flash of green and a strange woman's chuckle off to his right, but he could not be sure and right now he did not give a damn if he did. He reached under her shirt, feeling the heat in his body for the first time in a long time. It was the first time he did not think of the world's weight since before he could remember.

Gods, she feels so damn good.

His body ached like a starving man as he pulled her closer to him. Killian of house loyal had been with women, but since Melodia, they had all been nothing more than distractions. With Lara now, he felt the similar way he felt when he was with the fair priestess, long ago. He felt like it was right and he got lost in the flesh and soul as he reached around her back and laid his hands flat on her burning skin. He kissed her again and then pulled his head away to look at her. Her long dark hair had pulled out of its bindings and hung over her face, hiding everything but her dark eyes and even the dim light could not hide the fire there. Neither spoke but they stared a moment more before

149

collapsing into each other breathlessly and holding each other as if they were the last and only thing left in this cold dark world to hold onto.

CHAPTER 19

He had no idea why he was running. He had been carrying rocks in a basket just like he had so many times before this. His daily routine now consisted of collecting stones and then, by any means possible, getting it to a pile indicated by the big Barbarians who were always watching. Sometimes he could carry the heavy baskets and other times he could only drag them. All Ishma knew was that if he were to stop, he would be lashed unmercifully by a whip that was, ironically, almost identical to the one he had not long ago. For all he knew, *it was* the one he had owned. The thought put him into such a depression that he had to try to bar it from his mind. His only comfort was in concentrating on the face of Sebastion and the way he would one day bash it in. He let his hatred for the young slave consume him and allowed hate to consume his very being. It was hate that would get him up and moving when the rocks' weight drew him into the ground. It was hate alone that kept him from dying on the rocks from dehydration, lack of decent food, and rest, like so many of the others who had arrived with him in the dark hell. Some he expected he ate along with the others in the Barbarians stew that they got maybe once a day if they were lucky. Yes, it was hate that kept him alive. But he even had to admit that was getting as stale as the stew. Sebastion's face that he saw in his head kept Ishma's legs moving as he passed under the caves' torch-lit byways.

Up ahead, he saw the crowds of people veering around something. He heard yelling, but he could not make it out over the pounding of his heart and the thudding of the feet of the people around him. He suspected it was a Barbarian trying to stop the wave and he decided to get close to look at what was running right through them like a blade through soft butter. His ears caught the words next to him, and it took a moment before he recognized the meaning. He slowed, trying to determine if he had imagined it. Then the crowd parted and the blood demon himself, the single source for his life of hate, ran right by him with the beast he had caught to sell beside him. Neither man nor beast even looked in his direction. Ishma felt the tingling as blood ran to his face, and every nerve in his body went cold. It had not been that long ago that he had been the only deciding factor whether those two that had paced him without even a glance lived or died. They passed him like nothing more than an insignificant toad not worthy of even a look— a mere piece of rotting meat to avoid and run past without even a fleeting thought.

Gods, I hate him!

Anger was pushing away the shock of seeing them here, now. His heart came fully alive again as it pumped the liquid hate through it. He had stopped running and leaned against the wall, watching them turning around a bend in the cave. The chanting of the blood demon was getting louder and he saw Sebastion turn back once with a look of amazement on his now-bearded and strangely drawn face. There was no mistaking that something was different about him. Still, Ishma would have recognized him a hundred years from now and in total darkness. His hate for the tall, light-eyed man engulfed him like a dried leaf in hot fire.

It's time to die, blood demon.

He followed them and the flow of the others. Some of them had turned as well.

Do these pathetic fools think he is some hero that has come to save them? Well, this son of a whore hero will not live long enough for that!

Ishma reached into his pocket and pulled out a razor-sharp rock he had been saving just for an occasion like this.

An older man crashed into him, and Ishma almost toppled, reaching for the wall to get his balance. He reached out and found a protruding rock in the wall that helped stabilize him. The older man was still trying to push around him; the crowd was becoming more chaotic. Ishma tried to control himself and moved forward, using the wall as a lever, pushing people aside with one hand, still gripping the sharp stone. His small stature allowed him to stay low and gain momentum as he went. His face, black with soot and grime and his many tattoos, could not be seen. But his eyes were bright with hate. Some who caught a glimpse of him moved out of the way. He wanted to yell out for them to stop so he could catch up, but Ishma knew that would spoil the surprise of jamming the rock in an eye … or maybe through the chest to the boy's rotten stinking heart. Oh, how he savoured that image as he pushed forward like some crazed animal.

Soon the boy was almost within arm's length, his grip tight on the rock. He knew he would get only one chance at this, so he concentrated on a spot on the neck. He could see the blood pulsing there as he lifted his hand for the thrust that would end the boy's life and give him release from whatever curse he had put on him. Just as he was stabbing down, he was thrown to the side like a rag doll. Before the world went dark, he saw a Barbarian standing where he had just been ready to strike. The colossal Barbarian was stabbing down with a dagger at the boy just where Ishma's rock was about to go. A new rage fueled by desperation came over the tiny slaver like an avalanche. He was about to lose the thing that had kept him going here, the only thing that made him get up each day, regardless of the pain and the loss of hope in his soul. Ishma's eyes cleared and opened wide like a raging bull. His body shook with the madness of losing the boy to the Barbarian before he could get at him, himself. It could not happen ... must not! No, he would not let the overgrown Barbarian deny him the death of the boy that had destroyed *his* life. It would be his eyes the boy stared into when he died and no other!

Ishma sprang off the wall in a howl with the strength of madness. He landed on the Barbarian's back with a thud. He did not even notice the sharp rock was still in his hand as he beat down on the Barbarian's throat. If the stone had not been there, he would have used his bare hands. When he realized it was still there, he sawed the tender flesh that was there. The big Barbarian screamed in surprise and twisted, trying to throw Ishma off his back, but it was no use. Ishma had used the same tactic before while fighting a bear long ago. Now he fought a man as big as a bear but the result would be the same.

"NO-NO! YOU WILL NOT! HE WILL BE MINE ... MINE!" Ishma screamed. Blood shot up into the air all around them. The Barbarian twisted around and around, trying to grab the little man. The other slaves stopped and stared, leaving a wide circle in the cave, unsure what to do. Ishma barred his little sharp teeth, hanging on with one arm and cutting deeper and deeper with the other. Finally, the Barbarian

154

fell face down. Ishma rolled onto his feet, ready to spring again onto the boy he lived to kill now. He looked around but the half-starved slaves staring at him wide-eyed were the only ones there now.

"Where did he go? Where!" He demanded of one closest to him. The man could only stare, shaking his head and holding an arm up as if expecting a blow.

"The boy! WHERE DID HE GO!" Ishma bellowed.

The man pointed further down the hall, and Ishma was about to follow when he heard it and realized the half-starved imbeciles were cheering him, some brave enough even patted him on his back. Ishma thought they were praising his murder of the Barbarian until the chanting started. At some point, he must have told someone his name as they were chanting it.

"You saved his life! You saved the blood demon!" A broken and filthy man said, smiling wide, with a toothless grin. "You killed the barbarian with your bare hands and saved the blood demon!" The man reached out and grabbed Ishma's shoulders in a surprisingly firm grip. "You are a hero!"

"No, you damn puck-" Ishma could not finish as the man pulled him into an embrace. Ishma pushed away and, for the first time, met the eyes of the crowd. He knew instantly that they were mistaking his rage for some attempt to save the disgusting boy. The line of slaves in the cave grew as more caught up and stopped to stare at the little man.

"THEY CAN BE KILLED! THE BARBARIAN BASTARDS CAN DIE!" Someone yelled out. It started as murmuring and then yelling as the slaves picked up rocks and ran back the way they had been running. Ishma watched the broken and starved fools change from doomed slaves to angry mob in what seemed the blink of an eye. They ran, chanting "ISHMA!" and "BLOOD DEMON!"

What has the maggot boy gotten me into now? How could this be happening!?

CHAPTER 20

Sebastion and Morakye moved quickly through the running slaves. They paid little attention to them as they wanted to get to Baran before it was too late. Constava said that Baran would be killed and Sebastion believed her. It would be like Baran to give his own life so that the Barbarians would not find the others ... specifically Lara.

As he ran, he heard the slaves start yelling behind him and, at one point, it even sounded as if they had started chanting something he could not make out. But he had no time to reflect on it if he was going to help Baran.

They heard a man's screaming in a corridor to their right, and they blindly ran into it, rushing into whatever was there, hoping they would be quick enough. It was only lit by a single torch on a wall. There was screaming and what sounded like the branches of a tree being snapped. Sebastion saw the shadows bouncing off the rock walls twist and jerk unnaturally. Then he heard silence. He and Morakye exchanged worried glances as they turned the last corner and what they saw made them stop short. Baran stood wide-eyed, staring at the broken and twisted bodies of the Barbarians around him. Each part of them was at an awkward angle. They stared at the mutilation before looking to Baran, who was still slack-jawed and unmoving.

"Baran, are you hurt?" Sebastion asked, but the big knight did not move. "BARAN!" Sebastion yelled out. Baran finally looked up and blinked.

"Are you hurt?" Sebastion asked. Baran shook his head no. "Good. Do you know where the others are?" Baran nodded his head, rubbing his face with his big hand.

"Uh, Yes." He said simply. "Do you know what-"

"Don't worry about it." Sebastion cut him off. "We need to get to the others before the Barbarians find them."

"Did you do this?" Baran asked with what Sebastion thought was a hint of accusation in his voice.

"We haven't-"

"Did you do this?" Baran asked, this time interrupting him.

"Not exactly," Sebastion said, reaching out to pull Baran forward, but the big man recoiled from him. "What in the dark hell are you?" He asked, shaking his head. "What has just happened to these men-"Baran shook his head. "I would not wish on my worst enemy … not my worst enemy." Suddenly the hall was full of a woman's cackling laughter. Sebastion and Morakye looked around for what they knew must be Constava.

"Brother," Morakye said nervously. "I think she must be crazed from the killings."

Sebastion nodded. "Yes, somehow I do know that she gets … drunk from it. We need to go."

"She?" Baran asked. But this time, Sebastion shot his arm out and pulled Baran forward. "MOVE!" He yelled at him. Baran decided to run ahead without question this time. Sebastion wasn't sure if the man ran to his friends or to get away from him.

As they entered the main cave, they realized that the slaves had changed direction and angrily held rocks, torches, or just fists over their heads. Sebastion thought they looked crazed, as the three of them moved against the wall to let them all pass by. A few curiously looked at Morakye as they passed. One of them saw Sebastion and stopped a moment as if trying to comprehend what he was looking at. He yelled, "BLOOD DEMON!" and pointed to him. Sebastion had his sword back and started to raise it, not knowing what would come next. Then the slaves lined the cave and chanted Blood Demon at him.

"Why are they calling you d'at?" Baran called out nervously from the wall.

"I-I killed some men in Endrea, and some of the people called me that."

"So, why are they all falling over themselves in front of you like that for killing people?"

Sebastion shook his head, not understanding.

"Methinks they want something from you, brother." Morakye offered.

"What could they want from me?" Sebastion watched as some fell to their knees. One of the closest heard them and pathetically squirmed towards him on the ground. Sebastion cautiously watched him.

"Please ... Blood Demon." The man said, looking up into Sebastion's eyes. "Take us from here. Deliver us from this hell." The man began to weep. "Please, Blood Demon ... save us from the Barbarians." Sebastion saw the desperation in the man's eyes and was taken back by the plea for help.

"We have seen what you can do, Blood Demon." The man explained, rising to his knees. "You could beat the Barbarians. You could help us. You and your ... animal." The man said, looking over at

159

Morakye. Morakye growled low in his throat. The man stepped back, eyes wide.

"Why me?" Sebastion asked, looking and seeing more of the men as they lined the narrow cave and fell to their knees. "How can-" But Sebastion could not finish the thought as the screaming started again as a handful of Barbarians began pushing into the crowd, yelling and kicking their way through. They looked up and saw Sebastion. The leader smiled and swung his spiked club in an ark, indicating a challenge.

"Me's do not think that is wise, brother," Morakye whispered, sensing what Sebastion was thinking.

"No," Sebastion said, stepping around the men on the ground in front of him. They suddenly cheered his advance, but Sebastion tried to ignore them. Instead, he concentrated on the big man's eyes. The Barbarian was older, but Sebastion knew what the man probably lacked in strength would be more than made up with battle experience.

The cheering men separated as Sebastion moved towards the Barbarian. The leader made another gesture with his club and backed through the cave. He kept indicating for Sebastion to follow until they moved to a spot where there was more room. Several of the slave men pulled torches from the walls and stood in a circle in the opening to watch what would happen. The Barbarian shrugged off the hides from his shoulders, leaving him only with a leather vest. The man was huge, and even with Sebastion's height, the barbarian towered over him. Sebastion spun his sword once and immediately attacked. The Barbarian quickly knocked the blade away with his club and shot out a foot faster than Sebastion would have thought possible for such a big man. It connected to his thigh, and Sebastion went down. The spiked club followed, and the crowd of men gasped. Morakye leaped forward, but the gesture was unnecessary. Sebastion rolled as soon as he hit the ground and was back on his feet. The Barbarian changed the angle of his swing, trying to hit Sebastion on the way up, but Sebastion jumped back out of the way. When the club cleared him, Sebastion jumped forward and punched the man in the nose. His nose cracked, and blood splattered across his face. The crowd cheered in delight. The Barbarian shot an arm out and grabbed Sebastion by his shirt and pushed as if nothing had happened at all. Sebastion flew into the group of people and tried to get his feet under him.

Sebastion realized he might have made an error in judgment in accepting the huge man's challenge. He looked around to gauge the possibility of escape, but all the entrances were packed solid with the slaves watching them. Even the Barbarians seemed to have forgotten why they were here and stood almost comradely next to the slaves watching the fight. The big Barbarian smiled, and Sebastion saw that the man only had a few sharpened teeth left in his head. The lack of teeth, however, did not make the old grizzly fighter any less intimidating. The slaves cheered and chanted. Then he felt hands on his back and was propelled forward. The Barbarian got ready to swing as the slaves that pushed him sent him right in front of his opponent. If Sebastion had not rolled under the swing, it would have splattered the contents of his skull onto the cave wall. When he got to his feet, he kicked back at the Barbarian's knee. He winced in pain as he thought it like kicking an oak tree, and Sebastion moved back, letting the pain in his aching foot subside. The strike did not hurt the Barbarian, put it did seem to put him in a furious rage. The big warrior roared like a bear and charged with his club above his head. Sebastion let himself go limp and rolled onto his back, remembering a trick Killian had once shown him. As the Barbarian started to pass above him, he leaned back and shot his feet up with all his strength. Sebastion caught the Barbarian in the crotch and lifted him into the air. The man yelled out as he sailed onto another group of slaves.

At first, there was stunned silence, then an explosion of cheers. Two of the closest Barbarians exchanged angry looks and started to step forward when a dagger appeared at each of their crotches.

"Let's keep this fair, shall we?" Lara said, sweetly smiling up at the two. The Barbarians nervously went onto their toes. "The kid better have some more of those tricks up his sleeve." She said, turning to Killian as he limped forward, pushing slaves out of his way.

"Who the puckering hell picks a fight with a Barbarian!" Killian swore as he came forward. "Dark blasted pig-headed idiot!" Killian shoved another slave out of the way. As he made it to the front, he watched as the Barbarian that Sebastion launched rose above all the men as he stood. The slaves scurried away from him like ants from a fire. Several of the slaves that the Barbarian had landed on were either unmoving on the ground around him or only just beginning to show signs of life.

The big man smiled and nodded his head in mock congratulations.

"It was nothing," Sebastion said in the Barbarian language. The big man looked at him, surprised. "Oh, yes. I speak your crude language. I

162

have to admit, however, that I find it about as stupid and lacking as your fighting skills." He said, feigning a yawn. He was hoping to put the Barbarian into a rage so that he would make a mistake. He was wrong, as the big man smiled. As Sebastion had feared, the man was far too experienced to fall for his tricks.

"You find my talk stupid, eh?" The Barbarian said in Sebastion's language now. "I will find your pretty *stupid* head a fine piss pot, heh?" With that, he ran forward, his club spinning in front of him.

"Keep him moving! Idiot! Keep him moving!" Killian yelled out.

"SO GLAD YOU COULD SHOW UP, UNCLE!" Sebastion yelled back sarcastically, backing up and keeping his eyes on the club.

"Never mind the attitude, fool! Just keep him moving and wait for your opportunity. He can't spin that thing forever."

"Thanks," Sebastion said flatly as he jogged backward in a circle with his sword in front of him.

The Barbarian suddenly changed direction with his club and nearly took Sebastion's head off a second time. He heard the crowd of slaves suck in a breath. The Barbarian was slightly off-balance from the swing, and Sebastion got his sword in for a slice on the man's back. The Barbarian swung back in anger which also sent him too far off his balance, and Sebastion sliced the man in the same spot on the other side. More barbarians showed up and were watching. They started pushing forward. Baran saw them and turned to Morakye to attack them together, but realized the Fangor was gone. "Damn cat!" He whispered to himself. He pulled his sword free and went to meet the two head-on. Suddenly one of the two dropped into the crowd as if in a hole. The men around him yelled and jumped back, and Baran

163

thought he saw a flash of fur as something jumped away from the now dead Barbarian. The one left looked around, realizing he was now alone. Baran took the opportunity and ducked his head low and ran. He connected with the unfortunate Barbarian with a thud. The unsuspecting Barbarian flew backward, taking slaves with him. There was another flash of fur, and Baran realized who it was and that the Barbarian he had hit would also not be getting back up.

Lara watched Baran as he connected, not knowing if he too would be knocked down. She was relieved to see the Barbarian go down. However, she did not have time to enjoy it. One of the Barbarians she held with the knife saw his opportunity and swatted Lara to the ground with one big hand. Lara didn't see it coming and hit the ground hard. The sound of it filled the cave and Killian looked to find that she was no longer there. Dread filled him as he watched one of the Barbarians staring down at the ground where Lara had been standing.

"Lara!" Killian yelled. Sebastion heard his uncle, saw him, and followed his eyes, realizing Lara was no longer standing there. Then he glimpsed a dark shape over the heads of the slaves. The torches' flickering lights made the image hard to see, but he knew it was Morakye. He then sensed more than saw the club coming down at him. He jumped out of the way, and it slammed to the ground. He leapt into the air, twisting as he went, and as his body came around he grabbed the mangy hair of the Barbarian with one hand and slipped his sword into his throat with the other. He heard the surprised gurgle, but did not have time to make sure he was dead. He pulled his sword free as he ran into the crowd of slaves to find Lara. He watched, horrified, as one Barbarian lifted a big-booted foot to stomp down on what was on the ground.

"NO!" Killian yelled, trying desperately to push through the crowd.

The dark image went up again and then bounced off a rock and into the face of the Barbarian who was about to slam down a foot on Lara's head. The Barbarian screamed and pulled Morakye off, leaving deep gashes on his face. He threw Morakye across the cave and into a pile of rocks that exploded into dust and fell all around Morakye's body. Then Sebastion was there. He had dropped his sword trying to get through the people. He jumped up to capture the bleeding Barbarian's head under his arm. As he went down, he twisted savagely, and there was a loud snap. The other one standing close by raised a club over Sebastion's head, but Killian kicked at the Barbarian's knee. It broke, and he and Killian went down screaming, with the Barbarian holding his leg and Killian holding his ankle.

"HELP HER!" Killian yelled. "DAMN DARK BLASTED PUCKERING..." Killian swore as he rolled around in pain. Baran ran up and stuck a sword in the Barbarian next to Killian.

Lara was lying motionless on the ground of the rocky cave. Her lip and nose both had droplets of blood flowing from them. The side of her face was red and already beginning to swell. Killian prayed it was just the light from the torches that made her look so pale. He crawled over and brushed her dark hair away from her eyes as he looked down.

"Lara? Can you hear me?" He asked gently as he took her hand in his and kissed it. "Lara? Wake up?" She did not move. He put his head on her chest and thought he heard a faint heartbeat there.

165

"You men are all alike." She whispered, reaching up and touching his head. "Always the first thing … you go for."

Killian sat up and took her hand and placed it on his face.

"You okay?" He asked.

"Not so sure I'd go that far." She whispered again. "I'm going to sleep now." She smiled up at Killian.

"NO! YOU MUST STAY AWAKE!" Killian said frantically as Lara's hand gently slipped off his face.

"no … no, no NO!" Killian yelled, shaking her shoulders.

"Me's can hear her heart," Morakye said, coming up to them with Sebastion supporting him. He had one arm that was hanging at an awkward angle tucked in close to him.

"She is alive," Sebastion said, putting a hand on Killian's shoulder. He had no idea his uncle had such feelings for the warrior woman. He looked over at Baran and saw he was looking at Killian with an all too knowing look. It seemed he was not the only one that didn't know about these two.

"Which way is out?" Killian asked Sebastion, wiping an arm across his running nose.

"I-I'm not sure." He answered honestly.

"But we know." One of the slaves said, stepping forward.

The slaves that were not in the caves during the fight were attacking the other Barbarians throughout the rocky terrain. They made a litter for Lara, and the group solemnly marched behind it in silence. Sebastion still had Morakye under his arm as the Fangor limped beside him. Killian marched right behind the litter using a stick the slaves gave him to support his weight off his ankle. Baran was last and

166

held a torch in one hand and his head hung low. They were all tired and felt the weariness in every part of their bodies and minds, and they were covered in dirt and blood. They were indistinguishable from the slaves now as they marched towards the soft light that awaited them at the end of the tunnel.

Sebastion did not even know how long they had been walking. It could have been hours and it could have been days. Somehow he knew that time did not have the same effects in the dark recesses of the caves. When they were outside, the sun was shining, but the air was cold. They were in a clearing surrounded by cliffs that were occupied by more slaves that looked like rag dolls. Their bodies were torn and near their breaking point, but it was their eyes that struck Sebastion as he walked. He looked into them, and he no longer saw scared men just waiting for death like those he had first seen in the caves. Now, these broken people of Torenium were returning his look with what could only be ... pride.

"BLOOD DEMON!" one yelled and then, like a wave, people fell to their knees. They watched as the people quietly went down.

"What is this?" Killian asked, looking around, wincing at the pain. A man in the centre stood holding someone in his arms. He slowly came forward to stand in front of Sebastion, who held Morakye under his arm to support him.

"He just wanted to see you before..." The man couldn't finish as tears made clean streaks down his filthy face. The man came closer and showed him the bundle in his arms. He held a small emaciated boy close to his chest.

"They said those that can't work couldn't eat." The man said, a hardness coming to his voice. "I hid him away so that those bastards wouldn't ... so they wouldn't..." Another man walked up and put a hand on his shoulder.

"They made us eat those that no longer could work." The other man said sorrowfully.

"D'ats insane," Baran spat on the ground and they nodded at him.

"Please, sir." The man said, holding the boy up. "He does not have much time left."

"He is alive?" Sebastion asked, surprised.

"Barely ... he wanted only to meet the Blood Demon."

"I am n-" Sebastion started, but Killian had come beside him and put a hand on his arm. Sebastion looked over, and his great uncle gave him a look that said a hundred words. Killian took Morakye's arms, and they both limped back a bit. Sebastion turned and watched them, feeling the weight of what was about to happen. He once again felt as if things were shifting without his control. When he looked back, he was looking into the eyes of a dying boy. Surprisingly, what he saw there was not pain or even sorrow. What he saw was reverence for him.

"Will you save us?" The boy asked from the man's arms. Sebastian didn't know what to say. How could he tell this boy that he could save all these people? He didn't even know how to save himself. Surely they could not expect him to take responsibility for all these people.

"Will you take us home?" The boy asked, desperate now. Sebastion wanted to look away from the big brown eyes in the starved face. But as much as he wanted to look away, he could not. He suddenly felt the other inside of him and thought he too was feeling what he was feeling. Without realizing it, he reached a hand out and put it on the boy's cheek.

"Yes, little man. We are *all* going home." Suddenly the crowd erupted into cheers. Sebastion stared into the boy's eyes as life left him with a smile on his face. Sebastion looked up and saw the man, too, smiling with more tears running freely down his face.

"What d'a dark hell just happened here," Baran asked, leaning in close to Killian. Killian laughed, looking around and taking it all in.

"Methinks," Morakye said, looking around. "Something bigger than *we* be happening here."

Killian looked down at his Fangor friend and nodded his agreement. "Me's could use the help keeping you human's alive." Morakye smiled. Killian laughed and let his eyes go to the litter with the still body of Lara in it. Morakye followed the man's eyes. "Let us check on her, yes?" Morakye asked.

"Yes," Killian answered back solemnly.

That evening they found themselves in a tent that once housed the Barbarians. They told the tattered men, now known as the Blood Army, that they did not need a tent and could be with everyone else, but the Torenium's would not hear of it. It was Killian at last that told the people that they graciously accepted their offerings. The next thing they knew, they had hot food and a comfortable place to sleep. It seems the Barbarians took a lot of pride in their horses and kept them close to them. The dead Barbarians would be happy to have their horses back to them in death as the Blood Army fed off of them.

Sebastion had no idea what to do next. He had never even led a group of people down a street, much less an army *of starved desperate men.* He sat on the cushions in the tent smoking a pipe he had found there. It reminded him of when he was young and thought how strange life was to have led him here. Strangely he missed the quiet forests of his youth. At least there no one expected much from him. As long as he did his regular daily routine, he was pretty much left alone. Now he had hundreds, maybe more, looking to him to lead them home through the northern region where he had no idea what waited for him. He rubbed his aching head with the ball of his hand.

"Hey, Blood Demon," Killian sarcastically called over. Sebastion puffed out a cloud of smoke and gave him a dirty look.

"Yes, *Rayer*?" He asked back. Killian smiled despite himself.

He's family, for sure. Killian thought, shaking his head.

"I have to set this." He said, indicating Morakye's arm. Sebastion got up and went to Morakye's side. "Me think's you are too enthusiastic, brother," Morakye said, giving him a look.

"What do you mean?" Sebastion asked.

Killian laughed. "You have to hold him when I pull the bones apart to set them." Killian pulled Morakye's sleeve up. "Grab me's hand and hold, brother." Morakye said between clenched teeth.

"Wait!" Sebastion said. "You're going to pull his arm apart first?"

"Yes," Killian answered in the same voice. "And as a leader of an army, especially one as decrepit as this one, you should know how this is done. Did they not teach you this in that school?"

"Guess I missed that day," Sebastion said, putting his other arm around Morakye's waist.

"Okay, I'm not going to lie to you, Morakye 'ole boy," Killian said, looking into Morakye's eyes. "This is going to puckering hurt."

"Methinks I-" But before he could finish, Killian pulled and Morakye roared. Killian expertly put two sticks on either side of the Fangor's arms and quickly spun cloth around it. When done, he let go, and Morakye lay back, staring up at the tent. "That was most-unpleasant." He said breathlessly.

"She's so pale," Baran said across the tent. They all looked over at him. He was brushing Lara's head with a cool cloth. "We have to help her." He said, looking up to Killian. "Is there not something you can do for 'er?" Baran asked suddenly to Sebastion.

"Me?" Sebastion asked, confused.

"Yes, you." Baran said, angry now. "You can speak in different languages, see in 'da dark and everything else, but can you save your friend? Can you do d'at?" Baran started to weep. "Can you?" He pleaded. Sebastion suddenly felt helpless. What good were the things he could do? The thing is, he wanted none of it … but … what good is any of it if he couldn't even help his friend.

"I don't…" Sebastion started.

"Leave him alone. He would do anything he could … if he *could*, Baran." Killian said in his commanding voice.

"So what good is d'at?" Baran asked, sniffling. "SHE'S DYING!"

Killian got up, sat next to the big man, and put an arm around him. "We'll think of something." He said soothingly. "She's still with us."

Sebastion got up and walked out. Outside he took a deep breath, letting the cool air fall into his lungs. The people outside cast him curious looks but were respectful of his privacy. He suddenly had an urge to get away from everyone and head to a trail that went up to a cliffface. He climbed up and got to the ledge with his back against the wall. The sun was almost down, and he watched it as it started to disappear behind one of the peaks of the black mountains. The wind blew and, although it was not necessarily cold, it was biting nonetheless. He could feel that the harsh cold of winter was not far behind. He closed his eyes and tried to clear his mind. As usual, in these rare moments of quiet, his mind went to the girl with the big brown eyes. It always hurt to go there, but it was always where he ended up. He felt the heat in his eyes and fought back what was about to come next. *Some Blood Demon,* he thought bitterly. He subconsciously put his hand on the crystal that hung around his neck. A thought then came to him. He knew Miska had gone to live in the service of the Lady of Light. So many fantastic things were happening; maybe it was also true that the Lady was real. He thought it couldn't hurt to try to pray that she take care of his Miska and keep her safe, especially from the man-eaters. They could have already found her. The thought sent a chill down him, so he decided he would try praying. He closed his eyes and faced the sky.

"Lady of Light, if you can hear me." He said, squeezing his fist tight. "Please watch over her. Please keep my Miska safe ... don't let th-"

"There you are." A woman's voice was suddenly close to him.

"I do not wish to be disturbed." Sebastion said irritably.

"Then why did you call me?"

"What?" Sebastion asked, opening his eyes.

In front of him stood the little girl he had seen in his dreams in what seemed a very long time ago.

"You?" He asked,

"I have been very concerned that I would never see you again." The girl said in a woman's voice. A thought came to him. He let go of the crystal, and as it fell from his palm, the image of the little girl blurred and shook until a tall woman stood in front of him. She wore a white gown that went from her throat to her bare feet. She had long features and flowing dark hair. She was easily the most beautiful woman he had ever seen. Not in a loving way but in a perfect way.

"That was a rather uncomfortable trick." She said, reaching out and grabbing the rock for support.

"I am sorry. I'm not sure what I did." Sebastion said, standing. "Are you her?" he asked nervously. The Lady of Light looked over the ledge and nervously moved closer to the rocks.

"I, uh, am feeling ... mortal at the moment." The Lady said nervously.

"I am sorry," Sebastion said. The Lady smiled up at him. However, she was tall and did not have to look up far.

"Sebastion, my dear." She said, smiling. The breeze blew her hair around her head. "Such things are indeed revolving around you." She said.

"I do not understand."

"Of course not, my boy." Sebastion felt heat rising at being called a boy. The Lady did not miss it. "No. No longer a boy."

"Is it you that has been controlling me? Are you the one that kept me alive after that monster tried to bleed me empty?"

"So that is true." The Lady said, more to herself than to him. "So how is it you are still alive?" She asked, reaching out a perfect delicate hand, but Sebastion stepped away. The Lady smiled sadly. "Your instincts are good for not trusting me." She said, crossing her arms and facing the sun's last as it passed behind the mountain. "You are part of something bigger than I."

"Bigger than you?" Sebastion asked, confused. "What can be bigger than the Lady of Light?"

"What indeed." She asked back and Sebastion thought he saw worry touching her face. He decided he did not like that look on a goddess's face.

"Look, I don't mean to sound rude to a god and all." He suddenly felt encouragement come from within himself. "But I don't care much about gods and all this mysterious goings on." He crossed his arms like his uncle did when he was about to give a lecture.

"What *do* you care about?" The Lady asked curiously.

"You have Miska in your church." He said carefully. "Is she all right?"

"She is fine." The Lady said, seemingly surprised.

"Will you keep her safe?"

"She makes her own choices." She said hesitantly.

"What exactly does that mean?" Sebastion asked.

"It means I can guide my people, but their choices are their own. I do not control them. They are free to make their decisions. I may influence, but I never interfere with free will." Sebastion felt himself getting angry.

"Interfere? So, if those man-eater bastards come to the great city, you will do nothing? Will you let them all die? You will let Miska die?"

"That would be most unfortunate." The Lady answered, looking sad.

"Unfortunate?" Sebastion asked, putting his hands on his hips. "-Unfortunate that your people will be slaughtered and eaten by those dark puckering monsters!" He took a step forward, and she took one back closer to the edge. She looked back, worried. The thing inside him warned him to calm down, but he did not want to. "I have a friend dying down there. Will you help her?" He asked, on the verge of exploding.

"Sebastion." The lady said calmly. "You must understand. I cannot change the things that are to be. The wheel is turning now with something greater than I."

"Greater than a god! Greater than the Lady of Light!"

She nervously looked down again.

"So you tell me Miska will die. Lara will die. And you will do nothing but watch?"

"That is what she does." Killian said from behind him. He stepped around Sebastion and grabbed her arm, pulling her more to the centre of the small ridge. Sebastion did not budge at first to move out of his way, but it only took a look from Killian for him to step back. "I do know what you are feeling," Killian said wearily.

"You have no idea what I'm feeling? Give me a break. What do you feel?" Sebastion asked bitterly.

Killian huffed out a bitter laugh. "I too once had my own Miska, boy."

"I am not-oh forget it..." Sebastion said, exasperated, and headed for the trail.

"Mine also left me for the church." Killian went on. Sebastion stopped in his tracks but did not turn around. "She chose her." Killian gestured to the Lady. "Over me." The old knight sighed as the memories came back to him. "She could not get past what I was … and she made her choices. I prayed to one day be with her. As time went by, I prayed that she would be happy with someone else. As more time went by, I prayed that I would see her once again, if even across a crowded street." Killian leaned against his stick and Sebastion turned around. He thought the pained look on his face made him look very much like the man he once knew as Rayor.

"What happened to her?" Sebastion asked.

"She was murdered by the one I once served."

"Bashor," Sebastion growled.

"She died trying to save you, Killian." The Lady said painfully.

"She died trying to save herself," Killian answered back with venom in his voice now. "She died because you let her become a whore and filled her with such conflicts that she sought an end to her pain. She felt no love for me! She wiped her hands clean of me many years ago."

"That is *not* true, Killian of House Loyal, and you damn sure know it." The Lady said, growing angry herself. "Do not cheapen her sacrifice with your internal conflicts, Ser Killian." Sebastion thought it strange that they would face each other like this after so many years. A god and a knight.

"Now another dies there below me. Would it even help if I were to fall to my knees this time and pray for your help?" Killian asked sarcastically. Sebastion saw Killian's knuckles turn white on the stick that held him up as he tried to contain himself.

"I cannot." She said, Killian looked away angrily rubbing away tears in his eyes. "Then my curse continues even now." Killian composed himself, pulling his hair back and breathing deeply. "What can you tell us about what is happening with my nephew? Why does your brother want him, and why did Bashor try to kill him?"

"He is part of something bigger than us all, and my brother fears him."

"The dark lord?" Sebastion asked. "The dark lord fears me?"

"Yes, He knows that many things reside with you. Though he now thinks you are dead, it will not take long before he knows you are quite alive."

"Yeah, no thanks to your friend, Bashor." Sebastion added.

"The dark mage is not my friend." The Lady said in a warning voice. "I intend to make him pay for his crimes against mine." Killian looked up at her but said nothing.

"By the way." The Lady asked, pointedly looking back and forth at them . "*How* is it that you are still alive?" She asked, raising a brow at them. Killian and Sebastion exchanged a look.

"Shouldn't a goddess like yourself already know that?" Sebastion asked.

"They cannot see within the black mountain," Killian answered for her.

"Is Shama still alive? Oh, please tell me that he is." She pleaded to them. Sebastion saw such concern in her beautiful dark eyes that it put him off some.

"Is Shama the dragon?" He asked her.

"Yes, and so much more. He is my friend."

Sebastion came forward, and not knowing why he took her hand in his own. He came close and looked into her eyes. Her eyes looked back and started to open wide until, finally, they were big with surprise. A smile began to spread across her face, small at first, then taking her over completely. When he let go, she excitedly clapped her hands together.

"My dear boy, it makes sense ... of course ... of course!" She said excitedly. When she recovered her composure, she looked again at Sebastion seriously. "It is not the man-eaters that are your problem. It is the other gods, I'm afraid. My brother and the thirteen."

"You mean eleven," Killian said, correcting her.

"Do I?" She asked Killian. "Thank you so much for correcting me, knight." The sarcasm was as thick as mud. "Please cover that crystal with your palm."

Sebastion did, and the Lady of Light leaned in and kissed his head. She then turned to Killian with pain in her eyes. Killian coldly returned her look.

"I suppose you also know about Bashor's deceit regarding my false memories of my brother's death?" He asked as She looked away. "Right."

She looked back to Sebastion, leaned into him, whispered into his ear, and then was gone. Sebastion looked surprised at Killian.

"I'm sure she told you something really useful?" He turned to leave the way he had come.

"She said the Barbarian healer could save Lara."

"What?" Killian nearly tumbled down the trail and swore at his injured leg as he turned.

"She said I must bring her to him."

Killian stared at Sebastion for only a moment. "Then let's get going!" Killian said enthusiastically, watching as Sebastion only stared at him. Killian could see the wheels were turning in his head. "What now? What is it?"

Sebastion scratched at the stubble on his chin.

"Spit it out, then," Killian said, getting annoyed at the delay.

"Look ... I know you're not going to like this, but-"

"The longer we stand here, the less chance we have to save her." Killian pleaded.

"You can't come."

"WHAT!" Killian coughed in disbelief.

"I'm sorry."

"Pucker that, lad. I'm coming." Killian headed back down the trail.

"I need your help," Sebastion said to Killian's back.

"As soon as she's better, you can have all the help you need," Killian awkwardly used his stick to get down the cliff. Sebastion moved on, hoping he would have better luck convincing his uncle of what he needed him for below in the tent and followed in silence.

In the tent, Baran slept next to Lara with a sword in his hand. Morakye leaned against a pillow, looking miserable as he held his bandaged arm against his chest.

"How are you, brother?" Sebastion asked him. Morakye put a brave smile on his face, but Sebastion had been with the Fangor long enough to see it was a facade. Baran woke up then and stretched.

"Have you thought of anything yet?" He asked Killian.

"I think we do have a chance, Bull," Killian whispered. Baran lit up. "As is our fortune, it won't be easy, but there is hope."

"When ... where?" Baran asked, getting to his knees.

"My nephew has more detail than I. Sebastion, would you care to elaborate?" Killian gave him a look that said there will be no more talk of not coming.

"I know only that the Barbarian healer can save her." He said, looking down at Lara's pale white skin and swollen red bruise across her face. The skin around her eyes was turning black and purple. He watched her chest as it rose and fell ever so gently. If he had not been looking for it, he would have missed it.

"Methinks our time for her is short," Morakye said from behind them.

"Okay. Let's go." Baran said, putting his sword in his sheath. He then put his metal helmet on, smacked the top of it to get it tight, and impatiently looked at them.

"I promised these people that I would get them home," Sebastion said, putting it out there and waiting for the tirade.

"And well, you should do d'at. Well, you should any way." Baran said, putting his pack on his shoulder. "Just as soon as we get Lara right d'ats what we should do ... a good plan, it is."

Sebastion nodded. "We have to split up." He waited again, but Killian stayed quiet this time, so he went on. "Baran and I will take Lara to find the healer."

"And what pray tell will I be doing then, nephew?" Killian asked between clenched teeth.

"I hope you will help me keep my word and lead these people home, uncle," Sebastion said, coming up to face Killian. "They will not make it through these northern mountains without you, and the snow is close." Killian ran his hands through his long hair and breathed. "I'm sorry. She told me that I had to bring Lara … and these people need you." Sebastion reached out and grabbed Killian's arm. "I need you, uncle. Please help me help these people. They need you."

"And what of her?" Killian asked, hanging his head, conflicted.

"I give you my word that we will find the healer and make her well again. I promise you."

"Oh, puckering hell," Killian swore, gripping his stick like it were his sword in battle. "You assume I can get these people across the mountains and into Torenium?"

"You are the only one of us that has led a group of men. I have not." Sebastion explained.

"Yes, a group of military men into battle, not a group of half-starved peasants who will probably starve or freeze to death on the way."

"I am relyin on you to make certain that will not happen," Sebastion said in such a way that made Killian look up from his deep thinking and catch his eye. Despite himself, he smiled slightly. "What?" Sebastion asked.

"It's just that there was only one other that could reason with me the way you do. One other that had a damn dirty way of speaking the puckering truth like that." Killian suddenly stood up straight and stuck his chin out. "I will do as you ask. I have your word you will save her?" He asked now like a military officer.

"You have it," Sebastion said, surprised by the sudden change. Killian clasped forearms with his nephew. "Remember one thing,"

181

Killian said, still holding his nephew close. "I will hold you to your word." Sebastion nodded, smiling.

"Alright wit all d'at then," Baran said, annoyed. "If you two girls are done swapping spit, can we get this moving?" They laughed, and Sebastion gathered up his things. Morakye painfully got to his feet. Sebastion knew the most challenging thing was yet to come. "Brother," Sebastion said, hoisting his pack on his back as Morakye winced as he leaned down to scoop up his things. Sebastion gently pushed the things back down to the ground.

"Ah, Morakye is to be left behind then too?"

"No. Not behind, brother." Sebastion said, putting his hands on the Fangor's shoulders. "I have a very large favor to ask of you. A favor I would only ask of you." Morakye cocked his head sideways in that way that Sebastion always thought made him look so ridiculous. His ears stood attentive on top of his head, and his yellow eyes beamed. Sebastion smiled … but only for a moment. "Please-please, brother. Find my Miska and keep her safe from the Barbarians. I don't know what I would do if she were … if she were to be- "Sebastion could not finish the thought.

"Do not worry, brother. Morakye will do this for you." Morakye said, nodding his head. "Morakye will find his little sister with the big brown eyes. He will keep her safe."

Sebastion smiled wide. "Thank you so much. You know this means everything to me."

"So I get stuck with your cat? That's how it is?" Killian asked.

"And me's gets stuck with the smelly uncle."

"Hey!" Killian said as if that hurt his feelings.

182

"We got's all the hugs and kisses worked out?" Baran asked sarcastically, again pulling at his straps.

"Almost Bull. We have a few more things to discuss. Like where we'll be meeting and how you will let me know that Lara is all right?"

Sebastion thought on that. "I say we meet at the Great City."

"It's bound to be well into a siege or ... perhaps worse," Killian answered gloomily.

"Then, if the Great City is lost, we will meet at what remains of Endrea. Yes?"

"Fine. How long?"

"No idea," Sebastion answered with a shrug.

"And how will I know about Lara?"

"I will find a way," Sebastion said, annoyed at having to answer all the questions.

"Hey, don't get mad at me." Killian shrugged. "You're the blood demon here. The leader makes these decisions. It's nighttime. You sure you want to travel out there at night?"

"Best if we're not seen where we're going," Sebastion said, adjusting his pack and ignoring Killian's comment.

"Might be it's a good time to tell us where da't place would be, lad?" Baran asked.

"We are headed to the dead plains."

"Ah, good. It sounds like da place to be. I'm sure it's beautiful d'er. Let's get there when my friend here still has breath in her, heh?"

Everyone clasped arms, and they were on their way. Outside the tent, several of the slaves stood waiting for them. It was dark now and the only light was coming from the fires scattered around. "Are you leaving, blood demon?" One of them asked, concerned. Sebastion did not know what to say.

"YES," Killian shouted as he exited the tent. "Listen up!" He said it loud for all to hear in the night. "I am Killian of House Loyal and first son of King Bastion." The slaves started exchanging shocked looks and comments. He let it soak in a bit for effect before going on. "The blood demon has put me in charge for the time being when he's off working his plan." He let them stir nervously. "What plan, you ask?" He stepped forward as if he no longer had a badly sprained ankle. Only those closest to him saw the strain in his face. He pulled his sword free and held it high. "A PLAN TO MAKE THOSE BASTARDS BLEED FOR WHAT THAY HAVE DONE TO TORENIUM!" The people erupted with cheers. Several started cheering blood demons, and soon they all were ... even Killian. Sebastion looked around in awe until he got to Baran and saw the pain in his eyes as he stood holding Lara's litter. Sebastion threw a fist into the air to the people's delight and walked away quickly with his big friend into the darkness.

"Seems to me's that my brother has become very popular," Morakye commented next to Killian as they watched the people enthusiastically cheer. Killian looked down and winked at his little Fangor friend.

CHAPTER 21

"I have never noticed you in this way, Mother," Lehgone asked, bowing and smiling into his long moustache.

The Head Mother, Doria, looked at the big knight like a mother would an undisciplined child.

"You may call me Doria."

Lehgone smiled down at her taking her in. "Did I hear you say something about a castle?" He asked.

"How long have you been spying on us, knight?" She bluntly asked him.

"Oh, long enough, *Doria*."

"Okay, so you know who I am and where we are going. Maybe you can tell us what you wanted to talk to us about?"

"I wanted to talk to the Head Mother," Lehgone said, winking.

"Are you going to make this more painful than it needs to be?" Doria asked, crossing her arms, annoyed.

"Certainly not, *Mother*." He said in the same voice, smiling.

"Can you tell me if Sebastion is still alive?" Miska asked, seeing her opportunity.

"I have no idea whether the boy or his pet is still alive, pretty girl," Lehgone answered honestly. The truth was that he would be surprised if the boy were still alive after this long. Bashor had wanted him badly, and he was pretty sure it was not for clever conversation.

"Do you know where I could find him if ... if he is-"

"I can tell if he is still alive, he will not be in Endrea," Lehgone said bitterly. "Everyone seems to be showing up here, so probably he'll be coming here as well, if he can."

"That leads me to my question," Doria said, walking over to the table and pouring herself a glass of water. "It does seem like this is the place that many of our Torenium brothers and sisters are running to. How can we get those gates open?"

"That is easy. They may all come in over my dead body." Lehgone said, smiling.

"You will leave them to be slaughtered?" She asked him.

"Yes." Lehgone shrugged as if the answer was so simple. "If they come in and go through our reserve supplies, we greatly jeopardize surviving the inevitable siege that is coming by the hands of our good neighbours from the north."

"We cannot just do nothing and let those people die by the hands of the Barbarians," Doria said as if the mere sound of it was ridiculous.

"Ah, that is why women do not rule in these matters, my pretty one," Lehgone said condescendingly.

"It is just like a small man to take the easy way out, my rugged coward," Doria angrily answered back. This time Miska watched as Lehgone's face turned red from the barb.

"They come in, and we all die. It's quite simple, woman, and I do not see how you cannot get that through your thick skull."

"Because it does not make sense," Doria argued. "Even you admit that eventually, the man-eaters will be getting in, yes?"

"It is, in my opinion, unavoidable," Lehgone answered, looking down his nose at her.

"Well then." Doria went on like explaining to a child why one needs to eat. "We will need every able body to fight, yes?"

Lehgone laughed at that. "Yes, that's what we need. A bunch of starving Torenium women and children fighting Barbarians. Come now, even one as obviously thick as you should see the problems with that logic."

"All I see is a servant of the Advisors too afraid to do what makes sense," Doria answered back, seemingly unscathed by the dark knight's words. "One other thing," Doria said in her patient voice. "From what I have heard about Barbariansthey are not the brightest and lose attention rather quickly. If they are left to slaughter the refugees at their whim, we may find we are inviting them to stay longer at our doors. Not to mention feeding them while they're here."

The last did make Lehgone think. He scratched his chin and looked at the ceiling. Doria and Miska exchanged an annoyed look when Lehgone took his time. Finally, he looked down again as arrogant as ever. "Thank you for your time, pretty ladies. You have given me some interesting things to think about with the people who actually make decisions around here."

Doria did not miss the message Lehgone was giving.

"You," Lehgone said, pointing to Miska. "I suspect somehow I will see you again. You have an uncanny way of showing up in the most extraordinary places for such a young woman."

Miska said nothing but returned his hard look as best she could as her skin crawled from even being close to the dark knight again. "And you, dear Doria," Lehgone said smiling. "Perhaps you should be more interested in keeping your own house safe rather than worrying about the people outside those gates that don't have the good sense to know they are already dead."

"According to you, we are all already dead." Doria countered.

"Perhaps not all of us." He winked.

Doria paused then sucked in a disgusted, shocked breath. "You do not mean to say..."

"I said nothing, *Mother*. We all have our secrets. Is that not what you said?"

Doria's face flushed red, and Miska saw such anger on the Head Mother's face that it made her take a step back. Lehgone winked again, smiling. "Enjoy your little adventure and please be sure to say hello to the old man for me." Lehgone whirled and left through the doors leading from her chambers.

"I do not understand, Mother," Miska asked.

The Head Mother of the light looked at the ground with a furrowed brow.

"Doria." She corrected absently.

"Yes, sorry-Doria."

Doria walked over to a bookcase and pulled at a book that was on a shelf of many. There was a click and the row of books folded down, revealing a hidden shelf. Behind it were many glass bottles and jars. She pulled one of them out and poured some of the contents into a glass. Then she put it to her lips and drained it. She sucked between her teeth as she forced it down. "What he is saying, my dear." Doria cleared her throat. "Is that the Advisors plan to negotiate with the Barbarians for safe passage at some point."

"What does that mean for us?" Miska asked, taking on Doria's shocked look.

"It simply means we all will be left to the whims of the Barbarian Man-Eaters so the Advisors and the rest of the rich can walk away."

"But that is not right!" Miska said, putting her hands on her hips.

Doria looked over and smiled weakly. "Yes. And what should we do about it, dear?"

"I say we start with seeing what the king thinks about this."

Doria nodded her agreement. "Yes, but I do not expect much help there, I'm afraid."

"Well, as my father says, it's feet that get you there, not tongues."

"Then let us follow your father's advice and be on our way," Doria said, taking another sip straight from the bottle and closing the shelf. "Grab that torch and let us go."

They found that the dark knight had thankfully broken most of the webs that hung in the dark corridor. However, many remained and hung all around them as they walked. The torch that Doria now held singed, and it gave off a foul burned smell as they moved through the damp darkness. Before long, they got to an old stone staircase where Miska could not see just how far down it went. As they silently descended, she could feel the air getting cooler and the dripping of water getting louder. That was when she first smelled it. It seemed to consume her as she leaned against the wall for support. Doria sensed her stopping and looked back.

"That smell … it is so horrid!"

"This passage will run parallel to the sewage tunnels. If we don't keep moving, we could be at risk of passing out here. I don't even want to tell you what would happen if we were to have that happen."

Miska heard a noise in the darkness where the stairs disappeared. It was like a high-pitched squeaking.

"You have to be brave, Miska," Doria said.

Miska did not like the tone in her voice. She said it like there was something about to happen. The squeaking noise got louder. "Press your back against the wall and do not move. You must be brave, Miska." Doria said again.

Miska watched the stone stairs for as far as the light would allow her as a brown wave of rats started coming towards her. She did what Doria said and pressed her back against the wall and tried to be brave. When the rats reached them, Miska sucked in her breath and held it as the rats ran over her feet. She was very thankful she now had thick man boots on. However, she could still feel the tiny little feet pushing across hers through the boots. At times, one of the rats would look up at her, but the many others always pushed it forward. Miska watched as a small rat tried desperately to keep up with the others but was trampled by the wave. She watched as it tried, again and again, to get up and move forward to no avail. In a frantic last desperate move, it jumped into the air and towards the wall. Miska watched helplessly as the rat jumped seemingly impossibly far and right at her. She could not move or be pushed over the side by the rats. The rat landed on her chest, and she let out a scream. The sharp claws did not gain purchase until around her belt. It slid down, clawing at her skin. The scratches burned until the rat held onto her belt. She wanted to run, but she knew she could not. She threw up her hands and the rat made a hissing sound at her that made her freeze. She stared down at it, locking eyes. The eyes were tiny and red. Its body was small for a rat, but that just made the little needle-like teeth seem more significant as it snarled up at her.

"Get it off." She said desperately to Doria. "PLEASE ... GET IT OFF!" She risked a look over at her Head Mother. Doria was holding out the torch in front of her and looking down the stairs intently at something. She then did the worst thing Miska could have thought. Doria threw the torch over the edge. Miska watched as the reflection of the light got dimmer as the torch fell. There was a splash and then total darkness. She thought she was going to scream. She felt movement on her belt, and she covered her face with her hands and sucked all the air she could into her lungs to let out a thunderous scream, but before she could, a hand clasped over her mouth.

"Do not make a sound. The rat that was on you is now gone." Doria said in a whisper by her ear. "Someone is coming up these stairs and they know we are here." Doria moved her hand away, and Miska was thankful to let out her breath. She hadn't even noticed that the wave of rats had stopped. She then noticed that she could see in the darkness just enough to make out the things around her. She looked around and noticed it was coming from whoever was coming up the stairs towards them. Doria cautiously peered over the edge again.

"Hello?" A male's timid voice said up at them. "We mean you no harm." He said gently. "We know you have been coming in from the river runoff. We are here to help you find your way."

Doria looked at Miska, surprised. "They think we are refugees. It seems they have found their own way into the city." Doria whispered.

"We're coming up now." The voice said, cautiously.

"Quick! Muss up your hair and roll around on the ground until you are good and dirty. Remember to get a lot of it on your face!" Doria did just that and, while on the ground, she saw Miska unmoving and staring at the ground with a disgusted look. "NOW!" Doria commanded urgently. When Miska still didn't move, Doria reached up and pulled her to the ground. "There's worse than rat dung to worry about." She scolded her as she pushed her novice priestess down. "On your face ... get it on your face!"

As the two men arrived where the two women were, what they found was just what they had expected. Two more refugees lost in the caves, dirty and frightened.

"You two are darn right lucky to be alive." One of them said, coming forward and handing them a skin of water. Doria reached out and grabbed it eagerly. She put it to her lips and drank like she hadn't tasted water in days. She handed it to Miska and Doria gave her a look so quick that the men did not have a chance to see it. It was a warning that she had better do exactly as Doria had and she did as best she could. "How long you two been lost in here?" The one who had handed them water asked.

"Can't be sure," Doria answered back, putting a hand against her chest and feebly leaning against the wall.

"Well, you were sure lucky to have that torch then. If you ain't had that, you would have been rat food for sure. Can't tell you how many bones only we are finding from those little beasties." The one with him grunted his acknowledgment. "Well, I'm Fritz and this is my brother Silth." Fritz said, reaching out a dirty hand. Doria took it and shook it.

He then reached out to Miska and she gingerly took it. "Why, you're a girl!" Fritz laughed. "Thought for sure you were a wee lad, I did. Reckon its best to be a boy these days." He said sadly. "Well, my ladies. There ain't nothing to fear from Silth and me here." Fritz said, smiling again. "Now Silth don't talk much but don't go thinking that's because he don't like you. Naw, that's only because he ain't good of thinking of things to say is all. One thing he is good at though. My brother be the greatest ratter that ever lived, he is!" Fritz said proudly. Silth stepped closer, and Miska sucked in her breath and stepped back. It was not the big shoulders, scruffy hair, beard, or sharp knives stuffed here and there that scared her. No, it was the twine with what looked to be around thirty or forty dead rats tied to it and strung around his neck.

"Now, don't get scared of them wiggly critters, My Lady," Fritz said, smiling. "We got's mouths to feed as you clever ones are coming in from the river and are growing every day. Let's go meet them, shall we?" Fritz said, indicating for them to follow.

"Yes, of course. Thank you so much for saving us." Doria said, graciously.

"We all need save'n from time to time. Just remember 'ole Fritz and his brother Silth when it's our time."

Doria smiled and let them lead the way. Doria snatched the blade tucked into Miska's belt with a quick move of her hand and hid it in her sleeve. Miska wondered nervously what she was going to do with that knife.

They followed the men for what seemed like forever and around so many dark bends that Miska was sure she could never find her way back again. She wondered nervously if that was precisely what these men were trying to accomplish. She did not get a bad feeling from Fritz and Silth, even if the dead rats did make her want to hurl, but she had been wrong about people before. For all she knew, these men meant to rape and murder them somewhere deep in a dark cave where no one would ever find them again. Suddenly, Doria stopped. Miska looked around her and saw Fritz talking into the darkness of what looked to be a slightly open space. Suddenly, a man's head poked out and looked at them and then disappeared again. Fritz looked back at them with a sad look.

"This way." He said, waving them on.

"Could you hear what he was saying?" Miska whispered to Doria.

Doria nodded. "That man is waiting for his family. They were separated and he has not seen them for some time now. Fritz brought us to him first to see if we were them." Doria wiped her eyes with her sleeve. "It is unfortunate. The man has been looking for them for a long time. There isn't much of a chance for someone lost in these crevices."

"We pray to the Light, and sometimes we receive her charity so we can help these people," Fritz said from ahead of them. "Forgive for overhearing, but one's hearing gets sharper when living in the dark."

"You live in the light even here in the darkness. That is very inspiring to see." Doria said genuinely. That's when the smell of meat cooking hit their noses and the sound of people murmuring. "The Lady of Light has been queen to us lost souls here in the darkness," Fritz said. "She gives us more than blessings." As they turned the corner, they saw a large opening and people were eating, sleeping, or whispering everywhere. Most were women and elderly with children. "You see, the Lady of Light has given us her." Fritz said, pointing and grinning with

194

pride. Miska followed his finger and locked eyes with Lithra, Miska's plain-faced friend from the church.

"Lithra?" Miska asked in disbelief.

"You two know each other?" Fritz asked curiously.

"She is uh ... my niece," Lithra said, seeing Miska's look of distress.

"Then this is your aunt?" Fritz asked, confused, pointing to Doria.

"Yes, of course, Aunt-" But before she could finish, Doria put her arms around Lithra and squeezed her tight. Miska thought she saw Doria whisper in her ear but couldn't be sure. "It is so good to see you, aunt. Please come with me so we can catch up." Lithra said, indicating that they follow. Doria reached out and grabbed Miska's arm.

"Thank you, Fritz and Silth," Miska said as she almost stumbled as Doria pulled her away.

"Please, Miska!" Lithra begged. "Do not tell the others about this. The priestesses would never let me forget it if they knew!"

"Calm down, Lithra," Miska said quietly, looking around to see if anyone else heard her outburst. However, everyone seemed to have problems of their own. "How did you find these people?" Miska asked, sitting with her friend and taking her hand.

"I found the passage..."

"Go ahead." Miska urged.

"I found the passage while cleaning in the library. I saw there were marks on the floor like someone had scraped them. By the angle, I found that there was an opening in the shelf. I found the book that moved the shelf and ... then ... looked around."

"You have been spying?" Doria asked, red-faced.

"OH, NO! NOTHING LIKE THAT. I SWEAR!" Lithra looked back at Miska, worried again. Miska gave Doria an angry look. Doria looked back with amused surprise.

"Do not worry, Lithra. I believe you. We are friends, right?" Lithra nodded, wiping her nose. "Now tell us the rest." Lithra nodded again, wiped her nose again, and went on.

It seemed that Lithra had gotten more comfortable with the twists and turns of the caves. She had investigated quite a bit of it before she first saw Fritz and Silth wandering about. They were the first to have come through the river runoff alive. She found them living in the caves, frightened and not knowing what they could do. Lithra heard them praying to the Light one day, and it was then that she decided to risk meeting them. At first, the two men thought she was a ghost as she was wearing the dull white of a priestess novice. As they talked, however, they became friends. They developed a partnership to help the people who wandered into the darkness from the river runoff. Fritz and his brother would help the people find their way to the big opening they were in now, and Lithra would bring them things she could get from the outside.

That got sharp looks from Doria, but she said nothing.

"I could not leave them to die here, Miska. I JUST COULDN'T!" Lithra explained, red-eyed. "Will you tell?" She asked, her head down.

Miska touched her head soothingly. "Do not underestimate the church of the Light, my friend. I cannot believe there would be much punishment for someone with so much compassion."

"I think I would like to hear more on how you have 'procured' things," Doria asked.

"Who are you?" Lithra asked, looking up into Doria's eyes. "I believe I would recognize all that live in the church." She said curiously.

"Well ... I am a priestess that has come back to the church," Doria explained defensively.

"My pardons, governess," Lithra said, bowing her head slightly from the ground.

"I am so proud of you, Lithra," Miska said, taking the attention away from Doria.

"What?" Lithra asked, confused.

"You dare to help people no matter what the obstacles are. You are a natural giver, and that is a good and noble thing, my friend."

"Thank you," Lithra said, looking up at Miska, confused. "So you won't tell the Head Mother?" She asked.

"We will tell her together. I will be at your side. She will understand. I promise."

Lithra nodded again, sheepishly.

"How well do you know your way around?" Doria suddenly asked. Lithra looked at her questionably. "There is something we need to do. How much of this underground do you know?"

"All of it," Lithra said, shrugging and without a hint of pride.

"Come now, my dear. These caves, caverns, and sewage lines run all over the city."

"Some outside the city as well," Lithra added.

"Nobody could know all of it."

"I cannot explain it, governess. It just seems that I have picked it up. Even in places I have never been, I seem to know which way to go."

"Have you had this ability before?" Doria asked curiously.

"I guess. I have never been in such an underground labyrinth before." She looked at Miska and she smiled.

"That's great, Lithra. So you could help us?"

Lithra thought a moment before answering. "Why are you two out here?" She asked innocently but with enough of a question that both Miska and Doria looked at each other.

"We are on a mission for the Head Mother," Doria whispered.

"I bet she would be very pleased with you indeed if you could help. I'm almost certain that your little nighttime quests and procuring would be only a distant memory to the great help you will be giving us."

Lithra looked up at Doria for a moment, silent, then turned to Miska. "I will do it if you ask." She said to Miska.

Doria made a sour face so funny that Miska had to swallow her laugh. "Yes, please help us, Lithra."

"Okay. But I have to make sure everything is all right here first." Lithra said, getting up and going to the nearest group of people lying on the ground and cuddled together for warmth under a blanket that came from the church. Miska knew Doria recognized it as well. "She did what she thought was right by helping these people," Miska said, not looking up to catch Doria's eye.

"I know that," Doria said, sounding a little tired. Miska looked over and, in the shadows of the torchlight, thought she could see the Head Mother's older features again. "Remember, my dear, that most likely we will be under siege for a very long time. All resources must be accounted for and used sparingly. I know her action seems justified by the goodness of her heart, but that does not mean that the same good intentions couldn't mean catastrophic consequences." The Head

198

Mother of the Lady of Light explained. "It seems the right thing to open our stores of food to let all that are hungry eat as much as it took until they were satisfied. Would that be the right thing to do?" Miska looked over, understanding her point.

"I see," Miska said, looking away from all the hungry and cold people living off of the rat meat that Silth could catch.

"Good and seemingly noble decisions are not always wise decisions," Miska said, almost to herself. She jumped a bit when she felt a hand on her shoulder. She looked over and saw Doria smiling at her.

"How is it that one so young could be so wise beyond her years?" She laughed. "And that look you gave me while you were speaking to Lithra silenced me … silenced me!" She laughed. "No easy task there!"

Miska laughed too. Even being covered in dirt and rat dung, she was decidedly having fun. It had been a long time since she could say that.

In a short time, Lithra was back and they were heading out, with worried looks from Fritz and Silth. It was quite apparent that they were very fond of Lithra. In fact, from the look in their eyes, it seemed to go beyond fond to something else altogether. Doria watched worriedly. She had been around worshippers all her life, and she recognized the look of devotion. It could be very dangerous for a person to have that much power over someone. Dangerous for the worshipper, the worshipped, and all the people around them. Doria also could tell that Lithra had no idea how deep this devotion went. She even saw it in the faces of the people in the cave with them. She made a mental note to revisit this potential problem with her little novice.

Lithra moved over the uneven ground with practiced ease. Miska came close, trying to stay within the light of the candle Lithra was holding. Doria came last and would, at times, stop and listen to make sure they were not being followed. Lithra's only instruction was to lead them as close to the castle as possible. The rest Doria was sure she could do herself. Doria was once again listening as Lithra and Miska disappeared around the bend. When she was satisfied, she came around to find Lithra and Miska standing there waiting for her.

"What?" She asked.

"We're here," Lithra said, shrugging again.

Doria looked around and recognized none of it. "I said to the castle, dear. Where are we?"

"This way takes you to the castle gates. And this way will take you to the castle kitchen."

"The kitchen? Are you sure?" Doria asked, amazed.

Lithra thought about that and then looked up and nodded. Doria was suspicious. The way she knew would have taken them to one of the royal barns, not inside the castle itself. She couldn't help wondering who else knew of this tiny entryway. "We will use the kitchen entrance then. Is there anything else?"

Lithra thought on that. "No." She said simply.

Doria suddenly had a thought. "Did you find any other hidden doors inside the church monastery?" She asked. Lithra looked back at Miska, worried.

"It's okay, Lith. Just answer her question."

"Y-yes. There are a few ... well ... a lot actually."

"I see," Doria said seriously. She thought a moment, then smiled. "Congratulations, novice." She said abruptly. Lithra looked at her, confused. "You have been awarded the honour to further participate in the church's holy work." She said, smiling wider.

"Participate?" Lithra asked, looking back and forth to them in the light of her candle. Miska rubbed her temples, feeling a tightness there, knowing what was coming next.

"Oh, I can't!" Lithra said, backing up from them.

"Look. It's not a big deal." Doria explained, holding out her arms as if to catch her If she disappeared into one of the holes like a frightened mouse.

"Please, Lithra. We need to get inside and see the King." Miska explained.

"THE KING!" Lithra yelled, looking like she was about to explode. "You want *me* to get you to the *king* of the great city! *ME*!"

"Yes, Lithra. We want you to help us." Doria said in her commanding voice. "Now stop your little tantrum and do exactly as I say."

Miska, at first, was angered by Doria's tone but then saw Lithra relax. Apparently, Lithra felt more comfortable in a more subservient role. Miska watched her friend settle, surprised by her reaction.

"Now, I want you to lead us to the castle kitchen. Do you understand?" Doria asked in her same commanding voice and leaving no room for disagreement. "Once inside, we will search out another hidden passage using your special talents. Do you understand that?"

"Oh, yes. B-but, but what if there are people in the kitchen?" Lithra asked nervously.

"Your questioning of our plans will only slow us down, dear. Please follow orders as I give them and keep quiet, yes?"

"Yes," Lithra said, back standing up straighter now.

"What if there are people in the kitchen, mo ... I mean Doria," Miska asked this time.

"It is still the middle of the night," Doria explained patiently. "We will be fine. Lithra, lead the way."

The novice timidly stepped past them and headed down the passage holding her candle before her. Their shadows danced on the rocky walls as they walked. It was not long before they were at what seemed to be a wooden door. A piece of metal was nailed to the door, and Lithra moved it aside like she had been doing it all her life. She peered inside and then gently let it go back in place. "I do not see anyone inside the kitchen."

"Okay, let's go in then," Doria whispered.

They stepped out of the wall that had looked just like any other wall moments before. Miska thought she heard the faint whispering of someone outside coming in. The kitchen was huge, with hundreds of pots and pans hanging over long rows of wooden tables. There were many fireplaces of varying sizes. Some of them were still glowing red from the embers left inside overnight. "I think someone is coming," Miska said, looking for a place to hide. "Lithra, where is the passage."

"I have to look ... I can't just know," Lithra said, desperate, her eyes darting around.

"Well, look then, girl!" Doria whispered harshly, pushing Lithra into the kitchen. Lithra looked around but became more flustered every time she turned. It was then that Miska realized that Lithra was wearing the uniform of a Lady of the Light novice. If someone were to find them there, they would recognize it and then accuse the church of snooping. Miska saw an apron hanging and grabbed it. She ran up to Lithra and tore at her dress until it was unrecognizable. She then threw the apron over Lithra's head. Lithra looked at her wide-eyed like a deer surprised by a hunter. Just then, the door opened, and two elderly women came in.

"What's this then?" One of them cried out with her hands on her huge hips. "Who said you could be poking around *my* kitchen." Miska had her back to them and made it like she was poking around a barrel with fruit in it. She finally turned, taking a big bite out of a pear. She opened her boy's shirt to allow her bosom to be almost fully exposed. She smiled and swayed on her feet.

"Hello, there, ladies!" She said, nearly falling on the floor. "I consider it to be a great-" She hiccupped. "onor ... er, honor to be in your kitchen." She belched and covered her mouth with a smile.

"Looks like we got another one." The other woman said, shaking her head with a pinched face as if what she saw was beyond disgusting. "Any more of you whores around here, d'en?" She asked, looking around.

"I'm sorry, sweat mudders," Doria said, following Miska's example and swaying back and forth as she walked to the centre of the room.

"You two are filthy! Get out of my kitchen before I call the guards!"

"Servant!" One of them called out to Lithra. Lithra bowed submissively. Miska was hoping that Lithra's gift of blending in would help and, by the looks, it was. "Take these *ladies* back upstairs and under the Advisors where they belong. OUT!" The big woman said, kicking at them. "Blasted dirty whores!" She yelled again as they hurried out of the kitchen, laughing and giggling as if they were drunk.

"That was brilliant!" Doria exclaimed enthusiastically.

"Thanks," Miska said, buttoning her shirt up.

"Okay, Lithra. It's up to you now. What do you think?" Doria asked.

Lithra closed her eyes and then opened them again, more focused. "We have to find a room. These stone walls will not help us. I need a … that way." She said, hurrying down the hall. Miska and Doria had to run to keep up. Then, to their surprise, Lithra went right up to a door, opened it, and went inside. They exchanged a surprised glance and ran after her.

"Lith!" Miska whispered into the darkroom. "Lith!" She tried again when there was no answer.

"Yes," Lithra answered calmly by her shoulder in the darkness. Miska nearly knocked Doria over, jumping. "Lith! What are you doing?" She said in a tight whisper.

"Finding the passages … as you asked me too," Lithra said as if Miska's reaction was obvious.

"Okay. You just startled me, is all." Miska admitted grabbing lithra's arm. "Which way?"

"Follow me," Lithra answered cheerfully.

"She is a strange one," Doria whispered in Miska's ear. Miska agreed but said nothing. They closed the door, and Lithra lit her candle. They looked around and saw more doors surrounding them.

"Where are we?" Miska asked in amazement, looking around, overwhelmed by the choices.

"These are the servant's stairs," Lithra explained, smiling. "These stairs lead all over the castle."

"I would still expect the king's stairs to be guarded ... at least at some level," Doria added.

Lithra got quiet. They watched as she once again closed her eyes and then focused on staring straight ahead. "I do not believe these stairs lead to the king." She paused and looked around as if she were looking through the walls. "But I think I know a way."

"Lithra," Doria said seriously. "This is some pretty amazing things you are doing." She said, meeting Lithra's eyes. "Is there something you would like to tell us?"

Suddenly Miska saw a desperate look come over Lithra's face, even in the dim light. "Perhaps we could discuss this later ... after we do what we came to do?"

"I do not think so," Doria answered back in a voice that was very much the Head Mother of the church again. "How are you doing these things?" She asked in way that demanded an answer.

Lithra looked again at Miska, but Miska looked at the ground, knowing there was nothing more she could do to help her friend. She knew Lithra did need to explain herself.

"Please..." Lithra pleaded.

"Now," Doria commanded again. Lithra lowered her head and went to her knees in the little room as if she was about to confess a great crime and began to weep. Doria went down to her knees too and gently lifted the girl's head to meet her eyes. "Child, It cannot be as bad as that. I have heard many things over the years. I doubt you will surprise me. Tell me now." She urged, this time more gentle.

"My parents said it is evil." Lithra wept. "They said I was a child of the dark."

"You are surely not that," Doria said confidently.

Lithra took encouragement from that and sniffed before continuing. "I was sent to live with my uncle here in the city. I found out later that he was not my uncle at all and that I was sold to him." She sobbed a bit more and then went on. "He had a house with another woman, but he could not use me. Because of ... because of it."

"Because of what, child?" Doria asked.

"Because when I use what is inside of me ... it ... hurts."

"What hurts?" Doria asked.

Lithra looked over at Miska. "I would give anything to be like you." She said to Miska with tears rolling down her cheeks . She then pulled the strap of her dress down, and Miska put her hands to her mouth with a gasp at what they saw in the sparsely lit passageway. "It gets worse when I use it," Lithra said, looking up at Miska. Miska could only stare at the frayed red skin that lay beneath the girl's dress. There were blisters and wet skin as if she were being burned in front of them.

"Oh, by the Light, child," Doria said, looking at the wounds. "Who has done this to you?" She asked in disbelief. "Did this uncle man do this to you?" She asked, this time with anger in her voice.

"No, you do not understand," Lithra said between sobs. "*It* does it. It has always done it." She said, sobbing harder now. "Every time I use *it*, It takes a piece of me as payment. It always takes more of me!"

"Alright, Lithra," Doria said, sounding patient, but Miska knew the Head Mother was running out of it. "What is I*t*?"

Lithra looked up into Doria's eyes. "It is ... magic."

Doria looked down at her for a moment, wide-eyed. Then she shook her head. "That is preposterous!" She said, standing and looking around as if to get support from somewhere. "Ridiculous!" She said with an angry look on her face.

"Why?" Miska asked nervously.

"What?" Doria shot at her.

Miska went down to her knees now, pulled Lithra's strap back over her shoulders, and held the weeping girl in her arms. "I said, why? Why would it be so impossible for her to have magic? Are there not people with magic like ... like what we saw together this evening?" Doria shot her a dangerous look. "All I am saying is maybe there is a chance she too has it," Miska explained.

"The two things are not related," Doria said with her arms crossed defensively. "The *other* is from *those* that have power and it is a *gift* from that power. There are no mortals with magic. The lesser gods made sure of that a long time ago, and no one can survive having the curse. There are some folk tales of some, but they are foolish nonsense told to small children so they will eat their greens. Nothing more."

"This *is* more," Miska said as if the answer was as plain as the nose on her face.

"Nothing but a good sense of direction and a lot of luck," Doria said as if trying to convince herself.

Lithra snapped her fingers then and the room filled with light. Miska watched with astonishment as a fire burned around her fingertips.

"AMAZING!" Miska cried out in awe. She felt Lithra jerk once in pain, and the light went out. "I'm convinced," Miska said, looking up at Doria with only the candle lighting the room now. Doria leaned against the wall and slid down. "This changes a lot of things." She said with a sigh. "If she has it, then others must as well."

"They do," Lithra said then.

"There are more like you?" Doria asked in a whisper.

"You met one in the tunnels," Lithra said, wiping her eyes and standing up now.

"The rat catcher," Doria said, thinking back.

"Close. It is Fritz. Please do not tell him that I told you that."

"How do you know that he too has these ... abilities?" Doria asked.

"He gives the rats suggestions to go this way or that. That is how his brother is so good at catching them."

Doria just shook her head. "Magic back in the world. How could this be happening?" She whispered to herself.

"Didn't it once exist?" Miska asked.

Doria nodded slowly before answering. "It did before the gods ... a long time ago when magic was shared among the people. Those who had it were revered ... even honoured. That was before the thirteen took magic from the world and kept it all for themselves.

"They let only two be born with the magic, right?" Miska asked. "...the twins?"

"Yes, one to represent the dark and one for the light ... to balance the world. One good and one ... not. The lesser gods thought they would bring the balance back to the world after taking the magic and ... upsetting it. But magic was a big part of this world, and it took a long time for people to learn to exist without it. But we did ... we did."

"Some world," Miska interjected. "Are we not surrounded by man-eating Barbarians and on our way to see the decrepit and absent king, Head Mother?"

Doria gave her a look and Miska looked back, confused. She looked at Lithra and she too was giving her a strange look.

"What? What did I say?" Miska asked innocently, spreading her hands. Lithra then looked at Doria with wide eyes. Miska thought to herself about what she had said and then blushed a deep red. "Oops." She said apologetically to Doria.

"You *both* will refer to me as Doria."

"Yes, absolutely. Sorry ... no problem." Miska put in quickly.

Lithra said nothing but just continued to stare. "Child, it is simply a gift from the Lady of Light. Do not lose your head over it."

"It is magic?" Lithra asked.

"It is a gift from the Light," Doria said again with a hint of anger. "I think we have had enough discussion for now. Let us do what we came to do, shall we?" She said, breaking the uncomfortable silence.

Lithra led them up one set of stairs and then another. From there, they crept down a long hallway that smelled of old dust. At the end of the hallway was a big wooden door. "We need to get in here," Lithra whispered. "I think there is a place that will lead us to the King."

Doria gently put her hand on the latch and gently turned. The door was locked. "It's locked." She to them, whispering. "Is there any other way?"

Lithra closed her eyes, and when she opened them again, Doria knew the answer. She put her shoulder against the door and started to push. The lock holding the door crumbled quickly. They all looked at it, surprised.

"Guess nobody has been here in a while," Doria said, shrugging. When they stepped inside the room and Lithra re-lit a candle, they knew why. The room walls and floors were covered with books. There were more books than any of them had ever seen.

"Wow..." Miska could only say, looking around.

"I guess we now know why no one has been here," Doria added sarcastically. "The men in charge of the castle now do not strike me as the intellectual type, if you know what I mean. Well, where from here?" Doria asked Lithra.

Lithra moved around the room, concentrating.

"Has to be one of these shelves, right?" Doria said confidently.

"No, I don't think so. I mean ... yes, there are hidden doors there but none that will take you where we want to go." Lithra answered, sitting on a chair behind a big heavy oak desk. Her hands went to work feeling underneath. The others looked at the nearest books with interest.

"The True Religion." Miska read out loud. She felt Doria's eyes on her and turned to her.

"Those were all thought to be burned," Doria said, coming to look at the book herself. "Why would anyone leave this lying around like this?" She said, more to herself than to any of them.

"What is it?" Miska asked. Doria made a perplexed look reading the first page. "It is like the Blessed Book of Light only for another religion. One that existed a long time ago before the lesser gods … or so they say. I can't tell you the truth about it because I was not around during that time. But some other books refer to this one from time to time." Doria smiled, stuffing the book into her shirt.

There was a click, and Lithra's elated "Ah, ha!"

"What did you do?" Miska asked.

Lithra grabbed the big desk and, with one hand, easily slid it aside, revealing stairs. She smiled triumphantly, and Miska and Doria looked into the darkness. "More cobwebs." Miska said more to herself. It was apparent that the passage had not been opened in a very long time. Lithra reached up and pulled the desk back into place when they started their descent. The desk rolled easily and clicked when it fell into place.

"Well … here we are again," Miska said miserably.

"Sorry," Lithra said apologetically. "There was no other way that I could … find."

"It's alright, Lith. Just lead the way. Maybe you can break the webs ahead of us." Miska said, smiling.

Lithra smiled back and took the lead with the candle. Twice the candle went out, and twice it was easily re-lit. She had wondered how Lithra was lighting the candles so quickly; now she knew.

So many amazing things! Miska thought, furiously pulling webs from her face. *And some damn right disgusting!* She heard Doria chuckling behind her.

"I'm going to take two baths … maybe three, when we get back," Miska said, pulling at the webs as she walked, trying to use Lithra as a shield.

"That would not be advisable as we are conserving with the siege a possibility.

"Yes, M-Doria," Miska said, quickly correcting herself.

"I know a place underground that has a natural runoff of spring water. It is naturally warm," Lithra whispered back behind her.

"Oh, you are a blessed good friend indeed," Miska happily whispered back.

They only went down a short while before going up again in a narrow opening that was right behind the wall. That's when they heard voices. They saw the light escaping from cracks and holes in the wall up ahead. Lithra moved quietly and cautiously forward. When they got to the wall, they peered out through the holes. What they saw was a large room with a tub with steaming water coming from it. The walls were covered in white tile. They noticed that some of the tiles had fallen off, leaving the wood walls behind. They realized that they must be looking through one of those walls.

Many men sat in the water drinking from goblets. Women gathered around at different stages of undress. Some of them poured wine into the goblets almost as soon as one of the men took a sip. Other women waved fans to keep the air moving, and even more were scattered around like ornaments for the men's viewing pleasure. The

212

floor looked to be made of some light tile, so the sound bounced around quickly. It made it easy for the followers of the light behind the wall to hear what they were saying.

"What was the brute's name again?" One of the men in the water asked. Miska recognized the man's voice as the Advisor with the greasy hair and new sandals she had met earlier.

"His name is Tok-morg, master Flaz." Another man said, stepping out of the shadows in the room. He had a long green cloak covering his entire body. He was standing so still in the shadows it was like he had not been there a moment ago. Lithra sucked in a sharp breath and put a hand to her lips. The man pulled the long hood from his face slightly and searched the room with his eyes as if he sensed something there. All three women held their breath as they watched as the sickly-looking man looked around as if searching for something. The man's face was so thin and the eyes so sickly yellow that he looked to be close to death.

"Ah, Cobras." The Advisor said, obviously also surprised that the man was there. "We did not see you come in."

"You were speaking of the man-eaters." Cobras reminded them, pulling his hood over his face again after casting one more sceptical look around the room.

"Yes … the brutes at our walls. Right, then." Flaz said, clearing his throat to go on as he adjusted himself in the steaming water. He gave Cobras a sideways nervous look before continuing. "I believe our friend here has spoken to this, Tok.Tok."

"Tok-Morg." Cobras said again.

"Yes, him. If I have this right, it sounds like this beastly man has come to terms."

"All of them?" The fat Advisor across from him asked enthusiastically.

"Yes, I believe so. We can lea-"

"Masters." Cobras interrupted with annoyance plain in his voice now. "Would this discussion be best served in a more private place?"

"What, them?" Flaz asked, waving a hand around, indicating the women. "They are among the chosen ones."

"They are people who live in the city. Do you not believe they have family and friends that would … take an interest in what you are planning?" Cobras asked in a whispered but menacing voice.

Flaz rolled his eyes like a spoiled child. "Fine." He said at last. "Everyone out!" He yelled.

The women around them started getting up. Cobras walked around the room. As he strolled by the wall where they were looking out, he the slowed and listened. It seemed to the women behind the wall that it took an eternity before he moved on. Miska let out a silent breath. She looked over at Doria and saw her face was pale and there was a shocked look on it. She knew then, looking at her, that asking her to keep moving away from this wall would be impossible. Miska looked over at Lithra and could see her looking through the crack in the wall with one hand on her throat. She looked ready to bolt at any second. There was no question that there was more going on in the room than she understood.

"They will need to let all of us leave with whatever we want." One fat Advisor said, pulling grapes from a nearby plate. Several fell into the water and floated away from him in the foamy water that bubbled. Cobras saw other food floating in the water and couldn't help thinking

214

the men outside the city walls would have perceived this as some kind of human stew.

"The leader has given his word." Cobras said, smiling a crooked smile inside his hood. What value is a promise from a man like Tok-Morg, he thought. Cobras was rarely intimidated by anyone, but Tok-Morg had an air about him that could put fear in anyone. The man was big, even by Barbarian status, and worse yet he had some degree of intelligence, not the kind that would write letters or read books but a type that could plan and scheme. He saw it there in his light-coloured eyes above the nearly healed long cut on his cheek. And why any man, a Barbarian or whatever, would tie rotting human parts to their beards and hair was far beyond his comprehension.

"Have his terms remained the same?"

"Yes." Cobras said, knowing this meant the end to them and the great city of the Torenium Empire. With the great city gone, the rest of Torenium will be quickly taken. The truth is Cobras would not miss the city that thought so highly of itself. Though it did provide a certain amount of entertainment from time to time. Slitting a throat here and there for a bag of gold was easy business in a big city like this. However, the bags of gold were few and in between these days. He sighed.

"Cobras?" Flaz asked, annoyed. "Are you listening?"

"Yes." Cobras answered unapologetically.

"We asked you to go back to the Tok... The Barbarian."

"Tok-Morg."

"Yes-yes Tok-Morg or whatever these animals call themselves," Flaz said, dismissively waving a hand in the air. "Tell them we accept *if*—

" Flaz held up one long waterlogged finger. "They agree that we can leave with all we can carry and with whom we desire."

"I am sure that will be fine." Cobras said simply from deep in his cloak.

"Do you not need to ask them before you answer?"

"Master, Flaz." Cobras said, almost successful in keeping the contempt from his voice. "Tok-Morg has told me that you may leave if you give up the city. I do not see him having a problem with you taking anything you see as valuable when you go. It is simply the city … and the ones that remain, that they want." The fat Advisor in the tub across from Flaz nervously cleared his throat.

"What is wrong?" Flaz asked.

"Well … how do we know they will keep their word?" He asked with his chins bouncing up and down worriedly as he spoke.

"Come now, Borgo, my friend," Flaz said, trying to sound brave. "Like Cobras says, they only want the city. They will be far too busy plundering whatever is left here to worry about what we have. And believe me, we will have enough to keep us living the way we should for many, many generations. So do not get your chins wagging. All will be well. Besides, we will be going to the Northern city of Murgoth and will live like kings." Flaz said, raising a glass above his head and smiling. "We can be quite sure that those northerners have never seen the wealth we will bring them. They will be falling to the floor at our feet for just the mere taste of the wealth we will have." Flaz looked over to Cobras. "Right, my friend?" He asked as a pointed question.

"Oh, yes, master Flaz. All has been arranged. The city of Murgoth awaits the King's Advisors with open arms and empty purses." He

216

answered with the lie easily coming to his lips. The fact was he had not even had any contact with Murgoth and suspected they too would be having their problems with man-eaters soon.

"You see?" Flaz asked, drinking a big gulp of his wine.

"And what of the peo-"

"Don't even say it!" Flaz yelled at him. "Who cares about the crumbs of Torenium! We are the only ones that kept the Empire running when the *great* King wasted away. We kept the trade and governed. And for what!" Flaz yelled with contempt heavy in his voice. "I will tell you for what. So they can come snivelling behind our walls for safety! They contribute nothing and always want more! So I say let the brutes have them for all I care. Let their Lady of White save them."

"Light." Cobras interjected.

"What? Oh, yes. Let their god, the Lady of *Light*, help them. We have done what we could. Now it is time to leave. It is that simple." Flaz put his nose in the air. "Perhaps when the mangy beastly men have had their fill of the place and run off for the better game, we will have it back ... who knows."

Miska looked over again at Doria. The Head Mother now pressed her fingers against the wall as if she were about to break it down and attack. She had bared her teeth and her blue eyes shone with an eerie light coming through the cracks in the wall.

"Mo-Doria," Miska whispered to her, but Doria did not move. She looked over to Lithra. She was shaking her head in disbelief.

"I think we need to go." She said, but knives exploded into the wall with a loud bang just as she finished. All three of them jumped back and pressed their backs to the stone of the wall behind them.

"GO!" Doria whispered frantically, still staring at the knife that protruded from the wall only a finger's width from where her eye was. She got up and followed Miska's bent-over shape in the dimly lit passage. Two more knives plunged through the wall, which only made them move faster. Lithra stopped and Doria looked around her to see what was the matter. What she saw was a solid rock wall in front of them. That was when they heard someone breaking through the wall behind them.

"What do we do!" Miska asked, looking around.

"Use the magic, Lithra! Hurry!" Doria desperately whispered back. There was more pounding and the sound of pieces of the wall falling. Lithra closed her eyes and tried to concentrate. She opened them and looked around, confused.

"Who's there?" An angry voice cried out.

"Lith..." Miska whined. She worriedly looked back the way they had come. The only thing that kept whoever was there from seeing them was the dust kicked up when they broke through the wall. Miska felt her heart racing in her chest, knowing the man would see them at any moment. When she looked back to Lithra, her friend was gone. Her racing heart skipped a beat as a cold chill ran up her spine.

"HERE!" Lithra's voice said, as a hand grabbed her ankle. Miska almost screamed. "Down here!" Lithra said again. Miska looked down and saw that there was just enough space for someone to squeeze through a hole between the floor and wall. Miska quickly got on her stomach and Lithra pulled her through. When she was out, she turned and pulled in Doria.

Inside there was even less light, and all they could see were dark objects looming around them.

"That was far too close," Doria said breathlessly. "We better keep moving." As if to extenuate her thought, they heard a man's voice yelling at them through the hole they had just crawled from.

"This way!" Lithra said, taking Miska's hand and Miska took Doria's so they could move in the darkness. They had no idea where they were going as the darkness swallowed them as they moved. Sometimes the air was stale, and other times it seemed cool and moist, but neither could explain why as they followed Lithra blindly.

"Are you sure, Lith?" Miska whispered, thinking she may have felt something cold and wet brush against her cheek.

"Almost there," Lithra encouragingly whispered back.

"Didn't she say that already?" Doria grumbled. A short time later, in the darkness, Lithra stopped. Then Doria and Miska gasped as light sprang up close to their faces. It was coming from Lithra's finger. They huddled close around it.

"There is a tricky spot coming up," Lithra said to them. Miska did not like the inflection her friend put on 'tricky'. "We will be alright as long as you keep your back against the wall at all times," Lithra explained.

"Why, Lith?" Miska asked suspiciously.

"There is a slight drop where we will be going."

"How is it that all these tunnels and such are under the castle?" Miska asked with astonishment, looking around at what she could see in the little bit of light from Lithra's finger.

"It is said that this city was built on top of a volcano ... a long time ago when the northerners occupied it," Doria answered back.

"Oh," Miska said blankly. Suddenly the light went out again. "Lith?" Miska asked in the darkness.

"I'm right here. You still have my hand." Lithra said softly.

"Oh, right ... okay."

"I need to," Lithra started but then stopped as if not able to find the words.

"What is it?" Doria asked.

"I cannot keep the flame and keep us on the right trail."

"You mean we have to go by this *slight drop* without being able to see!" Miska asked with her voice quivering.

"It's all right as long as-"

"I know." Miska interrupted. "We keep our backs to the wall."

"Yes, exactly," Lithra answered quickly.

"Okay, let us keep moving, shall we." Doria urged Miska forward.

"I'm not real fond of heights," Miska said back to her.

"Don't worry," Doria chirped. "You won't see a thing." Miska held her tongue, not wanting to let out what she said in her head to the Head Mother of the Light.

They made it over the drop and beyond quickly enough. Soon they could see but didn't know where the light was coming from. Lithra led them on a trail that looked like it was used relatively often at one time. Suddenly Lithra stopped short. Miska nearly knocked her over. "What is it?" She asked sharply.

"There is something there," Lithra said, pointing to somewhere in the distant darkness.

"What is it? Is it someone? Is it the man from back there?" Miska asked nervously, looking around.

"I think I need to go see something," Lithra said in a strange voice. "Just follow the path there, and you will find what you are looking for." She said, letting go of Miska's hand and walking off.

"But how will you find us?" Miska knew it was a stupid question as soon as it was out of her mouth. Lithra looked back and gave her a tight smile before disappearing into the darkness beyond.

"And just like that, we lose our guide," Doria said, throwing her hands up in the air. "What could be so important that she would leave us here and head back into the dark?" Doria asked, not expecting an answer.

"I guess we follow the path," Miska said nervously.

And they did in the tiny amount of light they had left. Soon they found themselves at another wall. This one was so cracked and worn that many beams of light streamed through providing abundant light for the two of them to look around. Beside the wall, there were piles of wax on the ground as if someone had stayed for hours watching through these cracks and holes. Miska and Doria leaned in on the wall and peered through.

They saw an older man sitting by the window and watching the sun come into the sky. He was slumped in the chair and looked like he had been there for a long time. They both looked around the room through the holes but did not see anyone else there with the man.

"Is that him?" Miska asked.

"Yes, I think so. I have not ever really seen him up close before. Mostly in paintings." Doria answered back.

221

"What do we do now?" Miska asked.

"Let's do exactly what we came to do," Doria said, looking over at the novice priestess. Doria then felt around the wall. When she found what she wanted, she turned her wrist, and there was a click. Doria swung part of the battered wall open and softly stepped inside. Miska hesitantly followed behind. The room was small, with some tapestries on the walls that were worn and falling off their hooks. There was a small fireplace that looked to not been used in a long time. The bed was neatly made and that too looked little used. The only sign of life were empty bottles on a shelf. Some still had a small amount of white liquid in the bottom.

Quietly and without a word, they crept up to the man. There was a thick red tie that held the man in the chair. His head was bare of hair except for a few white wisps and dark age spots covered his head and white-bearded face. His skin looked like worn leather and hung loosely around his eyes and jaw. He wore an old blue ragged robe.

"Are you certain he is alive?" Miska asked, looking down, discouraged.

Doria touched the man's wrist. "He's alive." She said, putting her hands on the man's shoulders. She pushed gently. "Sire." She said in a whisper. The King did not move, so she went a little harder. "Your majesty," Doria whispered into his ear. The old man in the chair slowly opened his faded eyes.

"Dreaming?" He whispered.

"No, Your Majesty, we are here to speak with you," Doria said, bowing slightly. The old man watched her and slightly raised his head.

"They-do not let me dream-this is very nice." He mumbled.

"Your Majesty, the Empire is in great danger. The Barbarian man-eaters are outside the gates as we speak."

The King looked up at her. "You have his eyes, you know?" Doria lifted her head and a dark look took over her face. "There is nothing here for us," Doria said, still looking like she was ready to tear someone apart.

"He-is-coming-to-me … my-S-bastion." He whispered and fell back into his sleep.

"Did he just say Sebastion?" Miska asked, looking wide-eyed at the already slumbering King.

"Don't be ridiculous. How would he know anything about your Sebastion?" Doria asked, already heading back to the opening in the wall.

"What did he mean about your eyes?" Miska asked, still not moving from the King's side.

"The old man is obviously too far gone to help us. His words mean nothing." She said, stepping through the wall.

Miska leaned close to the King and gingerly put a hand on his arm. He opened his eyes again, slightly. "What did you mean when you said he was coming?" She asked in his ear. The King smiled somewhat, and he looked up at her.

"He-will-release-me-as-he…" The King took a breath. "-as he promised he would."

"Who?" Miska prompted.

"You-know-him-don't-you?" The King said like he was close to running out of breath.

"Yes," Miska answered.

223

"My-Bastion..." The King sighed. Miska also sighed, now knowing that she must have misunderstood the man before. She gave the King one more sympathetic smile and turned to follow Doria through the wall.

"-will-guide-the-boys-hand." The King finished.

Miska turned back, surprised.

"He-will-finish-what-was-promised-me." The King finished, exhausted.

"Who will?" Miska asked.

"My-great-Grandson-my-dear ... Sebastio-nnn-" The King shut his eyes and breathed like one in a deep slumber. Miska stared down, letting the King's words wash over her.

Is that possible ... her Sebastion? The grandson of the King? She turned fast to call to Doria and jumped when she found her standing right behind her, her eyes wide. "Did you hear what he said?" Miska asked. Doria nodded, still staring at the old man. "He said his grandson is Sebastion," Miska said with wonder in her voice.

"Hold on, there," Doria said, turning to her and raising her arms. "We don't know if he meant your Sebastion. He could be talking about anyone ... or even just repeating what he heard in this room." Doria explained. "Who knows what those drugs are doing to his mind."

"I admit it seems incredible ... almost impossible." Suddenly a thought came to her. It was the image of the man's eyes in the painting in the room with the Advisors. The blue-gray eyes were peering out from under a knight's helmet and faceplate. It was the man that was holding back the creature as it lunged for the King. But it was the eyes in the painting that she remembered—Sebastion's eyes.

"The man in the painting ... the one with the knight and the King?" Miska asked Doria.

"Yes. I remember. The knight was Ser Bastion the Loyal. The King's one-time best friend and closest confidant. What of it?"

"The eyes were exactly that of Sebastion. Even the way the painter captured the way he moved in that painting ... it is him. I would know it anywhere." Miska said confidently. Doria looked at her, but Miska could see she was far away. "What does it mean, Head-I mean Doria?"

"The age is about right..." Then Doria shook her head as if waking from a dream. "No-no-no, that is just too far-fetched. There must be another explanation." She said, putting her hands on her hips like she was about to lecture her novices for doing something bad. "A simple resemblance because you *wanted* to see him and an old man repeating what he heard just moments before-that is all this is."

"It may not be." Came a woman's voice behind them. Doria pulled a knife from her sleeve as she turned.

"That will not be necessary." The woman said to Doria disarmingly and holding her arms out. She wore a long nightshirt and slippers. Her hair was black and gray and wild, like she had just woken up.

"May I ask who you are?" The woman asked politely.

"I would ask you the same question," Doria defensively said back.

"Fine." The woman said, stepping a bit closer.

"But first, let's get one thing out of the way." She said, crossing her arms and scowling. "Do you intend to harm my father?" Doria and Miska exchanged a confused look. "And do not lie to me. I will know the difference."

"If you are referring to the King, then no, we do not mean him any harm. We have come here to let the King know of the situation in Torenium ... and, more specifically, the great city. Did you say, father?" Doria added suspiciously.

"I am Kirra, the daughter to his Majesty the King."

When Miska did not hear anything come from Doria, she curiously looked over at her. Doria stared at the woman with a blank expression on her face. Miska frowned, thinking the reaction was quite rude.

"Hello, I am Miska," Miska said with a slight bow.

"Hello, my dear. A bold thing to sneak into the King's bed-chamber." Kirra said to Miska.

"We would not have to if we did not have to deal with the Advisors," Doria answered for Miska.

Kirra stepped up closer to Doria, looking into her eyes. "I ... know you," Kirra said, coming close. Doria knew the woman would eventually figure out who she was. There was a time when the two of them were very close. However, Kirra would only know her as a much older woman.

"Yes, Kirry. You do." Doria said in the voice of the Head Mother now. Miska watched as recognition came into Kirra's eyes. It was slow, but when it was finally there, it ran across her face like a wave of emotion.

"You? It cannot be." Kirra said with tears in her eyes.

"Yes, sweet friend," Doria said, her own eyes becoming wet. "I'm in disguise, you see." Her eyes filled up, and she scrunched her face with emotion. The two crossed the remaining space and embraced for a long time, both weeping softly. Miska watched the exchange in silence. She could see that these two women loved each other very much.

"They told me you were dead," Doria said, pulling Kirra to arm's length but holding her arms firmly as if to not let her go. I have never felt such loss in my life, Kirra. Why would they tell me this if it were not true?" Doria asked, her voice cracking.

"Most believe I still am dead, my friend," Kirra said, wiping her green eyes with her sleeve. "Believe me; I never meant to hurt you. It is quite the opposite." She explained. "There was whispering that the people wanted to see me on the throne."

"Yes, Kirry. I whispered these very same things. Although, if you remember, I was never much of a whisperer." Doria said, smiling.

"Yes, Dory. I remember that well." They both laughed at that.

"So you faked your death so as not to be on the throne?" Doria asked, confused.

Kirra shook her head. "No. Not exactly." She explained. "The Advisors had no intention of letting me make it to the throne. Oh, no. They were having far too much fun squandering my father's wealth and using his power. They meant to get me out of the way."

"That is even too low for those filthy puckering bastards. Lady forgive me." Doria added with a small prayer.

"Yes. It was even below them. Someone else more powerful was orchestrating the plot, I believe. Someone much worst."

"Who, Kirry. Who would have more power than the Advisors? Who else would want you dead?" Doria asked. Miska could hear the anger in her voice.

227

"-a dark man, an evil man that wanted nothing more than to keep Torenium in turmoil. He has a personal vendetta against the Empire and all that live in it. He is the one that first rotted my father's mind until it became dark and hollow of life ... like the man who was responsible."

"Who?" Doria asked again.

"His name is Bashor."

Miska and Doria looked at each other.

"You know of him?" Kirra asked, seeing their exchange. Then there was someone clearing her throat in the room. It was Lithra looking embarrassed for interrupting them.

"Yes?" Doria asked.

"Excuse me, Mother-" Suddenly her face got red realizing what she had said.

"It's alright, dear. What is it that you were going to say?" Doria asked in the patient voice of the mother of the church.

"Do you remember the man who threw the knives?" She asked shyly.

"Yes," Doria answered with a hint of annoyance now in her voice.

"Oh, right. Of course, you do ... well."

"Spit it out, child," Doria said, this time not masking her annoyance.

"Sorry ... right," Lithra said, jumping to attention and sensing she'd better be quick about it.

"There is ... you know, that man. Well, he is on the way up with some guards."

"WHAT!" Doria hissed. "That is the kind of thing you just puckering spit out, girl!" Doria swore, waving them all to the wall.

Just as the hidden door clicked behind them, the King's private chambers' entrance flew open. The man they had seen previously entered the room with his knives in each hand. The guards followed him, looking around.

"Stop moving, you stupid maggots!" He yelled at them. As they held still, Cobras came into the centre of the room and sniffed the air like a dog. "They were here. Search the room. Look behind the chest. Look everywhere. MOVE!" The guards quickly moved around the room, looking frantically for them but turned up nothing. Soon they stopped and blankly looked at Cobras. The skinny man with the yellow skin wiped his face with his hand, visibly trying to gain his composure.

"I do not mean find them because they are STILL IN THE ROOM. I mean, find the way they CAME into the room." Cobras' eyes grew wide as he saw them exchange glances and then continue staring at him blankly. "I swear to the darkness that I will slowly cut your head from your shoulders if you don't locate the hidden door. Give me that look one more time. Just one more time!" The guards started running around the room, tearing everything up, looking for anything that would help calm Cobras' rage.

Doria watched from the crack in the wall as the man in the forest-coloured cloak made her skin crawl. There was something not right about the man. She could feel it in her bones. She knew their paths were going to cross again at some point. She pulled her eyes away and saw Kirra waving them deeper into the caverns again. She gave one more look and saw the man they called Cobras walking towards the wall, and from what she could see of the man's bloodshot eyes under the hood, he had a suspicious look on his face.

"Let's go!" She whispered. "Lithra, lead the way."

"We should go back to my rooms," Kirra said to Doria.

"Lead the way, Lithra," Doria commanded, getting a confused look from Kirra. They followed Lithra through a maze of caves and into spaces between rocks that they would never even think were there. Soon they came to another wall, only this one had a door in it, and the wall was solid with no cracks.

Kirra turned the handle and light flooded in. The little bit that came from under the door allowed them to see the door and wall, but they were not prepared for the assault of light. They all walked in blindly, shielding their eyes. When their sight came back, they saw that they were in a large room, and one wall was the vast stained glass mural of the Lady of Light holding up the sun. Doria recognized it immediately. They were in the King's former private chapel. The only difference was that they were now in some between-room that was filled with light.

"The architects loved this glass window so much that they did not want it facing out towards the city. They were afraid it would eventually either be destroyed or would get worn from the seasons." Kirra explained. The woman stared at the inverted image of the Lady of Light as she stood huge on the glass above them. "They built this room behind it to house the light to give the effect that the glass is outside and letting in the light. Those windows allow the light most of the day." Kirra continued pointing up to the ceiling.

"Nobody knows of it?" Miska asked.

"Very few, my dear," Kirra said, smiling. "And besides, not many would care as the King's chapel gets little use these days." Doria frowned at that.

Kirra took them through another set of doors that led them into her private areas. The setup was very nice. Inside was a big room that had almost every bit of it covered in books. The only part that didn't was because there was a large fireplace in the wall that looked like it was in desperate need of cleaning. The room's light came from slits in the ceiling that let in light from the connected space.

"This is nice," Doria said, looking around but still frowning. "But it is still exile."

"The caves and other hidden places keep me pretty Informed of what is going on around the castle and beyond. And there are a few who know that I am here and visit me from time to time."

"Your people need you," Doria said in earnest.

"No, Doria," Kirra answered back sadly. "The people need a leader." She shook her head sadly, and the others could see she fought back the tears. "Bashor and my father broke me a long time ago, my friend. You of all people know that."

Doria came up to her and put her hands on her shoulders. "Wounded, yes." She said, looking deep into Kirra's eyes. "But I can see you are not yet broken. I have seen the most wicked of wounds heal and become only scars. Never forgotten … but well enough to go on."

They stayed in the room for some time, waiting in the hope that Cobras would give up the search for them. Doria spoke quietly with Kirra away from Miska and Lithra, who walked around looking through the books and talking. Lithra told Miska about her sad upbringing and how people seemed to hate the things they could not understand. when Lithra turned to reach for a book, Miska noticed the stained wet spots on the back of her dress. When Lithra's hair moved, she saw the blistered skin below the collar of her dress.

"Lith, is there nothing I can do for those?" She asked. Lithra just shook her head without a thought about it. Miska thought to herself about just how hard it must be living with such a power, and the only way to use it is with sacrifice to your own body. She was glad she did not have any magic. It was pretty obvious to her that the price was high.

"I am not familiar with the story of Kirra," Miska whispered, looking over at the two women as they quietly talked together. Lithra stepped away from the shelf and shot a gloomy glance at the women.

"It is a sorrowful tale," Lithra whispered back.

"Can you tell me ... please, Lith?" Miska pleaded.

Lithra smiled and walked towards the other end of the room, looking into her book as if it was suddenly interesting. Miska slowly followed behind.

"It all started when the Loyals came to the city for the tournaments." Lithra began with a light in her eye now. Miska could see that Lithra enjoyed the story and was excited to recount it back to her. The Dempsies were famous for their storytelling and she missed them and their wonderful stories very much. Miska was excited to hear this.

"At that time, Talion, son of Bastion, was the King of the north. He came to the city by orders of the great King himself. It is said that the Loyals did not like to come to the city as they believed the great King was possessed by some evil spirit ... or some such thing. Anyway, the King had a secret that was really not a secret. He had fathered a daughter with a woman that also lived in the castle. The King never openly admitted to having her but also never denied it. In fact, she was with him often."

"So why not just admit he had her and call her his princess?" Miska asked, confused.

"Because if he did, then her mother and her family would consider themselves part of the royal family, and the king was-"

"Is." Miska corrected her.

"-is a private person. And there is all sorts of politics. Anyway, that's what I guess."

"Did Kirra have a son?" Miska asked suspiciously.

"Hold on!" Lithra whispered wide-eyed and forcing down laughter. Miska laughed gently.

"Well, everyone came to the tournament. There were knights from all over Torenium, and they all wanted to impress the great King. All that is except the Loyals. They kept to themselves and did not participate in the games unless directly challenged by another king. And that soon stopped after their youngest Loyal thrashed whomever he was pitted against."

"What was his name?" Miska asked.

"Ah, you are most perceptive, as he is important to this story," Lithra said dramatically. Miska rolled her eyes. However, she was thoroughly enjoying herself inside.

"His name was Ryder," Lithra said slowly for effect. She suddenly realized she had said that too loud and looked over to catch Doria's eye. Lithra looked back quickly and continued in a quieter voice.

"People in the city did not like the Loyals as they were thought prideful and separatist from the rest. Everyone knew of their crazy theory about the King, so mostly everyone just left them alone. Mostly..." Lithra added in a more subdued dramatic fashion. "You see, being bored, young Ryder had a tendency to wander at night, especially with not being able to fight in most of the tournaments. One evening, his boredom led him to the wall that separated the castle from the city. That night he decided to walk along the top of the wall, and he did just that. He followed it, losing track of how far he was going, and ended up right above the King's private gardens. And in that garden of lustrous flowers of every shape, size, and colour, the young Loyal set his eyes upon the most beautiful thing he had ever seen."

"Kirra," Miska said, smiling.

"Yes. The King's only daughter. It was night, so Kirra did not see him there on the wall. She restlessly walked the garden and Ryder walked with her above, unseen … or so he thought. As Kirra passed beneath a peach tree, Ryder waited on the other side for her to come back into view. But she did not. As time passed, Ryder became worried that something had happened to her, and he jumped onto a limb of the tree and swung to the ground … but still, there was no sign of her. He walked to the other side, worried now, and what he found there was a rock hurtling towards his head. He ducked just in time but tripped over one of the tree roots and fell to the ground."

"How could you know all this?" Miska asked suspiciously.

"Everyone in the great city knows this story, Mis," Lithra said with her hands in the air, innocently. "It's a legend here."

"All right. Sorry, please go on."

"Well, like I was saying-" Lithra gave Miska a sour look. "Ryder went down and Kirra went right down with him. Only Kirra now had a

234

small knife in her hand and held it right under the young Loyal's chin. It is said that when he opened his eyes to look into hers, they fell madly in love right there under that peach tree." Lithra took a moment with her eyes shut and smiling blissfully. "Even with Kirra's knife still held to his throat. And I must admit, if Ryder was as handsome as Bastion, his grandfather, in those paintings, I would have fallen in love with him before he even hit the ground."

"Lithra!" Miska said, laughing.

"What? I'm just saying it is all."

Miska just laughed. She thought of the eyes in the painting that she thought could be Sebastion. She remembered what those eyes had done to her.

"Okay. What of the son?" Miska asked, looking over and thankful Doria and Kirra were still engrossed in an intense conversation. Lithra shook her head sadly. "What is it?" Miska asked.

"The rest of the story is quite tragic. Very sad..." Lithra said, looking glum.

"Please, Lith. I have to know the rest." Miska pleaded.

Lithra winked and went on. "Ryder and Kirra met every night during the rest of that tournament. They were inseparable in the evenings but had to meet in secret. The great King and Loyals were not on the best of terms, and neither would be too pleased to hear of their meetings in the King's gardens. But be that as it may, Ryder wanted nothing more than to marry Kirra even though they had only been together for a few short weeks. Kirra knew her father would disapprove, so they decided that they would run away together. They planned it all perfectly. At the end of the tournament, they would meet again on the wall. They would take a ship to the black mountains and seek out their adventures there together. Well, as the night came, Ryder waited on that wall, but there was no Kirra. He waited until he could wait no more. It is said Ryder headed back to the north, a broken man, now realizing his love was not shared by Kirra.

But on the second day, on his way back to the north, a rider came to him and gave him a note. The rider was Kirra's chambermaid. She handed him the message with shaking hands and a nervous smile on her quivering lips." Lithra paused, thinking.

"Lith-?"

"All right, some of this I may be fluffing a bit." She said, smiling guiltily.

"Did she have a son?" Miska asked again, but this time she was running out of patience.

"You see, she had not met him on the wall because she was too ill and could not get out of bed."

"Pregnant," Miska said at last.

"Yes. Kirra was with child."

"So what happened?" Miska asked now, enthusiastic about the story again.

"Ryder was so happy to hear of this that he turned his horse around and galloped back towards the city with all the speed his warhorse could muster. But he never made it as the King had caught wind of what was going on and had men on the road waiting for him. Ryder was ambushed, and the King's men filled him with arrows. They say his last words were 'Kirra ... I love you as he died alone on the dirt-covered road."

"Oh, my god. That's horrible!" Miska shouted.

"Everything all right, girls?" Doria asked from across the room.

"Oh, yes. Sorry." Miska answered with her face turning red. She tried not to make eye contact with Kirra. "That is a horrible story." She said in a quieter voice now.

Lithra nodded sadly. "And it gets even worst for her."

"How could it get worse?" Miska asked, shocked.

"But it does, my dear," Kirra said, walking towards them. Both Lithra and Miska sucked in a deep breath and lowered their heads.

"Kirra, you do not-" Doria started, but Kirra waved her off.

"It's all right. It was a long time ago." She said, coming to stand with the girls. "Would you like to hear the rest?" She asked Miska.

"Oh, yes, Your ... I mean My Maj-"

"Kirra will do, dear," Kirra said, smiling. "My story ends with my father. He thought it treason to bring into the world a child with our blood and that of a Loyal. Bastion was once my father's closest friend but later became his most hated enemy. Bastion did not believe my father was who he once was and was not afraid to tell anyone that wanted to hear it. Well, my father would not have a grandchild with Loyal blood." Miska saw Kirra's eyes start to water and suddenly felt guilty for wanting to hear the story. "My dear father killed my little boy shortly after I delivered."

"By the Light..." Miska said, her eyes wide.

"I think by something else entirely," Kirra said, wiping away the tears.

Miska somehow had thought that Sebastion could have been that son, but now that would be impossible. "Are you sure ... I mean ... do you know he's..." Miska stumbled.

"MISKA!" Doria barked.

"Quite certain," Kirra said, looking up to the ceiling, trying to get her emotions under control.

"It's just that I know this b-"

"THAT IS QUITE ENOUGH!" Doria yelled, stepping close to Miska. Miska stepped back, lowering her head. "My little novice here has a vivid imagination at times," Doria said apologetically.

Miska did not miss that Doria called her a novice instead of a novice priestess.

"My apologies, Kirra," Miska said with her head low.

"Oh, child. Do not fret." Kirra smiled. "I too have a wonderful imagination that I live in most of my life." Then Kirra did a much-unexpected thing and grabbed Miska and hugged her tightly. Miska was surprised but quickly gave into the embrace and hugged her back. Doria and Lithra exchanged a shocked look. "My son would have been around your age, my dear," Kirra said, holding Miska tight. "I would have loved for him to have a girl like you in his life." Miska patted the King's daughter gently on the back as she held her tight. Doria watched, shaking her head from side to side, watching the tender moment in disbelief.

CHAPTER 22

"Are you mad!" Taglien swore, feeling his dark skin prickle.

"Come now, my dear Taglien. You knew this day would come." Bashor said soothingly to him as he sat at the small desk in the room where the lesser gods permitted him to stay.

"There are spells here to protect against our voices being overheard, but what you say should never be spoken!" Taglien said nervously.

"Come now." Bashor went on. "There is no other way here. They have become far too powerful, and you all must have known that there would come a time when they would turn on you. Answer me this, my good man." Bashor asked, standing. "When will the *lesser* gods be done with being *lesser*? The two will destroy you all. You must know that by now."

"There is no reason for the twins to want us dead," Taglien said, crossing his arms defensively and walking to the door. "However, there are many reasons for *you* to want them dead. One of them, perhaps because you believe you could take their place. Was that not your plan so many years ago, Mage?"

Bashor sighed out a long breath through his nose.

"Yes, Taglien. That *was* my plan. But now I want to join with you and the others to keep us *all* alive. Together ... and only together could we defeat the twins. Now I am tired of trying to put reason into your thick heads." Bashor said, flicking a finger at the door. The door flew open.

"Do not forget that we are no longer whole, Mage. You do remember two of our happy family members have been destroyed?" Taglien smiled before stepping out of the open door. He turned once more for his last jab. "Have you factored that into your schemes, Mage?"

"Yes," Bashor said confidently. "And we will be chatting with them shortly."

"What?" Taglien asked, his mouth falling open. "That is imposs-" But before the lesser god could finish, Bashor flicked his wrist and the door slammed shut.

"Simpleton magicians!" Bashor swore at the closed door.

Bashor nodded at the little globe that hovered in the corner of the room and the light dimmed. He lay on the bed and massaged his temples. He knew working with the lesser gods would be difficult, but he had forgotten just how much. Bashor rubbed vigorously and tried to picture what things would be like when the pieces of his plan all came together. Not too long from now, he would have the absolute rule of everything this world had to offer. Torenium would only be a small piece of what the rest of the world would hold. The thirteen wizards that made up the lesser gods have always had a small vision. They found small groups of humans in only half of the world and made them theirs. Even the short-sighted twins chose to keep their influence on Torenium alone. Because it was there that those imbeciles believed those worthy to worship them lived, so they bicker and scrape for a piece of this world alone.

Idiots!

He had a larger plan in mind. When the lesser gods and the pesky twins were out of the way, he and he alone will rule this world in its entirety. He will become what a god should be, not a magician with a knack to stay alive but a significant divine entity of ultimate power. The world will be his garden to play in. And he could pluck or plant any flowers in that garden as he saw fit. He sighed again, but this time with a smile spreading across his face. It would only be a matter of time before all his plans came to fruition. There was one thing that would pull all this together. One thing that was the key to everything he meant to do. And that very one thing was last seen hanging around the neck of his one-time annoying servant. The Eye of the Gods, and It was the key to everything he was trying to do.

The Eye was the last of the magical items of significance left to this world. The lesser gods had been effective in destroying nearly everything that held magical properties. Bashor had collected all that he could still find in existence and hidden them away deep in the black mountains. Most, however, bore little magic and were just trinkets left behind from a distant forgotten time. The Eye, however, was something else entirely. It was a conduit for magic. It could either sap magic or, if used correctly, be a tool to enhance the magic. Those were the things known about the little crystal. He had it in his hands at one time but then lost it in one of the rare lucid moments the great King had.

The idiot actually gave it to the Loyal family for safekeeping. That family had a very unsettling way of getting involved in everything. Bashor closed his eyes and reached inside himself to feel the comfort of his returning powers. As annoying as the Loyal family was, Bashor had to admit the boy had helped him regain power, and he would always hold a special place in his heart. The blood was extraordinary. The boy had helped him put his plan into motion faster than he could have imagined. There was no longer any reason to use Sebastion as a tool to get control of the Torenium Empire and keep the Twins busy in their small world. All that was going to be a distraction as he gained strength and searched for the Eye. No need now as the boy turned out to be more beneficial than he could have ever imagined in another way.

Too bad there are not more like that one. Bashor thought grudgingly to himself. Oh, well. There was no use mourning the dead and gone. The powers this dull world holds will all be mine.

CHAPTER 23

They had been traveling nearly non-stop for three days. Sebastion's back, arms, and legs burned from the litter Lara lay unconscious on. The ground was uneven, so they had to carry her in the make-shift litter instead of dragging it. Baran seemed to be almost immune to the weight. He was single-minded in his trek forward. Here and there, Sebastion would correct Baran's path, not knowing or caring how he knew where it was. Sleep was just a short few hours against a rock or just collapsing. Time was getting short, and Lara's breathing was nearly non-existent now. Her face was turning a shade of blue that was making Sebastion nervous. He knew he had to consider the possible outcome if they didn't make it to the healer in time, and Lara would die. His uncle would be most disappointed in him, to say the least. Sebastion knew that Killian was very fond of Lara, and the thought of his loss helped keep his legs moving even when he thought they would just bend and never push him up again.

"Baran ... I need ... just a moment." Sebastion pleaded in the fading sun of their third day. Baran stopped without saying a word. Sebastion gently put his side of the litter down. His knees buckled, and he lay there on his back, looking up at the dimly lit sky through the dense forest. He could feel his heart pounding in his chest.

"If we keep going ... like this, we'll be ... no good if we run into ... Barbarians," Sebastion said, trying to get his breath back. Baran did not move but remained staring off into the trees toward the way they needed to go. "Baran ... are you all right?" Baran still did not move, and

Sebastion started to get worried. With all the will he had left, he pushed himself up and came around to look at the big man.

Sebastion felt terrible for his friend when he looked into his big broad face. Streams of tears ran into his beard as he cried like a child. When he saw that Sebastion had seen him, he no longer tried to conceal it and let his shoulders bob as he sobbed.

"Baran, just sit a moment."

"I can't do d'at," Baran said in a weepy voice. "If I sit d'en I won't be able to get up again ... I ain't got much left in me." Sebastion realized that that was what was making the big man cry. He knew his body was about to give up, and he thought he would be responsible for Lara's death if he couldn't go on.

"All right, bull," Sebastion said, putting his hands on his knees and leaning down to rest while he thought about what they should do.

He closed his eyes and concentrated. At all other times, the fleeting thoughts and hints of where to go just came to him. This was the first time that he had turned inward for an answer. There was a flash of light in his head, but still, he concentrated. Like looking through a cloud, he saw three figures standing together, no ... not standing. One was standing, another bent over, and another was lying on something and was still. He then realized with a shock that he was looking at them. Suddenly he felt himself slowly rising, and he watched himself get smaller as he climbed into the sky. When he was just a speck, he stopped. He was very high, and he nervously looked around. He saw not far off a massive opening in the forest with many tents and what looked to be temporary buildings with smoke coming out of them. But that was not the amazing thing he was now able to see. What was truly amazing was the endless number of Barbarians that moved around in that extensive clearing.

Sebastion couldn't believe how many were there. His heart skipped a beat at the thought of the implications of it. He pushed his vision closer, and he mainly saw men and many weapons either in piles or already strapped to the man-eaters. It was evident that this was another army of Barbarians other than the one already in Torenium, which worried him greatly.

He suddenly felt the other in him that the lady called Shama was putting in the healer's thought. Sebastion pushed the thought into the power that he felt around him. His vision narrowed into a tent so fast that Sebastion thought that he would crash into it. The tent was old and looked as if it would fall apart at any moment. Sebastion could not look into the tent no matter how he concentrated on it. He pushed, but he could not get his vision in. Just then, the flap of the tent threw open, and a man with a pointed hat and long beard came out and angrily looked around. He pulled nervously at the rags he wore as clothes while looking around. Finally, the man closed his eyes and then opened them again, looking right at him. Sebastion shot backward into the sky and then down to where he was still bent over. He came back to himself so quickly that he now felt his body being thrown back. He fell into some underbrush and down a slight hill.

"By the Light!" Baran swore, coming over to help him. "Take it easy, der kid!" Baran said, reaching out a hand to him. Baran easily pulled him off the ground. "You sick 'er something?" Baran asked, concerned.

"No ... I think I'm okay," Sebastion said, feeling a little dizzy. "We're not far, my friend." He said, putting a hand on Baran's arm. "Maybe quarter day's walk that way ... not far at all." He saw Baran's face light up.

"And d'a healer?" He asked enthusiastically.

"I think I saw him. And I think somehow he may have seen me too."

"I ain't gonna per-tend to understand dat," Baran said, getting in front of the litter and picking it up. Sebastion followed suit and took his end. Baran jogged in the direction Sebastion had indicated.

They arrived a short distance away from the extensive clearing. All they could see was a mass of small fires in the darkness that looked like a sky full of bright stars. They were on a high ledge, and there was a cool breeze that washed over them as they lay on their backs sucking in air. The insects buzzed loudly, and there was the occasional bout of laughter or scream of pain below them. Sebastion suspected he knew what games they were playing below and tried to steer his mind from it.

"She's ... hardly ... breathing," Baran said, still trying to breathe. His helmet was off, and his usually thick hair was flat and soaked with sweat. "We need to find him."

Sebastion looked over at him and saw that his clothes had been nearly torn to rags from the branches and prickly bushes they had to run through to get here in the dark.

"Okay." Sebastion started and swallowed hard. "I will try to find him-" He swallowed again. "And bring him back."

"Hurry ... please hurry." Baran pleaded. Sebastion clasped the big man's shoulder as he sat on the ground and then walked towards the vast Barbarian camp.

Since his awakening at the witch's hut, he'd had some flashbacks of what happened while he was with Bashor. They were more vivid when he slept and he found that he started to prefer less and less sleep because of it. He had no desire to feel the way he did back in that dark castle. Every time his mind would take him to that time, he would push the memory down. The mere thought of it made him feel like running. He didn't know where but the feeling was so intense at times he would have run anywhere. Now was one of those times. He sat between two trees watching the Barbarian's mill around in the dimly lit clearing. He knew what he must do, but Bashor's face kept coming to him, and that made it almost impossible for his body to move.

He did not remember the conversation in its entirety, but one fact made it through to the surface. He remembered Bashor saying that he had a brother. All other details were like a dim memory from a conversation many years ago ... but not this. He was sure he said that he had once had a brother, and that intrigued him. If he had a brother, was he still alive? Was he like him, and did he also feel like he did, like he was alone? He knew he needed to have a clear head to would sneak into the Barbarian camp and find the healer undetected, but the thought would not fade. The possibility of it was too big for him to swallow into his subconscious. He if couldn't get his thoughts under control, he very well would get himself killed and not even to mention Lara and Baran, who were relying on him. He had to regain control. He remembered a trick Keeper had taught him and focused his mind and tried to pull forward the image of the stream he used to sit by as a young boy. He imagined the water as it ran across the rocks. Soon he was able to hear and see it in his mind's eye. It was so real he felt as if he could touch it. He looked up and let the cool, calming breeze next to the stream soothe him. He curiously reached out and plucked a leaf off a sapling that grew nearby. He ran his thumbs across it, feeling the veins and soft ridges of it. It felt cool and smooth and *real!*

He opened his eyes and he was back between the trees looking at the Barbarian camp again. He quickly looked around to make sure he was still alone and saw someone standing beside him. He fell to his side, reaching for his sword before he recognized the eerie green glow.

"What the dark are you doing!" He whispered harshly. Constava just stood there staring accusingly at him. "What?" He asked in the uncomfortable silence. She shook her head at him.

"I was minding my own business when suddenly I was somewhere else far away ... what is going on?" She asked.

Sebastion desperately put a finger to his lips. "Oh, stop that! No one can hear me but you." She said, crossing her arms and looking angry. "Could you please appear with clothes on from now on ... please?" Sebastion asked, looking away from her irritably and back at the Barbarians.

"How did you do that?" She asked like she was talking to a child. Sebastion looked over again and now she was wearing a type of sheer material that did little to hide her body. He thought it even made it look better.

"Nothing ... it was nothing. I was clearing my mind is all."

"So you put in two locations?" She asked back at him.

"I do not have time for this. Go back to whereever you go. I have bigger problems right now."

Constava looked up and seemed to notice where they were for the first time.

"You're going in there!" She asked.

"Yes. I have to find the healer to save Lara. Do try to pay attention, will you?" He said, reaching into his pocket and pulling the rock statue of the woman's torso out of his pocket. "I do not have time for you. Go back."

"I can help you." She said, smiling at the Barbarians.

"Thank you very much, but I think it best we stay undetected."

"I can be discrete, dragon."

"Do not call me that and get back into your ... whatever this thing is. Now!"

Constava turned to him, scrunching up her face disapprovingly. "Fine!" She said, crossing her arms again and looking very much like a sulking child. "Make sure you don't drop that." She said and disappeared. *Drop what?* He looked down at his hands and noticed he was gripping something. He turned his hand over and opened it. Inside there was the leaf he had plucked from the sapling by the stream ... where he used to live with Keeper.

I haven't got time for this!

Sebastion crept along the border, keeping to the darkest sections. He had to make some noise as he noticed several animals were also watching the man-eaters, and he didn't want them to give away his position. They mainly were rodents and some slightly larger varieties of beasts hoping for an opportunity to get at some easy food the Barbarians might leave unprotected. They ignored him for the most part if he left them alone. He had a vague idea where the tent was located from his strange experience looking from the sky and circled the camp trying to see it. He knew it should be more challenging than it was to see in the dark but like in the dark caves, he could see very well if he concentrated. The smell coming from the camp was making him sick. It smelled what he would have imagined it would have with thousands of unwashed Barbarians. It was so overpowering that he was beginning to get lightheaded from it. He was about to move again when he saw it. The tent was about a stone's throw away from him. He watched it intently and saw just a few Barbarians walking across the path every few seconds. There were a few tents on the left and right on the way to the healer's tent, but he did not see anyone coming or going out of them. He assumed this was mealtime and most of them were out getting their share. There was a scream, and that confirmed his thought. It was dinnertime.

Sebastion crept up slowly to the first set of tents and knelt behind it to listen. When he didn't hear anything, he moved to the next and so on until the healer's tent was just a few short strides away. However, the problem was that those short strides would take him out in the open, and even though there were not many people walking about, he was sure there was enough to notice him. Everyone was dressed in thick layers of hides, and he still had the clothes he had bought at Endrea. He looked more like a farmer than a Barbarian. He decided the only way to cross that distance was to have everyone who saw him think he was just another unwashed Barbarian walking by. He needed to find some hides that would disguise him. He started going from tent to tent to listen. He was at the third one before he heard what he wanted. It was the soft breathing of someone sleeping inside.

Sebastion made a small incision with his knife and looked inside. Indeed there was an old Barbarian sleeping soundly inside. An empty plate of bones lay next to him.

Already fed and cosy in his bed.

He slowly and silently made the hole bigger with his little knife. When it was big enough, he stepped inside next to the sleeping Barbarian. He knew what he had to do and his heart pounded in his chest. The number of the dead by his hand was ever-increasing, but that was not what made him nervous. No, what was causing his heart to pound was what he needed to do for it to be perfect. He had to hit the Barbarian just right so as not to have him wake up and alarm the rest of the camp. He was taught how it was done on a normal-sized man, not on a Barbarian twice a normal man's size. Sebastion raised his fist high, concentrating on the spot he had to hit. He plunged the heel of his hand downwards towards the Barbarian's nose.

The hides stunk worse than he could have imagined. His shirt had torn in many places, so it was not hard to find a few cloth pieces to put into his nose. The Barbarian did not seem to wear anything that could conceal his face, which was a problem. He looked out of the tent and watched, thinking about how he was going to hide his face. His beard was still thin and not long. He watched and noticed even the men that seemed young had a thick beard. However, at times it was hard to tell as most kept their heads down into the wooden bowls like the one that sat beside the old Barbarian he had just killed.

Wait ... that's it!

Sebastion grabbed the wooden bowl and mimicked how the others walked with darting eyes above a protective arm around their food. He watched for when the fewest amount of them walked about and headed straight for the healer's tent. He walked on his toes to give himself as much height as he could. He was thankful for his size for the first time in his life. Always Keeper had told him he was getting too big for an assassin. Though as he walked towards the decrepit tent, he knew even the disapproving Keeper would have liked his method and success in killing the Barbarian in the tent. The thought made his stomach turn.

He walked purposefully and kept his eyes on the goal. He did not know if anyone had noticed him as he kept his face low and hidden as if he was eating from the bowl. When he got to the tent, he opened the flap and entered quickly. He realized then that he had no idea what he would tell the healer inside to make him help him.

"If you're not looking for a dose of evil cast upon yea, I suggest you leave the same way you came in." The man with the pointed hat said from across the tent. He was sitting on the ground and looked to be reading something by a candle. Sebastion said nothing. He stood there looking at the man with his face still buried in his arm as if he was eating.

"Your ailment best be your hearing because if it is not..." The healer said, standing to face him. Sebastion was shocked to see the man was shorter than he. He was not a Barbarian at all. Although he had a thick beard, minus the usual body parts the Barbarians tied in, and some heavy-looking furs across his shoulders, the healer looked like he could have been anyone from the streets of Endrea. "I do not have anything for shortness so just turn around and-" He stopped then and squinted in concentration.

"YOU!" He said finally in an accusing and surprised tone.

"Speak one more loud word, and I'll take your head," Sebastion warned, pulling his sword from underneath the mountain of furs on his back. "You are the healer, yes?"

The man frowned profoundly and crossed his arms without saying a word.

"I have no time for games," Sebastion warned. "Are you the healer or not?" The man turned his head sideways and sighed out of his nose.

Pucker this! Now, what do I do?

"Listen-"Sebastion tried again, lowering his sword. "I have a hurt friend, and I need your help." The man nodded knowingly. "Well? Can you help me?" Sebastion asked, spreading his hands with the sword hanging from one of them.

"Can I?" The man said finally. "Most likely I can ... but who knows."

"Okay, *will* you help me ... *please*!"

The man rubbed his chin, thinking before responding.

"No." He said finally and turned to his book again.

"WHAT!" Sebastion whispered harshly at him in disbelief. "Listen, whoever you are, I need you to come with me ... right, PUCKERING NOW. So pack up whatever you need, and let's get moving ... NOW!" Sebastion ordered menacingly, raising his sword again.

"No." The man answered simply again and without even looking at him.

"I don't want to hurt you, but I-"

"Will?" The man finished for him, not looking at him and still reading from his book. "That is a stupid threat." He finished.

"What?" Sebastion asked, feeling a wave of uncontrollable anger rising in him.

"Stupid, I said." The man in the ridiculously large pointed hat said, looking up. "If you hurt or kill me, how will I help you?"

"So you will help me?" Sebastion asked enthusiastically.

"No." The man said again.

Sebastion pressed his palm into his forehead, trying to contain his frustration. "Is there anything I can do to have you help me?"

"Yes." The man said, still reading his book.

"And what might that be?" Sebastion asked, trying to sound calm.

"You can get me out of here."

"That's it?"

"It is not as easy as you might think." The man said, turning and facing him. "I am bound to these filthy beasts ... have been for a long time." The man in the hat explained.

"You mean you cannot leave here?" Sebastion asked, feeling a sinking feeling in his stomach.

"I cannot." The man answered thoughtfully. "But one with power could help me do it."

"Power?" Sebastion asked just a little suspiciously.

"Come now, son. Do not be coy with me. You know very well I detected your little flight from the heavens just a short while ago. That was you, yes?"

Sebastion did not know how to answer. He knew the man seemed to have seen him somehow. He did not have time to hedge as Lara might already be slipping too far for even this strange healer to save her. "Yes. Whatever you want. But PLEASE, can we go?" The man smiled.

"Whatever I want? Do you agree to help me escape? To do whatever you need to do to have me *un-bound*?"

"Yes."

"Then what are we waiting for." The man said, beaming from ear to ear. He went around stuffing various things into a pack with a wide grin. In just a few minutes, he was ready and looking at Sebastion eagerly.

"What?" Sebastion asked.

"I'm ready now." He said, smiling.

"Okay..." Sebastion said, thinking about how he was going to get him out without being seen.

"Don't tell me you don't have a plan to get us out of here?" The man said, shocked.

"Don't worry, I'll think of something," Sebastion angrily said to him.

The man dropped his bag and sighed. "I knew it was too good to be true." He said miserably.

"PICK UP THAT BAG!" Sebastion hissed at him.

"For what? You have no idea how we're going to leave ... and in case you haven't noticed, this is not exactly a high-class inn here."

"I know that!"

"Why do you not use your powers? You could just send us where we need to go." The man said, looking to be on the verge of tears now.

"Send?" Sebastion asked, confused. The man sat back down on his cot. Just then, the flap of the tent opened, and a colossal Barbarian stepped inside, filling the tent as he bent to fit.

"One of us lies newly dead and could use your -" He stopped, turning and seeing Sebastion, who looked back at him wide-eyed.

"What?" The Barbarian said, but before he could finish, Sebastion spun, slashing at the man's throat with his sword. Blood sprayed across the tent.

"What are you doing!?" The man in the hat yelled. The big Barbarian opened his mouth to scream, but all that came out was a gurgle as he fell face first to the ground. He choked for what seemed like forever until he finally died.

"That was the nephew to the Chief!" The healer said in earnest. He ran to the dying Barbarian and started speaking in a language Sebastion could not understand.

"We're leaving!" Sebastion said, grabbing the man's arm.

"What! You will not get five strides before the entire camp is using your head for target practice."

"Enough of that! Grab your bag and let's go." Sebastion made his best impression of how he saw the Barbarians walking. He held his chin close to his chest to hide his face and walked like he was not to be messed with. He held the healer's arm firmly in his grasp and pulled him along when he was too slow. They headed towards the tent where he had killed the sleeping man hoping no one was there waiting for them. They were not that lucky. Two Barbarians were eyeing them suspiciously as they walked towards them. Sebastion purposely put the healer in front of him to hide his face.

The two who watched them approach knew something was amiss as the Barbarian who went to get the healer should have been towering over the healer. Sebastion knew he only had one chance at the surprise and marched the man ahead of him quickly before them could raise the alarm ... or even pull a weapon free. The one closest to them bent sideways to see around them and looked at Sebastion's face. Sebastion hid, and that was enough to have the Barbarian pull his fur aside and pull out what looked to be a thick stick with sharpened bones attached at different angles. Sebastion shot forward, swinging. He aimed at the hand and easily severed it. The Barbarian watched his hand drop to the ground with the weapon. The shock was enough to give Sebastion time to shove his sword through the Barbarian's neck.

The other Barbarian, however, moved quickly and kicked around his friend. His big foot landed on Sebastion's chest and sent him sailing backward, where he finally hit the ground with a thud. When he was able to open his eyes again, he saw a club headed for his head. He rolled and felt the impact the club made on the ground next to him. The Barbarian put a foot on his chest again to hold him still and raised the club again with a broad smile on his face. Sebastion shot his hand into his pocket and desperately felt around. He felt the coolness of the stone and pulled it out with a jerk.

"Constava! Constava!" He yelled.

"What is it?" Constava answered irritably as she materialized next to him. She looked down at Sebastion and followed the giant foot to the Barbarian holding the now still club.

"I think I see someone who needs a kiss." She said flawlessly in the Barbarian language. She seductively shook her body back and forth. The Barbarian smiled, and Constava flew herself to him and locked lips. The Barbarian first pressed into her passionately and then his eyes flew open. He tried to pull away but Constava did not move. He dropped the club and, with two big arms, pushed at her head. Constava did not move. She was like stone. Then there was a wet sucking noise and the barbarian screamed out of his nose. His face went white and then slacked as everything inside of him was sucked out. Sebastion closed his eyes, not wanting to see or hear the sucking and feeling the foot's weight on his chest get lighter and lighter ... then it was gone. Sebastion opened his eyes and saw Constava wiping her full lips with the back of her hand. She looked down at Sebastion and then at the healer ... she smiled.

"NO!" Sebastion said, getting to his feet. "We need him." Constava disgustedly looked at Sebastion. Just then, they heard someone stop short to look at them. It was another Barbarian, but his eyes did not even see the other Barbarians dead on the ground. His eyes were only on Constava. She looked over at Sebastion with desperation in her eyes.

"Okay. You did good." He said, picking up his sword and the healer's bag. "One more ... but don't let anyone see you." Constava and the Barbarian ran to each other like they were lovers. Sebastion didn't stay around to watch what would come next. He held the sword and bag in one hand and the healer in the other. He dragged the man through the forest more than led him.

"AMAZING!" The man kept saying as he stumbled over roots and brush in the darkness. "You do know they will be looking for you for what you did that to their men back there." Sebastion said, pulling the healer off the ground as he stumbled for the uncountable time.

"We're almost there," Sebastion added encouragingly. "Just try to keep your feet for just a short while more." He felt the adrenaline and knew that once he stopped and his muscles relaxed, they might not be working again until he got to sleep. He spotted Baran looking in their direction in the darkness. It was too dark for Baran to see them, but Sebastion saw him perfectly. He had his short sword in his hand, and he had to find a way to let him know he was coming without getting that short sword plunging at his head. Sebastion whispered,

"We're coming," And sent the words ahead with the same power he had used to find the encampment. He saw Baran jump and defensively throw his arms around himself before falling over.

Oops. Sebastion thought with a pang of remorse.

"What the dark blasted was dat!" Baran asked Sebastion as they entered the opening. The healer immediately went to Lara and put his hand on her head and shut his eyes. He opened them again, shaking his head.

"What?" Baran asked, coming beside him.

"I have not seen a woman besides a Barbarian in quite some time." The healer said, looking Lara over.

"Maybe dat this will be your last," Baran said, looming over the man. The healer looked up at Baran, and Baran winked as he impatiently tapped his sword onto his hand.

"I mean no disrespect-"

"Her name is Lara." Baran interrupted. "And she more d'en just a woman." Baran leaned in closer to the healer. "She be my very best friend in this puckering screwed world ... you get that?"

"Got it." The healer said, smiling and looking back at Lara.

"Can you help her?" Sebastion asked.

The healer put his hand on Lara's chest and closed his eyes again. Baran glanced over at Sebastion, and he made a motion for the big man to relax. He knew he needed to get Baran preoccupied with something.

"There may be some of those Barbarians coming. Can you listen over there and let us know if anyone approaches?" Baran nodded, looking as if he was fully aware of the ruse.

"She is nearly gone." The healer said, looking up. Sebastion could feel Baran's eyes on him from the trees.

"Is there nothing you can do?" He asked, feeling a cold chill coming into him. "Are you not the healer?"

"I can heal, yes. But that is not all I am. You may call me Sorko."

"Fine," Sebastion answered irritably. "Sorko, then. Can you help her?"

Sorko rubbed his neck, looking at the woman before him. He knew she was barely breathing and would be dead in the next few hours at most. "Here is the problem." He said, standing and straightening his pointy hat that had flopped again. "I could bring her back. The problem does not lie there ... exactly."

260

"Go on," Sebastion said, trying to sound patient.

Sorko crossed his arms and looked at Sebastion in the same way the teachers did at the school. Sebastion instantly found it uncomfortable.

"The problem is that when they come back from being so far gone, they don't always come back themselves or ... alone."

"Now, what does d'at mean?" Baran asked, making Sebastion jump a little as he didn't hear the big man approach him from behind.

"It means there is a risk that goes beyond us here. I am not sure if it would be wise to bring her or whatever else comes with her back here." Sebastion had to only think of the promise he made to his uncle to formulate an answer.

"Do it." He said simply.

"You must think about-"

"Do it, or I swear to everything and anything that I will drag you right back to that camp."

Sorko looked into Sebastion's eyes as if looking for something. At last, he must have found what he wanted and sat back down next to Lara.

"My powers are limited, and this may take a few minutes," Sorko said, rolling up his sleeves.

"A few minutes!" Baran asked excitedly. "You mean you can heal her, and she can be better in just a few minutes?"

"Yes, of course. I am a shadow of what I once was, but I can still heal a body. Her *body* will be well..."

Sebastion did not miss the point Sorko was making. "Did the Barbarians bring things back with them?" Sebastion suddenly asked,

261

not knowing where the thought came from, but an instant later knew it must be coming from Shama, the dragon.

Sorko curiously looked up at Sebastion.

"That is a very pertinent question, my boy. The answer is rather complicated but suffice it to say that they seldom come back as the ones' left when the Barbarian's die. The spirit that leaves always has another battle to fight for the body he wishes to reclaim. The difference, however, is that it is almost always another Barbarian's twisted spirit that comes forth. The distorted does not easily attract the others."

"Others?" Sebastion asked suspiciously.

"I think I better get started here," Sorko said, looking at Lara's face.

"Yes, of course."

"We will speak of it again. I hope..." Sorko closed his eyes and held Lara's head at the temples. Baran and Sebastion exchanged worried glances at Sorko's last comment.

I hope? What does he think could come back with her?

Sorko started chanting some words that Sebastion didn't understand, but strangely they began to make sense. Sebastion curiously watched the healer as the creases in his forehead deepened as he concentrated. Sebastion understood the words, but they seemed to fade again as soon as they entered his mind. He tried to make his mind keep the meaning, but the more he tried, the quicker the words disappeared. He watched as Sorko breathed in a big breath and blew it out over Lara's body. Sebastion looked over at Baran and then looked at Sorko with a raised brow and a sceptical look on his face. Sorko looked over at Sebastion and miserably shook his head. Sebastion shrugged, not knowing what to do.

"You boys want to stop with your adolescent looks and get yourselves prepared for who's coming?" Sorko asked like an annoyed parent.

"I been ready to see my friend from da moment she fell," Baran said, stepping beside the healer. "And how do we know you even mean to bring *her* back?"

"You don't," Sorko said, opening his eyes and looking up at the big man.

"Oh … I see d'en." Baran said, pulling his sword free.

"WAIT!" Sebastion said, pushing Baran back away from Sorko, who was getting up to stand.

"I've been around more intimidation than you can imagine. Do not even presume you scare me one bit with your fat body and little table knife there."

"Table knife, d'en?" Baran asked, trying to step forward with Sebastion holding him back with his hands on his chest. "How about we see how you like da table knife in your black heart, healer? Let us see what a good healer you really are? How about dat, d'en?"

Sorko laughed, and that just made Baran even angrier. "Dat's it!" Baran yelled wide-eyed. Sebastion's feet slipped on the ground as Baran stepped forward.

"You look just like my father." Lara's voice said then.

They all looked over to see Lara standing, watching them curiously. She stared at Sebastion.

"Dat you?" Baran asked, squinting at his old friend.

"Do not worry, Bull," Lara said, straight-faced. "She is still here with me."

The three of them stared at her. Sebastion still had his hands on Baran's chest, and Sorko had a part of his pointy hat nearly covering one of his eyes.

"If Lara is d'er with you ... d'en, who are you?" Baran asked.

"My name is Ryder." She said, stepping closer to them. "And I am this boys ... no ... man's father."

"My father?" Sebastion asked, standing up and then stepping back from her ... or him. "What have you done with my friend?" Sebastion asked, angrily crossing his arms.

"She has allowed me this short time to spend with my son," Ryder said through Lara's body. "Unfortunately, as much as I would like to, we cannot spend our time getting to know each other ... or at least you getting to know what I was."

Sebastion saw a sad look pass over Lara's face. "How is it you are here?" Sebastion asked suspiciously.

"That one could probably explain it better," Ryder said, indicating Sorko with one of Lara's long delicate fingers. "But I will give you my version. I died in a way that left my spirit here and not willing to cross over, you see. My head was full of possibilities and..." Ryder took a moment to look up at the sky to compose himself. Lara's dark hair hung around her face. Sebastion knew Lara was always brushing her hair away when it hung in her face and thought it strange to see it there a mess. "I died on my way to see your mother. I had just found out she was pregnant with you, and I could not wait to hold her in my arms again. You see ... I loved her very much. More than you will ever know.

264

And I have been with her many times since the day I died. I was there when you were born." Lara stepped closer, and this time Sebastion did not move. "I was there when you and your brother were born, Sebastion."

"My brother?" Sebastion asked, wide-eyed. What he remembered from Bashor's castle was right.

"Yes," Ryder said now, with Lara's eyes filling with tears. "Oh, yes. I watched him die. The King took his life like he has taken mine and so many others. I watched my son, your brother, slip from your world to mine, unable to do anything to help him. If I still had a heart, it would have turned to stone that day." Ryder reached out and took Sebastion's hand. Sebastion looked into Lara's dark eyes, trying to see the man who claimed to be his father.

"That is history, and there will be time to hear of it. But there is something else you must hear, and I do not have much time as the longer I stay it gets harder for the one who does occupy this body to come back." Sebastion felt more than saw Baran shift uneasily. "There is something you must do, my son." Ryder looked at Sebastion's hand in his own. "I am sorry to give you this weight, but there is no other way." He looked up at Sebastion, who was once again searching Lara's eyes. "This world is suffocating. I see it where I dwell now. I see it every day. The magic, for lack of a better term, has been captured by them." Ryder nodded towards Sorko. Sorko didn't say a word, but Sebastion thought he did see a pained look cross the healer's face. "They found a way to contain the magic and keep almost all of it for themselves. This world lives on it like it does the sun and rain. The world will die without it, and yet the others keep it for themselves like some greedy child not willing to share their toys."

"What does that have to do with me?" Sebastion interrupted.

"You have already met Bashor," Ryder said rather than answer.

"Yes. We have met, but I do not remember all of the details."

"Probably best if you do not," Ryder said, nodding Lara's head. "When he finds his way to me, I will have many things to repay him. Most of our family's pains come from that evil mage. Even your brother's death ... though it was not his hand physically, be sure it was surely his will."

"I still do not see what it is that I must do?" Sebastion asked again, feeling tyhe tiredness coming back to his body now.

"Son, you must release the magic and let the world take its first breath in far too many years. You are the only one that can save us all from ourselves."

"I am nobody. How can I do something like that? Why me?"

"Because you are the only one that can. You have that around your neck to aid you and, more importantly, you are a Loyal."

"A Loyal? I am not a Loyal. I am a man without a home. Where is my mother? Why has she let me grow up alone and with a wicked, cruel man? Why have all the other Loyals abandoned me!" Sebastion asked, stepping forward now. "A Loyal? A Loyal! That is ridiculous! Why should I do anything for you ... or for that matter, for this world? It seems to me that so far in my experience this world hasn't got much worth saving."

"I admit you have not had things easy, Sebastion. But there are still things worth saving. For one, your mo-"

"Mother? My mother? HA! What has she done for me?" Sebastion asked, feeling the pain of his own words prick his skin.

Lara shot in front of him so fast he was not able to move away. "Listen to me, boy. And I see now that you are still a boy. Do not judge her without first knowing *why*. Yours is a sad tale, but do you think you are the only one to have things hard? Do you think those people you brought out of the caves had it easy while they watched their loved ones being slaughtered before their eyes? If you were not my son, I would slap some sense into you." Ryder crossed his arms. "But you are my son, and that means I know you are not speaking with your head but with your heart. It has been our family's curse and greatest strength having such strong passion and love. Find your mother, and you will see why things are as they are. I will tell you this, however. You share the enemy with my uncle; he is mine as well and has been for a long time. Give Bashor a visit and know it will be my hand with yours that plunges my families' sword through his cold and twisted heart. Tell Bashor that Ryder Loyal gives his regards and will be seeing him real soon here in death."

"Father," Sebastion said, looking at the ground and feeling so tired he could fall to his knees. "You have not told me how to do this thing you have asked. Even if I could, I cannot if I do not know what it is."

"It is simple, my son." Ryder smiled, putting Lara's hands on Sebastion's face. "Destroy the thing that keeps the magic prisoner. You *must* kill all of the lesser gods and the twins."

"WHAT!" Sebastion could only spit out through his slack jaw.

"You cannot be serious!" Sorko asked with eyes as wide as Sebastion.

267

"My time here is far too limited not to be serious," Ryder said back to Sorko. "You have been long enough removed that if your immortality can be separated, you may not be a threat. But if your immortality remains..."

"I must be killed?" Sorko asked.

"Do not play the victim with me, Sorko," Ryder growled. Sebastion thought it strange how the anger in Lara's face could be used by someone else. "You have lived longer than most could even believe. You and the rest of your kind need to release the stranglehold you have on this world. You do not even know the effects your meddling has had on the world as a whole. There are many more places like Torenium and what you call the Outer Territories."

"Yes, but not much," Sorko muttered.

"YOU IGNORANT FOOL!" Ryder yelled, wide-eyed. "You have visited with your powers, what? A thousand years ago? Do you not think things have changed? Even with your raping of the power that holds this world together?" Ryder disgustedly shook Lara's head. "You call yourselves gods. You are nothing but ignorant children with a stolen gift."

"Do not think I don't agree with you, eh ... Ryder, is it?"

Ryder said nothing. "I have no reason to hold any favor for those that have abandoned me. I would enjoy seeing their demise. And so, I would suspect, would my brother."

"Your brother?" Ryder asked, interested now.

"Do you believe I was the only one to endure the twins' treachery and live?" Sorko asked, staring into the trees as if looking for something there.

"Milnor lives?"

"He does."

"Then will he, like you, help my son put back what was stolen?" Ryder asked, excited.

"I can only speculate that he would. I will be more than happy to seek out my revenge, and I'm sure he would as well. If enough of him remains, that is."

"What do you mean?" Ryder asked. Lara's body started to convulse slightly.

"The great spider Fok-Orga Tung holds him. His situation is far worse than mine. I am not even sure his mind could have endured all this time." Sorko said, removing his hat and exposing his bald head underneath. His long hair grew in a horseshoe shape around the balding spot. Lara's body started to shake more and Ryder took a step to regain his balance.

"Sebastion, my son. Find the spider and release Milnor. He and Sorko will help you. Together with your friends, you can destroy the ones that falsely call themselves gods. This world is worth saving." Ryder shook slowly and fell to one knee.

"I-I don't know." Sebastion could only reply.

"Kirra is worth saving, your mother. She too will help you. Be gentle with her, Sebastion." Ryder fell forward, catching himself with an outstretched arm. "She does not know you are alive. Be understanding. Do not tell her we have spoken. Tell her to find another to love and live what remains of her life … tell her to be happy."

"Yes." Sebastion could only reply, seeing the struggle.

"I am … proud … of … you." Lara's body suddenly stood up tall and angrily looked around. She brushed aside her black hair.

"You two look like a couple of fish sucking air." She said, pulling her long black hair back behind her head. "Which one of you stole my binding?"

Baran walked to her and she opened her hand, expecting to be handed her binding for her hair. Instead, Baran scooped her off the ground and hugged her tightly. She huffed out a breath, pushing on his big shoulders. "You're going break my damn ribs, you bull-headed…" But then she started to laugh and hugged him back. Baran laughed, choking back tears.

"Are those two together?" Sorko asked, looking confused.

"Not exactly," Sebastion said, smiling from ear to ear.

"I do not think Baran and I can keep walking," Sebastion said, only a few minutes after leaving the encampment overlook. Sorko reached out a hand to touch Sebastion's head, but Sebastion had a knife to his throat before his hand got anywhere near him.

"I can help you," Sorko said, holding his chin up so it wouldn't get pricked by the knife.

"Help from a lesser god? I think I will pass." He said, pushing the knife a bit more.

Sorko rolled his eyes and stepped away. "If I wanted to harm you, you would-"

"-be dead already." Sebastion finished for him.

Sorko made a disgusted sound in the back of his throat. "Fine, then. Let's rest and let our friends get closer."

"You are a bitter little god, ain't ya?" Baran said, smiling as he sat heavily on the soft grass in the dim light of dawn. Sorko rolled his eyes again and took off his hat to wipe his sweating bald head. "We rest, and then we set off."

"And where might d'at be?" Baran asked suspiciously.

"Get some rest. Even big smelly bulls need their sleep." Sebastion said, good-naturedly.

"Oh, pucker off," Baran suggested, lying down on his back and closing his eyes.

Sebastion couldn't help but smile at that as he dosed off for a much-needed and well-deserved rest.

In just a couple of hours, they were up and moving quickly through the forest again. Sebastion felt better than he had in a long time. His body felt as if he had slept for two days. He suspected that was not natural, but the man-eaters were getting closer. As much as he would have liked to punish Sorko, he grudgingly was thankful for the feeling.

"Which way are we heading?" Lara asked as they jogged down a deer trail.

"Back," Sebastion simply replied.

Lara looked at Baran and he shrugged.

"Back where?" She asked as she jumped over a log that lay across the trail.

"Back to Torenium, to the Great City."

"Ohhhh, I see." Lara said worriedly. "Last I checked, the Barbarians were on their way there," she added.

"That's where Killian and Morakye are going. I told Killian I would bring you to him just as soon as you were better."

"He said he wanted to see me right away?" Lara asked in what Sebastion thought was a strange voice that made him look over.

"Of course." He said simply.

"Did he say anything else?" She asked.

Baran groaned miserably.

"He made me promise that I would bring you back to him," Sebastion said, pushing aside a branch as he jogged.

"He did?" She asked excitedly.

"Now you two do know what we have 'der chasing us, right?" Baran asked, nearly tripping on a root that was poking out into the trail. He swore bitterly, re-adjusting his Helmut.

"Where is he now?" Sorko asked. "-this uncle of yours?"

"I would imagine he is somewhere still crossing the mountains." Sebastion dubiously shot back. "I could not know where exactly he is."

"Actually, you could. And have already done it before." Sorko said, jogging behind them like he never ran out of air or was ever fatigued. "Do you not remember how you found me?"

"I remember," Sebastion answered shortly. "But it does not matter because we are going to the great city."

"I thought we were going to find Milnor? Is that not what your father asked? Was that not the quest?" Sorko asked.

Sebastion slipped down a hill, losing his balance. Lara nearly landed on top of him.

"I do not plan to take on this quest, *lesser* god," Sebastion said with thick contempt. "I intend to return Lara to my uncle as I promised. I will then collect my Fangor brother and M..." He stopped, then looked back shyly. "I want no part of the god's plans. I will tell you the same thing I told the Lady of Light-"

"HOLD ON!" Lara yelled out as she skidded to a halt. "You *met* the Lady of Light?" She asked, wide-eyed.

Sebastion stopped to look at her as well. "Yes."

"The god? The goddess of light? You spoke to her?"

"She was the one who told me how to help you." He answered, looking through the trees behind them for any movement.

"The Lady of ight cared whether I lived or died?"

"Well ... actually, it was Ray-I mean Killian, who yelled at her about not helping you. He was pretty upset with her."

"Killian yelled at the Lady of Light because of me." Lara started as if seeing how the words sounded to herself. She then shook her head with amazement. She had doubts the goddess even existed, and now she finds out that not only does she exist but she also knows her name.

"I guess I shouldn't be so surprised. We already met the dark lord and now travel with a one-time destroyed lesser god. So why not have casual conversations with the Lady of Light? Oh, and let us not forget, I also had to share my body with a man who's been dead for years. That *was* a fun time!"

"I think she needs to rest," Sorko said, coming to stand beside her. "I can repair the body, but the mind needs rest as well, and there is nothing I can do for that."

"You know what, *Sorko*," Lara said, her face red. "I don't think I like you when you talk about me like I'm not standing right in front of you. What do you think about that Sor-ko?" But before he could answer her, an arrow shot through his body and protruded out the other side. They stared at it in shocked silence.

"Well, that's rather annoying ... I must say," Sorko said calmly, looking down. He reached up to it and pulled it out with a jerk. They all winced at the sucking sound as it came out. "I suggest we leave this discussion for later and run. What do you think?" They all started running again, with Sorko running in the rear as if nothing had ever happened to him.

When they stopped again, only Sorko was not gasping for air. They had expended a lot of energy to climb a hill to see those that were chasing them. When Sebastion was able to breathe, he climbed onto a pile of rocks to get higher and stared down at the trees behind them. The others heard his groan and did not need to hear what was there.

"So much for-them-giving up," Lara said, still trying to catch her breath.

"They will not give up until they find us," Sorko said, sitting comfortably against a tree. "My gifts are precious to them, and they will be ... steadfast in their pursuit."

"Then why don't we give 'em back." Baran offered. "We got what we wanted from 'em."

"Because, my portly friend." Sorko put in angrily. "It was my powers they used to make themselves the abomination they have become. A time long ago, the man-eaters were nothing more than a tribe of misguided Eaterners that had peculiar eating habits."

"Peculiar? D'ats one way of putting it." Baran interrupted.

"Be that as it may. That small group was nothing before they were given to me and the trace of magic I had left. They have twisted a

274

certain piece of immortality and have become the living travesty that they are today. Their kind was not meant for such long life."

"You saying they can't be killed?" Sebastion asked. "I have killed a few already, and they looked pretty dead to me."

"They die and I regenerate the body, and ... someone comes back," Sorko said, shrugging. "That is all I know of it."

"Or all you will tell of it," Lara said, getting up and stretching.

"Perhaps," Sorko added as he closed his eyes and spread his hands. They all immediately felt better.

"I know a way that our friends may not follow."

"Let me guess-" Sebastion started.

"They will catch up sooner or later. It is our only chance to lose them."

"You two want ta' share that bit of information?" Baran asked, getting up and hoisting his pack onto his back.

"You want us to find your brother, right?" Sebastion asked.

"I cannot help that circumstances leads us in that direction. It is the most prudent decision considering the present circumstances." Sorko offered unapologetically.

"Conveniently, that is our only hope," Sebastion said, shaking his head.

"So, what's it d'at would slow down a party of man-eating Barbarians, anyway?" Baran asked.

"Something that *eats* the man-eater Barbarian," Sorko said back, starting in another direction.

"Er, something that *eats* 'em? That's our only hope? Ain't you smart fellas able t'a come up with some'n else?" Baran asked, not hiding the worry in his voice and trying to catch up with them as they took off.

"Come on, Bull," Lara said, pushing the big man towards the way they were now headed. "We made it this far ... besides, how bad can something be that enjoys killing Barbarians?" Lara caught Sorko's eye and didn't like the look he gave her when she said that.

How bad indeed, Sorko thought as he adjusted his hat.

They ran on throughout the day and stopped at dusk, feeling like they had slept the whole day. Sorko gave them endurance and they knew they had to accept it or be overrun. Where they were now the trees were taller and further apart. The soft pine needles made running easier than the thick brush that had covered the ground when they started. However, the trees did not provide much cover if the Barbarians caught up with them.

Sebastion saw the steep dip in the land ahead of him and ran towards it as he had done many times already this day. The others followed him, trusting his uncanny ability to know where he was going. Even Sorko did not say a word as Sebastion led them in one direction and then another. The truth was that he had no idea where he was going. He was running by feeling alone. When he thought he should turn, he would turn. He did not hesitate but just ran on trusting what was inside him.

He suddenly felt the air around him get considerably cooler, and the feeling inside telling him where to go screamed STOP. He stopped, sliding on the pine needles and falling on his backside. Lara was beside him, with her sword in her hand, as soon as he hit the ground. She looked in all directions, ready for whatever was about to happen.

"What is it, lad?" Baran asked, throwing his pack down and searching the area with his eyes.

"We're here," Sorko said simply.

Lara thought she detected a hint of worry in the healer's voice and looked over at him. Her suspicions were confirmed as Sorko looked up at the trees, rubbing his hands together nervously.

"What are we looking for?" She asked him. Sorko looked at her but did not reply. "Sebastion, what is going on?"

"Shama said to stop."

"Who is Shama?" She asked, confused-looking around.

"Um, the voice inside of me."

"You gave it a name?" She asked, looking down at him with a raised brow.

"It's a long story."

"The dragon." Sorko put in, coming to stand next to them.

Lara shook her head and rubbed her eyes. "Are you fatigued?" Sorko asked her.

"No. That's not the problem; let's focus on the here and now. Like why we stopped, and why you are looking into the trees like we are going to be attacked any moment?"

"This is the home of Fok-Orga Tung," Sorko said, whispering as if the trees could hear him.

"I's don't suppose d'at is the name of the local baker?" Baran asked, following Sorko's gaze into the trees.

Sebastion got up off the ground and brushed himself off. "That's the name of the thing that is keeping Milnor prisoner. The name is in

277

the ancient language of Fatuga, and it roughly translates to 'The one that eats life.'"

"D'a thing eats life?" Baran asked, stepping closer to Sebastion and Lara.

"Sort of ... I think."

"The description is accurate if not a little obscure," Sorko said, still searching the trees. "The translation is correct. The-" He was about to repeat the name but changed his mind. "-creature lives off the fluids of the living."

"Like a spider." Lara offered.

"Not exactly," Sorko said, shaking his head. "It is not only immortality that is used by ... it. It also has found a way to use the magic to extend the life of its victims." They watched as Sorko's face became suddenly sad. "The magic is warped in the body of it. It has become something that we didn't believe could exist in the world." Sebastion thought he now saw regret on Sorko's face. "We thought the world was an oyster that we could crack. I'm afraid your father may be right, my boy. We may have changed things in a way that may never be fixed. Fok-Orga Tung and the Barbarians are just the beginning of what is to come. There is a ... sort of life force. It is affected by everything we do. We thought we could keep things balanced ourselves, but we were fools. Children playing with fire is all we were. Now everything is being thrown into chaos. Creatures like the one we are going to meet will be everywhere. The magic was the glue that held this world together, and now it's ... finding a new way back. I fear it is finding a darker path. A path we might call ... evil."

"Were you not one of those that created good and evil?" Sebastion asked.

"Some of us may have been called that, but we were just playing games in one realm of good and evil. Even the dark lord is just a flake of snow in the coming storm. A storm that did not come from us but is in response to us. What we are about to do to ready for the storm will not make a difference.

"Damn your storm and damn all this talk of things beyond our control, healer … lesser god … or whatever you call yourself now," Sebastion said, stepping closer to him. "All I want now is to get my friends back together and keep them safe. To dark puckering hell with the rest of it."

"Sorry to say, my boy," Sorko added sadly. "But I have a feeling you are the eye of that storm. You and your friends here." He said the last looking around.

"Alright, d'en." Baran interrupted, trying to lighten things. "I thought we gonna be squashing bugs or some'n, already."

"I'm with the Bull," Lara added. "And by the way. Has anyone thought of going *around* this buggy thing?"

"It knows we are here and will not allow it," Sorko said.

"Great," Lara said sarcastically. "And when were you going to tell us we had no choice but to fight it?"

"He wasn't. He wanted us here so we could free his brother, right?" Sebastion asked the healer.

Sorko said nothing and started looking in the trees again.

"I am t'ankful for healing my friend here, but I got ta' say-" Baran was cut short when Sebastion shot up a finger for silence.

279

"It's here." He said simply, pulling his sword from his back.

They formed a circle, looking for any movement. The sun was going down, and the shadows made it harder to decipher a shape in the trees. The birds they heard were few and far off. It was almost dead silent while they prepared to confront Fok-Orga Tung.

They heard it at once—the heavy footfalls of someone running towards them. Not far off, they saw a Barbarian man awkwardly running between the trees. His arms seemed to be bound to his sides with white rope. He stumbled once and got up and ran on as if the dark lord himself was at his heels. As he got closer, they could see that there was also white rope around his mouth so that he couldn't speak. Ten paces away, he stopped, looking at something they couldn't see. Then what looked like a long black spear shot out and went through the man's body. The Barbarian didn't even seem to notice the spear and stared, transfixed, at what was hidden from them by the trees. They watched as the man was lifted the length of the tree to the very top. Still, the Barbarian in the white rope stared. Then, in a flash, he was pulled into the branches at the top of the tree beyond their sight.

They could not take their eyes from the spot. There was suddenly the sound of something crashing onto the tree above them. Leaves and dead sticks fell on them, and then they saw the body of the Barbarian crashing on the limbs of the tree on the way down. They jumped as the man hit the ground with a thud right where they had been standing.

"We cannot kill it unless you separate Milnor from it," Sorko said to Sebastion, quickly looking down at the dead man.

"How do I do that?" Sebastion angrily asked back.

"Use the crystal, Sebastion. It is the only way!" Sorko said, stepping farther away from the tree.

"What do we do?" Lara asked, still looking up at the tree.

"You hope that your friend does what he has to," Sorko answered.

"Well, ain't gonna just let no creepy-crawly thing attack us and do nothing," Baran said, stepping up to Sebastion.

Just then, the branches moved and something large and dark fell from the tree. It hit the ground with a thump and a cloud of dust. When the dust moved away, Sebastion was looking at a spider about the size of a large cow. It faced him, unmoving.

"Why d'ay always have to be spiders?" Baran asked, staring and exasperated. "Why it ain't it ever giant kittens or butterflies or something?"

"Baran ... step back ... slowly," Sebastion commanded in a whisper. Baran started to refuse. "This is not a request. Do it ... do it now."

Baran did as he was told and slowly lifted his foot. Fok-Orga Tung moved slightly, and Sebastion stepped in front of his friend.

"A little puckering faster, Baran," Sebastion swore under his breath. Baran quickly moved back with the others.

"Release Milnor and we will leave you unharmed. You have my word." Sebastion tried. The spider jerked up as if surprised. Then it shook and took two steps back. It reached its long front legs up into the air and let out an ear-piercing screech before rolling on its back and convulsing.

"What's happening?" Sebastion asked, stepping back, confused.

"I have no idea," Sorko answered, just as confused.

Sebastion watched as the four corners of Fok-Orga Tung's torso seemed to be pulling apart. He could hear bones snapping. Tendons and muscles were pulled apart like snapping saplings. It let out another scream as the four corners finally split apart.

Sebastion looked to the centre as blood splashed to the ground and thought he could see something inside when two eyes opened on a face that was now there. Sebastion took several steps back, raising his sword.

"What the-"

"I-am ... Milnor." The face said to him. "Please ... help me!"

Sebastion heard a gasp behind him and looked back to see Sorko stepping forward with his hand over his mouth. Tears started to run down his face. "Brother?" He asked, coming closer.

"Sorko ... could that be you?" The face soaked in gore asked from inside the trembling spider body.

"Oh, yes, brother. It is I ... we come to help... Oh, Milnor. What can we do?"

"Please, brother ... please release me ... there is not much of me left ... kill me if you must but release me from this horror..." The bloodied face pleaded.

Sorko wept, falling to his knees. He looked up to Sebastion with his hands together, begging.

"Please ... please help him. I cannot look upon him like this." He grabbed Sebastion's pant leg. "Strike them both dead if you must, but do not leave him like this!"

"I thought you said I had to separate them?" Sebastion asked, trying to pull away uncomfortably.

"Yes-yes separate them! Only do something!" Sorko cried.

Milnor screamed, and Sebastion looked over and saw it was his face now being pulled apart this time. It cracked and flesh stretched and pulled apart.

"DO SOMETHING!" Sorko yelled.

Sebastion did not know what to do. He grabbed the crystal around his neck in his fist and looked around, desperately not knowing. Milnor screamed again in unbearable pain; out of desperation, Sebastion shot forward, letting go of the crystal, and tried to pull the face back together. Milnor silenced at once as Sebastion saw with surprise what he was doing was working. Milnor stared up at him in shock. Sebastion watched as the flesh did not only come back together but became pink and normal. Sebastion experimented by pulling slightly harder, and Milnor's head came out of the spider's body, followed by his neck.

"YES-YES!" Sorko shouted behind them.

Sebastion pulled until the man's arms popped out. Milnor grabbed Sebastion's hands, pulling himself as well now, all the time staring into Sebastion's eyes in awe. Sebastion gave one final tug, and Milnor's naked body dropped to the ground. Fok-Orga Tung righted itself immediately and screamed. This time it was not pain ... it was pure rage.

Sorko ran up and grabbed Milnor's wrist, and pulled him away.

"It's mortal again," Sorko said when his brother was far enough away. "It can be killed."

"I said I would not harm it if it let Milnor go."

"It did not let him go. You *pulled* him out!" Sorko angrily yelled back.

"Be that as it may ... if it does not attack us, then we will not harm it." Sebastion started to back away, and as he did, several arrows landed where he had just been standing. Everyone turned, including Fok-Orga Tung.

Five Barbarians were running towards them with weapons raised. They yelled, rushing them until they realized what was there with them. Sebastion suddenly had the image of Fok-Orga Tung eating the Barbarians, their large bodies wrapped in webbing. He gently pushed the thought to the spider. Fok-Orga Tung looked back at him with its huge hair-covered eyes as if knowing it was he giving him the idea.

"More to eat..." Sebastion shrugged at the monster.

"More da' what?" Baran asked, looking around, confused.

Sebastion pushed another message. Milnor was coming with them, and if the spider insisted on fighting, it would die today.

"Let's go!" Sebastion yelled, spreading his arms and prodding them to run.

"What about d'at?" Baran asked, looking at the spider as it lowered itself to spring.

"It prefers Barbarians." Sebastion said over his shoulder moving away.

"You sure about d'at?" Baran asked, unconvinced.

"It ... told me. I haven't time to explain. Let's go!" Sebastion led the way as they ran. Lara, Baran, Sorko, and Milnor, running with a blanket held around his shoulders. It was all they had to spare and he made do. Sebastion knew they would have to stop eventually as the man also had no shoes and the ground was littered with sharp rocks.

As he ran, he suddenly had the image of Miska, and he started to get excited with the thought of seeing her again. He had found the healer, and Lara was on her feet again, regardless of the strange encounter with the ghost of his dead father. He now travelled with the healer and had also saved his brother from a giant man-eating spider. He travelled with two more which, by the way, were once the lesser gods that were supposed to have been destroyed more years ago than he could even imagine. All he knew is he had done what he was supposed to have done and more. There was nothing left to keep him from getting to Miska. He knew he should have chased after her from the beginning and was ready to do the right thing. He was going to the great city to be with her no matter what. He did not give a damn about his strange lineage, Barbarians, or missions to kill gods. There was only one crucial thing and nothing would keep him from it. He was going to find her. Several times he heard his companions behind him swear as they tripped over rocks or roots, but he pressed on.

With the help of Sorko's magic, they stopped infrequently. Sorko was able to use his blanket to make Milnor suitable clothing for the time being. Baran had some rabbit furs tucked into his pack and they tied them into boots. Milnor said little, but when he looked at Sebastion, they could see the ambivalence in his eyes. Sebastion saw none of it, however. He held the image of Miska firmly in his mind and marched forward.

CHAPTER 24
The Blood Army

The wind seemed to bite to the bone. Every time a branch snapped back and hit the flesh, it felt like being flogged on bare flesh. The big thick trees surrounding the army had only the leaves that had forgotten to die and blow away in the wind. Even the sun seemed to give in the coming winter. The days were dim and dreary. The few birds that flew overhead would chirp indignantly at the army as they flew off to better weather. It was as if they laughed at the pathetic army of skinny men in rags.

Killian did not mind the flocks of little birds overhead so much. As he marched in front of his pathetic blood army, what worried him were the large, seemingly well-fed vultures that enthusiastically and continuously flew over them. That made him nervous. Twice he had steered the armies away from the way they were going, and both times the paths he was taking took him right back. He was sure he was going in different directions each time, but...

They had been marching now for many days. Each night, he would send Morakye ahead with his scouts to find a suitable place to settle down for the night, usually consisting of small fires and whatever they could find to eat. Lately, it was small game Morakye could bring down with his bow. Killian had to admit the Fangor was a better shot with an arm in a sling than he had ever been without injury. The fact was that they would not have even been able to get this far without the help of

286

Morakye. Killian was grudgingly becoming more fond of the little furry man.

"Commander," a man said, running up to Killian. He had rags tied all around him in an attempt to keep warm. Killian looked down and saw the blood-soaked rags around his feet. He knew they could not go much further like this.

"It's Killian."

"Yes." The man said apologetically, bowing. "Commander Killian, of course."

"No, no, it's … oh, forget It." He said, shaking his head. "What is it?"

"One of the scouts has returned with news."

"What news?" Killian asked, stopping to face the man.

"Best if you ask him, I think."

"Well, what are you waiting for? Bring him here then," Killian commanded, spreading his arms, exasperated.

"Sir…" He paused nervously. "The scout is um … wounded."

"Has he spotted the Barbarians?" Killian asked, stepping close to the man and grabbing his shoulders. "I have no time for games, man!" Killian growled.

The man looked down to see if his feet were still on the ground as he dangled in Killian's grasp. "I do not believe the Barbarian's know where we are. Please … if I may." Killian let go of the man and he stepped back quickly. "Please come, Commander Killian." The man pleaded. "All will be explained."

Killian growled, making Morakye's ears perk up to the top of his head. Killian waved a hand forward, and the man hurriedly led the way.

287

A short distance off from the blood army, there was a boulder in a small clearing surrounded by large trees with only a few leaves on them. Birds circled the opening, eagerly eyeing the man lying on the rock. When the wind blew, the rags the man wore flopped in the wind. Men dressed in armour waited nervously. They shifted from foot to foot, brushing their long blond hair back from their light-collared eyes. The leader, a tall man with long hair that flowed over his broad shoulders from beneath his war helmet, shifted his war axe from hand to hand. He reached up and pushed impatiently at the nose guard with a knuckle. He longingly back up the path where they had come. The problem was that he had given his word that he would return the man on the rock to the commander of some Torenium army. However, Gluten did not know why a scout from an army that sounded so fierce would be wearing rags. Unless, of course, it was to hide his identity.

Perhaps I do not give these Torenium warriors enough credit. They have always been crafty in their cruelty. He thought, putting his axe in his other hand and knuckling his helmet. Gluten looked over and saw the fifteen men with him eyeing him, waiting for an order. He also noticed they were looking anxious and ready to fight. Gluten tried to relax a bit but then heard the rustling of dried leaves that meant someone was coming. Gluten put up a mailed hand and signalled for silence. The fifteen well-trained soldiers ducked down in unison.

I will not die today without spilling the man-eater blood! Gluten swore to himself as he quickly switched hands with his battle-axe.

"I do not like mysteries," Killian grumbled as he cringed every time his feet went deep into the leaves. To him, the sound was like horns

288

announcing his presence. He was envious of his little friend's feet that didn't seem to make a sound next to him. He looked and saw that Morakye was gone. Killian looked up into the trees as a chill went up his spine. He was a seasoned warrior and knew to trust his instincts. Killian stopped and pulled his sword. He reached forward to the man who was leading them and he lowered his voice to a whisper.

"No more games." He said into the man's ear. "What waits for me beyond that hill?" Just then, there was a rustle of leaves as Morakye reappeared next to him.

"There be Barbarian's waiting for us just beyond the hill," Morakye said, eyeing the man in Killian's grasp with narrowed yellow eyes. "Methinks they seem ... different than the other ... different from the rotten ones."

Killian pulled and twirled his sword as he ground his teeth. "So you have betrayed your own?" Killian said with disgust in his voice. "You will have an eternity to contemplate your mistake." Killian drew his arm back to drive his sword through the man in rags. The man stared, wide-eyed, into Killian's eyes, unable to speak. Morakye gently put his hand on Killian's shoulder.

"Not like the rotten ones," Morakye said again.

Killian paused and looked over at his friend. "Are you saying that I should give this worm a chance to speak before I run him through?"

Morakye turned his head sideways and looked at the man's eyes that were dangling in Killian's grasp. "Methinks there may be ... more to this," Morakye answered.

Killian dropped the man. "This is why I hate mysteries," he said, kicking the man in the rump to move him forward. "If this is a trap, you are the first to die."

When Killian got to the boulder, he felt the pulse of the man that was lying there. He was alive, but not for much longer. Killian got close to his ear.

"What is going on here?" Killian whispered. The man opened his eyes slightly and sighed. "I know of the men hiding below us."

"They are not ... the enemy," the man on the boulder said.

"Explain," Killian demanded.

"I ... have only fought to stay alive ... to tell you ... they are like ... us ... just like ... us." The man whispered, and then died.

"What does that mean?" He asked, turning to Morakye, but once again, Morakye had disappeared. "Gods, I hate when he does that!" Killian grumbled. "You got any ideas?" Killian asked the man who had led him here. The man just stared up at the trees in awe. Killian followed his gaze and saw a flash of fur silently moving from tree to tree. "Sure would have been wiser if he were to get the rest of the men," Killian said, shaking his head. "Some army." He climbed onto the rock.

So, they are just like us. Well, let us see how Barbarians can be just like us, shall we? I would have liked to see Lara one last time, to feel her just one more...

"We know you are there," Killian called out. "We have you completely surrounded." He lied.

"Will they be beating us to death with their rags, then?" The Barbarian called back from beneath the hill.

"I am Killian Loyal of House Loyal. I am the leader of these men and would appreciate not speaking to dirt and leaves." Killian watched as a large man stood not far off. He was very large and looked every bit the Northern Barbarian he had fought in countless skirmishes in his past. Though he had fur lining his armour, it was apparent he was not one of the Man-Eater Barbarian variety. Killian was close enough to see that the man kept his armour and general appearance clean as a Northern soldier would, not a man-eating monster. Morakye's description suddenly came to him. The man was indeed not of the rotten variety. But he was still a Northern Barbarian.

"I have not the time or patience for a battle of insults," Killian irritably called back. He heard the man say something low and heard low laughter. Killian felt the blood rushing to his face.

"What is your reason for hiding there in your rabbit hole?" Killian asked. He knew he had hit a nerve as the men suddenly became silent. Killian could feel the anger in the Barbarian's eyes as they silently watched him. Suddenly the man that had led Killian and Morakye there stepped between them with arms raised. Killian curiously looked down at him from the boulder.

"Please, sirs." He shouted in the cold air. "May I suggest we meet halfway to discuss?"

"No need." The Barbarian called out. He growled an order to his men who were still out of sight and started forward.

Killian jumped from the rock and pushed the man out of the way. "If I die, tell the men to continue West and find their Blood Demon there."

"Yes, sir," the man said. However, as he said it, he glanced up to see the wink of a yellow eye, knowing the message has been sent to the one who needed to hear it. He held still, letting the Barbarian lose distance from his men. Killian had been in enough battles to know that bravado almost always meant death. If the stupid brute wanted to show off, then let him. However, the truth was that Killian had fought the Barbarians enough to know that they were skilled fighters. The fact was, if there were fifteen trained fighters out there, as Morakye had said, they could be in serious trouble. Any by the comment about the rags, the Barbarians knew it.

"I am Gluten of Murgoth." Gluten said, simply coming to stand in front of Killian.

They stood staring at each other for a few moments, sizing each other up before Killian spoke back. "What is your intention?" Killian asked in the same to-the-point way.

"I am going to find the Mech-Flashom-" Gluten spat on the ground after he said it. "-and kill as many as I can until my hand leaves this axe or my soul leaves this body."

"Why do the Easterners' fight with themselves?"

"The Mech-Flashom are not *one* of us." Gluten said, his eyes blazing. "They are something that should not be. And my men and I will be sending many back to hell where they came from."

"Will the men without souls fear hell?" Killian asked.

Gluten looked at Killian, impressed that he knew what Mech-Flashom meant in the Eastern Language. Gluten stepped forward slightly and looked closer at Killian.

"There is some Eastern blood in you." Gluten said, looking him up and down. "You have our height and eyes. You will need that strength when you meet the Mech-Flashom."

"I have met the Man-Eaters and left their bodies to rot," Killian said, putting his sword away and crossing his arms with his chin in the air.

"I see." Gluten said, nodding. "Then there is no denying the blood that flows in ya' veins."

"I am Torenium," Killian said defiantly.

"Aye." Gluten said, putting his axe away. "This man-" Gluten gestured to the dead man on the boulder. "Had told us you could tell us where the, eh … Man Eaters are going. Where-" Gluten stopped and looked at the sky a moment before going on. "Where they are taking our people … taking … my son."

Killian nodded knowingly. He had been away from the military type so long that he was suddenly enjoying being around another like him. He thought he could hear his father, Bastion, rolling over in his grave at that thought. A Torenium enjoying the company of a Easterner, unheard of!

"I suspect they are taking the prisoners to the same place they had taken the Torenium. But before we get to that." Killian paused and Gluten raised a brow. "Why is my man lying there dead?" He asked, crossing his arms near his sword.

Gluten nodded at that. "That man saved our lives."

"How does a man in rags help fifteen armed Barbarians?" Killian did not miss the surprised look that came over the man's face.

Gluten explained how the blood army scout had come into the decimated city. As he followed the road, surrounded by silence other than the occasional ticking of rodent's feet or the flapping of vulture's wings as they scavenger fed off the dead, he heard what sounded like distant yells. He walked up and down the cobblestone road, trying to find where it was coming from. He found a small barn that looked to have housed horses at one time. He followed the muffled yelling to one of the stalls and then he had stood there awhile trying to pinpoint it. He slowly walked to a corner near the barred window and kicked the old hay away. Under a layer of dirt, he found an iron door on the floor. He yelled back, and suddenly the yelling beyond became more excited. The scout found a rake and worked to pry the door open. After much struggling, the door slowly opened. The man stepped back as a dirty, mailed hand came out and pushed the door the rest of the way.

The scout watched as fifteen armoured men slowly pulled themselves from the ground, lying on their backs and sucking in the air. Before long, they tried to ask him questions in the Eastern language. It was not until Gluten started communicating in the Torenium language that the others started getting up, concerned. The scout explained what was outside and then they ran into the streets where they fell to their knees, weeping among the dead.

"He saved us from the dark hell only to let us into another." Gluten said, going over to lean against the boulder where the man lay. "But he did not have to let us out. He could have just left us there, but he did not."

"That is fine and good, but it does not explain why he is dead," Killian asked.

Gluten stood, taking off his helmet. Killian was surprised at how young the man was and how much he resembled Sebastion. It took him off guard and he stared.

"Never before have the Mech's left their dead behind. This time we found some scattered here and there. Your scout got too close to one not quite yet dead and found a knife jammed into his leg. You are a soldier and know there are places on the body that do not allow for healing - this was such a place. I tried to stop the bleeding as best I could, but..."

"He was knifed in the leg, then?" Killian asked again.

"Aye."

Killian walked to the dead man and started lifting the rags. Sure enough, he found bloody rags wrapped around his left leg. Killian put his hands in the air and moved them rapidly. Gluten eyed him suspiciously.

"It's time you met my friend," Killian said, smiling. Seconds later, Morakye dropped to the ground near them. Gluten stepped back, reaching for his axe.

"Whoo there, big man," Killian said, raising his hands. "This is my friend."

Suddenly fifteen Barbarians appeared on the hill with weapons ready.

"Your story being true-" Killian started quickly. "It seems we have a common enemy."

Gluten turned away from Morakye and nodded quickly before turning back. "What is it?"

"It?" Morakye asked indignantly. "Morakye be a *who* not *it*."

Gluten looked back and forth from Morakye to Killian. "You've trained it to speak?"

"Morakye-" Killian said, making the point to stress the Fangor's name. "-is a friend and a skilled warrior."

Gluten doubtfully looked at Morakye.

"We will explain this more at length," Killian said, his hands at his side. "But for now, we need to trust each other, yes?"

Gluten waved a hand at his comrades who were coming closer. They stopped suddenly but looked ready to charge. "I have no time for games." Gluten said, putting his helmet on again. "Tell us where the Mechs are taking the people, and we will leave you."

Killian frowned, looking at the men behind the Easterner. "You will die along with your men." He said simply.

"We died when we came from that hole and saw our brethren slaughtered on the ground." Gluten said miserably. "I only choose to catch up with those that survived and die with them as we fight for their freedom."

"So-" Killian sighed. "You only choose to die against the power bigger than yourself?"

"We will take many with us." Gluten said menacingly.

"But you plan to die? Killian asked.

"We are dead already."

"And your son?" Killian asked.

Gluten stood up straight, holding his axe.

"What of him?" Killian asked, going on. "Will you throw your life away for him? Are you sure he is even dead?"

Gluten frowned deeply. "If he is not dead already ... I think I fear his future more."

Killian looked at the prominent Easterner, surprised as tears freely rolled down his face.

"He was everything I had always wanted to be." Gluten said, running a finger under his nose. "He was smart, strong, and had no need for cruelty. He was a born leader and led the other boys by being patient. When some would test his mettle, they learned quickly that this boy was not kind because he was weak." Gluten gripped his axe proudly. "He had the strength of an ox in those arms."

"They turn them into slaves," Killian said abruptly.

"What?" Gluten said, turning his head sideways.

"If your boy is as strong as you say, they are probably using him to dig."

"You mean he could be alive?"

"I mean, there is a chance he could be alive. And that throwing your life away ... even for an Easterner-" That got a laugh from the men behind Gluten. "-makes no sense to me."

"It does not need to, Torenium." Gluten said, adjusting his armour as if preparing to leave. "You have provided a great service and given me something I never thought would have come from a-"

"A Torenium?" Killian asked.

"Yes." Gluten said, stopping to look at Killian. "There really may be a chance he might be-"

"Take the hope," Killian said, coming forward, his hand outstretched. "In these times, I fear it is all we have." Gluten took it and clasped it firmly. "We have little food, but what we have, we will share."

"That is very kind … Killian." Gluten said with a half-smile.

"I ask that you stay the evening so we can speak of this further," Killian asked.

"I fear time is not on our side."

"Neither is rashness going to save your boy," Killian said, letting go of the big man's hand and facing him like a soldier again. "I can see in you a soldier," Killian said, frowning. "You must know that charging headlong into battle without a plan is-"

"Not going to help my son." Gluten finished.

A chill ran up Killian's back as Gluten looked at the ground, frowning and deep in thought almost precisely as Sebastion would.

"We will stay and ask of you your help in the way of a plan." Gluten finally said, raising his head to meet Killian's eyes. "In return for what you know and what you provide in the strategy, we will give you a map that helps you get through the mountains undetected by the Mech-Flashom. But for now, let us fill our bellies and drink to the dead before we speak of plans. Tomorrow my men and I will be sending many of the Mech-Flashom back where they came from!"

"As I said, we have little, but what we have, you and yours are-"

"We have more than we could ever eat." Gluten said sadly. "The Mech-Flashom … what you call the man-eaters, did not touch the cities' stores of food. They were … after other things."

Killian ran a hand through his hair, thinking.

A city of food and provisions. Enough for … an army!

Gluten suddenly looked around at the Torenium men that were coming up to the rock to see them. He frowned at them as if seeing them for the first time.

"This army of yours-" Gluten said ominously. "-they plan to kill Mech-Flashom?"

"They will die." A man close to Gluten said sadly.

"They killed my family." The man said, limping towards Gluten, his rags flapping in the wind. "I-" The man stopped, swallowing the tears. "I saw them die before my eyes. I saw-"

Gluten stepped forward and grabbed the man's skinny arms. "We are the same in this." Gluten said, almost lifting the man into the air. Everyone was silent, watching the exchange. "Brothers in a way to this ... horror." Gluten swallowed hard but did not let the man loose. Instead, he continued to look into the man's eyes for a moment. "Yes." Gluten said, finally allowing the man to go.

"We are brothers in this!" He said for all to hear now. "And my brothers will have all they need to fight the monsters that are doing this to us all."

Killian and Morakye shared a confused look.

"Not far from here, you will find many of my dead brothers scattered around the ground," Gluten announced. "Take their armour and weapons and continue where they have left off. Wear their things and remember all our brothers and sisters as you send those bastards back to hell FROM WHICH THEY WERE SPAWNED!"

The men in the clearing erupted in a cheer. Soon they were chanting blood demon again, and Gluten turned to Killian, confused.

Killian waved him off to follow, smiling, thinking that perhaps fortune had finally come their way ... for once.

Later that night, Killian and Gluten sat together in an empty tavern in the closeby town taking turns getting up and pouring each other drinks from the now empty bar. Some other people were milling about looking for things to take with them. Killian thought he might never forget the look on Gluten's face as they stepped over the dead laying on the ground as birds and insects fed from their flesh. He had announced again for the Blood Army to take what they wanted and leave the men where they had fallen. The Torenium slowly pulled off armour and took the weapons as they made their way to the empty town.

The town itself was silent other than the birds feeding and fighting over the dead scattered where they had fallen. A small number of dogs and other farm animals slinked around the dark recesses of the alleyways. As if they, too, were trying to respect the dead by staying hidden and silent. The Blood Army had entered the open gates with heavy hearts and deep in their memories as they stepped over the dead. At times, one of the men would reach down and pull something from one of the deceased. Some wept openly as they were crushed by the events running their course through their minds.

"By now, there will be more," Killian said, putting the drink to his lips. "They will not be so easy to sneak up on."

"What choice do we have?" Gluten asked, running his fingers down the metal helmet that sat next to him.

Killian nodded solemnly, emptying his glass.

"I do have a question that has been weighing on my mind," Killian said carefully.

Gluten looked at him but did not say a word.

"You said you were locked underground by a heavy door when all those around you-"

"Were being killed." Gluten finished for him.

"Well, yes." Killian took a sip of his drink but searched Gluten's face.

Gluten sighed and rubbed at his eyes. "There was a girl."

"There always is." Killian added.

"No." Gluten shook his head spreading his hands. "It makes no sense really. A girl I have never seen before. She was the prettiest child I have ever seen. Though her hair was dark which is unusual for Easterners. She was ... beautiful and innocent."

"A little girl locked you all in a hole?" Killian asked, curiously leaning towards Gluten.

"No, she told us there was a way for the women and children to escape but we needed to clear the way. She led us to the opening in the ground. I told my men to leave me but they would not. We were going to clear the way to bring the woman and children from the church to this place when she..."

"She what?" Killian asked.

"She closed the opening door and plunged us into darkness. So many of us and we could not budge that door above us. We were desperate to fight, but..." Gluten groaned. "Not until that Torenium man showed up did we come out. We could have turned the tide of the-"

"You would have died. But now you live. So many strange-Killian jumped as suddenly the door opened and Stal, the man Gluten had picked up and searched with his eyes back in the woods, came in wearing mis-matched Eastern armour. It hung all around him, and he rattled like a wind-chime as he entered.

"Sir." He said from deep inside his metal helmet. "I think we may have a problem with the armour."

Killian started laughing at the ridiculous-looking man ... then stopped suddenly, not wanting to disrespect Gluten and his men. When he looked over, however, he saw a smile spread across the man's face.

"Seems we have some big shoes to fill," Killian said, getting up and slapping Gluten's shoulder good naturedly. "Best see to the others," Killian announced, heading to the door.

"Perhaps when we are gone you can spend some time sizing those." Gluten said, leaning back in his chair.

"Not for me," Stal said, pushing his helmet back and putting his hands on his hips. "I'm going with you."

"WHAT!" Killian yelled, turning back from the door.

"I will save the boy from the Mech ... Mech-"

"Mech-Flashom." Gluten said, sitting up straight in the chair.

"Yeah, them." Stal nodded. "I will fight to get his son back. I will save that boy as a tribute to my son who could not be saved."

"And who else thinks this way," Killian asked dangerously, looking at the man.

"There are ... uh ... more," Stal said, stepping away from Killian.

302

Killian growled and threw open the door. Outside everyone else was dressed much like Stal and all were wearing the same determined look in their eyes.

So much for puckering good luck!

"I will not tell them that." Gluten said, his hands on his hips.

"Then we all will die," Killian said, throwing his hands up, exasperated. "This is madness!"

"Why do you doubt us so?" Gluten asked, walking to the bar and filling his glass. "You have already defeated them once."

"Morakye would enjoy killing more Mech-Flashom." Morakye smiled, showing his fangs. Gluten looked over and Morakye winked a yellow eye. Gluten awkwardly smiled at him, unsure about the Fangor yet.

"That was sheer luck ... plus, we had..." Killian stopped rubbing his face with his hands.

"What?" Gluten asked, now interested.

"We had ... Sebastion."

"The blood demon." Gluten said, nodding.

"More than that," Killian added, coming to sit at the table. Gluten pulled a chair out and sat across from him.

"What is this *more*?" Gluten asked.

Killian sighed before going on. "Sebastion is part of something ... big." Killian tried to explain. "Things just seem to happen around him. He is like a magnet that attracts things to him, not always good things."

Gluten nodded as if understanding.

"We, a group of us, are in something bigger than us."

Gluten now looked at him, confused.

Killian explained about the gods and, in a small part, Bashor. He hesitantly added the dragon and their meeting with the Lady of Light and the Dark Lord. Killian looked over at Gluten many times, waiting to see a sign of disbelief, but it never came. That in itself was worrying him as he went on. When he ended with them parting ways and Sebastion, The blood demon, leaving with his beloved Lara, Killian stopped and waited for a response.

Gluten leaned back and drained his mug. He looked up and stared at the ceiling awhile. Killian and Morakye exchanged looks, waiting for a response.

Finally, Gluten got up and gingerly put his mug on the bar before turning to face Killian. He removed the armour on his forearm and pulled up the sleeve to reveal the image of a dragon tattooed there.

"I was sick with fever many years ago." Gluten explained as Morakye came over to take a closer look. "I dreamt of a dragon that watched over me. I dreamt I was living far in the forest with a cruel man that always appeared in gray. He would beat me and make me learn to kill in the most dishonourable ways."

Killian now felt that familiar chill run up his spine.

"But through it all," Gluten went on, looking into Killian's eyes. "I knew this dragon watched over me. Connected to me in a way." Gluten turned his head sideways as if Killian was not telling him something. "Can you tell me more of this Blood Demon of yours?"

Morakye suddenly stepped closer to Gluten. The Fangor looked like a child so close to the large Northern man. He closed his eyes and put his nose in the air. Seconds later, Morakye opened his yellow eyes wide, smiling.

"What?" Killian asked.

"I believe this man and Morakye's brother have met before."

"Where?" Killian asked.

"That is for them to find out, me think's."

"This is puckering madness," Killian said, walking out of the room.

"You were raised here, yes?" Morakye asked.

"Yes." Gluten said. "My mother and father were followers of Felster. They travelled throughout the East looking to convert the Barbarian hordes to the Light. They were killed when I was training to be a soldier. They thought they could calm the Mech-Flashom with religion." Gluten frowned deeply. "They were wrong."

Morakye nodded his head. His long ears folded solemnly. "Me's will come with you to get your son," Morakye said, and suddenly he raised his head as a thought came to him. "How old is your son?"

"He is of twelve years."

"But-" Morakye asked, his head cocked sideways.

"Yes." Gluten nodded knowingly. "He is not of my blood. He came to this city after the Mech-Flashom destroyed his village. He was alone and only a child. I was also alone with ... my parents no longer alive. Together we are all we have." Gluten narrowed his eyes, looking at Morakye. "I will take him from them."

"And Morakye will help you," Morakye said back, leaving no room for discussion.

Killian suddenly opened the door. "You better come out here." He said to Gluten. They went outside and saw all the men packed and

305

prepared for departure. They had gathered what they needed and looked anxious to be on their way.

Gluten looked over at them, at first confused by their steadfast stares, but as the realization came over him, tears came to his eyes. The other of his men came up beside him.

"They are stubborn." One of the Easterners said, looking over them and nodding.

"No, they are stupid men." Killian corrected, but Gluten thought he heard a hint of pride in his voice. "Ask them to please at least get their rest tonight," Killian said. "Tomorrow, we can walk into the fire ... again."

"They are your men." Gluten said only and backed away a step.

Killian angrily looked at the man and then let out a sigh. "I can think of only one other that gets me to this place." Killian ran his hand through his hair, thinking before stepping forward.

"LISTEN UP." He boomed. "We are at a crossroads for what this ... *army* represents." Killian paused to let that sink in. "We could run back to our lands to fight. There is no doubt there are many that could use our help right now. Toreniums like us that are watching their families being killed before their eyes as you have seen. We could move through the mountains fast and attack them from behind. Or-"Killian paused again as rumbling started among the men. "-we could do the unexpected and go back and re-open those wounds we started to bleed. We could send a message to all the Man-Eaters that Torenium *and* the Easterners have come together, and the gods their bite KILLS!"

The men started yelling out encouragement.

"AND LET THOSE BASTARDS KNOW THAT THE THIS BLOOD ARMY BRINGS THEM PAIN AND DEATH!" Killian yelled loudly in the darkness of the night. The group of men, Torenium and Easterns, exploded into cheers.

CHAPTER 25

The knights had found some horses hiding in fields not far from the city. Most were workhorses but they were all right to carry supplies. Luckily for the Blood Army, there were plenty of provisions to take with them. Two days on their way back, they got word that the Man-Eaters had caught up with them and that they had started shadowing them. There were not many and the Blood Army waited patiently for them on the trail. As they approached, utterly unaware that their slaves would have turned around to fight, they were quickly killed. They even took one alive to question him. However, he did not last long as he traded barbs with Gluten. Killian could only roll his eyes at the big man's youthful mistake at separating the Man-Eaters head from his shoulders.

Back on the trail, they made good time. Killian stayed close to Gluten, trying to devise a way to attack the Man-Eaters and get the people out safely. The prospect was not sounding easy.

"We can only hope that the army has left to find other game." Gluten said, knuckling his helmet nervously. "We would be no match against the whole army."

Killian grunted his agreement. "What happened to the bravado?" He laughed bitterly.

"I think I left it back there with my empty glass of mead." Gluten smiled over at him.

Killian laughed, shaking his head.

"My guess." Gluten went on. "Is that the Man-Eaters fortified the ones watching over the slaves and left."

"What's your reasoning for that?" Killian asked curiously.

"The Mech-Flashom are using the slaves to find something they must want in that mountain. You and the Toreniums-"

"Blood Army." Someone in earshot corrected him.

"Right." Gluten said apologetically. "You and your Blood Army took all the slaves and that work has stopped." Gluten rubbed the fine hair on his chin. "I would guess that the Mech-Flashom would want more slaves to make up for the ones they lost. They will be looking for another city or town to take hostages. That means leaving the slaves they acquired and leaving quickly to get more.

"Let's hope you're right." Killian half-smiled at the young Eastern warrior.

"How much longer until you think we are in sight of them?"

Killian thought to himself, looking at the fire. The thought of Lara suddenly came to his mind. He closed his eyes and tilted his head back. He breathed in through his nose and smelled the cooking meat and the crisp fall air. Then he knew that it would not be long before the snow fell. This was, however, not where he wanted his mind to go. He furrowed his brow and concentrated harder. He breathed in again, and he found it. Faint at first, but as his mind took him there, he could smell Lara's sweet scent. Suddenly his head was full of her. A smile spread across his bearded face as he pushed his nose towards the full moon, seeing none of it. He imagined how his lips felt on the soft flesh of her neck. He breathed her in again and felt the hairs on his neck stand up. He could hear her sighs of pleasure close to his ear.

"Eh, Sir Killian-" Gluten asked uncomfortably.

"What is it?" Killian asked without looking over and barely paying attention.

"Shall we come back?" The young warrior asked.

Killian sighed heavily but looked over to Gluten with a smile on his face. "I was thinking of a woman," Killian said without a hint of embarrassment. "A special one, at that."

Gluten uncomfortably started to sway like he wanted to leave suddenly.

"This woman is intoxicating." Killian smiled widely, pulling his long hair from his face. "Do you know a woman like that?"

"No. Not really." Gluten said quietly.

"Take the advice of an old man," Killian said, looking the young Easterner in the eyes. "Do not mistake love for weakness. The love of a woman can be the one thing that gets you off the ground and fighting when all else is lost. It can keep your legs moving when the muscles scream for you to stop. I look young, but my life is old. When I have looked death in the eyes ... and I have too many times to count. It was not my battles, accomplishments, wealth, or deeds that I sought. No, it was love I sought. The kind that makes your head swim and your parts ache. Not lust, per se-" Killian smiled and winked. "Though that too is better with love. Look for it and hold on to it when you find it. It's worth waiting and-" Killian sat up straight. "And it's sure puckering hell worth fighting for."

"I do not think I have heard it better." Gluten nodded. "There is definitely Eastern blood in you, Sir Killian." Gluten smiled and ran a hand across his eye. "How long until we start killing the Mech-Flashom?"

"You already have but … three days." Killian smiled. "We'll be wading in Man-Eaters in just three days."

"Not soon enough," Gluten added and turned to leave.

Killian watched him leave, thinking as he did that he hoped the young warrior was alive on day four. The odds were that none of them would be. But as time had been teaching him ... odds didn't mean a dark load of dung these days.

CHAPTER 26
Home

Bashor spat on the dirt ground from within his deep hood. Several Man-Eaters in the tent looked his way at his sudden unexpected reaction. They could not see his face and so they reluctantly ignored his seeming insult.

"You need only wait a short while longer," Bashor said, thinking the Barbarian words even felt dirty in his mouth.

Tok-Mork absently rubbed his cheek where the scar now ran from his eye to his chin. He did not like waiting and knew his Armies outside liked it even less. They had been promised the city many months ago. Though he did have to admit the Mage kept all his other promises.

"What of the Healer?" Tok-Mork asked, scowling at the skinny man hidden in his cloak.

"He will be returned." Bashor hissed. "My gift to your people will be returned."

"How is it he was able to leave us?" The prominent Barbarian leader asked, feeling the anger rising in his stomach. "You told us he would never be able to leave us."

"He will be returned, and all will be as it was." The truth was that Bashor had no idea why the Lesser God was able to escape the Man-Eaters. He was bonded to the Barbarians with powerful magic that should not have been broken ... ever.

"My men are not patient," Tok-Mork said not as a warning but as a simple fact. "We have lost many that have not been returned."

Bashor nodded in his hood. He knew what was coming and was already planning what would be needed. "I will return as many as I can before I am missed. I will use this tent." Tok-Mork started to object but stopped before the words left his lips.

"Bring me the newly dead, no more than two days ago."

"There are not many that new."

"Do you still have Eastern prisoners?" Bashor asked.

"Yes," Tok-Mork replied miserably. The Barbarians did not like adding new bodies to the hoard ... but at times, it was useful. "I will bring the ones that can be used."

"Also, bring me any of the religious ones you are keeping. Tie some rope to those beams above us and as many containers, cups, basins, barrels, or whatever you can find."

"I do not understand."

"And you never will," Bashor said in a whisper in his hood. "Bring me these things and I will bring back some of the ones you have lost."

An hour later, Bashor sipped from a cup he would occasionally dip into a barrel underneath several hanging corpses that occasionally twitched as blood dripped from them. He had already brought back the twisted souls of the ones that occupied the newly-dead Man-Eaters. The hard part would be getting the Man-Eaters into the Eastern slave's bodies. The ones that occupied the bodies always fought hard to reoccupy their vessels. He had to stay off these and, at the same time pull in the ones he wanted. Only once, he had been beaten; that was the boy with the blood that had helped return his power. That day it was almost what he had done that seemed to make perfect sense. He was sure that when he brought the infant's soul back it was not the same but somehow entered as if it had always been there. It was a strange night.

"We have slit their throats, Mage," Tok-Mork said, laying down dead Eastern slaves in the tent.

"Don't call me that here," Bashor said absently, as he had dome many times already this evening. "I cannot promise which one will be in which body." Bashor came to stand in front of the bodies. "This one is still alive." He pointed to one on the left. The Eastern man's eyes flew open, and he made for the tent opening. Tok-Mork grabbed the man by his ragged shirt and thrust a large knife into his neck. The man tried to scream, but his slit throat did not permit him. Instead, he just slowly collapsed onto the ground.

"Ok." Bashor rubbed his hands together, getting ready for the task ahead. "-wait outside and do not come in until invited."

"I cannot promise that this will make the others wait for long before attacking the city." The big Barbarian said, heading for the exit.

Bashor stopped and slowly turned to the leader of the Man-Eaters. "You cannot promise?"

"I-"

"You will do as I ask of you, or I will *promise* you that I will bring the Blood Demon to your very tent this night." Bashor hissed. It was all he could do to swallow down laughter at these imbeciles' superstitious twisted lifeforms. He knew this Blood Demon being rumoured about like gossiping women. Blood Demons were mythical creatures that came to the ones that had spilled blood unjustly. If there were anyone this Blood Demon was to come for, it would be him for spilling blood. And yet ... where was this creature? It was all Bashor

314

could do not to laugh as Tok-Mork bowed his head and left the tent without a word.

They are barely able to form a thought.

Bashor shook his head, disgusted, and watched the Barbarian leave.

Sebastion lay against the tree high up on a branch. He had picked an evergreen as that was the only tree that still had enough foliage to hide him. For two days, he had spent his time looking over the massive army of Man-Eaters. Each passing hour his frustration was building. He was so close to his Miska, and he was stopped cold in his tracks. He blew out a blast of air in frustration and looked at the white buildings that made up the city's centre beyond the high gates. He imagined Miska there right now, locked away in a church cell for trying to get back to him. He imagined her crying his name, and he unable to get to her. He ground his teeth and slammed a fist into the tree.

There has to be a way inside.

But he knew the problem was that the Great City was trying to keep everyone *out*. He closed his eyes and leaned his head back.

"Hey," Lara said from below. Sebastion did not even acknowledge her. "Why don't you use that-."

"I'm not doing it." He answered miserably.

"I know how you feel." Lara sat on the cold ground and leaned against the tree far below. "When my father was alive, I would have to dress up every weekend and holiday," Lara grunted, miserably remembering. "He'd make me wear puffy dresses and have women do terrible things to make me look what he called *presentable*. I wanted to do very terrible things to *them*!" Lara could feel the hot blood

315

coming to her face as she thought of them. "I would have wrung the life out of them if I could have."

"I believe you," Sebastion said, still staring off in the distance.

"If it were today … I might well do it." Lara took a second to reflect. "Well, the point is sometimes we need to do things we don't want to do."

"I've been doing that all my life." Sebastion countered. "-and still doing them. From my dead father from the grave to a horde of crazed slaves."

"Yeah." Lara agreed. "That is completely insane." Sebastion coughed out a laugh at that. "But at least you don't have to wear a dress." Lara countered back.

"Give it time." Sebastion added miserably.

"Actually-" Lara said, getting up. "With that nice hair and long legs, you might look good in one."

"Thanks," Sebastion answered sarcastically.

Lara sighed again and decided to try one more time. "We need to get into that city. Killian and the rest may already be in there waiting for us."

"I know."

"Then we need you to reconsider, and please try the magic stuff … please."

Sebastion suddenly grabbed the branch and swung to the ground, hitting it with a thud. He crossed his arms and frowned down at her. "Fine." He breathed out like an angry bull. "One condition."

"Anything you want." Lara agreed. "Just get us out of this freezing puckering field!"

"I want you to put on a dress for when we meet with Killian."

"WHAT!?" Lara's mouth fell open.

"You think I like having the feeling that my soul is leaving my body and flying away?"

"I'm not wearing a dark blasted puckering dress."

"Baran!" Sebastion called out. "Might as well start building a shelter as it looks like we will be here for a while."

"Ohhh..." Lara said, looking at him through dark narrow eyes and hands on her hips. She was wearing furs that they had stolen from the Barbarians along the way. Sebastion noticed that by putting her hands there they were closer to her short swords on her waist. She swung her head to Baran and then back to Sebastion. Her long braid down her back dangerously whipped around her head.

"Do it." She said simply.

"Then we have a deal?" He asked.

"I swear you Loyals get under my skin like no others have."

"Then we have a deal?" Sebastion asked again with a hint of a smile.

"Yes," Lara growled. "I will wear a dress when we meet up with your puckering uncle." She walked away, muttering under her breath, and Baran jumped out of her path. He looked at Sebastion quietly, laughing to himself.

Sorko and Milner sat across from Sebastion, encouraging him as Sebastion closed his eyes and concentrated. It was getting near dusk and they were letting their small fire burn down for the evening. There was no sense in having the Man-Eaters see the fire. Sebastion kept

317

trying to concentrate on clearing his mind, but all he could think about was how cold and hard the ground was under his crossed legs. Every time he tried to think of nothing, something would pop up.

"Just think of nothingness." Sorko offered. "How did your mind become clear when you did it to find me?"

"I don't remember," Sebastion said lamely. "It just happened."

"Were you thinking of something in particular?"

"I thought I needed to find you or Lara would die. I was getting desperate."

Sorko and Milner shared a look that Sebastion caught as he peeked through his closed eyes.

"Perhaps if he thought of the one he wanted to contact." Milnor offered. Sebastion thought it strange when the tiny wizard spoke because he so rarely did.

"Yes." Sorko agreed, nodding. "Think of someone you want to see in the city. Perhaps your uncle, if he is there. Is there any..."

Lara threw a pebble at Sorko that bounced off his hat. He looked at Lara, confused. She nodded in Sebastion's direction, eyes wide as if to say; *open your eyes, you idiot.* Sure enough, Sebastion was in deep concentration, not saying a word.

Sebastion felt himself lift out of his body. He looked down and saw himself sitting there with Sorko, Milner, and Lara watching him closely. He looked over and saw Baran leaning against a tree, watching the army below them. The feeling made him nauseous and at once he considered just returning to his body. Then the image of Miska came to him again. He grabbed onto it as if it were a lifeline out at sea. He grabbed it and pulled himself towards it. Suddenly he was being flung towards the city. As he moved towards the Man-Eaters, he had the strange sensation of feeling his heart quicken somewhere else far off from where he was. He thought it was not a good feeling.

As he came to the Man-Eaters he saw a man in a cloak step out of a tent. Sebastion flew right over him. He looked back and saw the man he knew as Bashor remove his hood and look in his direction as if he was searching for him. Sebastion felt a coldness run through him at the sight of the Mage. Then he felt himself slowing. The voice inside him yelled for him to keep going forward, but he found with terror that he might be going back to Bashor. The man that had drained him of his blood and left him to die. The thought was terrifying. The voice inside screamed to concentrate, and Sebastion immediately thought of the big brown eyes. He thought of her smile and her touch on his skin. Suddenly he was moving towards the city again. He kept her image firmly in his mind.

At the gates there were Toreniums hiding by the river that ran around the city. They hid, terrified, in the high-growing grass. Many looked to be already near death. There were several Man-Eaters also lying dead with arrows in them. He could see that high on the wall soldiers watched over them. He did not understand why they did not let them into the walls. They could have even lowered ropes for them to climb. It made no sense.

He flew over the wall and inside and saw that people were sleeping everywhere. The city was already packed with people. He thought they moved about without purpose as if they were already dead. Most did not look any better than the ones in the tall grass outside. Seeing them made him feel terrible, and he concentrated on Miska, trying not to see them. He saw that he was floating to a large building with statues of the Lady and became excited that he might be getting close. He flew through a wall and thought he would cry out at the sensation. Inside, the corridors were plain, and the floors wooden and shined with cleanliness. Many more statues adorned the halls, but that was about it. He came to large double doors with the Lady's sculptures on either side and passed through them, closing his eyes and thinking he would slam into them. Inside he was drawn to another wall and passed through it as well. He was starting to feel nauseous again. Inside was what looked to be a sitting room or library with a strange painting of what looked to be lovers. Sebastion thought that odd within a place like this. He concentrated again and was hurtled towards a fireplace. He tried to close his eyes but found it was impossible as he passed through that too. Then he was in some kind of corridor heading fast through the darkness. He knew somewhere far away he was getting sick. He tried to put Miska's smile in his mind's eye, and then she was there. Just like that, he was close to her.

He watched her hovering above as she pulled what looked to be people like those from the river from the dark water. She and others were in some underground cavern. There were torches on the walls surrounding them, giving off light. Much of the light was bouncing off the still waters of the small underground pool. Miska was wearing a dress of what looked to him to be a priestess of The Lady. She was not as he remembered. Her hair was long and tied tight behind her, but that was not what seemed so different. He saw his Miska pointing and giving orders. She seemed older and more in control than he would ever think. This was not the same weeping Miska that left him at Endora. No, this Miska appeared to be in control and able to take care of herself.

At this point, Sebastion began to think that perhaps she did not want to see him. That maybe he was just a passing phase in her life and she no longer wanted anything to do with him. Was it not she that had left without saying a word? Then, without warning, she looked up to where he was and he no longer cared. He looked into the big brown eyes in the light of the torches and just wanted to be in her presence ... to be really in her presence. Then he was opening his eyes and feeling sick as he lay on the hard cold ground.

"Did it work?" Lara asked enthusiastically. Sebastion rolled over and looked at the darkening sky. He wasn't sure whether to be exhilarated by seeing Miska or to be terrified of Bashor. He decided to close his eyes and just breathe. A couple of minutes later he opened them again to see them all standing over him, staring with concern on their faces.

"I'm all right." He said, sitting up. "It worked."

"So you found a way in?" Sorko asked.

"I think so, but ... there is something else."

Lara breathed out a heavy sigh, knowing there was always something else.

"I saw..." Sebastion did not even want to mention his name. "I saw Bashor."

"The Mage?" Sorko asked.

"Yes." Sebastion got up and stretched. He was thankful that none of his vomit had gotten on his clothes, found a water skin, and drank deeply. "He was with the Man-Eaters and-" He took another big gulp. "-and he looked pretty comfortable."

"Did he know you were there?"

"He looked up in my direction – that is all I know."

Sorko took off his pointed hat and rubbed his bald head as he stared at the ground.

Lara said. "Did you see her?"

Sebastion smiled, thinking of her. That was all Lara needed to see to know.

Baran handed Sebastion what looked like a root. "It for 'da taste."

"Thanks," Sebastion said, thankful for it.

"Do ya think we can get 'n there, then?"

"There is a way some of the ones by the gates are getting in."

"Some of 'da ones?" Baran asked.

"Yeah, they have closed the gates to the people. Not letting anyone else in. They are hiding in the tall grass by the river."

"They're just leave'n them 'dar?" Baran asked, his brow almost reaching his hairline.

"Most are nearly ... well ... you know."

Baran nodded his head with an anger that Sebastion rarely saw on the big man's face. "Yeah, I do know." He said, looking back towards the city.

"So, what's the plan?" Lara asked.

They were going to follow the river, disguising themselves as refugees. When they got to the part closest to the gates, they would look for the place that led into the caverns. They got some rest and planned to start their trek an hour before sun up.

The weeds near the river were dry and brittle. Their cracking and snapping sounded to them like thunder cracks in the quiet darkness. They had not anticipated this, and it slowed them down. As they got closer, they saw signs of other refugees. It was Sebastion who finally noticed the reflective eyes near the water. There were many just there waiting by the water. Families covered in mud and muck huddled together like frightened animals. They were so silent that they had gone unseen since they started their journey. Sebastion's heart twisted inside, seeing the children who were afraid grasping their parents with wide, terrified eyes. They all looked starved and close to death. He wanted to speak to them, but he was afraid of making any more noise. So they just moved on by each pair of eyes gleaming in the approaching light in the sky.

When they saw the hulking figure of the gates in the distance, it seemed they were going to make it. That was when the reeds in the soft mud stopped. The Man-Eaters had cleared out a section, and guards were sleeping near a fire. Sebastion made out another figure sitting a few yards away from the fire, and he could see his head moving from side to side, listening. He doubted his friends could see him. His ability to see at night was still much better. He held out a hand for them to stop. Baran came up to whisper into Sebastion's ear. "We can't just leave 'em there."

"Man-Eaters." He whispered back, indicating with a nod of his head.

"Da' bastards are blocking their way," Baran said, understanding. "I will's go kill 'em." He started to get up, but Sebastion grabbed his arm.

"It has to be quiet." Sebastion indicated for him to stay there and moved to the clearing like a stalking cat. The others caught up, and Baran filled them in.

Sebastion moved slowly, keeping an eye on the Barbarian sitting closer to the water. Every time the Man-Eater looked away, he made progress. The entire clearing was covered in bones. He knew what kind of bones were turning under his hands and feet as he crawled, but he tried not to think about it. Near the fire, he could see the rising and falling of the two slumbering Man-Eaters. Sebastion crept up to the first one and waited. The one by the water turned away, and Sebastion struck his nose straight up with the butt of the big knife. The Man-Eater did not even move. He lay next to him, hidden by the big fur-covered body. He watched and then snuck up to the next one. He meant to do the same thing but saw that the man was sleeping wearing a helmet with a nose guard. Sebastion did not want to do it this way, but he quietly slit the man's throat. He hoped he wouldn't wake up, but the man did look around confused. Sebastion looked over to the water but did not see the other there.

Pucker!

He stabbed the Man-Eater in front of him in the chest and rolled onto his knees, looking around. The Man-Eater wasn't anywhere. Sebastion started turning in every direction to find him. Nothing! He was afraid that he had gone to get help. That's when he saw the outline of the Man-Eater rise again by the water. The rising light was behind him, but it looked like he was facing Sebastion with something like a bucket in his hand. Sebastion was about to throw his knife as the Man-Eater tossed something in the air. As it came down, rolling towards him, he paused; it was the head of the Man-Eater looking up at him. Sebastion looked over and saw the crouching form of Baran coming towards him. Sebastion hung his head and breathed out a sharp laugh. He wasn't sure if he should be happy or mad at the big man. He had told him to stay put.

"What happened?" Sebastion asked him in the coming light.

"Wouldn't ya just know the big bastard ran 'is neck against me sword ... four times, he did." Baran smiled. Sebastion shook his head. The way after that was pretty straightforward. Nearest the gates, the Man-Eater army was loud as they woke from their sleep. They had to crawl to the water's edge, and they were all freezing by this point. They thought they should have started earlier in the evening. They no idea it would have taken this long.

"What now?" Lara asked, miserable lying in the mud with her hair plastered to her head and face. "If I lie here any longer in this coldness, I will be no use in a fight." Sebastion nodded, understanding. He searched the water, looking for some sign of the way to the cavern. He decided he had to swim out and see if he could find it. He took off the clothes that weighed him down and told them what he was going to do. They huddled together in the mud for warmth and waited.

Sebastion did more floating than swimming as he didn't want to splash around too much. The bridge led to the main gate. The gates were, of course, closed but the bridge remained. He swam slowly towards it. Underneath, he saw words painted above him. They read:

325

tThose that follow with faith shall breathe again.' Sebastion did not know why but the words seemed important. He stared at them, trying to make sense of it. *—breathe again.* He looked at the water and wondered. He put his head underwater and looked around. All he saw was a green haze. He took his head out and wiped the water from his face. What could it mean? The cavern he had seen had to connect to this water. The other side must join it.

Those that follow the faith shall breathe again.

In frustration, he dove down and swam deeper. He thought he saw something white below him. He swam deeper. The water was even colder here and he wanted to go back to the surface; as he got closer, what was there looked to be a white rock ... no, not a rock. It was a statue. Sebastion nearly lost his breath as he realized what it was. It was a white statue of the Lady pointing the way ahead. He swam a bit further and saw another statue leading under what looked like a great rock with a cave. Someone had put a talisman of the profile of the Lady above the dark entrance. Sebastion decided to try it. He knew he didn't have enough air in his lungs to go far, but he could look in. He swam towards it and poked his head in, looking up. Sure enough, there was light above him. He knew that was it. He left to swim to the bridge. When he surfaced, he sucked in the cool air. It felt great to his lungs.

When he returned, his small group had tripled. There were nine of them now huddled together in the mud. Baran had two people who looked to be children tucked into his arms, sharing his warmth. Lara was with two others that Sebastion could not make out to be women or men as they were so covered in mud. As he got closer, he could see that they were all shivering and miserable. He swam closer, and one of the refugees pulled a knife that fell from his blue shivering grip. Sebastion plucked it from the water and handed it back. The man looked at him, confused, and Sebastion realized that this must be his family.

"I'll get you out of here," Sebastion said, patting the man's shoulder. "Just hold on a while longer." He noticed the familiar look of admiration and uncomfortably crawled through the mud towards Lara.

"They just popped up out of the mud." Lara tried to smile, but her blue lips and chattering teeth didn't let it come entirely to her face.

"I think I found it."

"Well, if you didn't, then I'm offering myself to the fires," Lara said and wished she hadn't when the people around her looked at her with sad eyes.

"Everyone, come with me *quietly*," Sebastion said, indicating the way with his head. "We need to get to the bridge. I will explain the rest when we get there." He didn't want to say too much now, just in case they were caught. He didn't want to compromise the only way that led back to the city and Miska. "I know you're cold, but you must be silent and follow what I tell you."

Everyone nodded and were shivering heads as they crawled forward. It was slow going, but once there, Sebastion explained what they needed to do. Everyone was less than enthusiastic about the swim. The family, in particular, looked doubtful. The children began to weep in Baran's arms. He tried to console them.

"It's the only way," Sebastion said, trying to convince them.

"Did you see it," Lara asked?

327

"Well ... not exactly."

"Oh, puckering hell," Lara swore, holding herself in the water as she shivered.

"Take some deep breaths and follow the statues below. I will go last in case anyone gets lost." Sebastion said. "No more talking. Let's get this done." Lara looked at him, surprised.

"Lara, you're first, then Baran and the children. Then the rest of you. Follow the statues, and you will find the cave. Go in and swim to the surface. Let's go."

Lara grunted and dove down, disappearing. Baran took a few more seconds convincing the children but then dove down as well. The man stood a moment looking at Sebastion before diving as well. Sebastion stood there a few minutes more, looking back at the way they had come wondering how many other families lay in the mud, lost and freezing to death. He meant to ask the ones that were personally letting this happen. This was the centre of the Torenium Empire. Perhaps if this was the way Torenium treated their own, they didn't deserve to be an empire. He sadly dove down and swam. It was slow going as he pulled their packs behind him. He didn't see the others and hoped they had all made it. At the cave, he looked up and saw the man coming back for him. He grabbed a pack and helped pull it inside. Sebastion was grateful for the help.

Once through, they floated to the surface well enough. The cavern was alight with torches. Women were surrounding them, wearing white and others were in the corners and crevices of the rocks. Some held swords and bows at the ready as Sebastion pulled himself from the water. He held himself, shivering. He saw that the others were being stripped and covered in blankets. He saw one of the women coming towards him and then stopping. He rubbed his eyes and looked at her. He was looking into the very eyes he had been dreaming of since the day she had left. Everyone else in the cavern had stopped and watched.

"It seems we keep meeting in the same way." Sebastion smiled, unsure what to do but keep talking. "The Prince of Dirt has returned." He said between chattering teeth.

He watched as large tears fell from Miska's eyes as she looked at him. Sebastion dropped all reservation at that, crossed the last few steps in the water, and scooped her up into his arms. They laughed and cried, holding each other close.

"You left," Sebastion said, breathing her in and feeling his own tears.

"I know." Miska wept. "I won't again ... I promise."

The people in the cavern started moving again. One of them watched the exchange with a heavy heart. Doria was happy to see Miska so happy but knew the Lady of Light would need to come first. It was not uncommon for the women in the Lady's service to take a lover, but it was always a second thought to their duties to the church. She hoped that Miska understood that. Seeing them together now, she had serious doubts that she did.

CHAPTER 27
War

They stayed in the caverns that evening, feeding on rodent meat and warming by the fires like so many other refugees. They were in an enormous underground room surrounded by fires. There were holes in the ceilings that whisked the smoke away. Lara had been asking if they had heard from Killian, but no one knew. When she asked the tall woman with the fierce blue eyes about Sebastion's uncle her reaction bordered on rude. She worried but knew there was nothing she could do. From what she had gathered from Sebastion, he led an army of ragged Toreniums that called themselves the Blood Army. She knew it was a big name for a small bunch of starved farmers. She worried most that Killian would get the fool notion that he did have an army and do something which he would see as noble or honourable or what she would describe as plain stupid. Yes, she worried as she rubbed life back into her frozen arms while munching on rodent meat on a stick.

Damn, I never thought I would miss the wall.

The group was filled in on what has been going on. Doria had taken it upon herself to get them up to speed. They introduced Sorko and Milnor as brothers that possessed some valuable qualities and could be helpful. That was all the information given, and Doria did not ask for more ... however, she did cast suspicious glances at them when they thought she wasn't looking.

Sebastion and Miska were missing. They had disappeared a few minutes after seeing each other, and none had seen them since. Lara was not worried, but Doria seemed quite perturbed by Miska's absence. Lara, Baran, Milnor, and Sorko slept underground that night. Their clothes had dried, and they slept soundly for the first time in a long time. That morning, Lara felt better than she had in a long time. Even Sorko's magic was nothing compared to a long, restful sleep. When she got up and stretched, she saw how many people were in that cavern. There were hundreds, and she couldn't believe the Lady's followers would show so much compassion. She wondered if she was wrong for judging the religions so harshly. The whole world was falling apart, and it was only here that she saw any compassion. If by answer, Doria came up to stand with her.

"It is sad to see all these people that have lost their homes," Doria said sadly. Lara nodded her agreement, taking it in. Families have become just huddled masses of rags in corners of the cavern.

"The Advisors would not let them in." Doria continued. "They said they were expendable as there was no more room inside the gates. They left them to die." Doria turned to Lara. "The people they left to be slaughtered like pigs by the monsters outside." Lara could see the anger in those blue eyes. She also thought she saw something else. Perhaps something she'd seen before but was unable to put her finger on. "So we bring them here."

"You are doing a good thing," Lara said softly. "We have seen so much death and ... unbelievable things that it is good to see humanity still exists somewhere, if even hidden underground where few can see it."

"Above ground is bad and getting worse."

"It's just a matter of time before the Man-Eaters take this city," Lara said matter of factly.

"I will be above fighting for my city." Doria crossed her arms, frowning and looking at the people around her. "There are things here yet to fight for."

"What is the tactic for fighting the Man-Eaters back?" Lara asked.

Doria looked at her, still frowning. "I do not believe there is one."

"WHAT!?" Lara said loud enough to make people stop what they were doing and look at them.

"Do not concern yourself," Doria said, smiling for the people around them. "These things are complicated." Lara took this to be a jibe at her and bristled.

"Look," Lara said low again. "It seems I have not properly introduced myself. I am Lara O'Lankin, Commander of the Eastern Wall."

"I have heard the Wall has been taken," Doria said without looking at her.

"It has." Lara crossed her arms, getting them close to her swords. "But we took many Man-Eaters before we ... left."

"You mean abandoned."

"That's it!" Lara pulled a sword from her belt. "Many people gave their lives in that battle, and I will not have some underground blowhard disrespect their name." Lara got into a fighting position. "If you do not have a weapon, then I will provide you with one. Either way, you and I are going to dance."

Doria looked at her, expressionless and without movement.

"Loss of words?" Lara asked.

"You will see that the men by the walls will kill you before your sword could fall," Doria said, still as a statue.

"'em sticks won't stop me, then," Baran said, standing to his full height with his sword in his hand. "Do appreciate d'a shelter, but you kill 'er, and I kill you." He smiled, shrugging.

"What is the point of this?" Sorko asked, standing.

"Great, it seems everyone is getting to know one another," Sebastion said, coming into the cavern from a side entrance. "I'm so glad that at this time when we need to work together all of you are getting along."

"Do not try to shame me, boy." Doria said, still staring at Lara.

"Shame you?" Sebastion asked, stepping up to her and looking at her. He stared until Doria switched from Lara to him. Then it was as if they both saw something they recognized in their eyes.

"I saw you in a dream," Sebastion said, staring slack-jawed. "Wait ... not you but ... you look so mu-"

"ENOUGH!" Doria yelled. "You and your-" She paused, looking at Lara. "-group can come above. I believe we have some things to discuss." She headed for the exit giving Miska, in the shadows, a quick look before leaving.

"Well, she seems like fun," Lara said, returning her sword. "I suppose that's how you get when you don't get your share of men." Several of the women in white who were following Doria stopped a moment before continuing. Sebastion put his hands on his face as if rubbing the comment away.

"What?" Lara asked, innocently looking around.

Above was no better. The group sat in the Mothers' Library, sipping spiced wine and talking in small circles. Miska and Sebastion exchanged glances from where they stood in their respective groups. They were separated by only the space in the room now, and still, they could not hide their angst from being separated.

"You two make up then?" Baran asked, smiling. Sebastion looked to the ground, embarrassed.

"Ain't d'at cute." Baran laughed. "This one faces death nearly daily and now he can't handle a 'Lil fun."

"Give him a break," Lara said, grabbing his arm. "I'm sure his thoughts are pure." She wrapped around his arm and looked deep into his eyes. Sebastion immediately looked over at Miska, who now seemed to be ignoring them. "Oh, she sees us, sweety." Lara laughed.

"Enough," Sebastion said, shrugging her off. This just made Lara and Baran laugh louder. Sebastion noticed the group of priestesses had stopped talking and were looking at them. With his anger giving him the courage, he cleared his throat.

"There are things happening here bigger than us." He said, frowning at them all. "There are people out there living in the weeds of the great moat who have lost hope." He paused to make sure that they were all listening. "I will see that they are getting within these walls as we have. If they are to die, they will die with us and not forgotten like leaves blown away by the death wind." He saw the look of shame go over Lara's face. "We came this far," he said, taking her arm this time. "We can still do something. We can still do *something*."

Lara looked up into his eyes and nodded her agreement. "Yes, let's do something." She said, smiling and narrowing her eyes. "I think I'm done running."

"-me too," Lithra said sheepishly and everyone turned to look at the plain-looking girl in her grey dress. "I just..." She cleared her throat, trying to gain courage. "I just think we should not let those outside die alone. I mean ... if we are to ... if we're going to..."

"We're going to live." Doria finished for her. "It's time for secrets to end and our survival to plan. I am the Mother of the Church." She looked around, letting them digest the information. "It is time that we start doing the right thing here. Sebastion is right." Doria glanced over to see the proud look on Miska's face. "However, it will take us all to save those outside. Let us use what is in our power and get those people inside these gates."

"There are more coming, eh Mother," Lithra said, looking a little pale.

"More?"

"Yes, umm ... I think they are like our friends here."

"My little Novice ... I do not like riddles." Doria threatened.

Lithra closed her eyes and concentrated. "I can feel the ground. I hear people's footsteps and sometimes I can get a feel from those treading those footsteps. I feel ... they are ... similar to them." She nodded to Sebastion. "And..." Lithra paused. "There is one that walks differently." Lithra closed her eyes and concentrated. "It walks on two legs but with the ... softness of a cat."

"MORAKYE!" Miska and Sebastion said together, looking at each other wide-eyed across the room and smiling.

"The Fangor?" Doria asked, looking back and forth. "Oh, this *is* getting interesting!"

CHAPTER 27
The Rot

The Lady of Light sat at her big table and rubbed her forehead. She sighed heavily and looked again at the stone that was thought to have been carved by an ancient civilization that had some clairvoyance into the future. She knew it could just be coincidence but she kept coming back to the feeling that it was not. She shared half with her brother and friend, Shama. Now, considering her current predicament, she wished she had shared it all to both. Something had been put into play since her meeting with the one called Sebastion and, for the first time in forever, she felt out of control andv...vshe suspected even, mortal.

"Again with the rock, sister?" The Dark Lord said as he materialized. "Surely you can find something else to amuse yourself."

"The rest is there." She said simply and leaned back in her chair to look at it.

"All of it or-"

"All of it." She said, cutting him off.

The Dark Lord let his boots echo a little louder on the stone floor to accent his annoyance. He stood there reading the half he hadn't seen and rubbing his chin. Finally, he laughed bitterly and walked to a nearby chair to lean on.

"More ancient drivel." He said, but this time a bit more gently, looking at his sister and sensing her distress.

"I believe they created us as a buffer … or a filter to what might happen if it found its own way back.

"The Power?" The Dark Lord asked. "Our power simply moved their-"

"They are using us," She cut him off again. "The dwarves used to use small birds in cages when they dug deep. If there were gasses that could harm them … the bird would die first."

"You think we are the bird?" The Dark Lord laughed. "What has come over you?"

The Lady of Light slowly rose from her chair and came close to the large rock floating over her table. "I believe we were born as mortals and were given these powers … or at least enhanced."

"Ridiculous!" The Dark Lord snorted.

"How did we get here?" She asked. "What memories do you have before being what you are? The Dark Lord and The Lady of the Light. That's what is ridiculous! They filled our heads. They added memories."

"You can't be serious."

"What have you seen of the world beyond Torenium? I we know it's there but-"

"Nothing but barren land and animalistic tribes!" The Dark Lord said, cutting her off now.

"The whole world, brother?" She asked. "All of it? Try to look and see. Use your mind's eye. Use the power of The Dark Lord."

"I DO NOT NEED TO!" He yelled. "What game do you play here?"

"Not my game, brother." She said, pulling her hair back from her face. "See for yourself." She waved her hand and the image of half of her face and the pale skin of her shoulder shimmered revealing dark

338

crusty tortured flesh. "this is new and you know from that rock-" She pointed to the engraved words. "-what this means!"

The Dark Lord looked upon his sister without a word or an emotion before shaking his head.

"I wish it was some trick." The Lady of Light said sadly, sitting back into her chair.

"I see." The Dark Lord said and turned as if to leave.

"You were right in one thing, brother." The Lady in Light said to his back. "It is time we get involved. I am getting much more involved."

The Dark Lord turned back and the Lady of Light gasped. She was holding his shirt open and she could see a puncture wound with dark rotting skin around it.

"A gift from the Mage." He said simply.

"So, it has truly begun." She said, leaning back and looking to the rock to read the second half of the inscription once again.

Few to bring back what was took

Failure dangled on a baited hook

Without the world is to rot

Only they the darkness to stop

The one with few a world to heal

The magic the trespass means to steal

The end of all is yet to see

End of tomorrows it to be

The rot return will be the start

As the world enchantment comes apart

THE END

Watch for Book 4 of the Torenium Chronicles.

Made in the USA
Middletown, DE
14 July 2023

35170826R00195